DELORES FOSSEN

THOSE TEXAS NIGHTS

WITHDRAWN

HQN™

ISBN-13: 978-0-373-80187-9

Those Texas Nights

Copyright © 2016 by Delores Fossen

The publisher acknowledges the copyright holder
of the individual work as follows:

Lone Star Cowboy
Copyright © 2016 by Delores Fossen

Recycling programs
for this product may
not exist in your area.

This edition published by arrangement with Harlequin Books S.A.

For questions and comments about the quality of this book,
please contact us at CustomerService@Harlequin.com.

® and TM are trademarks of Harlequin Enterprises Limited or its
corporate affiliates. Trademarks indicated with ® are registered in the
United States Patent and Trademark Office, the Canadian Intellectual
Property Office and in other countries.

www.HQNBooks.com

Printed in U.S.A.

Praise for Delores Fossen

"Clear off space on your keeper shelf, Fossen has arrived."
—*New York Times* bestselling author Lori Wilde

"Delores Fossen takes you on a wild Texas ride with a hot cowboy."
—*New York Times* bestselling author B.J. Daniels

"In the first McCord Brothers contemporary, bestseller Fossen strikes a patriotic chord that makes this story stand out."
—*Publishers Weekly* on *Texas on My Mind*

"Fossen delivers an entertaining romance between two people with real-life issues."
—*RT Book Reviews* on *Texas on My Mind*

"This is a thrilling and twist-filled read that will keep you guessing till the end."
—*RT Book Reviews* on *Lone Wolf Lawman*

**Also available from Delores Fossen
and HQN Books**

The McCord Brothers

Texas on My Mind
Lone Star Nights
Blame It on the Cowboy

And don't miss the upcoming novel
in Delores Fossen's
Wrangler's Creek series

No Getting Over a Cowboy

To see the complete list of titles available from
Delores Fossen, please visit www.deloresfossen.com.

CONTENTS

To my husband, Tom. Thanks for all you do for me.

THOSE TEXAS NIGHTS

CHAPTER ONE

SOPHIE GRANGER WIPED her eyes with the back of her hand and squeezed her mud-splattered Elie Saab wedding dress into the Wrangler's Creek Police Department.

It wasn't easy getting ten yards of ivory tulle through the doorway, especially while crying and being light-headed. Sophie had to gather up the sides of the dress into puffy balls and turn sideways to manage it. Even then she stumbled, and her big toe got caught in the netting so she stumbled again. With all the mumbled cursing that accompanied the stumbling, it was no surprise that she got everyone's attention in the squad room.

Everyone in this case was Ellie Stoddermeyer, the weekend dispatcher/receptionist, and the two deputies— Rowdy Culpepper and his sister, Reena. What she got from them was silence.

And stares.

"I need to see Chief McKinnon," Sophie said with as much dignity as she could muster. Which wasn't very much.

Reena had her mouth open so wide that Sophie could see the quarter-sized wad of pink chewing gum on her tongue, but she hitched her thumb in the direction of the office all the way at the back of the squad room.

"He's in there," Ellie added once she got her mouth working. "But he's not officially the chief until his trial period is up and Lordie knows when that'll be. Right now, he's just the interim 'cause the mayor and city council haven't given him a permanent contract yet. Is, uh, there anything I can do for you?"

Since Ellie was one of the biggest gossips in town, Sophie considered asking the woman to refrain from mentioning this visit, but Ellie had already gotten herself unfrozen from the shock and was taking out her phone. No doubt to text every single human being she knew to let them know that Sophie Granger was having a breakdown along with looking like something the cat had dragged in.

That meant Sophie didn't have much time.

Her family would find her.

Sophie declined Ellie's offer of help, and she made her way through the squad room. Again, not easily. Like a white fluffy plow going through a farmer's field, Sophie cleared the edges of desks and toppled over trash cans. Ink pens pinged to the floor, rolled. So did a plastic bottle of Diet Coke, and the cap gave way to the pressure of the fall and started spewing.

She tried to do a cleanup, but there was no way she could fully bend down in the dress, not with the overly cinched corset bodice vising her ribs and stomach. However, she did grab a Kleenex from one of the desks, and she put it to good use wiping away a fresh round of tears.

The door to the *interim* chief's office was even narrower than the front so Sophie wadded up the dress again. Squeezed. Turned. Grunted. Until she finally broke through to the other side. She must have looked like a vanilla custard oozing through pie crust.

And there he was.

Clay McKinnon. Or the cute cowboy cop as folks called him.

Even though she didn't make it back to Wrangler's Creek very often, Sophie had seen him around, but she'd never seen him quite like this. Sweet heaven. There was blood in his cocoa-brown hair, a cut on his forehead and scrapes and scratches on his knuckles.

"Are you all right?" She used her bouquet to point toward the first aid kit on his desk. Little bits of petals and leaves fluttered through the air and fell to the floor.

He nodded, slid his gaze from her tiara headpiece to her muddy bare feet, before he got back to dabbing his knuckles with some hydrogen peroxide.

"I'm having a bad day," he confirmed. "But something tells me yours is worse."

"Possibly."

He didn't really look at her, but he lifted an eyebrow. *"Possibly?"*

"Grading on a curve here, but at least I'm not bleeding." Sophie wasn't a fan of tears or mud, but the sight of the blood made her queasier than she already was. "Were you attacked?"

This time he lifted his shoulder. "You wouldn't believe me if I told you."

Sophie was sure she'd hear the details of the incident soon enough. Well, maybe. Her situation was likely such a hot topic that folks wouldn't bother to jabber about a puny altercation where the interim Chief of Police had been injured.

"I need a date," she said, wiping back more of the blasted tears.

Judging from the look he gave her, he was either about to call the mental hospital or laugh at her attempted joke. Nope, no laugh. She hoped this idea of hers sounded better than it was. Actually, she hoped it not only sounded better, but that it *was* better. Because it didn't sound very good in her head.

"Date as in the fruit or a date?" he asked.

"Date." Which, of course, would require some clarification. Chief McKinnon had moved to town several months ago, but their paths hadn't crossed enough for an actual introduction. "I'm Sophie Granger. I'm head of marketing for Granger Western."

"I know who you are. You're getting married—" he checked his watch "—in about fifteen minutes. But judging from your dress and the fact that you want a date, I'm figuring things didn't go as planned."

"No." And that single-word answer was a huge understatement. It also brought on more crying. "My fiancé, Brantley Barnwell, came by the dressing room at the church and said he couldn't marry me after all."

Sophie was sure she was still in shock. Exhausted, too. And hungry since she'd been dieting for two months to fit into this breath-choking dress. Maybe she should have asked for a date of the fruit variety after all. But sadly that shock wouldn't last, and she needed to fix this before she fell into a puddle of despair and more tears.

And anger.

Really, really pissed-off-bad anger.

Anger that she hadn't aimed at Brantley since he'd hightailed it out of there only minutes after delivering the worst news that Sophie had ever heard.

I don't love you.

He'd added a whole bunch of *I'm sorry's, I'm an asshole, I can't believe this happened.* Which hadn't helped. But then that was asking a lot of mere apologies and ramblings. Nothing would have helped except his saying this had all been just a prank and that he loved her after all.

"I didn't want my family to see me like this," she went on. And she just kept going on and on. "Right after Brantley left, I wrote a note saying that I needed a little alone time and hung it on the dressing room door so my family would see it. Then, I climbed out the window of the church. It's muddy from all the rain and I landed in a new flower bed. My shoes got stuck so I had to walk here barefooted."

"And no one stopped to give you a ride?"

She shook her head, dabbed at the tears again. "The streets are empty. Nearly everyone in town is already at the church waiting for the wedding."

Just saying that punched away at some of the shock. Punched at her gut, too. Thankfully, she hadn't eaten anything or she would have driven down her dignity another notch by puking.

"Are you, uh, drunk?" he asked.

"Maybe a little. Brantley brought me a bottle of Jose Cuervo when he delivered the news, and I had some sips."

Actually, she wasn't sure just how much she'd downed before climbing out the window. Sophie also suspected the tequila was the reason she hadn't noticed the mud until it was too late to save her shoes.

And it had almost certainly influenced her decision to come up with this date plan.

Chief McKinnon huffed, scrubbed his hand over his face and then winced when he encountered that cut on his head. "Look, Miss Granger, I'm sorry for what happened to you, but instead of looking for a date, you should just go back to the church and be with your family."

"God, no!" She couldn't say that fast enough. "That's the last place I need to be without a plan. One of my brothers is there. My cousin, too. My best friend. And my mother." Especially her mother. "They'd go after Brantley and beat him up. Then, you'd have to arrest just about everyone in the vicinity who's related to me."

He nodded. Stood. Handed her a fresh Kleenex. "I'll go to the church and calm them down."

"You'd stand a better chance getting this mud off tulle. Once they learn what's happened, there'll be little chance to calm them down. No, the best way to handle this is my date idea."

He cocked his head to the side, studied her as if he were indeed about to call the mental hospital to come and get her.

"Don't you see?" she asked, but didn't wait for him to answer. "If you and I leave now, I can say I ran off with you. We wouldn't really run off, of course. We could just go somewhere for a couple of hours, but I could tell my family I had second thoughts about marrying Brantley and that I couldn't help myself, that I had to have one last fling."

"That's the tequila talking," he insisted.

Possibly.

Probably, she amended.

Sophie didn't usually have to make critical decisions and plans while under the influence, and once she sobered up and got out of the dress so she could breathe, she might be able to come up with something better. For now though, this was all she had.

"If your family thinks you're with me, it'll make you look bad," the chief added. Clearly, he was grasping at straws here.

"I don't think I can look any worse, do you?"

He didn't argue, not with that anyway. "Basically, you want me to lie for you?"

She nodded. "But it's for the sake of keeping peace and preventing an assault. I hate Brantley for what he did. Hate him with every fiber of my being."

That shock was finally wearing off. Some of the tequila, too.

Fast.

Hell in a handbasket.

How had it come to this?

The hurt shoved away the anger so fast that Sophie didn't even know it was coming. She caught on to the desk to steady herself. That didn't help, either, and since her knees were too wobbly to stand, she just sat on the edge of the desk. Of course, she knocked things over, but she couldn't help it.

She was no longer an engaged woman. No longer about to become Brantley's wife. In fact, she wasn't sure who she was and prayed that was a temporary effect of the hurt and the lack of oxygen. Because at this exact moment, she felt something she'd never felt before.

Broken.

"I would ask if you're okay," Chief McKinnon said, "but I already know the answer. You're not. And that's why you're not thinking straight. If you just go to your family with the truth—"

"But I don't want them in jail," she added, just as the eighteenth round of tears came.

He glanced up at the ceiling as if seeking divine guidance. "Why me? Isn't there someone else in town who'd have an easier time lying about this?"

It was hard to give someone a flat look while you were crying, but Sophie thought she'd managed it. "There are no other eligible straight men in town."

He was it, period. All the others were married, too

young, too old, or else they worked at her family's ranch. Dating someone who technically worked for her was a huge no-no in her brother's eyes. Hers, as well. And there wasn't a single breathing soul in Wrangler's Creek who would believe she'd ditched Brantley for some wild-oats sowing with the pig farmer that everyone called Skunk. Or Ned the pharmacist, who had a germ phobia and wouldn't touch anyone unless he was wearing latex gloves.

Sophie kept trying despite the sobs. "Plus, folks don't know you that well since you've only lived here a couple of months—"

"Nine months," he corrected. He gave her four more Kleenexes, and she needed every one of them.

"In Wrangler's Creek time, that's only a couple of minutes. Skunk, the pig farmer, has lived here since before I was born, and people still call him the new guy."

At least the chief didn't just shoot down her idea. He bunched up his forehead as if giving it some thought. Thought that ended in a head shaking. "No one has ever seen us together before now. No way would they believe you'd run off with a man you didn't know."

"So we could embellish the lie and say we've been secretly meeting."

"Now you want embellishment?"

"It's for a good cause," she pressed.

But then Sophie had to consider something that she was certain she would have considered earlier if she'd been thinking straight. "Uh, are you seeing anyone, engaged, gay?"

"None of the above. That doesn't mean I want to buy into a lie that would snowball."

He still clearly wasn't on board with this so Sophie

just went for broke. "I don't want my family to see me looking this pathetic. This muddy," she added, glancing down at her feet. "While I'm crying. Do you have any idea how hard it is to be the only sister in a family of alpha cowboys?"

"Not really." He finally gave in and just handed her the entire box of Kleenex.

Even though he looked so ready for this conversation to be over, Sophie continued. "Well, it's hard. I've had to fight and scrape for every ounce of power and responsibility I have, and if they see me like this, I'll lose that. They'll walk on eggshells. They'll treat me like a hurt woman."

"Uh, aren't you a hurt woman?"

"Yes, but I don't want them to know that."

More ceiling glancing, more huffing. "Follow this through. If we pretend we're dating, the pretense will continue because there'll have to be a fake breakup. Your family will definitely look at you as a hurt woman then. And what kind of example would that set for me? I've got two nephews, and I don't want them to think I'm the kind of guy who'd carry on with an engaged woman."

He was making sense, but Sophie still wasn't giving up on this plan just yet. This was one of the things she had to do often at Granger Western. She had to tweak sales proposals, marketing plans and personnel assignments. This was just another situation in need of a tweaking.

But what? How?

Sophie was asking herself those very questions when she heard something she didn't want to hear. Voices that she recognized.

Oh, God. They'd found her.

"Is my sister here?" someone barked. Garrett, her oldest brother.

Garrett sounded both concerned and pissed. Not a good combination. He was the one most likely to kick Brantley's butt, but he would also berate her forever about getting involved with the man he'd always said was all wrong for her. Of course, any man who wasn't a cowboy would have been wrong for her in Garrett's eyes.

"Is my baby girl all right?" Voice number two.

Her mother, Belle. The one most likely to coddle her, but the coddling would quickly turn to smothering. Then nagging. Then, she'd go after Brantley with a vengeance.

"We know she's here. We followed her muddy footprints." Voice number three. Lawson. Her cousin. He'd berate her, coddle her and then assist Garrett and her mother with giving Brantley a serious butt-kicking.

The only Granger missing was her other brother, Roman. He'd been invited to the wedding, of course, but he hadn't shown and probably wouldn't. Too bad, because if Roman had come, then it would have taken some of the ugly spotlight off her. A black sheep brother could do that.

"We need to see her." Voice number four. Her best friend, Mila Banchini. There'd be no nagging, butt-kicking and only minimal coddling from her, but for the next decade Sophie would have to listen to Mila's attempts to find her a suitable husband.

"I'm sorry," Sophie said to the chief.

"For what?"

"This is the only tweak I can think of." And despite it being a stupid tweak, Sophie launched herself into Chief McKinnon's arms.

From the corner of her eye, Sophie watched her family and friend trickle in. She also felt the chief's muscles go statue-stiff and expected a similar reaction from the others.

That didn't happen.

They were standing there. Three Grangers and Mila, who was wearing her champagne maid of honor dress. Each of them looked at her not with sympathy, exactly. There was something else. Something that caused her to go still.

They didn't rush to coddle her. Didn't issue death threats about Brantley. And they especially didn't ask what she was doing in Chief McKinnon's arms. The chief remedied that, though. He backed away from her, staying by her side and studying her family.

"We know about Brantley," Garrett said. "He came and talked to us right after he spoke to you."

Oh. Sophie hadn't expected that from the man she was now thinking of as freshly dropped cow dung.

"I know it's hard," her mother added. "You're crying."

It was the right thing to say. The right tone, too, but the four were still standing in the same spot as if someone had magnetized their feet to the floor. And Lawson and her mother were dodging her gaze. Definitely not a good sign.

"Did someone die?" Sophie came out and asked. Then, she got a horrible, gut-twisting thought. "Did one of you kill Brantley?"

"No," Garrett answered. He didn't add more because his phone buzzed. He mumbled something about having to take the call and walked out.

That knot in her stomach got worse. Because here she was jilted and broken, something Garrett would have almost certainly realized, and yet he'd taken a call.

"Did Brantley do something to harm himself?" the chief asked.

Evidently, he was also aware that something wasn't right about this visit. Something other than the obvious, that is, since she'd just been jilted and her family had seen her with her arms wrapped around the police chief.

"As far as I know, Brantley's okay," Lawson said.

There was a huge *but* at the end of that. Sophie could hear it. "What's wrong?" she asked.

Her mother, Mila and Lawson volleyed glances at each other, but they didn't say a word. They appeared to be waiting for Garrett to return, which he did a couple of moments later.

"Anything?" her mother said to him.

Garrett shook his head and drew in a long breath as if he would need it. He went to Sophie, taking her by the shoulders. "I know this is a shitty day, but I'm about to make it even shittier."

Not possible.

But a moment later, Sophie learned she was wrong about that. A whole new level of shitty had been added to her life.

CHAPTER TWO

A FAILED WEDDING. Now a funeral.

Not a literal funeral, but to Sophie it certainly felt like another sucker punch of fate. This couldn't happen. It had to be a mistake.

"It's a mistake," she repeated, this time aloud, but Garrett didn't react. Probably because she'd already repeated it a dozen times, and he'd likely gotten tired of telling her that it wasn't.

That something very bad had indeed happened to Granger Western.

Just how bad, they didn't know yet because they didn't have answers. Answers they needed from their chief financial officer, Billy Lee Seaver, who'd seemingly taken money and lots of it from the company.

Sophie held on to the *seemingly* part, figuring this was all some kind of banking error or a computer glitch, and she made a call to the next person on her contact list. The first sixteen calls hadn't produced much, and this one was no different. Saturday evenings apparently weren't a good time to reach business associates who would perhaps know Billy Lee's whereabouts.

When she struck out with the next two calls, Sophie looked at Marcum Gentry, their legal advisor, to see if he'd had any better luck. Judging from his body language that would be a no. He was pacing while having an intense conversation with someone at Austin PD. Marcum's pricey shoes clicked and tapped on the hardwood floors as he went from one side of Garrett's office to the other.

Her brother wasn't pacing, though. Garrett was seated behind his desk, looking very much like a troubled cowboy rather than a concerned CEO. He was in his usual jeans, his Stetson sat on the corner of his desk and he'd ditched the two items he rarely wore—a jacket and a bolo tie. Sophie hadn't even tried to talk him into wearing dress pants for the wedding because she was reasonably sure that her brother didn't own *dress* anything. However, he had put on his good boots to attend the ceremony, which he'd also already swapped out for his usual ones.

The boots and his clothes were the only thing usual about this day, though. Garrett was having his own intense conversation with one of their accountants he had managed to reach. Sophie watched Garrett's mouth move, and she was hearing him say the words. But her brain just wasn't processing what he was saying. Perhaps it was the tequila aftermath or maybe her mind just couldn't handle two major shocks like this in the same day.

At least she wasn't having to deal with this shock while wearing her wedding dress. Once they'd arrived at the Granger Western building in downtown Austin, Sophie had made a beeline to her office and changed into one of the spare business suits she kept there. Thankfully, none of their employees had been around to see her.

Of course, having their employees see her was the least of their problems.

If the initial reports were true, then Billy Lee had basically screwed them six ways to Sunday by embezzling a fortune. And after doing that, he'd disappeared.

Much as her ex-fiancé had done.

Too bad her heart hadn't done a vanishing act along with them because she wasn't sure how much more she could take. The panic was rising inside her. The pressure in her chest, too, and if this was some dream, she prayed she'd wake up from it soon.

Sophie forced herself to her feet, and while dodging Marcum's pacing pattern, she walked to the floor-to-ceiling window in Garrett's office. It was identical to hers, which was just next door. The view of downtown Austin was one of the best in the city, and it normally gave her a jolt of pride.

This was theirs.

The company their great-grandfather Zachariah Taylor Granger had built from the ground up. To remind them of that, there was a massive twelve-foot-high oil portrait of Z.T. on the wall of Garrett's office. Not an especially good portrait, Sophie had always thought, what with his stern gaze, slightly narrowed eyes and a "don't screw this up" sneer.

Garrett and she hadn't screwed it up. They'd nearly doubled the size of what customers affectionately called Cowboy Mart, had put it on the Texas financial map. It'd made them wealthier. Happier. It'd made them who they were.

It had to stay that way.

Marcum finished his latest call, but he didn't stop pacing. He kept moving until he was right in front of Garrett's desk. That cued her brother to make a quick end to his conversation.

"You want the good news or the bad news first?" Marcum asked them.

"Bad," Garrett and she said in unison.

Despite their quick agreement, Marcum still took a

couple of moments to answer. "Billy Lee robbed you blind. We don't know how exactly, not yet, but he embezzled nearly ninety percent of the company's operating funds."

Sophie decided it was a good idea to sit down, but since there wasn't a chair nearby, she just sank to the floor.

"Fuck," Garrett growled.

Sophie wanted to growl something, too, something equally as bad as the f-word, but she couldn't get her mouth working.

"How?" Garrett added. It was also growled.

Marcum shook his head. "That will take some time to unravel, but Billy Lee must have had the pieces in place for a while to do this. I don't suppose you had any checks and balances on him?"

"No," Garrett and she answered in unison again.

"He's my godfather," Sophie added. "Our late father's best friend."

Garrett had his own adding to do. "Billy Lee's worked for the company for forty years and never gave us any reason not to trust him."

Until now.

God, until now.

"What's the good news?" Sophie asked Marcum.

"I don't think Garrett and you will have to go to jail."

Sweet baby Jesus in the manger. "Is that stating the obvious, or was there actually a chance of that happening?" she pressed.

"A chance," Marcum answered without hesitation. "It appears that over the past couple of months, Billy Lee might have dabbled in some money laundering with the funds he was embezzling."

Sophie thought she might not be able to stave off that

puking any longer. Her stomach balled up into a knot, started dribbling like a point guard on the basketball court and she got to her feet in case she had to make a run to the bathroom.

"Billy Lee must have snapped," Garrett mumbled.

That stopped her for the time being, and she latched on to that like a lifeline. Yes, that had to be it. Because with the stomach knot and crushed heart, Sophie couldn't grasp that a man who was part of their family had done this to them.

"Maybe someone set Billy Lee up?" she suggested.

Both Garrett and Marcum made sounds of agreement. Weak agreement, though. But it was another lifeline that Sophie was choosing to grab.

"What do we do now?" Sophie asked.

"Get drunk," Marcum readily answered.

"Will that help?" And she was serious.

Marcum shrugged. "Only if you drink enough to pass out."

Sophie decided to keep that as an option.

Her phone buzzed at the same time that Marcum's rang, and Marcum stepped into the hall to take it. Maybe because he didn't think it would be wise for them to get another dose of bad news so soon after the last one.

But it was too late for that.

Brantley's name was on her phone screen.

She debated letting it go to voice mail. Debated answering it just so she could curse him. Debated the getting drunk option again. But after five rings, Sophie hit the answer button.

"Are you all right?" Brantley blurted out before she could curse him.

No, she wasn't, but her pride prevented her from saying that. "If you're calling to grovel, it won't work. I won't take you back after what you did to me. How could you do this to me? How?" Now, she added some of that profanity.

"I'm not calling to ask you to take me back," Brantley interrupted. His words sounded a little slurred or something. "I meant it when I said I can't marry you."

That stomped on her pride and her heart some more. "Then why the heck did you ever propose to me?"

Silence. Which was just another form of heart stomping. The least Brantley could do was apologize and call himself some of the names she'd just called him, but the silence dragged on and on.

"Look, I'm busy," she finally said in the same moment that Brantley said, "I thought I loved you, Sophie. But I was wrong."

Mercy. Each word was like another little dagger. He hadn't loved her? "You did a darn good job of faking it, then."

"I know. I'd fooled myself, too. It's because we'd been together so long. I kept thinking it was time for the next step, but the next step should have been for me to break things off."

That stomach ball started to bounce against her other internal organs. She was definitely going to puke.

"I should have never let things get as far as they did," he said. At least that's what she thought he said, but he was slurring.

"Are you drunk?" she snapped.

"Uh, no. It's nothing. I'm fine, really."

"I don't care a rat's butt if you're fine or not. And I have to go," Sophie insisted.

Brantley blurted out something just as she hit the end call button. Something about a belt. She probably should have been concerned that he was about to hang himself, but her concern meter for him was tapped out. Besides, Brantley had plenty of faults, but he wasn't the sort to kill himself.

Sophie put her phone in her pocket, looked at her brother, and that's when she realized he had his attention nailed to her. Marcum did, too, though he was still talking on his phone.

"Anything about Billy Lee?" she asked Garrett as a preemptive strike. Sophie definitely didn't want to talk about Brantley and what he'd just said to her.

He hadn't loved her.

The anger ripped through her. A better feeling than the soppy tears because she didn't need to blow her nose, but she needed to blow off some of this rage. She yanked off her two-carat engagement ring and threw it against the wall. Probably not the smartest idea she'd ever had because it hit the oil painting of their great-grandfather and made a dent in the canvas just below his left nostril.

"I'm guessing that call didn't go well," Garrett said on a heavy sigh.

"But please tell me your call went better."

Garrett lifted his shoulder. "It was Chief McKinnon. He was checking on you."

Great. Now, her *date* was chiming in on this. She didn't want anyone checking on her. Especially anyone who'd seen her make a fool of herself. At the moment, though, that included pretty much everyone in Wrangler's Creek. Later, in a day or two, she'd need to call him and apologize. Perhaps blame what she'd done on the tequila and temporary insanity.

Marcum finished his call, glanced at the two-carat ring that was now on the floor, before his gaze volleyed between Garrett and her. "You want the good news or the bad news first?" he asked again.

"Bad," Garrett and she said in unison for a second time.

Marcum nodded. "The company's assets will be frozen while the feds investigate the money laundering charges."

Sophie's mouth opened but no sound came out.

"Frozen?" Garrett snapped. "For how long?"

"I'm not sure. These things can take awhile."

"Define awhile." Garrett's snap was even snappier that time.

"Months. Maybe years. And it's possible everything will be seized if Billy Lee really was using this company as a money laundering operation."

Still no sound. Her breath had vanished, and she figured it was a good time to sit back down on the floor again. Good thing, too, because the bad news just kept on coming.

"The frozen assets include both your apartments here in Austin since they're company holdings," Marcum added. "Your cars, too."

No car, no apartment. It wouldn't be as great of a loss to Garrett as it was for her because he split time between Austin and Wrangler's Creek. And she doubted he'd ever even started the company car since he still drove their late dad's truck. But for her, the apartment was, well, home.

"The investigators will be going through everything in the offices," Marcum continued. "The vehicles and apartments, too."

They wouldn't find anything. Well, they wouldn't unless Billy Lee had truly gone bonkers and stashed some stuff there. Though with the way her luck was running, there'd be a counterfeiting machine, a kilo of cocaine and Jimmy Hoffa's body beneath her bed.

"Your personal bank accounts are also frozen for the time being," Marcum went on. "But I feel that's something we can resolve faster than the company assets."

There was no way for the ball in her stomach to get any tighter or bounce any harder.

"So, basically everything we own, including where we live, has just been taken away from us, and we might never get it back?" she asked.

"Pretty much," Marcum agreed.

"I'd like to hear that good news now," Sophie grumbled.

"The ranch." And apparently Marcum thought that was enough of an explanation. It wasn't. Sophie motioned for him to keep going. "The ranch and the operation there aren't part of the company or your own personal assets. That's because Roman legally owns it, and he has no connection to the company."

She gave Marcum a very blank look.

"So, you know what this means, right?" Marcum asked.

Sophie thought Marcum might be trying to tell them something more than the obvious here. "We won't lose the ranch," she concluded.

"It's more than that. It means you'll have a place to live. I just got the okay from Roman, and you and Garrett will be closing things down here in Austin and moving back home."

HOME SUCKED.

This was not what Clay had in mind when he'd moved to Wrangler's Creek. He'd come here to take over for the retiring sheriff. Also for some peace and quiet and to keep an eye on his kid sister, April. At the moment, neither was happening.

There was a toilet in the corner of what was supposed to be his living room. The bathtub was where he'd hoped to have a sofa. The toilet was obviously hooked up to some sort of plumbing because it was making a loud gurgling sound that Clay could hear even over the tile saw that was screeching in the kitchen.

"Yeah, I know," Freddie said, scratching his head. Freddie Shoemaker was the only contractor in Wrangler's Creek, and that's the reason Clay had hired him to renovate the old house he'd bought.

Freddie was clearly an idiot.

"The guest bathroom's not right," Freddie conceded. "They put the plumbing in the wrong place so they just hooked it up where the fittings stopped. I left instructions with my crew, but they musta read it wrong."

Yeah, or else they were idiots, too. Since the crew consisted of Freddie's two sons and a nephew, that was a strong possibility.

"I don't guess you could get used to having it this way?" Freddie asked. "It'd save you a lot of money if we didn't have to undo all of this."

No one had ever accused Clay of having a friendly face. It was a by-product of having been a cop for twelve years. First in Houston. Then, here in Wrangler's Creek. And Freddie got a whopping big-assed dose of that nonfriendly face.

"Put the guest bathroom fixtures in the guest bathroom," Clay snarled. "And no, it won't cost me a lot of money because I'll only pay for the work you do right."

Freddie mumbled an "okay, you're the boss" and headed toward his rust-scabbed truck parked just outside. Apparently that meant he was done for the day even though it was barely 3:00 p.m.

Clay tried to call April again. Again, no answer. He wasn't ready to sound the alarms just yet because April wasn't the most reliable person, but it'd been two days since he'd heard from her. Her boss at the hair salon where she worked had said April had asked for time off. She hadn't been at her house, either, when he'd dropped by, which meant something was up. With April, *something was up* usually went hand in hand with trouble. She was twenty-three, eleven years younger than Clay, but plenty of times she still acted like an irresponsible teenager.

Clay growled out another voice mail for April to call him, and he followed the sound of the tile saw into the kitchen. The saw was going all right, but no one was cutting the backsplash tiles. In fact, no one was in the kitchen at all. Clay unplugged the saw to kill the noise and went in search of any signs of progress or intelligent life.

He found neither.

There was still a hole in his bedroom floor marked with a scrawled sign that said *hole*. No windows, just tarp where they should be. And there was a fridge in the master bathroom, something that hadn't been there that morning. That didn't qualify as progress.

The fridge door was open, and one of Freddie's sons— Mick—was peering inside. Not foraging for food apparently but rather using it as a makeshift air conditioner to stave off the already sweltering April heat. He looked to be having an orgasmic moment with his eyes closed and his head going back and forth like an oscillating fan.

Clay cleared his throat, and Mick jumped nearly a foot off the floor. It was the fastest Clay had ever seen the man move.

"Shit," Mick repeated a couple of times. "You scared the dickens out of me, Chief."

Ditto. But Clay wasn't afraid of Mick. He was afraid he was going to have to live with these clowns for the rest of his life.

And learn the meaning of *dickens*.

Mick didn't close the fridge door. He just stood there enjoying the cool air on his backside and was seemingly oblivious to the fact that Clay wanted to rip off his arm and beat him with it.

"Why's the fridge in here?" Clay asked.

"Oh, it's temporary," Mick said as if that explained everything.

Clay decided to give very specific instructions and use small words. "I want the fridge in the kitchen, and the toilet and bathtub out of the living room and into the guest bath."

Mick looked at him as if that were a tall order but then nodded.

Even though Clay figured this was going to be just another exercise in frustration, he still wanted some answers. "Why *exactly* is the fridge in here anyway?"

"The plug." Mick hitched his thumb to the outlet.

"Did the electrical plug in the kitchen quit working?" Clay pressed when Mick didn't add more.

"Nope. I needed it for the saw, and since I wanted to keep my Pepsi cold, I brought the fridge in here. Didn't think you'd want it in your bedroom."

"I don't want it anywhere but the kitchen."

Again, Mick made it seem as if that would be a tall order. "Say, in case you didn't notice, the phone next to your couch is blinking. Guess that means you got a message or something."

Yeah, or *something*, but Clay didn't want to deal with that right now. The landline had come with the house, and while he hadn't given the number to April and didn't use it as his contact information, his neighbors sometimes called him on it. Along with one other person who'd managed to get hold of it.

And that particular person did leave messages.

Apparently, this was Clay's day to receive one. But not now. He'd listen to it when he was alone.

"Your face and hands are healing," Mick remarked. "Those chickens messed you up real good, didn't they?"

Yeah, and it pained Clay to admit it, but he'd actually checked for the feathered critters to make sure they weren't around before he got out of his truck and went into the house. The chickens weren't his. They'd sort of come with the property, but as soon as Clay could catch them, he was having a barbecue.

Clay shut the fridge door, hoping it would spur Mick to get back to work, and the man did follow Clay back into the living room. But apparently it wasn't to work. It was to chat.

"Guess you heard all about Sophie and Garrett having to move back a couple of weeks ago?" Mick went on.

Clay nodded. Hard not to hear what was the number one gossip topic. It had even surpassed Sophie's jilting and the talk about Sophie showing up at his office and asking him on a date. Of course, it was possible the date-thing was still the hottest topic, but the townsfolk were keeping quiet about that around him.

"I heard the FBI fellas took all their money and stuff." Mick followed him when Clay went out the back—after he checked for the feral chickens.

Apparently, they were still on the topic of the Grangers, but Clay ignored him and walked to the pasture fence. Now, here was why he'd bought the run-down place that folks called the old Pennington ranch. The land and the barn. No more boarding his horses, Sal and Mal. The pair were in the pasture and looked a lot more content than Clay did at the moment.

But Clay did have plans for the place. Plans that included a house where everything was in the right room. That way he could get on with the peace and quiet part of his life.

Man, he needed it bad.

"Don't know how their cousin, Lawson, is taking Sophie and Garrett coming back and being right under his nose," Mick continued. "Guess you heard about all the bad blood there?"

"I heard," Clay settled for saying, and he hoped that put an end to this conversation.

It didn't.

"Sophie and Garrett's great-grandpa was Zachariah Taylor Granger, or Z.T. as people called him," Mick explained. "Lawson's great-granddaddy was Jerimiah, Z.T.'s brother. Both of 'em made a fortune to pass onto their kids and grandkids. Z.T.'s kin live here on the Granger ranch. Jerimiah's kin live nearby, but they don't come into town much at all. The two families own so much land that it almost bumps right up against each other."

"Are you telling me this for a reason?" Clay asked. He used the same tone he did when interrogating felony suspects.

"Sure am. I'm telling you because there might be trouble with Lawson. Ever since he had a falling-out with his brothers about five or six years ago, he's been working the Granger ranch on Roman's behalf. Roman doesn't want to work it because of a falling-out he had with his mom and on account of him being so busy." He paused. "A lot of the Grangers have falling-outs."

"And you're telling me this for a reason?" Clay repeated.

"Yeah, it could be real important that you get the whole messy picture when it comes to the Grangers. Roman won't be trouble. He lives in San Antonio and owns a rodeo business. But Lawson's a different story. He might not be so happy now that Sophie and Garrett are back to take over things."

Maybe that was true, but Clay still couldn't find any angle that connected him to this situation. This all sounded like gossip.

"You figure Sophie Granger and you will get back together now that things are off with Brantley and her?" Mick asked.

So, that was the *angle*.

Clay gave him an annoyed glance. "Sophie and I were never together."

Mick made a *yeah right* sound, and Clay didn't bother to set him straight since it wouldn't do any good. Because Mick, like most other people, believed that Sophie and Clay had had a "thing," and that's why her ex-fiancé had called off the wedding. Apparently, Brantley was still well liked in town, and Sophie was getting the blame for ruining things with Mr. Perfect.

Other than Sophie launching herself into his arms the day of the jilting, Clay had never laid a hand on her. And wouldn't. Sophie wasn't exactly the peace-and-quiet-inducing type.

Plus, there were her eyes.

Clay figured a lot of men looked at Sophie and saw an

attractive woman. And she was. But Clay just couldn't get past those eyes because they reminded him, well, of things he didn't want to be reminded of.

He mentally put those eyes back in the memory box in his head that he'd marked as "shit to forget." It worked, but in those couple of seconds that it took him to move it there, the images came. He felt the sick feeling of dread in his stomach.

And he saw *her*.

Hell. He saw her, her face way too clear for just a tiny piece of a nightmare.

"Say, are you okay?" Mick asked.

"Fine," Clay lied, and he tried to look normal. Whatever that was. Maybe he needed to create a *normal* box in his head that he could pull out and use to fool people. Of course, it probably wasn't hard to fool an idiot like Mick because he seemed to buy right into Clay's "fine" lie.

"They haven't found Billy Lee." Mick again. He paused. "Since you're a cop, you'll probably know the answer to this, but what would make a fella run off with all that money?"

"Greed." And you didn't need to be a cop to know that.

Even though Billy Lee didn't exactly fit the profile of an embezzler and money launderer. The man didn't have so much as a parking ticket, and from what Clay could gather from the gossip, Billy Lee had been a father figure to Sophie and Garrett since their dad had passed away about ten years ago.

If Clay were leading the investigation, he would look for mitigating factors. Like maybe Billy Lee was being blackmailed or something, but this wasn't his rodeo, wasn't his bullshit to shovel.

Peace and quiet.

And a job where someone around him didn't get killed because of something he'd screwed up.

He'd trade the adrenaline rush of the *rodeo* for that.

"Guess you'll get more horses soon." Mick again. "Maybe make it the way it used to be."

"Yes, and that includes not having a toilet in the living room. You need to go take care of that now. I'd actually like to have a finished house before I reach retirement age."

Mick laughed as if it were a fine joke rather than one of Clay's genuine concerns. Clay would have spelled out his concerns—in both writing and while using sentences with small words—but the sound of a car engine snagged his attention. He got a jolt of relief then anger when he saw that it was April's powder blue VW convertible.

She stepped from the car as if all was right with the world, and she wasn't alone. His two-year-old twin nephews, Hunter and Hayden, barreled out the moment their mom freed them from their car seats, and they ran toward Clay as if he were a major prize at the finish line.

That's exactly how he felt about them.

They owned his heart, and the little shits knew it.

Clay scooped them up, kissed them both and got some sweaty, sticky kisses in return. Judging from the smell and stains on their shirts, they'd been eating chocolate ice cream. Of course, the ice-cream kisses and cuddles didn't last. The moment the boys spotted the horses, they wiggled to get out of his arms so they could get closer to the animals.

"Don't climb the fence or I'll arrest you," he warned them.

Hunter giggled like a loon, and Hayden immediately tried to climb the fence. Clay took hold of him like a wiggly football and tucked him under his arm while he gave April a once-over. She wasn't hurt, but she did have new purple streaks in her dark brown hair. And a hickey on her neck.

"Obviously, you're not dead in a ditch," Clay growled.

She was still smiling when she kissed his cheek and grabbed Hunter when he tried to climb the fence. "Nope. Not dead. And I don't go near ditches. According to you, they're death traps for kid sisters."

"Then there'd better be a good reason why you didn't return my calls." Normally, Clay would have punctuated that with a curse word or two, but he was in the little pitcher, big ear zone.

Still smiling and still with a kid in her arms, April twirled around like a ballerina. She sort of looked like one, too, in her pink dress.

"I do have a good reason." She stopped twirling long enough to thrust out her left hand for him to see the diamond ring sitting on her finger.

Clay sure didn't smile. "Please tell me that's a fashion statement and not what I think it is."

"No fashion statement." Another twirl, and she set Hunter back on the ground. "I'm engaged."

"For shit's sake." Clay mumbled it again when he realized he'd said that out loud. "The ink's barely dry on your divorce," he reminded her. "And you haven't been dating anyone that I know about."

"I've been divorced three months. That's plenty of time for the ink to dry."

"Yes, but not enough time to meet someone, fall in love and get engaged."

"Maybe not for a stick-in-the-mud like you, but for me it was like that." She snapped her fingers. "Love at first sight."

"More like lust," Clay grumbled, but he didn't grumble it softly enough because both Hayden and Hunter started a babble fest with *shit* and *lust*. "Where were the boys during all of this?" He snapped his fingers to imitate April's description of the joyous event.

"With their dad. Spike and I worked out a custody schedule. We'll alternate weeks."

Clay thought a week was too long for the boys to go without seeing one of their parents, especially since it would be Spike's, aka Ryan's, folks who ended up taking care of the boys when it was his week of custody. Ryan's folks were decent enough people and were well respected in Wrangler's Creek, but like April, Spike had some growing up to do. But that was another debate for another day. Right now, Clay had bigger fish to fry.

"Who's your *fiancé*?" Because as soon as he had a name, Clay would run a background check on him. He loved his sister—most of the time anyway—but April was a turd magnet when it came to men.

April quit smiling. "Now, before you bad-mouth him, or me, just hear me out. I'm in love with him, and he's a decent man."

Hell. That couldn't be good. "What's his name?"

"When I tell you, you've got to promise not to curse or yell. This could work out good for you, too. Well, since rumor has it that you're seeing Sophie Granger and all."

He pulled back his shoulders. "Sophie? I'm not seeing her. And what the heck does she have to do with this anyway?"

Clay looked at the ring. At the hickey on his sister's neck.

And the answer hit him like a fully loaded Mack truck exceeding the speed limit.

CHAPTER THREE

CLAY PULLED TO a stop in the circular drive that fronted the Granger ranch. To say he was dreading this visit was like saying it got a little bit hot in Texas during the summer.

This was his first trip here, but he'd driven past the place plenty of times. Hard to miss it with the sprawling house, sprawling pastures and miles of white fence. It looked the way he wanted his own place to look one day. Scaled down, of course, and with a real house with stuff in places where stuff belonged.

He was betting the Grangers didn't have a toilet in their living room.

Clay got out of his truck, taking his time and hoping this went better than the scenarios playing out in his mind. Of course, there weren't any good scenarios in this situation except that maybe Sophie had already moved on with her life and didn't give a rat's ass about anything.

He certainly did, and in Sophie's and his case, they had a rat in common.

Brantley.

Sophie needed to know that Brantley had proposed to April. That didn't mean the marriage was going to happen. For Clay, this qualified as one of those "over my dead body" situations. Brantley was only a month out of a long-term relationship with Sophie. A relationship he'd apparently ended because of some "love at first sight" shit with April.

Yeah, definitely over Clay's dead body.

He made his way up the porch steps but before he could ring the doorbell, Clay heard something he didn't want to hear. It sounded as if someone was crying. He went to the end of the porch and looked in the side yard and spotted the crier.

Sophie.

She was standing beneath a massive oak while she brushed down a bay mare. A tabby cat was coiling around her legs. No wedding dress today. She was wearing jeans and a white top. But like the day of the failed wedding, tears were streaming down her face.

Hell.

That wouldn't make this visit any easier, and he got out his handkerchief and went to her. She must have heard him coming because when he was still several yards away, her head snapped up, and she immediately started wiping away the tears with the back of her hand. He spooked the cat, too, because it jetted out of there as if Clay had scalded it.

"Don't tell Garrett," Sophie said, moving away from the horse.

He handed her the handkerchief. "Don't tell him what?"

She motioned toward her face. "He feels I should be over this by now, that my ex isn't worth the tears."

He's not.

But Clay kept that to himself for now.

"It's stupid," she went on. Since she didn't ask him why he was there, it was obvious that Sophie had some things she wanted to get off her chest. "I'm over him. I really am. And I hate him. But sometimes, things close in around me like a dark cloud, you know?"

He did know. Clay had a dark cloud of his own. One even darker than Sophie's.

She looked at him then, her gaze connecting with his. He glanced away but not before practically getting lost in those deep blue eyes. The color of a fancy stone in an equally fancy ring.

The color of *her* eyes.

Until he'd seen Sophie's, Clay had been sure there'd been only one pair of eyes like that. He'd been wrong.

"I went to the old gypsy lady who lives in the trailer just up the road," Sophie continued. "You know about her?"

Clay nodded, made sure he didn't make direct eye contact with Sophie. The woman's name was Vita Banchini. She was a local legend, like Big Foot, except she supposedly doled out curses and love potions. She was also Clay's nearest neighbor.

"Vita's my best friend's mom," Sophie went on. "Mila. But if you see Mila, don't mention I went there. Don't mention you saw me crying, either."

"Wouldn't dream of it." Besides, he doubted Mila and he would ever have a conversation about anything, especially this. The few times he'd seen Mila at the bookstore she owned, she hadn't spoken a word to him. Rumor had it that she was the town's thirty-year-old virgin.

"You're going to think I'm crazy, but I had Vita read my palm." Sophie groaned softly. "And she said it was over between me and my ex—that I needed to look elsewhere for the future I've been planning. That tells you how crazy I am to do something like that. I don't even believe in fortune-tellers."

She must have taken his grunt as a conversational green light because she kept talking. "Today would have been our one-month wedding anniversary. If the wedding had actually happened, that is. On top of everything else, it just got to me."

Clay grunted again. If he kept this up, she'd think he had indigestion. Maybe social anxiety, too, what with him not actually looking her directly in the eyes.

"How is everything else?" he risked asking.

Sophie opened her mouth, maybe to give a polite "fine" answer, but it must have stuck in her throat. "I've avoided going into town. Gossip." She hadn't needed to clarify that. "And I've banned anyone on the property from saying my ex's name."

Which meant she probably hadn't heard the news about Brantley and April's engagement. Their temporary engagement, that is.

Clay wasn't sure why he felt the need to come and tell her in person. This certainly wasn't a police matter, and after the date debacle at the station, Sophie likely wanted to avoid him as much as her ex.

Or not.

That wasn't exactly a get-lost gesture she was giving him, and just as she'd done in the police station a month ago, she launched herself into his arms. "Play along, please," she whispered.

Clay glanced around to see what had put her up to this and soon spotted the source. Her cousin, Lawson. The lanky cowboy was making a beeline toward them. Clay knew him, of course, and vice versa. Knew plenty of gossip, too, and not just what he'd heard from Mick. Lots of people were concerned that Lawson would feel pushed out of the place he'd worked. He'd made his home in

Wrangler's Creek as well, since he and his girlfriend lived in a house just up the street from the police department.

"Chief McKinnon," Lawson said. "Or I guess that's still interim chief?"

"It is, but call me Clay." They exchanged nodded greetings despite the fact that Sophie still had her arms around him.

Sophie finally stepped back, but she stayed right by Clay's side. "My allergies are bothering me again," she told her cousin. No doubt to explain the red eyes.

Lawson shook his head. "Bullshit. But as your older male cousin, I have a genetic responsibility to ask if the bawling is about the numb nuts whose name we're not allowed to mention or if *Clay* is responsible."

Since Lawson said Clay's name as if he were an incurable toenail fungus, it was possible he believed the latter. Or maybe this was just more of his obligatory genetic responsibility. If so, that was good, because it meant Lawson wasn't harboring any ill feelings about Sophie's return to the ranch.

Of course, there was another possibility.

Even though Sophie hadn't been into town to hear the gossip, Lawson likely had been, and Lawson's stink eye was possibly for the part Clay had in this relationship mess. Not that Clay actually had a part in it, but maybe Sophie's cousin thought he was guilty by genetic association.

"It's about the numb nuts," Sophie admitted. "But don't tell Garrett."

Lawson made a locked motion over his mouth and shifted his attention to Clay. "Did you really get attacked by chickens?"

Hell. Was that going to follow him around for the rest of his life? "Feral chickens," Clay corrected.

Sophie shifted her attention to him, too. "The Penningtons didn't take those hens with them when they sold the place?"

"No." Clay could say that with absolute certainty. They were there and in the attack mode whenever they saw him. Something he'd never admit. His manhood had already taken a nosedive because of the little bastards.

"Heard, too, that you were renovating the place," Lawson went on.

Yet another pride-reducing topic that Clay wanted to avoid. He settled for a nod.

"When you're done with your visit," Lawson said to Sophie, "Garrett wants to see you. He's in the barn right now, but he needs to go over some business stuff. Heads up, though—he's not in a good mood. Paperwork," he added.

Sophie made a sound of agreement. "Garrett hates paperwork," she explained to Clay. "Actually, he hates anything that requires a desk. And pens. Computers, too."

Strange, considering Garrett was the CEO of a business. But in a way, that didn't really surprise Clay. The few times he'd seen Sophie's brother, Garrett had looked more like a ranch hand than the boss. Plus, even before their financial mess, Garrett had actually spent plenty of time here. Unlike Sophie.

"Take your time before you see Garrett," Lawson went on. "Get your *allergies* under control first."

She nodded. Huffed.

"By business stuff he means cows," Sophie said when Lawson strolled away. "Lawson normally runs the day-to-day operation of the ranch, but things are far from normal right now. Apparently, we're buying a big herd of cows with money from our trust funds. Long story," she grumbled.

From what Clay had heard it wasn't that long. Sophie and Garrett needed an income, and the ranch would provide that if they worked it as it should be worked, that is. A ranch meant livestock. While it was a subject that interested him, he'd already wasted enough time on small talk and catching up. Best to go ahead and tell Sophie the reason for his visit.

However, once again she spoke before he could say anything. "I owe you two apologies. One for the hug a month ago and another for the one I just gave you."

He lifted his shoulder. "No apology needed, but FYI, I don't think the hugs are convincing anyone that we're together."

"Probably not." She glanced up at him. "But thank you for coming out here to check on me. After the fool I made of myself, I figured you'd want to keep your distance."

He did want that but not for the reasons Sophie was thinking. "You didn't make a fool of yourself," he said, and maybe that would help with what he had to say next. "You know I have a sister, right?"

She looked at him. Clearly puzzled. Probably because she didn't have a clue what a fool and his sister had in common.

A lot.

Sophie nodded. "April. She moved to Wrangler's Creek a couple of years ago when she married Spike Devereaux, and she works at the Curl-Up and Dye Salon."

"She still works there, but Spike and she got a divorce."

"I'm sorry to hear that." Fresh tears sprang to her eyes, maybe because it reminded her that her own marriage hadn't worked out. "Didn't they have kids?"

Clay nodded. "Twin boys. They're two years old."

And he felt another punch in his gut. Something that he'd been feeling since April had shown up at his house the day before with the news. His nephews were the main reason he'd moved to Wrangler's Creek, so he could make sure they weren't getting jacked around.

Clay had failed big-time.

And he was failing now, too, because he just couldn't think of how to tell Sophie what he didn't especially want to tell her. He opened his mouth to blurt it out when her phone buzzed. She yanked it from her jeans pocket and grumbled something he didn't catch when she looked at the screen.

"I'm sorry, but I have to take this. Roman," she greeted the moment she hit the button to answer it.

Her other brother. The one with a police record. Judging from the fact that he hadn't come to his only sister's wedding, Clay figured it wasn't much of a stretch to say their relationship was strained.

And one-sided.

Other than her greeting, she didn't manage to say anything. Clay was close enough to hear the chattering on the other end, but he couldn't hear what her brother was saying. Whatever it was though, it clearly didn't please her because her forehead bunched up.

She stepped away from Clay, maybe to give herself some privacy, and she even glanced at him to see if he was staying. He was. That caused her to put a little more distance between them.

"I really would like you home right now," she said to her brother. "At least for a little while."

Clay decided it was a good time to stroll toward the back to get a better look at the place. Unfortunately, the breeze didn't cooperate because it sent the sound of Sophie's voice right at him.

"All of that happened years ago," Sophie argued. "Garrett and I need you here if for no other reason than to sign all these papers." She paused. "You can't give us the ranch—you know that. You know the terms of Daddy's will as well as I do, and you can't give or sell it to anyone. It's yours until you die."

Clay walked even farther away. Apparently, Sophie was getting hit on several fronts, and Clay had heard at least some of the story with Roman. From the bits and pieces he'd heard, it wasn't the first time they'd argued about the terms of their father's will. Whatever the problem was, it was big enough for Roman to stay away.

"No, I don't want you to kill Brantley for me," she continued. She shot a look at Clay, who tried to pretend he hadn't heard what she'd just said. "Don't even joke about something like that… Of course, you're joking. And no, the ranch won't fit up that particular cavity of Brantley's body. Just consider coming home. *Please.*"

Sophie finished her call, and she joined him at the corral fence. "Sorry about that. My brother. Another long story."

Clay hated to get in the middle of this, but there seemed to be an obvious solution. "Roman lives in San Antonio. Less than an hour from Wrangler's Creek. Since he doesn't want to be here, maybe you could hire someone to courier the paperwork back and forth?"

She nodded. "That works when he's home, but he's on the road a lot for his rodeo business. By choice. He's got people who can travel for him, but he likes doing that himself." Sophie took in a quick breath. "Now, what were we talking about before we got on the subject of my brother?"

Clay didn't get a chance to say because they were interrupted for a third time when someone called out her name. It wasn't a voice that Clay immediately recognized, but Sophie apparently did. Her shoulders snapped back, and she caught on to Clay's arm.

"Oh, God. It's Brantley."

Shit.

This was about to get ugly. Well, unless Brantley had had a change of heart and was here to grovel at Sophie's feet. Even then it could still get ugly.

"Clay," Brantley said, extending his hand for him to shake.

Clay tried not to break his fingers. All right, he didn't try that hard, and it felt a little too good to see the man wince.

Still wincing and wiggling his fingers after Clay let go, Brantley volleyed glances between them. "So, you told her, I guess?"

Clay had to shake his head. "Not yet," he said at the same moment that Sophie asked, "Tell me what?"

Clay debated what to do. The news should come from Brantley, but he honestly hadn't expected the guy to show up and do this face-to-face. Maybe he did have some balls after all.

Good. Because it would give Clay something to bust.

For now, though, he had to tell Sophie the news that would likely make her cry again. Not here in front of them. But as soon as she could get somewhere private, she would.

"Brantley proposed to my sister," Clay said.

Clay gave her a moment to let that sink in. Sophie's mouth was slightly open, and her stare was fixed on him.

"My sister said yes," Clay went on, "but I've asked her to reconsider."

Truth be told, he'd demanded it. Because there was no way she should be getting involved with a man like Brantley, especially this soon after her divorce.

Still no reaction from Sophie. Damn. She might be going into shock.

"Did you hear me?" Clay asked her. "Brantley and my sister are engaged."

Brantley shook his head. "Actually, we're not."

Thank the Lord and anybody else who'd had a part in this. April and Brantley had come to their senses and called off this nonsense. Clay didn't whoop for joy, but he would later. For now, it was time to get out of there so Sophie and this clown could perhaps work out a reconciliation. Even though Sophie deserved a hell of a lot better.

"Are you engaged or not?" Sophie asked Brantley just as Clay turned to leave.

"No."

There was something in Brantley's one-word answer that had Clay stopping in his tracks, and he turned around just in time to see Brantley reaching out to Sophie. Except he wasn't reaching. He was extending his left hand.

To show her the ring he was wearing.

"Not engaged," Brantley clarified. "April and I are married."

CHAPTER FOUR

SOPHIE'S THROAT SNAPPED SHUT, and that's why she was surprised she'd managed to make a sound. Unfortunately, the sound that came out of her mouth was profanity. Stupid, G-rated profanity.

Turd on a turkey.

It wasn't the right thing to say, of course. Not just now but in any situation whatsoever. Nor was it good for her to have what was no doubt a thunderstruck look on her face. She should have steeled up, put on the best mask she could muster and pretended that Brantley hadn't just ripped out her heart. Clearly, she'd failed at that.

"I know this is a surprise," Brantley continued.

He didn't continue talking, though, because Clay came back toward them and got right in Brantley's face. And Clay cursed, too. His profanity was a lot better suited to the situation than Sophie's.

"That'd better be a fucking joke, you dickhead piece of shit," Clay growled.

Brantley lowered his hand, dropped back a step, and his eyes widened. He looked genuinely surprised that Clay was upset with his news. That took some of the spotlight off her, and Sophie used that time to try to get control of her emotions.

"Uh, I thought April told you," Brantley said to Clay. Sophie moved to Clay's side but not too close. He looked ready to implode. A first. Every other time she'd seen him, he'd been cucumber-cool. Now he was more like lava-hot.

"No, she didn't tell me," Clay answered. He whipped out his phone, no doubt to call his sister, but he was gripping it so hard she was surprised it didn't shatter. He also didn't make the call. Maybe because his grip was too tight to make his fingers work. "How the hell did this happen?" he snarled.

Even though Brantley likely wanted to drop back another step, he held his ground. "I love April," he said.

All in all, it was a good answer. Possibly the best one he could have given a new brother-in-law who looked ready to rip off every protruding part of Brantley's body.

Brantley turned to Sophie. "You knew how I felt about April," he added.

"Uh, no I didn't."

But Sophie certainly knew how *she* felt. The ache came. And thankfully vanished because the anger roared in behind it to push it away.

"I didn't know," Sophie stated, but she had to do it through a clenched jaw. Though her jaw was practically slack compared to Clay's.

"I told you," Brantley insisted, "when I called you... well, a few hours after we were supposed to be married."

Sophie remembered the call that had come in while she'd been at the office. She'd hung up on Brantley but not before he'd said something she hadn't caught.

"You mentioned a belt," she offered.

Brantley shook his head and seemed confused before an *aha* look went through his eyes. "I didn't say belt. I said *bolt* as in lightning bolt. Because that's the way I felt when I first saw April. It was love at first sight. Real love," he tacked on as if it might help.

It didn't. It didn't help Sophie with her anger, and judging from the way Clay looked, it didn't help him, either.

"Real love?" Clay repeated. His voice had a dangerous edge to it that sent Sophie's pulse skittering. "My sister's barely out of one bad marriage. She doesn't need another one. Her boys don't need another one." The edge in his voice had gone up a notch.

"This isn't a bad marriage," Brantley argued. He huffed. "Look, I didn't think this news would be such a shock. In fact, I thought it'd be welcome now that Sophie and you are seeing each other. Sophie has moved on, and that's a good thing."

Oh, if only that were true. Then again, she had moved on from the raging anger to wanting to throw that turdy turkey at him. But that probably wasn't the direction Brantley was looking for her to go. Nor was it the direction Clay was taking.

Clay's index finger landed on Brantley's chest. "If you hurt my sister or my nephews, this badge will come off and I will make you pay. In fact, I might make you pay even if you don't hurt them."

It didn't sound like a bluff, but Brantley didn't have time to call him on it. Garrett came strolling out of one of the nearby barns, cursed, his profanity waffling on the air so they caught every word, and made a beeline toward them.

Great. Now, he'd get involved. At least she wasn't crying, though. Maybe it would stay that way.

As Garrett got closer, Sophie caught his usual scent. A mixture of bullshit from his boots, sweat and the woodsy aftershave he sometimes remembered to use on the days he remembered to shave. It was hit or miss, but he'd hit today, and there was the added aroma of leather from his saddle. Heaven knew where he'd been riding, but he was always looking for any excuse to be anywhere but inside his office.

"It's true?" Garrett snarled, looking not at Clay or her but at Brantley. "You're married? Meredith told me," he added to Sophie before she could ask how he'd found out.

Meredith, Garrett's wife. Apparently, the gossip flow had taken the direct route to her. Ironic since Meredith spent more time at her dad's house in Austin than she did at the ranch, but she did spend more time on the phone than Sophie did.

Brantley bobbed his head in a series of nods, a motion that mimicked the movement of his Adam's apple. He lobbed some very concerned glances between her brother and Clay as if debating which of these two were about to end his existence on Earth. It was a toss-up, but since she didn't want either to go to jail, she stepped between them.

"Yes, Brantley is married," Sophie volunteered. "And he was just leaving."

"No, he wasn't," Clay argued. "Not until he explains to me what the hell he was thinking by marrying my kid sister."

"And when the shit bag is done explaining that, he can tell me why he jilted *my* kid sister." That from Garrett. "You've been dodging me. Lawson, too. And it's high time you grew a pair and manned up about why you did this."

Brantley looked at her as if she might have the answers to prevent him from getting a butt-whipping. She did. Well, she had answers to her brother's question. Brantley hadn't loved her. Not enough, anyway. But while that was true, it might not stop said butt-whipping.

This was what she'd tried to avoid that day at the police station, and part of her knew she had to grow her own pair and stop it from happening now.

"I have moved on with my life," Sophie said to no one in particular and hoped they didn't ask for proof of that. She also hoped this next part didn't stick in her throat. "Brantley did me a favor by breaking things off."

Clay and Garrett stared at her, and both looked about as unconvinced of that as anyone could.

"See?" Brantley added. "It's all okay. Sophie and Clay are together, and April and I will start our lives as newlyweds."

"We're not together," Sophie said.

Clay talked right over her, though, so she wasn't sure anyone heard her. "You're not starting anything," he warned Brantley. "Where's April?"

"My house here in Wrangler's Creek. *Our* house," Brantley corrected. "I just moved her and the boys in." And despite Clay's intense glare, Brantley managed to hike up his chin and look as if he'd located his backbone.

The backbone display didn't last long, though.

The color bleached from Brantley's face when Clay took hold of his arm. Hard. The kind of grip he no doubt used when making an arrest. "Come on. You, April and me are about to have a little talk."

TALKING SUCKED, TOO.

At least it did when a big brother was talking to a knotheaded kid sister. After an hour of trying to drill home why marrying Brantley was a stupid idea, Clay had left to regroup and try to come up with an argument that might get April to come to her senses and annul the marriage. Or at least rethink it.

In the meantime, he hoped Brantley didn't a) break her heart b) stunt the emotional development of his nephews or c) knock April up. Just in case of the latter, Clay made a mental note to send April a jumbo box of condoms.

That hadn't worked with Spike and her, but maybe this time April would remember to have Brantley use them. Even though he wouldn't trade his nephews for the world, his sister needed another kid to raise even less than she needed another dickweed husband.

Clay walked into the police station, and of course, all eyes immediately went to him. Ellie's, Rowdy's and Reena's. The gossip had probably already reached them, and they might be concerned that he'd assaulted Brantley.

"Brantley's alive and in one piece," Clay greeted to put their minds at ease and to stop them from asking him anything. But it was clear that it eased nothing.

"Uh, you got another of those envelopes," Reena said, scrubbing her hands down the sides of her jeans, and she immediately looked away. "I put it on your desk."

Clay didn't ask for any details because he knew what she meant by *those envelopes*. Reena and the crew had no idea what was in them, though. They only knew he got one on the first of each month and that he only opened them behind closed doors. They also knew the envelopes put him in a shit-kicking mood. Since his mood was already at the shit-kicking level, it didn't bode well for workplace morale.

He made his way to his office, and right off he spotted the large document-sized envelope in the center of his desk. Hard to miss it since it was Pepto-Bismol pink.

Like the others, it was addressed to Detective Clay Mc-
Kinnon, care of the Wrangler's Creek PD and was post-
marked from Houston. Also like the others, the sender
had made a heart of the *o* in his surname.

Because he needed a minute—he always did when it
came to these deliveries—Clay sank down into his chair
and considered a drink. He kept a bottle of cheap Irish
whiskey in his bottom drawer. It was on top of a copy of
his resignation papers from Houston PD, which in turn
was on top of his last case file when he'd worked there.
Beneath that were more pink envelopes, one for every
month he'd been at Wrangler's Creek PD.

Just opening the drawer was like going into his "shit
to forget" box in his head so he decided to pass on the
whiskey. Good thing, too, because there was a knock at
the door, and it opened.

Before the woman even stepped into his office, he
caught a whiff of her. Garlic, for sure. Limburger cheese,
maybe. And Listerine. It was his neighbor, Vita.

Clay wasn't sure exactly how old Vita was, but she
had to be a lot younger than she looked because she had
a thirty-year-old daughter, Mila. Yet she looked to be a
hundred and sixty. Or maybe that wasn't actually wrinkles upon wrinkles but instead she was smearing her face
with Limburger cheese.

Like the other times he'd seen her, Vita was wearing
a long brown skirt, so long that the hem was dusting the
floor, and enough cheap bead necklaces to act as an anchor if she ever got caught in a tornado.

"I came," Vita announced as if he was expecting her.
He wasn't. But then you never really expected Vita. She
was like a cold sore and just showed up.

Best to cut her off at the pass and make this visit as

short as possible. The longer she stayed the more air freshener he'd have to use. "If this is about my sister and Brantley—"

"No. There's nothing to be done about that." Her attention landed on the pink envelope. "Or that, either."

Well, this was a cheery visit. Not that he had any faith whatsoever in Vita's future-telling/ESP powers that she claimed were in her gypsy blood, but if she'd offered him any hope, he might have latched on to it.

"I came about the chickens," Vita said. "They'll attack again soon."

That got his attention, and Clay frowned over the way his gut suddenly tensed. "How do you know this? Have the chickens been talking to you?"

The woman didn't crack a smile at his bad joke, but she did take something from her skirt pocket. An egg. Not a clean one that came in a carton from the grocery store. This one had what he was pretty sure was a smear of chicken shit on it and a bit of a feather.

"It belongs to one of them," Vita went on, her voice all low and dramatic. "Keep it with you at all times, and they won't attack. Their scent is on it, and they won't risk hurting one of their own."

Clay had no idea how to respond to that so he just grunted. Vita must have taken that as an agreement that he would go along with this because now she smiled. The joke hadn't amused her but a grunt had.

He made a mental note to talk to her daughter about getting her some psychological help.

Vita pulled something else from her pocket. A massive can of Mighty Lube. It was shaped like a penis but double the size.

"For Sophie," Vita said.

All right. Clay wanted to know why Vita believed Sophie would need glorified vegetable oil and why the woman couldn't just give it to Sophie herself. But he was afraid this was meant to be a sex aid, and like feral chickens, he didn't want to discuss that with Vita. He just thanked her, said goodbye and asked her to close the door on her way out. She did those things but not before uttering what sounded like a threat.

"If you hurt Sophie, you'll be sorry. I've read her palm so I know your paths cross."

"Of course they cross. It's a small town."

But he seriously doubted that Vita meant that.

"They'll cross," she went on, "but it'll be up to you which direction she takes after that. Hurt her, and you'll have to deal with me."

As the interim chief of police, Clay supposed he should remind her that it wasn't a good idea to threaten a cop, but instead he reached for the air freshener in his bottom left drawer. It was next to the whiskey. Once the Limburger smell had been cloaked with the scent of fake flowers, Clay turned back to the envelope. Best not to put this off. He reached for it, but reaching was as far as he got because there was another knock at the door.

Hell.

"Yeah?" he snapped, not bothering to sound even remotely receptive to a repeat visit from Vita. But it wasn't her. It was Garrett.

"Got a minute?" Garrett asked, coming in before waiting for an answer.

Reena was right behind him, and since she was frantically trying to fix her hair, it was obvious she wanted to impress their visitor. Clay had noticed that a lot whenever he'd observed women near Garrett. Even though he was married to the town's former prom queen, Sophie's brother caused women to primp, flirt and do other things that were normally directed at good-looking, single men.

Clay had seen a whole lot of eyelash batting going on.

"Vita," Garrett remarked, glancing at the egg.

Maybe the air freshener hadn't done its job. Or else Garrett guessed that Clay wasn't the sort to have a shit-streaked egg on his desk. Thankfully, his attention didn't seem to land on the Mighty Lube, or Garrett might have had some questions that Clay couldn't answer.

Garrett looked at Reena. Smiled. It seemed a little forced to Clay, but he wasn't exactly a smile expert. Still, it started the eyelash batting, and Reena coiled a strand of hair around her finger.

"I need to speak to Clay in private," Garrett added to the deputy.

"Oh, sure." Reena stuttered out a few more syllables, and eyelash batted her way out the door. Which she closed.

Clay had already done some bud-nipping with Vita, but he figured he was going to need another round of it with Garrett. "If you're here to threaten me not to hurt Sophie—"

"I am. In part. But since you're not involved with her, not yet anyway, just keep the threat for future reference."

It probably wasn't the average response, but Clay liked the guy. It's something he would have said to anyone getting involved with April. Of course, Clay's threats hadn't worked, and in Garrett's case, it wasn't needed. Clay wasn't getting involved with Sophie.

"The other part of why I'm here is something I'd like to keep just between us," Garrett went on. "I'd like for you to question Arlo Betterton."

Clay knew the name. Arlo owned the run-down gas station on the edge of town. He was in his sixties and re-sembled Santa Claus in grease-splattered overalls. "Has he committed a crime?"

Garrett shrugged, put his hands on his hips. "He was Billy Lee Seaver's best friend when they were kids." No need for Garrett to clarify who Billy Lee was. "The feds have already talked to him, but Arlo probably didn't do much talking back. He might know something, though, and you might have better luck getting it out of him."

"I doubt it. To Arlo I'd be as much of an outsider as the feds or Skunk the pig farmer."

Garrett didn't argue with that. "Lie to him. Cops can do that. Tell him you're sleeping with Sophie, and you're worried about her. Tell him that you need to find Billy Lee because you're afraid Sophie's about to fall apart."

"Is she about to fall apart?" Clay asked before he could think about why he shouldn't ask it.

It was a personal question, not related to this investiga-tion. And it was what his granddaddy would have called a red pecker flag. Pecker as in dick. Flag as in Clay's dick that had prompted the personal question about Sophie. Garrett picked up on it right away and scowled.

"No, she's not about to fall apart," Garrett assured him. "She's a lot tougher than she realizes, and that means she doesn't need a shoulder to cry on or a fuck buddy to console her. She just needs time to realize that Brantley is cow shit and that she deserves a whole lot bet-ter. Sorry," he added, no doubt because Garrett remem-bered that the cow shit was now Clay's brother-in-law.

Clay was sure he scowled, too, at that thought, but it was easy to push cow shit aside when Garrett had just dished up some official business. "Wouldn't you have better luck talking to Arlo than I would?"

"No. He doesn't trust me. He thinks all I want is to find Billy Lee, lock him up and throw away the key."

"Don't you?"

Garrett opened his mouth as if he might say something to contradict that, but he shook his head. "Just talk to Arlo when you get a chance."

"Okay. I will." It was the closest thing to any real police work as Clay might get. Plus, he might get lucky if he played the fake dating-Sophie card. Of course, that would only keep the rumor mill spinning about them, but as long as Garrett seemed to know the truth, that was okay with him. "And for what it's worth, I'm sorry about what happened to your business."

Garrett shrugged. "It was something my great-granddad started, a family legacy of sorts. Personally, I thought the ranch was legacy enough, but my dad and granddad wanted to keep the business going so we did. But it meant more to Sophie and my wife than me. And it's not like we're homeless or broke."

No, even though the gossips were divided on the Grangers' adjusted net worth. It varied from ten million to six billion. Clay figured it was on the lower end of those estimates, which meant they were still rich but had perhaps fallen out of the stinkin' rich tax bracket. With all the work Garrett was doing at the ranch though, they'd be back in that bracket in no time at all.

Garrett tipped his head to Clay's desk. "Sophie has one that looks exactly like that."

It took Clay a moment to realize Garrett was looking at the envelope, and his ribs nearly cracked when his heart slammed against his chest. "Sophie got a letter like this?"

"Similar to it."

Garrett kept on talking, but Clay could no longer hear him. That's because his pulse was drumming in his ears. Hell. Sophie wasn't part of this. Clay was about to snatch up the phone, but then he caught some of Garrett's words.

Father. Thirtieth birthday.

"What did you say?" Clay asked.

Another head tip toward the envelope. "I was saying that my father died ten years ago when I was twenty-four, but he left us letters to be opened on our thirtieth birthdays. Sophie'll open hers in November. For some reason, he put hers in a pink envelope. Mine and Roman's were in white ones. For a second there, I thought maybe Dad had left you some kind of instructions, too."

"No," Clay quickly assured him. "It's not from your father."

Garrett leaned in, had a closer look, and he must have noticed the heart *o* because the corner of his mouth lifted into a near smile. "Good. Because so far my dad's letters have been, well, a mixed bag of news, and you've already had enough of that."

Yeah, he had. And Clay didn't want to include Sophie in any of his personal mixed bag.

As Vita had done, Garrett left and shut the door behind him. Clay waited to see if there'd be more interruptions, but when a couple of minutes crawled by without another knock, he knew he should just get this done. Fast. Like ripping off a bandage. It would still hurt, but at least it'd be over.

For another month, anyway.

The sender, however, probably wouldn't wait a month to leave a message on the landline phone at Clay's house.

Those didn't come with the same regularity as the letters. But still, they came.

Clay used scissors to open the envelope, and he eased out the three pieces of paper. Two were pictures. One before. One after. He looked at both with the same reverence a good priest would look at a dying patient getting last rites.

Seeing the pictures was a sort of penance. They told a story, but they sure as hell didn't change anything.

Neither did the third paper.

But he studied it anyway. Not that there was much to study. Like the other three pages in the other envelopes, this one had a single word handwritten on it.

Killer.

CLAY PULLED HIS cruiser to a stop on the side of Arlo's Pump and Ride. He wanted to think that Arlo Betterton hadn't had a dirty mind when he'd named the place back in the early '70s, but since Clay had gotten complaints about Arlo's too-prominent display of adult magazines, the name had likely been intentional.

Before Clay even made it to the front, the door opened, the bell attached to it clanging, and Arlo stepped out. "If you're needing some gas, you're parked in the wrong place, Chief." Arlo was wiping his greasy hands on an equally greasy rag.

There were no other customers, no employees, either, which meant Arlo and he might be able to have a private conversation. Clay wasn't holding out hope that it would be a productive one, but he wanted to be able to tell Garrett that he'd tried.

Clay glanced around, taking in his surroundings. Old habits. The only danger here was slipping on some motor oil and throwing out his back, but after so many years of being a cop, it was hard to turn off his cop's eyes. Hard to turn off his brain, too, and since the contents of the pink envelope were still plenty fresh he hadn't been able to wrestle away the demons.

Killer.

Not a pretty label.

"If you're not needing gas then," Arlo went on, "come inside, and I'll get you some coffee. Made it myself just a couple minutes ago. It'll give you something to drink when you tell me why you're here."

"I'll pass on the coffee." And not because he didn't want to drink anything Arlo had made with those hands but because Clay's nerves were already jangling. No need to fuel those nerves with caffeine.

"Suit yourself. I'll pour myself one." Arlo went to the counter. Also grease stained. Ditto for the coffeepot. Probably the coffee, as well, since there seemed to be a mini oil slick swirling on top of the cup. "So, are you here because of Vita?"

Clay tried not to look surprised and held back from saying "why the hell would I be here because of Vita?" He'd learned that some folks gave him more info when he didn't actually question them so he just raised an eyebrow.

Arlo huffed. "Vita was in earlier, whining about feed. She accused me of feeding those chickens that've been pestering you out at your place. She said she saw feed on the ground. Well, it wasn't me. I got no reason to want chickens to stay around so they can go after you."

All that from a raised eyebrow so Clay raised his other one. Later, he'd check and see if there really was feed on the ground near his house.

"It's true." Arlo huffed again. "But there are some folks who might want to see you…pecked a little. But not me. I'm not bothered by cops, even when they're just an intern one, but some folks are."

Clay just kept his eyebrows raised and didn't correct "intern" to "interim."

Arlo added some profanity to his huff. "Ask Ordell Busby about the feed 'cause I'm betting it was one of his boys. They're always up for a good prank."

Clay knew about the Busby boys' penchant for pranking. It was harmless stuff like TP'ing yards and trying to tip a cow. To the best of his knowledge, they'd never actually succeeded at a prank without getting caught, but it wouldn't be hard to get away with tossing out some chicken feed.

"I'll talk to them," Clay said, and he didn't budge. He just stood there, eyebrows raised and perhaps looking as if his forehead had had a run-in with some extra potent Botox.

The seconds crawled by. And crawled. But Arlo eventually huffed. "So, you're really here about Sophie."

Clay made a sound that could have meant anything. Or nothing. Arlo opted for the something because he started huffing, cursing and talking again.

"I heard Sophie's down in the dumps. Heard it might be more than just down, that she might have that depression people have to take pills for. Guess you haven't been able to cheer her up any?"

Clay had to lower his eyebrows because his facial muscles were starting to twitch, but Arlo must have taken it as a cue to continue.

"Don't guess anything but getting her business back would chase away those blues. Well, I can't help you there, *intern* Chief. I don't know anything about where Billy Lee is right now at this moment."

You didn't have to be a cop to hear the slight pause Arlo made before *right now at this moment*, but Clay decided it was time to do more than offer up facial gestures. "Do you know where Billy Lee is, was or has been in the past month since he's been missing?"

That brought on more cursing from Arlo. "I already told those FBI fellas I didn't know, and now I'm telling you the same thing. Billy Lee's not here, and I haven't seen him."

Clay decided to use his cop's voice for the next question. "Have you communicated with Billy Lee in any way in the past month?"

Arlo looked him straight in the eyes. "No."

Clay studied him, trying to decide if he was lying. Strange but he didn't seem to be. Just in case though, Clay upped his stare a while longer, waiting to see if Arlo would break down and start blabbing. But he was literally saved by the bell. The one clanging over the door.

"Gotta go," Arlo said. "Got a customer."

Clay didn't stop him, but he did make a mental note. There was something going on with Arlo. Maybe something connected to Billy Lee. And he needed to keep an eye on it.

CHAPTER FIVE

THIS WAS A new level of Hell. Sophie was sure of it.

It was barely 8:00 a.m.; she hadn't even finished her first cup of coffee and had paperwork to do on the sperm and the bull pump Garrett wanted her to purchase. But she wasn't doing paperwork. Mila was on one side of her, Sophie's mother, Belle, on the other, and they both had opened tablets to show Sophie what they'd found through their internet search.

They'd found Hell aka dating sites.

"It's been six months since the *unfortunate incident*," her mother reminded her. "It's time to move on before winter sets in."

Maybe winter was a metaphor for life passing her by, but knowing her mother she could simply be thinking of Sophie needing someone to snuggle with once it got cold. And she did miss snuggling. But she doubted she'd find that on a site called Type-A-Businessmen.com.

"They're all professionals," her mom said as if that would help.

"Brantley was a professional," Sophie pointed out. A lawyer. On paper he was perfect for her, but Sophie hadn't been able to marry the paper.

Her mother hesitated, no doubt thinking up a comeback. "Well these are professionals who haven't jilted anyone."

Sophie had no idea if that was actually in the bios or if her mother was just making that up to get her to take that first step into Hell.

"There are plenty of other sites," Mila piped up. To prove that, she promptly showed Sophie the page for Cowboy-Match.com.

After one glance, Sophie concluded that not all cowboys were hot. Some were downright ugly and one had what appeared to be a lump of chewing tobacco in his jaw, complete with brown spittle on his chin.

"You like cowboys," Mila added, frowning at the spittle guy.

Sophie did. When she was looking at shirtless pictures of them on the internet. She liked the snug jeans, boots and hats. She liked the way chaps framed their junk. But those cowboys who'd posed for man candy pictures probably didn't need dating sites.

"How about this one?" Her mother pulled up another site. "This one is Well-Endowed-Hunks.com."

Both Mila and Sophie turned to her mother, giving her blank stares.

"What?" Belle protested. "There's nothing wrong with a man being large in that area." She pointed to her own nether region.

So, her mother did know what it meant. Sophie had considered that maybe she thought that meant they'd inherited a lot of money.

You couldn't always tell if her mother was clued into reality or not. She looked prim and proper as if she should be on one of those TV shows from the sixties, the ones where the moms wore high heels to do housework. Not a hair out of place. Lipstick was a necessity, and she wore hard padded bras that could bruise you when she gave you a hug.

"Well, if you don't want a large endowment," Belle went on, "I'll look for a site for men with small weenies."

Sophie groaned. "Don't. Please don't. In fact, you both need to leave so I can get some work done. Mila, shouldn't you be at the bookstore?"

"It doesn't open for another hour."

Sophie groaned again. "Well, I need you both to leave. I have to order a machine to jack off the bulls. After that, I have to order some sperm." If she'd had her coffee, Sophie was certain she would have phrased that better. Supplies for the ranch would have sufficed.

The color blanched from her mother's face. Not a pretty sight since that only made her bright red lipstick glare like a baboon's butt. "God, Sophie, you're not thinking of artificial insemination."

She wanted to groan again, but her throat was getting sore. "No. It's bull semen for all those cows that were delivered yesterday. Garrett wanted the machine so the hands could, well, get some from the bulls we already have. But it apparently won't be enough so I have to buy more. And I really do need to get it ordered this morning to stop the cows and Garrett from getting testy."

Sophie might as well have been talking to her coffee because once her mother got back her color she just continued advancing into those levels of Hell.

"Here's one I bookmarked. NicheDating.org, and you put in exactly what you want, and it matches you with your dream guy."

Sophie laughed and didn't bother to take the sarcasm out of it. She drank some more of her coffee and started filling out the sperm order, hoping it would prompt her best friend and mother to leave. It didn't.

"Go ahead," her mother insisted. "Tell me your dream man, and I'll type it in for you."

"Tall," Mila answered for her. "And dark hair." She stopped, snapped her fingers. "What about Shane Whitlock, the hand who used to work here? He owns his own ranch now near Bulverde, and I'm pretty sure he's single."

Shane. The guy Sophie had had a semicrush on in middle school. Because her attention had turned to Brantley in tenth grade, the crush hadn't led to anything, and it wouldn't now.

"I'll look up his number for you." Mila opened another browser screen and got started on that.

"I don't want Shane's number," Sophie said. "And I don't want my dream guy from Niche.com."

They didn't listen so Sophie ignored them, too, and got busy on the paperwork. Hard to tune out their comments, though.

Her mother: "You really should get serious about this. You're only weeks away from your thirtieth birthday."

Mila: "You're not like me. You like having a man in your life."

Her mother: "And I'll never get grandchildren if you stay a virgin like Mila."

Mila was indeed a virgin, but Sophie didn't tell her mom that she'd lost her virginity when she was eighteen. Not to Brantley, either. They'd just broken up for the umpteenth time, and Sophie had met a bull rider in San Antonio. Lucky McCord. She had some sweet memories of him, but even if she'd wanted to reconnect with him, she couldn't because she heard he'd gotten married.

"If these dating sites are so great," Sophie argued,

"then why haven't the two of you used them? Mom, you've been a widow for ten years, and Mila, you could certainly find that special someone you've been looking for on a site called NicheDating.org."

Her mother: "I don't want another man. Your father was more than enough for me."

Which could be taken several ways since her father could be an overbearing control freak. He was still controlling them in a way with letters he'd written and had arranged to be opened after his death. Heck, he'd even left her mother appointment calendars with reminders of birthdays, to schedule physicals, etc.

Mila: "I'm not looking for a man."

Oh, yes, she was. But she was looking for Mr. Special.

Sophie wouldn't bring it up in front of her mother, but Mila was obsessed with a BDSM *Fifty Shades of Grey* guy and wanted that kind of experience for her first lover. Sophie had figured her friend would give up by now, but the obsession was hanging on a little longer than her previous obsessions with Mr. Darcy, Captain Jack and assorted *The Lord of the Rings* characters.

Mila had somewhat eclectic tastes when it came to her fantasies.

"Seeing someone will help you get over Brantley," Mila said, obviously moving this conversation back to her.

"I am over Brantley," Sophie insisted.

But they ignored her again.

Her mother: "People feel sorry for you. *I* feel sorry for you."

Sophie suddenly felt sorry for herself. And not because she'd been jilted six months ago but because two people she normally loved were making her insane.

"What about Chief McKinnon? He's hot, and you like him," Mila asked.

This was an easy argument to win. "He's Brantley's brother-in-law."

And it didn't matter that last she heard he still wasn't happy about his sister's marriage. Sophie didn't want to get involved with someone who had that close a connection to a man she now saw as navel lint. Of course, she'd seen Clay since then. Hard to miss anyone in a small town, but thankfully he'd seemed as eager to avoid her as she had been to avoid him.

Man, oh man, she'd made a fool of herself twice in front of him. Once the day of the wedding that didn't happen and again when she'd gone mute after hearing that Brantley and April were married. It was best if she didn't get close enough for round three. Her foolery seemed to escalate whenever she was near him.

"Probably for the best that you aren't looking in Clay's direction," Mila went on. "There's something a little off there."

That got Sophie's attention. "What do you mean?"

"Well, there's almost nothing about him on the internet. No social media accounts, only a smidge of info about him being a cop. You'd think there would be plenty more since Reena said he'd been a Houston cop for twelve years."

Sophie shrugged. "Not everybody splashes their lives on social media." Though it did seem off that there'd been nothing about his investigations.

"Reena thinks maybe Clay did hush-hush cases, like undercover stuff," Mila went on. "But whatever he did, something must have happened for him to give it up and move here."

"He moved here for his sister." At least that was the main reason. But maybe there was something else.

"Ohmygod," her mother blurted out. "Look who popped up as a match when I put in all the things you wanted in a man."

Since Sophie was reasonably sure her mother didn't know what she wanted in a man, she didn't hold out much hope for an accurate match. Still, she had no choice but to look because her mother put the tablet right in her face. And she saw a familiar face.

Shane's.

Mila squealed. "It must be fate because I just found his phone number." She scribbled it down on a piece of paper and tried to hand it to Sophie, but when she didn't take it, Mila stuffed it in the back pocket of Sophie's jeans.

Fate. Was this really some kind of cosmic sign that she needed to start dating? She didn't have to think long on that.

No.

It wasn't a sign. It was a coincidence, and she wasn't ready to risk her heart again on an eerie happenstance.

"Am I, um, interrupting anything?" someone asked from the doorway.

It was her sister-in-law, Meredith, looking her usual perfect self despite the fact Meredith wasn't a morning person.

"Not interrupting a thing," Sophie assured her.

"Sophie's going on a date with this hunk," her mother announced, turning the tablet so that Meredith could see Shane's picture.

"No, I'm not," Sophie mumbled, but she must not have said it loud enough because Meredith didn't seem to hear her.

"Uh, that's nice." Meredith barely looked at the tablet. Barely looked at any of them. "I just wanted to let you know that I'll be back in Austin for a while."

Something was wrong. Of course, something had been wrong for a while because it was obvious Meredith didn't like being at the ranch.

Sophie slowly got to her feet. "Does Garrett know?"

"Yes. We just finished talking. He just left, too, for a cattle buying trip to Laredo." Meredith tried to scrounge up a smile. It wasn't the sort of smile that'd won her all those beauty competitions. She glanced around as if she might have forgotten something and then waved. "I have to go. Daddy's expecting me."

Meredith walked away, leaving Mila, her mother and her to stand there gaping at the empty doorway. "Poor thing," her mother said, "she's still trying to get over that baby she lost."

Maybe, but that had happened nearly two years ago, and Sophie had never been convinced that Meredith was thrilled about becoming a parent. Unlike Garrett. He'd been over the moon about it, and if anyone was still trying to get past the loss of the child, Sophie would put her money on her brother.

"I hope she and Garrett can work it out," Mila added. "I think of them as that couple in the bull riding movie with Clint Eastwood's son. Opposites, yes, but crazy in love."

Sophie hated that this might be the split that she had felt coming. Hated that Garrett might be going through his own version of hell right now, but at least this got the attention off her and those blasted dating sites.

Or not.

"If you don't want to go out with Shane," Mila continued, "here's another dating site for ranchers."

Sophie went to the window and watched Meredith get into her silver BMW and drive away. She also looked around for Garrett's truck, but it wasn't there. She had no idea when he'd be back from the trip and even when he returned, he probably wouldn't want to talk, but Sophie would try.

Hell. Now, there'd be two mopey Grangers under the same roof.

"Garrett will be fine, I'm sure," her mother said. "Meredith, too. They just need a little time to make their way back to each other. Unlike Brantley and you. You know that door's closed for good so that's why Mila and I are trying to help."

Sophie managed one of those fake smiles like Meredith, and she grabbed her purse. If she couldn't order sperm in peace, then she'd go in search of her brother. "Garrett will likely stop in town before leaving for Laredo, and if I hurry, I might be able to catch him." She raced out the door as fast as her feet would carry her.

"We'll look at the dating sites when you get back," her mother called out to her, assuring that Sophie would make this trip as long as possible.

After she returned, Sophie might even set up a base camp office at the guesthouse or one of the barns. There was also a house on the sprawling stretch of Granger land, a Gothic monstrosity that Z.T. had built decades ago. Her mother made sure the place didn't fall in, but that was one of the few good things Sophie could say about it. Unfortunately, the easiest way to get to it these days was on horseback, but heading there was a better option than going another round with the matchmakers.

Sophie got into one of the ranch trucks, and she drove straight into town. A short trip of less than two miles, and she slowed when she got to Main Street so she could look for Garrett. No sign of him so she turned on one of the side streets, hoping he might have stopped in at the Maverick Café for breakfast before heading out on his trip.

Nope.

She tried his cell. No answer. But with Garrett that could mean he was simply on the phone with someone else. Then again, he wasn't the sort to want to share his feelings. With anyone. Including her.

Since she didn't want to go back home so soon, Sophie pulled into the parking lot of the Maverick to get a coffee to go. It was a risk because it was packed, and someone would perhaps give her the "poor, pitiful Sophie" routine where the jilting would be rehashed to make her the victim. It was a testament to how much she needed caffeine that she decided to go in anyway. However, she hadn't made it to the door yet when the sound of laughter stopped her.

But not just laughter. Giggling.

She whirled around and immediately spotted Clay coming out of the café. Not giggling, though. Two toddlers were responsible for that. He had what appeared to be a goblin under one arm and some kind of pint-sized superhero under the other.

Clay stopped when he saw her. The kind of stop a man guilty of something might make. Probably because these were no doubt his nephews. And therefore Brantley's stepsons.

The boys continued to giggle and poke at each other when Clay stood them on the ground. "Halloween costumes. They're heading to playgroup over at the library."

She'd forgotten that Halloween was coming up. Actually, she'd forgotten it was October. She really did need caffeine. And a life.

Maybe sex, too.

But she only had that thought after seeing Clay.

"If you try to run, I'll arrest you," he warned the boys, causing the giggles to escalate. One immediately started to run, and Clay scooped him up so easily that he must have done it dozens of times. The other clamped onto Clay's jeans-clad leg and stared up at Sophie as if she were a deranged killer holding a blood-soaked machete.

"What are their names?" she asked just to be saying something.

Best not to stand there, thinking of sex and caffeine with the kiddos around. It was best not to think of those things with Clay around, either.

"Hayden," he said, tipping his head to the leg hugger. "And this is the troublemaker, Hunter."

Their faces were smeared with assorted colors of makeup, but she figured that they were cute beneath. Cute and perfect. The kind of kids that Brantley and she had planned on having. Of course, they already had a father, Spike Devereaux, but Brantley was probably having a ball playing part-time daddy.

"Are you okay?" Clay waited until her gaze came to his and he looked away.

"Sure." And because she felt she owed him more than that, she added, "I'm over Brantley. Really." She paused, shifted the conversation a little. "How are things with you and your sister?"

"S-h-i-t-t-y," Clay spelled out with a smile. "I'm sure you've heard all about it from the gossips."

Sophie shook her head. "I've been avoiding the gossips. Avoiding town, too. And phone calls from anyone and everyone who wants to spill things that I don't want to talk about." She could add life and sex to that list of avoidances.

Mercy.

She wished sex would stop popping into her head.

"I'm trying to make sure none of that *s-h-i-t* falls on these guys," Clay added. Hunter, the troublemaker, repeated the *shit*, letter for letter, causing Clay to groan.

"You're a good uncle." And then she remembered her conversation with Mila. "Good brother to your sister, too. I mean, you gave up your job in Houston to move here to be closer to her."

She'd meant that to sound casual, but a muscle flickered in Clay's jaw. "Yeah," he said, but she got the feeling there was more.

Maybe he'd gotten fired. Or had burned out. It didn't matter—it wasn't any of her business. Even if it felt as if it was.

"So you're taking them to playgroup?" she asked. Not that she wanted to hurry along this conversation, but they were starting to attract a crowd. Some of the diners in the café were gawking at them through the window.

Clay didn't nod, didn't shake his head. "No, I'm here with April and Brantley. The boys were getting restless so I brought them outside."

"Oh." Probably not the best response she could have come up with, but Sophie figured she should get out of there. She fluttered her fingers in the direction of her truck. "Well, I should be getting…somewhere." Anywhere but here.

Now Clay nodded.

And that prompted Sophie to say something. "I really

am over Brantley, and I'm happy for him and your sister." The first part was true. The last part not so much. She wanted them to make the marriage work for the sake of the toddler goblin and his superhero twin. "It's just it might make them uncomfortable if they see me."

Too late.

The café door opened, and Brantley and April squeezed out together. Squeezed because they had to make their way through the gawkers and also because they were practically wrapped around each other, making it difficult to fit through the door. Like the boys, they, too, were giggling, but those giggles froze when their attention landed on Sophie.

Sophie did another finger flutter toward the truck. "I was just leaving. It was good seeing you, Clay."

She lifted her foot to get moving, but her foot froze in midstep. That's because Sophie noticed Brantley's right hand. It was on April's belly. And while it was an average-sized belly, there was something about Brantley's hand placement that had big bells clanging in Sophie's head.

Good gravy.

"Yes, we're expecting," April announced. Her voice was crisp, her eyes slightly narrowed. "Other than Clay, we haven't really told anyone yet, but I'll be showing soon, and it won't be a secret much longer."

At least she didn't assume that Sophie would be thrilled for them. In fact, April was sort of glaring at Sophie as if daring her not to be happy.

Oh, it took some doing, but Sophie scrounged up a smile though it must have looked on the creepy side because Hayden cowered even farther behind Clay's leg.

She even managed a nod that she hoped seemed like some kind of approval.

Sophie looked at Clay to see how he was handling this, and he seemed a little shell-shocked. The fact that it was only a little meant he was either very good at masking his feelings or else this hadn't hit him as hard as it was hitting her.

"This should show you that it's really over between Brantley and you," April added. "We're a happy family now and don't want anyone from our pasts trying to spoil our future."

"Rein in your insecurities, sis," Clay grumbled.

"Just stating the truth," April grumbled back. "Brantley and I are committed to each other, to this marriage. I've quit my job to be a full-time mom to the boys and this baby."

"I really have to go," Sophie said, and she put her feet on autopilot, hoping that they would get her to the truck. Somehow, they did, and she got the engine started so she could leave fast.

She didn't get far. Sophie made it to Main Street and pulled into one of the parallel parking spaces outside Mila's bookstore, which her friend had given the odd name of Sniff the Pages. If anyone saw her, they wouldn't think anything of her stopping by her best friend's business. Well, they wouldn't think anything unless they looked closer and saw her shaking.

"I am over Brantley," she repeated. "I am."

But it was going to be a bitch to deal with the fact that he was not only truly over her, but he'd also moved on to the life that he'd always wanted.

Sophie didn't cry. She made a promise to herself then and there that she'd never shed another tear over Brantley or what might have been. Instead, she fished around in her back pocket and came up with the slip of paper that Mila had put there.

Shane's number.

And Sophie called him before she could change her mind.

CLAY STEPPED OFF the walkway to his house and ducked behind a scrawny hackberry tree. He only hoped that no one saw him doing surveillance of the chickens.

There were three by the side of his house, and they were doing what appeared to be normal chicken things by pecking at stuff on the ground. Maybe feed that someone had maliciously strewn, maybe just bugs and such.

Occasionally, one of them—the biggest one—would lift her head and look around as if doing surveillance, too. Clay didn't want to believe they could recognize him and want to use him for chicken ninja training, but after three attacks to date, his pride couldn't stand another go-round with the little bitches.

He considered just shooting them where they pecked, but the shots would spook his horses. Plus, it might spook Freddie or one of his sons if they were inside the house actually working. Clay doubted they were since there was no other vehicle around, but maybe he'd get lucky. He didn't hold out hope, though, that whatever Freddie and the boys might be working on would be done right.

After all these months, Clay had given up on *right*, but he hadn't given up on the remodeling. Even if it took him the rest of his life, he was going to hold Freddie's feet to the fire and get the projects done. To the best of Freddie's and his son's abilities, anyway. Which wasn't much.

After he was satisfied that the chickens were staying

in the same general area, Clay left the cover of the hackberry, and yeah, he hurried to the porch. He threw open his front door and nearly had a heart attack.

"Surprise!" someone yelled.

He cursed and reached for his gun before his brain shifted from the cop to the brother mode. This wasn't a threat that his body had prepared itself for. It was April with Brantley by her side. Brantley had some yellow balloons in his hand, and his sister thrust out a cake she was holding.

A birthday cake.

It took Clay a moment to realize that the cake was for him. And that this was indeed his birthday.

"FYI," Clay said, taking his hand from his gun, "it's not a good idea to start any conversation with a cop by yelling *surprise*. Nor is it a good idea to hide in his house and yell at him when he walks in."

"How else were we going to give you a surprise party?" April answered. "We parked in the back so you wouldn't know we were here." She grinned, kissed his cheek.

Clay didn't grin back. In fact, he narrowed his eyes, his normal reaction when it came to his kid sister and her husband. He'd accepted the marriage because he didn't have a choice, but he hadn't accepted that they'd been stupid enough not to use those condoms he'd sent them.

Hell.

His sister would be the mother of three—maybe four if she had another set of twins—before her twenty-fourth birthday.

April and Brantley had told him the *happy news* at the café the same day Sophie had found out. Clay had to hand it to her—Sophie had kept her cool despite his sister's witchy comment. He'd kept his cool, too, but only because he hadn't wanted to act like a horse's ass in front of his nephews.

Of course, now he'd have another nephew or niece, and he would love him or her just as much. But since he didn't have stars in his eyes like April, Clay knew she had a tough road ahead.

"Hayden and Hunter fell asleep so I put them on your bed," April explained when Clay looked around for them. "Say, did you know you have a toilet in your closet?"

Clay could only sigh. No, he hadn't known. The last he'd seen, it'd been in the corner of his bedroom, waiting to be installed in the guest bath. He hoped Freddie and/or his offspring had only moved it there to get it out of the way and that they hadn't actually misrouted the plumbing again.

"So, is your mood better today?" he asked April, and he didn't clarify what he was referring to because she knew.

April's chin came up. "I meant it. I don't want Sophie interfering in our lives. That includes your life."

"I'm thirty-four. Last I checked, that makes me old enough to decide who I see or don't see."

"And you want to *see* my husband's ex?" She didn't wait for him to answer. "Brantley and I have enough adjustments to make without Sophie Granger watching our every move."

"I doubt she's watching anybody's moves. She's got her hands full with the ranch." But he was talking to air.

"I don't want her in our lives," April declared.

The silence came. So did Clay's temper, and he considered telling his one-and-only sister to take a hike. But he remembered this level of bitchiness. It'd happened with the last pregnancy so maybe it was just the hormones.

"We got you some presents." Brantley tried to sound happy and not like he'd just got caught in the middle of a sibling shit-storm. He tied the balloons to the leg of the coffee table and took a couple of bags from the sofa. "The first one is from Vita."

Clay's hand hesitated in midreach.

"Vita saw us in town and said to give it to you but to be careful because it could break," Brantley added.

Clay was certain that put a fresh scowl on his face, but he took the bag, looked inside and saw yet another crap-streaked chicken egg.

Brantley had a look at it, as well, though Clay doubted it was his first look. "Vita said the other one she gave you was too old and that you needed a fresh one."

Even though he didn't come out and ask, there was a definite question mark at the end of that information. Brantley and everyone else in town probably knew about Vita helping him with the feral chicken problem. Or rather what Vita considered to be helping. But Brantley must have guessed that if Clay didn't volunteer anything, then it was a subject best not discussed.

But the first egg hadn't exactly gotten old, not on his watch, anyway.

He'd tossed it the day Vita had brought it to his office, but Ellie had fished it out with the claim that she would keep it for him, that it wasn't a good idea to diss Vita's cures. So, Ellie had put it in double Ziploc bags and shoved it in the tiny freezer of the office fridge.

This one was going in the trash.

Clay put it aside for now and took the other bag, this

one tagged from April and Brantley. There was a bottle of his favorite whiskey inside and an envelope.

"Now, don't get mad," Brantley said before Clay could open it.

Like the word *surprise*, that was not something he'd especially wanted to hear. At least it wouldn't be news of April being knocked-up since she already was. And he doubted it was a divorce announcement since she was clinging like a vine to Brantley.

"It's a subscription to a dating site," April blurted out. She sounded considerably less bitchy than she had a couple of seconds ago. Maybe the shit-storm had passed. Maybe her hormones had leveled out.

"It was April's idea," Brantley quietly added.

No doubt. It was exactly the kind of thing his sister would do, and Clay would toss it out with the egg as soon as they left.

"It's time you started dating again," April went on, "now that things have cooled between Sophie and you."

Things were never hot between Sophie and him. Well, they were, but only in a lustful sort of way. Hell, he'd never even kissed her.

Something he suddenly wished he'd done.

Clay frowned at that thought. He already had enough complications without adding his brother-in-law's ex to the mix. Plus, Sophie hadn't exactly stayed in touch or anything.

"The boys have gifts for you, too." April made air quotes around *gifts*. "And I can't wait for you to hear what Hunter told us."

"He said he wanted to be a *top* like his Nunk Cay," Brantley provided, followed by a laugh. "It was cute as all get-out."

Cute, maybe, but also confusing. Clay got the Nunk Cay part because that was Hunter's attempt at Uncle Clay. But it took him a second to realize that *top* was *cop*.

"No," Clay snapped, a little sharper than he'd meant to. "You talk him out of that." It made his stomach twist to think of a grown-up Hunter going through what he'd been through.

April rolled her eyes. "Yeah, right. As if I've ever been able to talk Hunter out of anything. He's like a mini version of me."

He was, and that was even more reason to steer Hunter in another career direction. The next time he was at the bookstore, Clay would pick him up some kiddie doctor books. Lawyer books, too, if they published such a thing. Even books about cowboys. Anything but a cop.

"I'll put the cake in the kitchen," April volunteered. "We can cut it when the boys wake up. Oh, and we bought some steaks and burgers to grill for dinner."

Clay thanked her and would have gone into his room to change if Brantley hadn't caught onto his arm. "Can we talk?"

Hell. That was yet something else he hadn't wanted to hear. "You'd better not be about to tell me that you're dumping my sister."

Brantley's eyes widened to the size of salad plates. "No. Of course not. I love April. I love the boys, and I love our unborn child."

"Good. And you'd better keep on loving them, or I'll kick your ass into the next county."

Brantley stared at him. "Has anyone ever told you that you're scary?"

"All the time. And I also carry through on my threats."

Clay waited. When Brantley didn't say anything he

asked, "Was that what you wanted to talk about—the threats?"

"Uh, no." Brantley glanced into the kitchen as if to make sure April was still there. She was. "This is about Sophie." He lowered his voice to a whisper. "I was, well, hoping you'd ask her out."

Clay huffed. "First a dating site subscription and now this? I can handle my own love life." Or lack thereof. "And didn't you hear what your wife just said? She doesn't want Sophie anywhere near her gene pool."

Brantley huffed, too. "I'm not saying to ask Sophie out for your sake but for her own. She could be headed for some trouble."

Until Brantley added that last part, Clay was about to tell him to mind his own business, but that got Clay's attention. "Explain that."

"Shane." And Brantley must have thought that was enough of an explanation because he paused.

"Shane, the guy she's got a date with tonight. Yeah, I know about it." Clay had heard it from at least a dozen people who doled out sympathy over his and Sophie's *breakup*. Apparently, Sophie was meeting this guy in a couple of hours at the Longhorn Bar at the end of Main Street.

"Shane Whitlock," Brantley provided. He made another of those kitchen glances and leaned in closer. Clay was reasonably sure there was nothing Brantley could say that would interest him about Sophie's date.

But Clay was wrong.

CHAPTER SIX

SOPHIE HADN'T KNOWN there was a level of Hell below the internet dating sites, but she could say for certain that there was.

It was the date itself.

She'd been so hopeful about seeing Shane. Or at least curious. And eager to get on with her life and dipping her toes back into the dating pond so that her mom and Mila would get off her back. But what she hadn't counted on was that she didn't have much in common with a boy she'd crushed on in middle school. A boy she hadn't even actually known that well.

Shane looked pretty much the same. An older version of the blond, blue-eyed kid who had first stirred her girl parts. He still had that little gap in his front teeth, a tiny flaw that she'd once thought of as a perfect imperfection. It was around the time she'd started reading Jane Austen books so she had been in somewhat of a romantic phase. In fact, maybe she should credit Jane's books for helping stir those parts.

Her parts weren't stirring now though, unless she counted her butt going numb from sitting so stiffly on the hard leather seat in the booth.

"And so after I got back from Italy, I moved in with a modern artist in Soho," Shane went on. He was forty-five minutes into answering her question: *So, what have you been up to for the past seventeen years?*

From what Sophie could tell, he was on year seven or eight now.

"You know modern art?" he asked, gobbling down one of the nachos they'd just been served. It was the best one on the plate, loaded with jalapenos and dripping with cheese. Sophie had had her eye on it, but she apparently wasn't fast enough because Shane had moved the plate closer to him.

"Not really."

"Well, you should study up on it. Interesting stuff. There's nothing like seeing a really good painting and just looking at it for hours to try to see what the artist saw."

She made a noncommittal sound, reached way across the table to retrieve a less generously topped nacho. She also checked the time again on her phone. It wasn't even eight yet.

Time had apparently stopped in this level of Hell.

"Anyway, after Soho," he went on and on and on, "I moved to Merida down in the Yucatan. Hooked up with another artist there. Man, she was amazing." He paused only long enough to drink some of his beer to wash down that nacho and move the plate even closer to him. "You're sure you're not into art?"

"Not really," she repeated, and she prayed for an earthquake or something. Nothing major, just enough to shake things up so she could say she needed to leave to check on the ranch.

At least Shane hadn't brought up the family business and their financial troubles with Billy Lee. Maybe because he already knew all the details from the gossips. Maybe because he didn't want to bring up such a sour subject on a date. Or perhaps because her life in no way interested him.

"Merida was incredible," he continued after wolfing down another nacho. He talked around the crunching and the swipes of his napkin to get the cheese drippings off his mouth.

Sophie listened in case she had to grunt in response or something, and she looked across the bar at the back booth where Mila was sitting. As planned.

Well, as Mila had planned, anyway.

She'd told Sophie that she wanted to be there for moral support, but Sophie figured Mila had also wanted to make sure she stayed put and went through with the date.

The door opened, bringing in a gust of the October wind. Not cold exactly, but since she was wearing a thin top—which she'd chosen because it was flattering—with her jeans, Sophie shivered a little. Her shiver turned to a shudder when her mother walked in.

Belle didn't own any bar/clubbing clothes and had perhaps never been in the Longhorn, but she'd tried to dress to fit in. She had on mom jeans, one of Sophie's work shirts and cowboy boots that she'd likely taken right out of the box. She smiled at Sophie, gave her a toodle-do wave and made her way to Mila's booth. Apparently, her mom was there for moral support, too.

"…and after a year in Merida," Shane was saying, "I stayed a while in LA. Great place. You know LA?"

Sophie caught enough of that so she could answer, "I've been there a couple of times on business. We distributed rodeo gear to—"

"Amazing city. Of course, I got involved with another artist." He chuckled, flashing that tooth gap. Sophie wondered if she could throw a dart through it. "Also did some work as a sushi chef. Yes, me a sushi chef. And yes, I wore this." He put his thumb beneath the brim of his tan cowboy hat and tilted it back on his head. "Everybody called me the Sushi Cowboy. Sushi's like art in a way because it's not just the taste but the visual experience. You like sushi, Sophie?"

"I do." And she'd had enough of this. "But I prefer books and reading. Do you read, Shane?"

He chuckled again as if it were a fine joke. "I love books." But he didn't linger even a second on which books he loved. "After LA, I made my way back to Texas—"

"I know Texas," she jumped to say.

Another chuckle from Shane. Sophie imagined driving a Mack truck through that tooth gap.

The door opened again, and since Sophie was more attentive to anything other than her date, she looked in that direction. And in walked Clay. He looked around, spotted her. Spotted Shane, too, because he scowled and made his way to the bar. Sophie wasn't sure if the scowl was for her or Shane, but it was probably all over town that Sophie had made this date only after learning that April was pregnant. Maybe Clay didn't approve.

Maybe he was jealous.

But she had to admit that was a stretch, considering Clay had spent a lot of the past five months avoiding her.

"Now, where was I?" Shane asked after eating more nachos. "I was telling you about being a sushi chef. Well, when that gig was over, I moved back to San Antonio and connected with an old friend who got me into graffiti art. You know graffiti art, Sophie? Probably not since there won't be any around here." He laughed. "Most of the yokels here would just consider it graffiti."

Enough of this. She could overlook the nacho hoarding, but if she stayed, she would end up saying things that wouldn't be very nice.

She wolfed down a few nachos. "I should hurry and finish this so I can get back."

"Get back where?" he asked.

"Home. I'm sure I mentioned I had some work that I had to get done tonight." It was a lie. She hadn't said a thing about work, but Shane made a sound of agreement.

"Yeah, I guess you've been busy with the ranch. How's that going?"

She nearly choked on a jalapeno because she hadn't anticipated a question about her. "Fine," she managed. "We own lots of cows now, and we're expanding our markets." She wouldn't mention the bull sperm, but they did own a lot of that, too, especially now that they owned the "sperm extraction" machine.

"Your great-granddaddy would be proud," Shane said. "Of course, he left Garrett, Roman and you with a pretty good nest egg what with all that land, trust funds and the big sprawling house. All you had to do was not screw it up." He added a passive-aggressive wink to that.

What he'd said was true, and she was certain others felt this way. The Grangers and those giant silver spoons in their mouths. Some, maybe even Shane, didn't know that Garrett and she put in plenty of hours to keep things going. Plus, the company they'd worked so hard to grow had nearly landed them in jail. Sometimes, they'd had to use those silver spoons to clean up buckets of crap.

An analogy that unsettled her stomach.

She put her napkin aside and was about to get up, but Shane beat her to it. "Gotta run to the little boy's room," he said. "If the waitress comes by, could you order me another beer and some more nachos? We seem to have gone through most of the whole plate. Love a woman with a good appetite."

Sophie had an appetite all right, but it hadn't been satisfied with the one nacho she'd gotten. Shane was off before she could even respond, but the moment he got back, she was leaving. In the meantime, she settled for nacho crumbs since she was starving.

Mila didn't waste time scurrying over to her, and she slid into Shane's seat. "So, how's it going? Any sparkage?"

"I want to kill him. Does that count?"

Mila frowned. "It can't be that bad. You're just not used to being on a date, that's all. Brantley and you were in the old hat stage. You didn't have to work at dinner conversation."

No, and she hadn't had to work for dinner, either, but it had been a battle getting that nacho plate away from Shane.

"There's something off about him." Sophie looked up and saw that Clay was no longer at the bar. Maybe he'd gone to the *little boy's room*, too.

"Well?" her mother said, hurrying toward them. She nudged Sophie over with her hip and dropped down on the seat beside her.

"No sparkage, she says," Mila repeated. "But I'm hoping she'll give him a second chance just to make sure."

"I don't need a second chance. He's boring and self-centered. We have nothing in common, and he ate the best nacho."

That last part didn't seem to convince them, and judging from their blank stares, they were focusing more on that than the other two things. Important things since she didn't want boring and self-centered. She wanted—well, she didn't know exactly, but her want list didn't include Shane.

"If you can hold out for a *Fifty Shades of Grey* guy, then why can't I?" Sophie asked Mila. But she wished she hadn't asked it in front of her mother.

Her mom snapped to Mila. "You mean that naughty book where the man uses feathers, ice and stuff like that?" She didn't wait for Mila to answer. She shifted her attention back to Sophie. "Are there men like that around here? Maybe there's a dating site to find them?"

There was no good answer to that. Not to her mother, anyway. But yes, there probably were sites, and maybe Sophie needed to turn the tables on Mila and find her a date on one of them.

The waitress, Marcie Jean Garza, must have realized that it'd been a while since she'd been to the booth because she hurried toward them.

"My date wants more nachos and a beer," Sophie said, nudging her mother off the seat so she'd be able to get out. "But can you tell him I had to leave? Something's come up." Not a lie exactly. Something had come up— her lack of desire to spend another second with Shane.

"Sure, I'll tell him, but you probably shouldn't go just yet. I think you should check on him first."

That comment and Marcie Jean's dour expression got Sophie scrambling to her feet. "Did he slip in the bathroom or something?"

Marcie Jean hitched her thumb in the direction of the back door. "No. He's out in the back alley with Chief McKinnon. And it looks like the chief is about to beat your date to a pulp."

CLAY HADN'T PLANNED on punching this clown, but maybe he needed to rethink that. If anyone needed punching, it was Shane. Clay had spent less than a minute with him and had already figured that out.

"This is police harassment," Shane protested. "I know my rights."

"Yeah, I know them, too, and you don't have a right to swindle rich women out of their money."

"I didn't do that, and I'm leaving. You've got no grounds to hold me."

Shane started to walk away, but Clay stepped in front of him. That's when Clay spotted one of the Busby boys at the other end of the alley. The boy was taking a leak, but he quickly zipped up to hurry back inside the Longhorn. No doubt to tell everyone that Clay had Sophie's date cornered. By the time the gossip made its way to Sophie, she'd think there was a murder in progress.

"You did do that to several women," Clay argued. "That's how you got your ranch and everything else you own. And you're not going to do it to Sophie. She's vulnerable right now, and she's been through enough."

Shane smiled. "Are you fucking her?"

Yep, Shane needed punching all right. "Not that it's any of your business, but no. What is your business though, and mine, is that I'm not going to let you pull your scam in Wrangler's Creek."

Shane just kept on smiling. "Are you running me out of town, *interim* Chief McKinnon?"

Rarely did the interim label bother him, but it did now. Then again, everything about this guy was bothering him. "Pretty much. Or you can stay, and I'll arrest you. Your choice."

That finally got that smile off his stupid face. "Arrest me?" Shane howled. "For what?'

"Loitering, public intoxication." He leaned in. "I smell

alcohol on your breath." And jalapenos. In fact, there was a chunk of what appeared to be jalapeno stuck in that big-assed gap between his front teeth.

"I'm not drunk. Not loitering, either. The only reason I'm out here is because you forced me into this alley."

Clay had forced him, in a way, but it hadn't taken much doing. He'd merely tapped his badge and said they needed to talk either in the bar or outside. Shane's choice. Shane had opted for outside maybe because he didn't want Sophie to hear Clay's accusations of his being a gigolo. One who'd resorted to everything from forging checks and fraud to theft.

"Besides, those charges won't stick," Shane went on. "I don't even have a record."

True. But that's because his victims had been too embarrassed or unwilling to file charges against him. That didn't mean he was innocent.

"Well, if you want to keep that record spotless, you need to get in your rental Hummer and head out now," Clay insisted.

The staring contest started. Clay figured a lot of Old West shoot-outs had started with this sort of glorified stink eye. But there'd be no shoot-out. Shane didn't have a permit for a weapon, and Clay was keeping a close eye on Shane's hands. If Mr. Gap-tooth really was stupid enough to pull a gun on a cop, then Clay could stop him and arrest him. There'd go that perfect record Shane was bragging about.

Clay didn't ease up on the glaring, and he knew for a fact that he was good at it because of all the practice he'd had with raising his kid sister. And he obviously hadn't lost his touch because Shane dropped back a step.

"Fine," Shane spat out. "I'm leaving, and then you

can explain to Sophie that you ran her new boyfriend out of town."

Those words were still coming out of Shane's mouth when the door opened, and Sophie walked out. Great. Now, he was going to have to explain to a riled Sophie what was going on.

Or not.

"You're not my new boyfriend," Sophie snapped. Apparently, her scowl was meant for Shane, not him. "And your teeth aren't perfect imperfections. They're stupid."

Clay agreed about the stupid teeth, but he wasn't sure where the remark was coming from. Maybe it'd been part of their conversation when they'd been chowing down on nachos.

Shane slashed his gaze between them, and he must have realized this was a lost cause because he flashed that bust-my-face-please grin. "You're wasting your time with her, Chief," he gibed, and Shane said the rest of his gibe from over his shoulder. "She was a bad fuck anyway."

"What?" Sophie howled. She nearly went after him, but Clay hooked his arm around her waist and pulled her back. He didn't want to have to arrest her if she tried to claw out Shane's eyes. "I didn't...do what he said with him."

"You had sexual relations with that man?" Clay heard someone ask. Sophie's mother. She was in the doorway with Mila, and behind them, every person in the bar had come to watch.

"No!" Sophie insisted. "I had a crush on him when I was twelve. I didn't even know what sex was."

Her mother nodded, seemed relieved, and then she turned that relieved gaze on Clay. "Did you make Shane leave because you were jealous and want to win Sophie back?"

Sophie groaned. "No," she repeated.

Clay hated to disagree with her, especially since the disagreement was a lie, but he'd given his word. "Yes," he said.

That got everyone's attention, and the only one who smiled was Sophie's mother. Mila just stared. And the others got out their phones, no doubt to text everyone in the known universe that Sophie and the interim chief were really an item.

Sophie stared at him a long time with those intense eyes. Thankfully, there wasn't much light in the alley so he didn't have to look away. "Excuse us a minute." Sophie didn't seem to be saying that to anyone specifically, and she reached behind her and shut the door. "They'll probably stand there and try to listen," she added.

Clay still had his arm around her so when she started walking toward the front of the building, he let go of her and followed. "I can explain." He used the softest voice he could because Sophie was right about the eavesdroppers.

"No need." She whispered, too. "Shane is some kind of con artist who preys on rich women, but you didn't want to spill that to everyone in town because you're investigating him."

Close. It hadn't taken Sophie long to pick up on that because according to the bartender, Sophie and Shane had only been in the Longhorn about a half hour before Clay arrived.

"He's been implicated in three cases where he allegedly stole or embezzled from women," Clay explained. "But I'm not investigating him. I got a tip."

Clay had hoped that Sophie might just accept all of

that at face value, but that wasn't an acceptance expression she got. "Who gave you a tip about him?"

"Brantley told me."

That wasn't an acceptance expression, either. A quick breath left her mouth, and she leaned against the building. It wasn't cold, but there was a nip in the air so maybe that's why she scrubbed her hands up and down her arms.

"Why did Brantley go to you with this and not to me?" she asked.

"He thought I could scare off Shane." Clay paused, tried to figure out the best way to say this. "Brantley violated attorney–client confidence by telling me, but Shane milked one of his clients out of a small fortune. The woman didn't want to file charges because she was embarrassed. Brantley did some digging, and he found a couple more women Shane had scammed."

Sophie nodded, mumbled something under her breath that he didn't catch. "So, Brantley thought he needed to look out for me, and he did it by proxy through you. I'm trying to decide if I should be grateful or pissed off." Her gaze snapped back to him. "I wouldn't have fallen for Shane's con."

Clay could see that now.

"But it was your job to warn me so I do appreciate that," she added on another sigh. "Thank you."

Now, he wasn't sure if he should be grateful or pissed off. And Clay wasn't sure why he was feeling these things. She was damn straight that it was his job, but he would have done this even if he hadn't been a cop.

Hell.

That wasn't a good thing to admit to himself. He'd made this personal, and he knew from experience—one really bad experience, anyway—that it wasn't a good idea to mix work and personal feelings. Especially since being involved with Sophie would mean her getting a daily dose of salt in the wound because she would also get daily doses of Brantley, April and their new family.

So, why didn't he just say good-night and move away from her, then?

Because he was stupid, that's why.

Maybe it was the cool, dark night. Maybe it was because Sophie's eyes were partly closed while she likely tried to figure out how she was going to tell her mom and Mila that she wasn't really involved with him after all. Or it could be her scent that'd made its way to him.

And maybe it was just this damn heat that kept flaming up inside him.

If he'd had the nachos, he would have blamed it on that, but this was heat from a nonfood source.

"So…" she said as if trying to prompt something—either him or herself.

But Clay didn't budge. "So," he repeated.

His hand was stupid, too, because it moved toward her. To her arm, and he brushed his fingers over her skin. If he was the sort of man who lied to himself, he would have said that was to check and see if she was cold. But as a general rule, he preferred to face up to the truth.

He just wanted to touch her.

And she was indeed cold. He could feel the goose bumps riffling over her skin.

Again, he could have lied to himself and pretended that he moved closer to give her a little heat, but Clay wanted to feel just how hot that slam of attraction could be when his body brushed against her.

It could be damn hot, he decided.

"I'm pretty sure this is a bad idea," she said. Her voice

was all shivery and sending out some kind of pheromones that went straight to his dick. Pheromones and
dicks weren't a good combination, either.

That didn't stop him. He was going to kiss her. And
yes, it would be a bad idea. "It's been a while since I've
had something to regret, but this should take care of that."

She laughed, not laced with nerves as he wanted it to
be. If there'd been nerves that might have caused him
and his dick to back away. But that laugh was laced with
pheromones, too.

"Just how much do you think we'd regret it?" she
asked.

"This much."

Clay moved in, sliding his hand to the back of her
neck, inching her closer. Not that she had to go far because he'd already positioned himself too close. His
mouth lowered to hers, and he caught her scent again.
Not those blasted nachos, either, but Sophie's scent, and
he figured she would taste as good as she smelled.

Probably better.

He started with a simple touch, his lips brushing
against hers. That packed a wallop, too, and Clay moved
in to make this a mistake worth regretting.

Instead, though, he got a regret of a different kind. It
came in the form of a man's voice.

"Sophie?" someone called out. "Clay?"

Hell, it was Brantley.

Sophie and he moved away as if they'd electrocuted
each other. Which might not be far from the truth. And
they did manage to move apart just as Brantley came
around the corner.

"There you are," Brantley said. "I was worried when
I didn't hear from you, but one of Freddy's boys told me

that Shane had left." Brantley just kept walking toward them until he was close enough that even in the dim light, he could probably see the guilty looks on their faces.

"Did Shane give you any trouble?" Brantley asked, and then he turned to Sophie. "Oh, God, you're upset. Please don't be."

Clay studied her face. She was breathing through her mouth, and her breath was too fast. Signs that Brantley had obviously misread as her being upset.

Good.

Clay had already come close enough to kissing her, and it was best if he didn't have to discuss that with Sophie's ex-lover who was also his brother-in-law.

Nothing complicated about that.

"I'm okay," Sophie assured him. "Shane and I weren't hitting it off anyway."

"Oh. Well, that's good." Brantley touched her, too, on her arm. Much as Clay had done earlier except this was more of a pat than a finger slide as Clay's had been. If Brantley had seen that finger slide and the near kiss, he wouldn't be hanging around right now.

Brantley quit patting Sophie and turned to Clay. "Ordell Busby's boy also told me what you said about being jealous and wanting to win Sophie back. Thanks for covering for me."

"Thanks for giving me the tip about Shane. But Sophie was already onto him by the time I got here."

"Good," Brantley said, and he repeated it. "And I'll figure out a way to set the Busby boy and everybody else straight. I'll convince them that you really weren't jealous and that you two aren't together."

Sophie mumbled a thanks, but it wasn't any louder than Clay's.

Brantley was also looking at them as if trying to figure out if anything was wrong. "Well, I'll be going, then."

Clay finally released the breath he'd been holding when Brantley turned, but the man hadn't made it even a step before he whirled back around. "I nearly forgot," he said, taking something from his jacket pocket. "It's a little early, but it's for your birthday. You'll be the big 3-0. Say, did you know that yours and Clay's birthdays are only two days apart? His birthday is today. We celebrated with him earlier."

Sophie shook her head. "No, I didn't know. Happy birthday," she added to Clay before she turned back to Brantley. "But you didn't have to get me a gift. In fact, I don't want a gift from you—"

"Oh, this isn't from me." Brantley pulled out an envelope. A pink one.

And he put it in her hand. "It's the letter your dad left you in his will. April and I are headed out of town for a little getaway first thing in the morning, and I wanted to give it to you before we left. Don't read it, though, until your actual birthday."

Brantley started to leave again and then stopped just as he'd done before. However, he didn't look at Sophie this time but rather Clay. "In case this letter's anything like the ones he left Roman and Garrett, I'll make sure someone is with her when she reads it." He gave them a wave that was much too cheery considering the news he'd just delivered. "Good night, guys."

Brantley had no sooner left when Sophie's phone dinged with a text message. She groaned when she looked at the screen and then showed it to Clay. It was from Shane.

Thanks for a rotten evening, bitch. I left the bill on the table for you. You can pay for it out of your trust fund. Hasta la vista, baby.

Sophie shrugged. "Being called a bitch and paying the bill is a small price to get rid of him."

Clay agreed and decided it would be a good idea to keep his eye on Shane, just to make sure he didn't come back to town and try to cause trouble for Sophie. And he thought that trouble might have already started when her phone dinged again. Since Sophie already had her phone angled so he could see it, Clay read the message at the same time she did.

Not from Shane.

But from April.

Ian Busby just called to tell me you were in the Longhorn alley with my husband. Brantley's married to me now so why can't you just leave him alone? There's a word for women like you, Sophie Granger. BITCH.

CHAPTER SEVEN

CLAY'S "SHIT TO FORGET" box was wide-open. If he'd been awake, he might have had a chance to snap it shut before the images escaped, but it was hard to fight a nightmare when you couldn't wake the fuck up.

He was trapped. Just as he had been that day. And just like that day the shit had started, he felt the fear crawl through him. Fear that he would fail.

And he had.

He'd failed when it had mattered most.

Delaney.

He saw her eyes. The panic in them, the silent plea for him to help save her. That image froze as it always did once the box was open, and in that moment he hadn't failed yet. There was still hope. That didn't help, of course, because the feeling of hope only made the next set of images even harder to stomach.

But for that moment, he could see the life in her eyes.

It didn't last. It never did. Because there was the sound of the blast from his own gun. Other sounds, too, of Clay failing and failing and failing.

And just like that, the life in her eyes was gone.

Gone because Clay had killed her.

GARRETT TOSSED THE cantaloupe-sized rock onto the small flatbed trailer that he'd hitched to the tractor. It landed with a thud on top of the other eight million rocks he'd already picked up from the south pasture. It wasn't a fun chore, but it was a necessary one because the rocks played havoc when checking the cattle on horseback. And for some reason the chore soothed him.

Right now, soothing was a good thing.

When he was a kid, he'd thought rocks grew like crops since they just seemed to appear on the ground. It made sense to a seven-year-old kid. Made sense, too, that the tiny rocks must be seeds.

Roman, who was two years younger but somehow always wiser about stuff like that had laughed like a loon when Garrett had told him about his rock seed notion. Then his brother had swallowed some pea gravel to prove Garrett wrong. Of course, Roman being Roman, he had later stuffed some rags under his T-shirt, arranging them in his midsection to make Garrett believe the rocks were growing in his belly.

Sophie had sobbed over the thought of her brother's stomach exploding, and when Garrett had realized what was going on, he'd punched Roman in his rag-padded belly. Because while Garrett might not have been wiser about such things, he was the older brother and had bigger hands. Plus, he was stronger from picking up all those damn rocks when he'd been a kid.

Garrett smiled at the memory of Roman, but the smile didn't last. Somehow, he had to fix this feud between Roman and their mom. He had to keep an eye on Sophie, too, to make sure she wasn't still bawling over the horse's ass who'd jilted her. There were also still things that needed attention on the ranch. And with the search for Billy Lee. Garrett needed to hire more PIs and push the feds to dig harder. Amid all of that, he had to work on his marriage and try to sort out what was going on with Meredith.

Yeah, there was plenty that needed fixing in his life. And some were outside his skill set as a big brother, the CEO of Granger Western and the alpha male of the family. Some of the things might be irreversible and unfixable.

Garrett heard a sound, looked up and saw a rider approaching. He hadn't told anyone he was coming out here, hadn't brought his phone with him, either, but apparently that hadn't stopped Lawson from finding him.

"You do know we pay hands to do this," Lawson greeted. He eased out of the saddle, walked closer to Garrett.

"I'm not doing paperwork today," Garrett told him right away. "And I'm not sitting in on any business meetings. Or looking over tax stuff. And I'm not going to soothe over any ranch hand you've managed to piss off."

"I can see that. But I can also see you won't be picking up rocks much longer." Lawson pointed to the iron-gray clouds. Rain was moving in, chillier temps, too, so Garrett would eventually have to go to the house.

But eventually wasn't right now.

"Did you ride out here to give me a fucking weather report?" Garrett snarled. Thankfully, he could be a dick with his cousin, mainly because Lawson could be an even bigger dick right back. Plus, he was blood, more like a brother than a cousin.

When Lawson didn't jump to reply with a dick-ish remark, Garrett tossed the rock he'd just picked up and looked at his cousin.

Hell.

Something was wrong.

"Is it Sophie?" Garrett asked. He had a good reason to suspect his sister was on the receiving end of that *something was wrong*. Her thirtieth birthday was tomorrow, but he'd heard that Brantley had already given her the pink envelope. The one that would almost certainly have some kind of shit-message from their father.

Lawson frowned. "Did something happen to Sophie?"

"I asked first." But it was a good sign that this wasn't about the letter after all. Garrett would need to make sure he stayed near the house tomorrow because she might need his big-brother skill set after she read the message from beyond the grave.

"Roman called," Lawson said. "You'd left your phone at the house so he called me."

Garrett mentally repeated that *hell*. "What happened to him?" Better yet, had something happened to Roman's twelve-year-old son? "Is Tate all right?"

"He didn't mention Tate so everything must be okay with him." Lawson paused. "Roman actually called about you. He's worried about you."

Garrett had learned never to be surprised by anything Roman did, but he was surprised now. "If he's so worried, then why doesn't he get his butt to the ranch to help with the paperwork?" Even better, Roman should do the paperwork.

Everything inside Garrett went still. Because it would have taken more than Garrett's general well-being to prompt Roman to call.

Lawson paused again and took out his phone. "Roman has a friend over at one of the TV stations in San Antonio, and he sent Roman this. A reporter and his cameraman were filming a story on a planned dog park, and the cameraman accidently filmed this instead."

Garrett couldn't imagine why Lawson would be showing him anything about a dog park forty miles away, but he took the phone and pressed the play button on the video. It took him a few seconds to see past the reporter. A few more seconds to see what Lawson had brought to him.

"I'm sorry, Gare," Lawson said. To the best of Garrett's memory, that was his cousin's one-and-only apology.

Garrett's mother was always going on about life turning on a dime and the world tipping on its axis. Until recently, Garrett hadn't had a true understanding of that—maybe he still didn't—but he'd certainly gotten a taste of it. Lives could indeed turn. An axis could indeed tip.

And it'd just happened to him again.

SOPHIE CURSED THE rain that was just starting to spit at her. She also cursed the flat tire and the lug nut that wouldn't budge. While she was at it, she cursed the text message she'd gotten from April the night before. This had been a crappy week, and the crap didn't seem to be leveling off any.

Why did this have to happen today and on this stretch of the road? It was a dead zone for cell service, and the only traffic was that coming in and out of the ranch. With a storm moving in fast, it wasn't likely that any of the hands, her cousin or brother would be headed this way. They'd no doubt hunker down until the weather cleared.

Sophie had considered waiting it out, too, but it might be morning before anyone came this way, and Garrett might think she was staying the night with Mila as she sometimes did.

Still cursing, she put the wrench on the lug nut again,

and this time she tried to stand on one leg of the wrench, hoping that her weight would cause it to give way. It didn't. The only thing that gave way was her footing, and she splatted onto the ground. At least she was wearing jeans and not a dress that would have landed over her head, but now the back of her jeans and butt were wet.

She tried once more and got the same results. This time her tailbone landed on a rock, and Sophie could have sworn she saw stars. Knowing it wouldn't help, she still threw the wrench at the lug nut, and because it alleviated some of her frustrations, she picked it up and threw it again.

And that's what Clay saw her doing when he pulled up beside her in his truck and let down his window.

"Who taught you how to use a lug wrench?" he asked, sounding way more amused than she was.

"Your mama." Which, of course, was a childish thing to say, but her fun meter was tapped out.

She thought maybe he chuckled, something she'd never seen Clay do, but she couldn't be sure because he turned to the side to get out of his truck. By the time he made it to her, there wasn't a trace of a chuckle on his face.

His pretty face, she amended.

A face that'd nearly kissed her the night before. At least the lips on that face had nearly kissed her. Sophie had been telling herself that Brantley's interruption was for the best, but it had put her in a sour mood. April's text had only added more sourness, and that had clung to her like rain all day.

"The lug nut's stuck," she said. She retrieved the wrench and handed it to him so he could have a go.

"Why don't you get inside the car, and I'll see if I can fix this?" he suggested.

"Nice offer, thanks, but I don't think I can get any wetter." She frowned because that sounded a little sexual.

Clay thankfully didn't seem to notice. He twisted the wrench. And twisted. He gave it an adjustment and tried again until the veins on his neck were bulging.

"Yep, it's stuck." He stood, his gaze meeting hers, but he immediately looked back at his truck. "I've got some Mighty Lube. It might work on this."

He leaned over the truck bed, giving her a nice view of his butt. Since he didn't notice that she was noticing, Sophie took in the view, too. All in all, it was good viewing material and a reminder that a butt like that probably looked as good out of the jeans as it did in them.

"For the record, you probably could get a little wetter," he commented. "But you could also get inside the car just to stop that from happening."

Sophie was fresh out of return insults so she just repeated, "Your mama."

Clay made a sound that could have possibly been a chuckle and fished around in his tool box so Sophie kept watching. He wasn't overly muscled, but there was enough of them to strain nicely against his shirt. The rain helped with that because, like her, he was quickly getting drenched. A reminder that he probably looked just as good out of that shirt as he did in it.

After a few more seconds of watching him, she'd mentally undressed him and had sex with him. She was probably flushed, and that's why he did a double take when he turned back around.

But Sophie did a double take, too.

Not because of straining muscles and butt-framing

jeans but because Clay was holding a huge can of Mighty Lube. Not the size you'd buy at a gas station but rather one from the big box store.

"Uh, you always carry that in your truck?" she asked.

"No. But Vita gave it to me a while back. Actually, she said it was for you." He looked a little unnerved by that. "You don't think she had a vision or something?"

"No vision. Over the years, I've had several flats on this very road. I suspect it's Ordell Busby's boys. They salt your property with chicken feed, and they salt the road with nails."

He frowned again, but this time it was a cop's frown. Sophie figured that he'd soon be having a chat with Ordell and his pranking offspring.

Clay sprayed the lube on the nut, but the lube bottle had such a phallic shape to it that Sophie decided it was best to look away. She'd already had enough mental foreplay. Still, she could hear Clay struggling, struggling some more and then cursing.

"It's really stuck on there." He glanced at the ground, and for a moment she thought he might throw the wrench there in frustration, but then she noticed he was looking at the little white pellets that were starting to land around them.

Hail.

Great. Now, in addition to being soaked, she was going to have welts on her body.

Sophie scrambled into the car, climbing over into the passenger's seat so that she could pull Clay in with her. He still had the Mighty Lube with him, and he tossed it on her dash so he could start the car and turn on the heater. Of course, the air was cold since the engine hadn't warmed up yet, and suddenly the car felt as if it'd shrunk to half its original size. That's because Clay had a way of taking up space.

A good kind of way since his shoulder was practically touching hers.

She looked at him. He looked at her. And she got those foreplay thoughts again. However, as Clay usually did, he glanced away, his attention landing on the backseat. And he frowned. She doubted the frown was because he'd realized it was too small an area for comfortable sex so she had a look for herself.

And saw the pink envelope.

He recognized it, of course, since he'd been there when Brantley had given it to her.

"I thought you would have gone ahead and opened it," he said.

"Nope. I'm putting it off until B-day which isn't until tomorrow. I'm not exactly looking forward to what's in it."

"So Brantley said. He called a little while ago to see if you'd opened it and if so how you were handling it. That's why I came out here, to see if you were okay."

It riled her that Brantley was still concerned about her. She didn't want his concern. But it did make her wonder if her ex knew what was in the letter. Brantley hadn't been a lawyer ten years ago when her father had written it, but it was possible that Brantley had opened it and then resealed it since it'd been in his law firm's files all this time.

"You're expecting it to be bad news?" he asked.

Sophie nodded. "My dad's messages from the grave can be unpredictable, and that's why Roman burned his when he turned thirty. But the lawyer's office had other copies, and they said they would keep sending it until he read it."

Clay slid her a confused-looking glance. "How would the lawyers know if you'd read it or not?"

"My dad liked to play games. Or rather liked to play God, and he must have known that Roman wouldn't cooperate. There was a password at the bottom of Roman's, and he had to give that password to the lawyers to turn off the flow of future copies."

Clay cursed under his breath. "What was in Garrett's that was so bad?"

"Well, he peppered the bad with the good first. He left Garrett a collection of rodeo buckles from our grandfather. Garrett had always treasured those as a kid, but we couldn't find them after Dad's death. Turns out Dad had locked them away in a safe-deposit box. But he also made Garrett the CEO of Granger Western."

"Garrett didn't want that?"

"No way. Garrett wanted me to have it so he could run the ranch. I was eighteen when our dad first got diagnosed with cancer, and Garrett made him promise that I'd be CEO once I was old enough. But our dad obviously reneged on that."

"He knew Garrett didn't want the business, but he forced it on him anyway," Clay concluded.

"That's exactly what he did, and to make sure Garrett carried through on his wishes, there was a codicil to my father's will in the letter. If at any point Garrett walked away from the company or didn't fulfill all his duties as CEO, then Granger Western was to be sold to a nonfamily member. No friends, either. In fact, there's a long list of people who wouldn't be able to buy it."

Her father had done that to make certain Garrett and

she didn't set it up as a dummy company that she could then run.

"In addition," she went on, "if Garrett steps down as CEO, a lawsuit would immediately be filed against our cousins, Lawson and his brothers."

Judging from the surprised glance Clay gave her, that was one bit of gossip he hadn't heard yet. Or maybe folks genuinely didn't know. If so, it would be the one-and-only thing her family had managed to keep secret.

"There's an old feud between the two branches of the Granger family," she explained. "We own the land east of the town. They own nearly equal acreage on the north side. The creek and a sliver of land divide the properties, and that's what's in dispute. Who owns it—them or us? There's no way Garrett or I want to bring the lawyers in on that. It would be a nasty public battle that neither of us want."

Clay stayed quiet a moment. "Your father was a sick bastard."

"Yes, he was. And it didn't get better with Roman when he got his letter from the grave. Dad set up a trust fund for Roman's son, Tate, and then he sprang another codicil to his will on him. He made Roman the owner of the ranch. Until then, all of us, including our mother, had been co-owners, but Dad gave it to the one Granger who wanted no part of it."

"Obviously that didn't work. That didn't bring Roman back here."

"No. But you can see why I'm not so anxious to read mine." Enough about her problems, though. Then Sophie remembered something she'd been meaning to mention to Clay. "Reena said you get a pink envelope every month delivered to the police station. My father didn't know you, did he?"

"No. They're not from your father." He shook his head, looked out the window. "I talked to my sister about that text she sent you. I'm sorry about it and wish I could say it won't happen again. She's young, immature and dealing with mood swings from the pregnancy."

Well, this change of subject wasn't any more pleasant than the letters. "April's right in a way. If I'm around, it won't make her life pleasant. That's why I was trying to avoid Brantley. And you. Obviously, I'm not doing a good job of that when it comes to you," she added in a mumble.

Clay continued to look out the window. Sophie figured he was going to confirm that she wasn't doing a good job but they needed to keep trying, for the sake of his sister.

But he didn't say that.

"Close your eyes," he said, his voice all low and manly.

Sophie glanced around to make sure there wasn't something she wasn't supposed to see, like a pervert flasher or an animal about to be hit on the road. But there was nothing like that. Only Clay, their vehicles and the hail.

"Close your eyes," he repeated, and this time she got a better clue as to why he'd wanted her to do that.

He turned, and in the same motion his mouth came to hers. And he gave Sophie exactly what she'd been fantasizing about for months.

Clay kissed her.

KISSING SOPHIE WASN'T STUPID.

Nope.

It was well past that. Clay should be doing everything

to keep some distance between them, and yet here he was, hauling her across the seat and planting a kiss on her.

She made a little sound of pleasure—which didn't help—and she kissed him right back. That didn't help, either, and it should have been Clay's signal to put an end to the lip-lock. Then, he could apologize and step out into the hail so the ice chunks could maybe knock some sense into him.

But he stayed put.

In part because Sophie took hold of his jacket collar and held on. Also in part because he didn't want to leave. Not with that slam of pleasure making its way from his mouth to other parts of him. One part in particular was pleased with the sensation, but Clay didn't intend to let that part have a say in this.

The kiss went on and on, and since he'd already launched into this bad decision, Clay decided to keep launching. He deepened the kiss, dragging Sophie even closer to him until she was practically in his lap.

It was too much, too soon for a first kiss, but then Sophie and he had been skirting around this attraction for a while now, and it had clearly built up. Like a pressure cooker, hissing and chugging and ready to go off. The problem with that was it was not a good location for him to make this anything more than just a kiss. They were on the side of the road where anyone could come driving up, and it was daylight. Added to that he was a cop, and if this went beyond the kiss stage, he might have to arrest himself for indecent exposure.

Despite those good arguments, Clay didn't stop, and Sophie played dirty by sliding her fingers up his neck, running her fingers through his hair, tugging gently on his ear. Normally, those weren't hot spots for him, but apparently everything was a hot spot where Sophie was concerned.

Somehow, he managed to get her even closer though it came at a cost. Clay banged his funny bone on the steering wheel. Definitely not funny. And he had to pause the kiss so he could curse. Good thing, too, because that's when Clay realized he was getting light-headed from lack of oxygen.

"Wow," she said. Gulping in some fast breaths, Sophie lowered her head to the crook of his neck. "I mean I'd expected a wow but not this much of one. My toes are tingling."

"If that's the only thing tingling, then I didn't do it right."

She laughed, her warm breath brushing against his neck. Now, that was a hot spot for him, and she must have sensed that from the grunt he made because she kissed him there.

"This is wrong," she added. It probably would have been a more convincing argument if she hadn't tongued the spot on his neck that she'd just kissed.

"Yeah, it is," he verified. It probably would have been a more convincing argument if he hadn't taken hold of the back of her hair and angled her so that he could kiss her again.

Somehow with all the maneuvering and kissing, her breasts landed against his chest. It hadn't been easy. It had required him to twist in the seat, and this time he banged his knee on the gearshift.

He'd have bruises. Sophie would, too, because her elbow had an encounter with the steering wheel. With the horn, as well, the unexpected sound so jarring Clay nearly stopped what he was doing. But he didn't until he heard something else.

A tapping sound on the glass.

It wasn't the same sounds the hail had been making. This was slightly louder and more rhythmic.

"Oh, God." Sophie scrambled to get off him, but it took Clay a moment to turn and see what had caused her to look as if she'd just seen a ghost. Just in case it was a real threat, Clay drew his gun.

And he came face-to-face with a man.

The guy was right there, staring in at them from beneath the brim of a black cowboy hat. How the devil had this clown gotten so close without Clay noticing? And when had it stopped hailing? He didn't know a lot of things right now other than Sophie repeated that *Oh, God* a couple more times.

"Back up some so I can open the door," Clay warned the Peeping Tom.

The guy smiled in a lazy but cocky way that only he and a rock star could have managed, and he lifted his hands in the air. He sort of resembled a rock star, too, in that black leather jacket, but the rest of his clothes were pure cowboy right down to that big shiny rodeo buckle.

Clay got one of his questions answered about how the man had gotten there. There was a truck parked just behind Clay's. Of course, the reason Clay hadn't heard the truck, or the man approaching, was because he'd been kissing Sophie.

"What are you doing here?" Sophie asked the man, so obviously she knew him.

"What are *you* doing here?" the man countered. His voice was as cocky as the rest of him. "Wait, don't answer that. I can see what you were doing. What I want to know is who you were doing it with." He extended his hand to Clay. "I'm Roman Granger, Sophie's brother."

Brother. The one with the police record. The one who'd refused to come home yet here he was. Well, the timing of his arrival sure sucked. Clay hadn't exactly been setting a stellar example for the badge.

Sophie fixed her shirt that had ridden up some, and she got out of the car on the passenger's side. It was still drizzling, but she made her way to Roman and pulled him into her arms. She kissed his cheek, then punched him on the shoulder when she pulled away from him.

"That's for not coming home when I asked you to," she snarled, but then she hugged him again.

With the sibling "greeting" out of the way, Clay knew it was his turn. He got out of the car, not easily, since he was having a little trouble moving what with his bruises and his semihard dick.

"I'm Clay McKinnon," he said, and he shook Roman's hand.

The corner of his mouth edged up into a smile, and Clay saw the resemblance between him and Garrett. "The new interim chief. So, you two are…seeing each other?" Roman asked. He sounded like a big brother now.

"No," Sophie quickly answered. Then she huffed. "If anyone asks, Clay and I aren't seeing each other."

Clay didn't correct that, either. But what did it mean? Did she plan for them to see each other on the sly? If so, that wasn't going to work in a small town.

"You don't want anyone to know because his sister wouldn't like it." Roman shrugged when Sophie stared at him. "Hey, I might not live here, but I still catch some gossip now and then. Plus, Tate keeps in touch with Mila."

It seemed strange that Roman's son would have a

friendship with Sophie's friend, but Clay wasn't exactly in a position to judge. Hell, he still wasn't in a position to walk right after that make-out session with Sophie.

"Did you come home because of that?" Sophie asked her brother. She hitched her thumb to the pink envelope on the seat.

Roman followed her hitched thumb and frowned. "No. I'm here because of Garrett."

Sophie did more staring at him. "You mean because Meredith is staying in Austin for a while?"

The staring continued, this time on Roman's end. "You haven't heard?"

Sophie looked at Clay to see if he knew what Roman meant, but Clay had to shake his head.

"It's all over the internet," Roman continued. He took out his phone, and while there was no cell service out here, Roman was able to play a video he had apparently saved. "I tried to stop it, but some folks knew they had a story."

"Oh, God," Sophie repeated, and this time it wasn't because Roman had shown up. It was because of what was on that video.

Garrett's wife, in the backseat of a car. Not alone, either. Nor was she dressed. She was buck naked and had her hands and mouth on some guy's dick.

CHAPTER EIGHT

As ROMAN MADE his way up the steps of the ranch house, he contemplated a couple of things about his place, or lack thereof, in his family. Garrett was the golden boy of Wrangler's Creek. The winner of the town's annual bronco riding competition for fifteen years running. Prom king. Star football player.

Men wanted to be like Garrett. Women wanted to marry him.

Then there was Sophie. Smart, beautiful. The prom queen. And a six-time winner of the town's barrel racing competition. Women wanted to be like her and some men, dickhead Brantley excluded, wanted to make out with her on the side of the road.

And then there was Roman right in the middle of them.

He had been arrested twice for underage drinking because he clearly hadn't learned his lesson after the first time. Then arrested for reckless driving. Lesson learned there. Another lesson learned when he'd knocked up his high school girlfriend and had become a father just a few weeks shy of his twentieth birthday. Despite fatherhood, he'd continued his bad boy ways. Some of them, anyway. Men hated him, and women wanted to fuck him.

Not a bad trade-off, all things considered.

"I can't believe this happened," Sophie said.

Sophie was right behind him, coming up the steps. Not with Clay, though. The cop had wisely opted out of this visit when Roman had offered to give Sophie a ride. Clay might be stupid enough to carry on with Sophie on the side of the road, but he was smart enough to know not to walk into the middle of a family shit-storm.

"Poor Garrett," Sophie added.

Yeah, poor Garrett.

But Roman put himself in the "poor" category. To a lesser extent, of course. There was a reason that Roman rarely made it home, and the reason was waiting for him in the entry of the ranch house.

His mother.

For such a sweet-looking lady, she had developed a good stink eye, and as she had done for the past twelve plus years, she was aiming that stink eye at him.

"How'd she even know I was coming?" Roman grumbled to Sophie.

"Once I was out of the dead zone, I texted Garrett, and he must have told her."

"He didn't," her mother's voice was coated with a little stink eye, too. "I heard Garrett tell Alice that'd you would be here soon and that she should probably put on a fresh pot of coffee."

Alice was their longtime cook and housekeeper, and unless she was filling that coffeepot with Jim Beam, Roman would pass. He didn't especially want to be any more alert for this visit.

"Is Tate with you?" his mother wanted to know.

Roman shook his head. "He's in school today." And just in case this visit involved taking Garrett to the bar to get drunk, Roman had arranged for a sitter to pick up Tate and take him to their home in San Antonio.

"Where's Garrett?" Sophie asked their mother.

"In his office."

Sophie and Roman started there, but their mother stepped in front of them. "You didn't come home for Sophie's wedding. Your only sister, and you missed her wedding."

Sophie huffed. "Really, Mom? We're going to rehash this now with what Garrett is going through?"

Apparently, they were because his mother launched right into the rehashing. Roman tuned her out, but his brain had no trouble filling in what she was saying. Because she'd said it so often it was like a broken record.

Your family needed you, and you weren't here.

You've always been so irresponsible, and that obviously hasn't changed.

And the biggie—*why haven't you married Tate's mother yet?*

The last was the easiest to answer. He hadn't married Valerie because they'd decided not to say "I Do" when she'd gotten pregnant with Tate at the tender age of eighteen. Roman had been only a year older. They had decided to raise the baby together, which had lasted until Tate was about six months old and Valerie skipped out on them, never to be seen in Wrangler's Creek again.

Rumor had it that Roman had murdered Valerie and buried the body. Second most popular rumor was that Roman's father had murdered her. The truth was Valerie just hadn't wanted to be a mom and had tucked tail and run. She sent occasional cards to Tate, called him on his birthday, when she remembered. On the years she didn't remember and when Roman saw the disappointment on his boy's face, he wanted to find her and wring her neck.

As for the first two rants from his mother, the answer

to both of those was yes. His siblings had likely needed him, and yes, he was irresponsible. By his mother's standards, anyway, but he'd quit living by her standards when he'd left Wrangler's Creek eleven years ago.

What his mother didn't know was that he had gone to Sophie's wedding with plans to watch it from the back of the church, and when it'd been apparent that Brantley had skipped out on her, Roman had hunted down the man and punched him in the face. It hadn't been a very mature reaction, but it'd felt damn good.

"Well?" his mother asked. Obviously she wanted some kind of response, and while she wasn't tapping her foot with impatience, it looked as if that was something she wanted to do.

Roman gave her a response, but it likely wasn't the one she wanted. And it definitely didn't involve groveling. He kissed her on the cheek, flashed his cockiest smile and headed toward Garrett's office.

"Oh, and why don't you ask Sophie why she was kissing a cop on the road?" Roman added.

Sophie glared at him, and yeah, it was bad to throw her to the wolf that way, but if he hadn't, his mother would have followed instead of staying in the entry to find out what was going on. This would buy Roman a few moments alone with his brother.

He'd always thought the house was too big. Twenty-three rooms. And it felt as if he had to walk past at least twenty of those to get to the office. The door was shut, but Roman didn't knock. He went right in, closed the door behind him and saw about what he expected to see.

Garrett, seated behind the massive oak desk.

His brother was sprawled out in the chair, legs stretched in front of him, his head against the back of the seat, and he had a highball glass dangling from each hand. The glasses were filled nearly to the brim with brown liquid.

Roman was betting it wasn't Diet Coke.

"You didn't have to come," Garrett said. Judging from his speech pattern, he wasn't anywhere close to being drunk. Too bad because while the booze wouldn't help, it might make him pass out so he could forget for a couple of minutes.

"I know. But every now and then I like to do something that surprises people. Keeps them on their toes." Roman located the whiskey bottle on the floor next to Garrett's chair and took a sip.

"I take it you tried to stop the video from going viral?" Garrett asked.

Roman nodded and pulled up a chair so they'd be face-to-face for the heart-to-heart they would have. Not that it would help. Nothing would at this point. But they would have it anyway.

"First of all, I'm sorry," Roman said. "And no, I didn't have a clue Meredith was cheating on you. Did you?"

"No." Garrett cursed, shook his head. "I knew she wasn't happy about being here. She hates the ranch, hated that we aren't at the business in Austin. Hated that we might never be back there."

Yeah, Roman had figured out that much. Garrett had been the prom king because his classmates had elected him and he'd reluctantly accepted it. Meredith had been prom queen because she'd lobbied, begged and prayed for it.

"Meredith left yesterday," Garrett went on. "Said she was going to be in Austin for a while. I asked if that meant we were separating, and she said no, that she just needed some space."

They both winced at that. *Space* was code for *you'll get the divorce papers soon.*

"Is this the part where you tell me I shouldn't have married her?" Garrett added.

"Nope." Roman took another sip of whiskey, a small one since he'd likely have to drive soon. "She was pregnant. You two wanted a baby, and you'd been dating a long time—since high school. And after hearing Mom harp on me for years about being an unwed parent, you probably didn't want to put yourself through it."

The difference was that Meredith and Garrett had been eleven years older than Roman had been. And Meredith and Garrett would have probably married eventually anyway. The baby had just moved the date up a bit. Then, fate had pissed on their lives because the baby girl had been stillborn.

As a father, that still cut Roman bone deep, and the cut went even deeper for Garrett.

"What about you?" Garrett asked. "Have you recently had your heart stomped on, or have you found a woman who'll put up with you for more than a one-nighter?"

Roman didn't mind the shift in conversation. His brother might be looking for a "misery loves company" kind of thread. Then again, they so rarely talked that maybe Garrett just wanted to know if he was close to becoming a brother-in-law or uncle again.

"No to both," Roman answered. "I was involved with the owner of the motorcycle shop where I get my bike parts, but she broke off things because she said I had a commitment phobia." And because he thought they could use some levity, he added, "I told her I didn't have a phobia, that being with someone on a regular basis scared the shit out of me."

It worked. Garrett smiled a little. Then, that vanished when his phone rang, and his brother hit the button to decline the call. "Meredith again. She keeps calling."

"Have you talked to her yet?"

"Some. I took the first call, and she said she was sorry. But I think she means she was sorry she got caught on camera blowing some guy."

Yeah. It wouldn't be good for her socialite image, and coming on the heels of the mess with Granger Western, Roman was betting Meredith would no longer be on Austin's A-list for parties and charity events. Her name would be mud in Wrangler's Creek, too, because she'd basically just cheated on the town's golden boy.

"We can do this a couple of ways," Roman started. "We can sit here and drink with the constant interruptions from Mom, Sophie and Alice. They'll want to feed you and smother you with love. I, on the other hand, want to get you shit-faced at some secondary location of your choosing. We can trash-talk Meredith, and if you're up to it, you can have a revenge fuck from just about any woman who crosses your shit-faced path."

Garrett stayed quiet a moment, swirled the drink in his left hand, took a sip from the one in his right. "Got any other options?"

Roman had to think about it. "We could saddle some horses, ride out to our great-granddaddy's old house and hide out the way we used to do when we were kids."

Though the place had been a lot more appealing way back when they didn't know how butt-ugly it was. The Gothic house was an architectural mess complete with some gargoyles, staircases that led to nowhere and secret passages. And it was painted a dull shade of purple with equally dull yellow trim. It looked like a giant bruise in various stages of healing.

A movie studio had once wanted to use it to film a horror flick, but their mother had declined, saying she didn't want to disrespect the place. It seemed to Roman that the place had pretty much screamed disrespect from the moment the painter had slapped on those colors.

"I could sneak some food from Alice," Roman suggested. "And threaten the ranch hands so they won't tell anyone which direction we're heading. We can grab some sleeping bags. Some liquor…"

"But what about Tate? He'll be expecting you home."

That was his big brother. Always looking at the big picture. "I'll call the sitter and have her stay with him."

Tate hated her. Well, actually he hated sitters in general because he thought he was old enough to stay alone, but if Roman explained that Uncle Garrett was in a bad place, then Tate would understand. Maybe. Tate was so surly these days that it was hard to tell if he was riled or if a grouch bug had crawled up his butt and taken up permanent residence.

"All right," Garrett agreed on a weary breath. "Let's get the shit-face session started."

Roman took out his phone and went through the contacts to find the sitter, Misty Joyner, and he wasn't really surprised when Misty answered on the first ring. That's because she was supposed to be picking up Tate right about now.

"Is Tate with you?" Misty blurted out before Roman could say anything.

Roman's heart skipped a couple of beats. "No. He's at school."

"He's not. I'm here now, and the lady in the office said he didn't show for his sixth-period class. She thought maybe you'd picked him up and forgot to check him out."

"No," he repeated, already getting to his feet. Thank God he'd had only a sip of the whiskey and was good to drive. "I'll get there as fast as I can."

"Wait. Hold on a second. The office lady was checking his locker, and she's walking toward me right now."

Roman cursed when Misty put him on hold, and the bad thoughts started to fire through his head. He'd learned over the years that parents could have some really god-awful thoughts about what could happen to their kids.

"What's wrong?" Garrett got to his feet, too, and Roman could see that he was already steeling himself up. No doubt so he could be the one to steel up Roman.

Roman didn't get a chance to answer his brother because Misty came back on the line, and his heart did more beat-skipping when he heard the first three words she said.

"I'm so sorry."

He could hear the concern in the sitter's voice, but it was a drop in the bucket compared to what Roman was feeling. "What happened?"

"Tate left a note in his locker," Misty continued a moment later. "Mr. Granger, Tate ran away."

ONCE AGAIN SOPHIE was driving up Main Street looking for a Granger. Tate this time instead of Garrett, but she wasn't having any better luck spotting her nephew than she had when she looked for Meredith the day her sister-in-law had walked out. Of course, the difference was Garrett was able to take care of himself, but Tate was barely twelve.

Garrett, Roman, their mother and Sophie had divided up the search so they'd have a better chance of finding him. According to one of his friends, Tate was on his way to Wrangler's Creek. God knew how, since it was miles away from his school, and besides it was possible Tate had told his friend that just to throw them off his trail. That's why Roman had gone back to San Antonio to look for him there, and Garrett was on his way to San Antonio PD to file a missing person's report.

Sophie tried to call Mila again but got no answer. That wasn't so unusual since Mila often didn't take calls on her cell while she was at work, but her friend wasn't answering the bookstore phone, either. Sophie hoped that meant it was because Mila had already gotten the word about Tate running away and was out looking for him. Too bad there were no guarantees that the boy was actually in Wrangler's Creek.

She pulled to a stop in front of the bookstore and wasn't surprised when Clay pulled up, as well. Sophie had called him within minutes after learning that her nephew might be headed this way, and Clay had gone out to the highway to see if he could find Tate hitchhiking.

"Anything?" Sophie immediately asked him.

Clay shook his head. "But I remembered Roman mentioning that Mila and Tate stayed in touch so I came here."

"That's why I came, too, but Mila isn't answering her phones. She's not at her house, either, because I drove by there on the way here."

Sophie hurried to the door, but it was locked, and the blinds were all drawn so that they couldn't even see inside. She searched through her purse for the spare key Mila had given her, and she used it to open the door.

The first thing Sophie heard was music, an old song from the fifties. It sounded familiar, but she didn't know the title. It was pouring through the speaker system which normally played Mila's preferred Celtic tunes. And then Sophie saw something she certainly hadn't been expecting.

"Would Tate have a key, too? If so, maybe he let himself in," Clay asked, but his words died on his lips when he saw what had caused Sophie to freeze in her tracks.

Mila was on all fours in the reading area, but she had pushed back the sofa and chairs that were normally there. Her friend was wearing denim shorts, a midriff white top that she'd tied in the front and white tennis shoes.

And her friend wasn't alone.

There was a man, someone Sophie had never seen before, and he was dressed in black pants and a black muscle shirt. Like Mila, he was on all fours, too, and they were facing each other, their mouths nearly touching.

"Shit," Mila said, scrambling to get to her feet. The guy scrambled, too, and his profanity was significantly worse than Mila's. "You're not going to arrest me, are you?" he said to Clay when he spotted the badge. "Because I'm only doing what Baby wanted. Uh, I mean Mila."

"Why are you here?" Mila asked Sophie and Clay at the same moment that Sophie had been about to ask, "What's going on?"

But Sophie knew those clothes, knew the music, too. "This is from *Dirty Dancing*," Sophie provided, and then she repeated, "What's going on?"

Mila huffed. "It's from one of the dating sites. You told me I should try one."

That was true. "Uh, this is a date?"

"A reenactment," the man quickly provided. "I found *Baby* on the Make My Fantasies Come True website. Mila was looking for a Dirty Dancing experience, too. Not the sex scene, of course, because I'm gay, but she wanted the *Love Is Strange* experience, followed by Baby in the corner."

Ah, that explained why the song was playing over the speakers, but it didn't explain much else. This was the first Sophie was hearing about that particular fantasy, but Mila did tend to obsess on anything romantic. At least she wasn't acting out a *Fifty Shades of Grey* scene because Sophie didn't want images of her best friend like that in her head.

Later, she would remind Mila that it wasn't a good idea to meet strange men in nonpublic places, but that could wait, especially since "Johnny" was gathering up his things to hightail it out of there.

"Tate's missing," Sophie said. "Did he get in touch with you?"

Mila's eyes widened. "No. How long has he been gone?" She grabbed her sweater and threw it on as if she might bolt out of there to go find him.

"He left school about four hours ago. Could you check your phone messages and see if he called you?"

Mila hurried to the checkout counter, where both her cell and the landline were. She turned the landline to Sophie so she could look for messages. Other than the ones from Sophie, there was nothing. Mila shook her head, too, after listening to the voice mails on her cell.

"None from Tate, but you called three times," Mila

said, still shaking her head. "I'd turned off my phone for the fantasy. God, I'm so sorry." Tears sprang to her eyes, and since Mila wasn't a crier, Sophie knew this had shaken her as much as it had the rest of them.

"When's the last time you heard from Tate?" Clay asked Mila.

He sounded like a cop, which in this case was both bad and good. They needed a cop to help them, but Sophie knew that Mila would probably just get frazzled if she was interrogated right now. Of course, Sophie hadn't realized her best friend was into fantasy role-playing, either.

"It's been a while." Mila blinked back tears. "Two weeks, maybe. Wait, no. That's the last time he called me, but he sent me an email day before yesterday." That caused Mila to scurry to her office, which was just a small cubby off the main floor.

"Tate and you were close?" Clay, again. And the cop tone had gone up a notch. He didn't come out and ask if anything inappropriate had been going on between Tate and her, but after what he'd just witnessed, Sophie could see why he'd have doubts.

"Yes, we were close." Mila was still battling those tears, but she sounded defensive, too.

"Mila and Tate's mother, Valerie, are first cousins," Sophie explained. "But Vita raised Valerie so they're really more like sisters. Over the years whenever Tate's wanted to talk about his mom, he'd call Mila."

"Then, he got into reading, and from time to time, he has me order books he's interested in," Mila added as she booted up her laptop. "In fact, that's what the email was about. He wanted me to see if I could get him an advance reading copy of a YA series that he's really into. Here it is." She turned the computer for them to see.

Clay and Sophie nearly banged heads when they both leaned in to read it, and Sophie frantically searched through the email. It really was just about a book order—until Sophie scrolled down past Tate's name. There was a PS.

Might be leaving soon to see my mom.

"Oh, God," Mila repeated. "I didn't even notice that. I just hit Reply and told him I'd see what I could do about the book."

"Do you have a way to get in touch with Valerie?" Clay asked.

Mila shook her head. "I haven't spoken to her in years."

Clay took out his phone, stepped away and pressed in a number. "What's Valerie's last name?"

"Banchini," Mila provided, and she spelled it for him. "If she's still using that name. She might have gotten married." She turned back to Sophie. "I'm sorry I can't be of more help. God, do you think Tate's all right?"

"I'm sure he is." Sophie wasn't sure of that at all, but if Mila fell apart, Sophie might fall right along with her. It was crushing her heart to think of Tate out there, especially at this late hour. And it was cold. He could have taken a ride with a stranger. He could—

"Sophie!" Mila practically yelled. "Are you hyperventilating?"

Probably, but Sophie quickly tried to level her breathing. Tried to focus, too. Passing out wouldn't help Tate.

Mila's near yell got Clay's attention as well, and even though he didn't end his call, he put Sophie in the chair

behind Mila's desk. Sophie assured him that it wasn't necessary, but it was. It helped with some of the dizziness.

"Would Tate go to your mother?" Sophie asked Mila.

"Not a chance."

Mila was right. Vita was scary enough to adults, and
a boy who had just turned twelve would give her a wide
berth.

"I'll call my mom just in case," Mila said. She gave
Sophie a "pray for me" look that Sophie had no trouble
understanding. A conversation with Vita was never short,
and if she was in a bad mood, you might end up on the
receiving end of a gypsy's curse.

Mila started that call just as Clay got Sophie's attention. "Roman didn't have a current number for Valerie,
but I was able to find one through DMV records. She's
in Santa Fe, but she didn't answer when I tried to call
her. A cop friend is trying to contact her now." He'd no
sooner said that when someone must have come on the
line because Clay put his phone back to his ear.

Santa Fe? Mercy, she prayed Tate hadn't tried to get
that far.

"I see," Clay said to the caller. He paused. "Shit."

Sophie's stomach clenched, and she got to her feet
even though she was still a little dizzy. She waited, holding her breath so long that her lungs started to ache. It
seemed to take an eternity for Clay to finish his call.

"Tate did have his mother's number. She'd posted it
on Facebook because she was selling something and he
saw it and phoned her this morning," Clay started. "He
told her that he wanted to go see her."

"Gotta go, Mom," Mila quickly said, and she hit the
end call button even though Vita was still talking. Sophie caught the words "location spell."

Clay shook his head, mumbled another *shit*.

"Valerie told him no, that it was a bad time for a visit, and she hung up on him."

Since Sophie didn't know what else to say, she doled out her own *shit*. "And Valerie didn't think she should tell Roman about that conversation?"

But she waved off this question. This was the woman who'd abandoned her baby, and Sophie doubted she'd recently gotten doused with a bucket of maternal love and instincts. Still, she had to be an idiot not to realize how this would affect the boy.

"I'll call Roman," Sophie said, taking out her phone.

Clay glanced around. "Does Tate have a key to this place or to your house?"

Mila was shaking her head before Clay even finished the question. Then, she stopped. "But he knows I keep a key in the verbena plant on my back porch."

Clay huffed, and if circumstances had been different, he might have lectured her on stashing a key where a burglar could find it. But instead of a lecture, they all hurried out the door. Since Clay made it to his truck first, Sophie and Mila followed and piled in the vehicle after him.

He took off the moment they had on their seat belts. It was only a short ride to Mila's, less than five minutes, but that was more than enough time for the silence to close in around them. Sophie considered using the time to call Roman, but she decided to wait until they'd checked out Mila's place.

"I was going to tell you about the fantasy stuff," Mila whispered to her. "But you've been so busy, and I figured you were dealing with the fallout from what happened with Meredith and Garrett. The fallout from April, too."

Until Mila added that last part, Sophie had been about

to assure her that she was never too busy to hear what was going on in her best friend's life. Especially this. But she stopped. "April?" Clay and Sophie asked in unison.

Mila looked at them as if the answer were obvious. It wasn't.

"April came by the shop a couple of hours ago," Mila explained. "She said she'd been by Clay's office, but Reena told him he was on his way out to the ranch to see you."

Clay groaned. "I didn't tell Reena where I was going, but she passed me on the road when I took the turn to Sophie's."

And Sophie knew why Clay had been going there— to make sure she wasn't a wreck from the letter in the pink envelope. Well, she was a wreck all right and hadn't even gotten to what was certain to be another dose of bad news from dear ol' Dad.

"Anyway, April was pissed," Mila went on. "She said she'd tried to call you," she added to Clay. "Then, she tried calling Sophie."

"Dead zone," Clay and Sophie answered in unison.

"That's what I figured, but then April had a fit that you two might be together. I assured her that nothing was going on, but she didn't believe me."

There was a good reason for April's disbelief. It's because something was going on between Clay and her. Well, some kissing anyway, but considering the firestorm their relationship was causing, there probably wouldn't be any future kisses.

A thought that had Sophie feeling even worse than she already did.

"Anyway, after she ranted for a while, April said she was going home to pack. She said if her brother was going to carry on with Brantley's ex, then she was going to have Brantley move the boys and her far away from Wrangler's Creek."

This time it was Sophie who groaned. "You can drop us off at Mila's and go to her," Sophie suggested to Clay.

He shook his head, pulled to a stop in front of Mila's house. "I want to check for Tate first."

Sophie knew this was already eating away at him. Yeah, definitely no more kisses. Heck, if April moved, then Clay might follow her just to make sure his nephews were okay. She got that. Because at the moment Sophie was worried about her own nephew.

"April called you a name," Mila continued as they headed up the porch. She glanced back at Sophie to indicate the name-calling was for her.

"She called me a bitch," Sophie supplied.

"How'd you know?"

"Lucky guess," she grumbled.

Mila unlocked the door, threw it open, and Sophie got ready to call out Tate's name. But it wasn't necessary. That's because she saw him asleep on the sofa.

Tate, who looked identical to Roman when he was that age, lay there with a bag of chips on his chest and a can of soda on the floor next to his backpack. He must have heard them because he opened his eyes, slowly. Eyes that doubled in size as his gaze slipped from Mila. To Sophie. Then to Clay.

Her nephew's gaze lingered a moment on Clay's badge.

Tate stood, the bag of chips toppling to the floor, and he lifted his hands in the air. He swallowed hard. "You can go ahead and arrest me," Tate said. He was probably trying to sound brave. And he was failing. His hands were shaking. "But please don't tell my dad where I am."

CHAPTER NINE

FROM THE MOMENT Tate had asked them not to tell Roman where he was, Sophie had known that was not going to happen. She called Roman, and as she expected, he said he'd be right there.

Sophie had insisted instead that Clay and she drive Tate to the ranch—where there'd be more space for Roman to deal with his son. The real reason, though, was that she hadn't wanted Roman behind the wheel in his state of mind. She wasn't exactly sure what that state would be, but she was certain it wouldn't be good.

"You shouldn't have told Dad," Tate grumbled as Clay got them into his truck. Mila stayed behind in the doorway, giving them a wave and then making the "call me" sign to Sophie.

"Your father loves you, and he was worried something bad had happened to you," Sophie grumbled right back to her nephew.

"Something bad did." Even though Tate was in the middle of the seat and strapped in with the seat belt, he managed to slump.

Sophie's heart sank, seeing him like this. Since this was the calm before the storm, she put her arm around him and looked over at Clay. He had his own storm to face.

"After you drop us off at the ranch, you should go ahead and check on your sister," she offered again.

"I can wait a while longer," Clay answered. "There was a missing person's report on Tate so I'll need to handle that."

"You gonna arrest me?" Tate asked him.

"Not at the moment."

"Wish you would," Tate said under his breath. "Then I wouldn't have to face my dad."

"Oh, you'd still have to face him. Trust me, it's best for that to happen when you're not behind bars. Mind telling me, though, how you got to Mila's?"

Good question because if he'd hitchhiked, Tate was about to get a lecture. Then he'd get another one from Roman.

"I don't want to get anybody in trouble," Tate said.

"Trouble's already here. Best to tell me what happened," Clay insisted. He wasn't using his cop's voice, though. This was more like the tone he used with his own nephews, and Sophie was thankful for it.

Tate took his time answering. "My friend has a big brother, he's sixteen, and I paid him to drive me out there. I used the key Mila keeps in that smelly plant to unlock the back door. I was going to have her take me to see my mom. I figured since they were cousins and all that she'd have my mom's address."

Sophie sighed. "You know she couldn't have done that."

Tate just shrugged.

"How'd you get your mom's phone number?" Clay pressed.

"Internet. She makes stuff out of trash. Like art, you know. And I saw where she was selling things in this shop. I called the shop and told them I wanted to get in touch with her so I could maybe buy some stuff from her as a present for somebody. They gave me her phone number." He paused. "She didn't know who I was. I had to tell her it was me."

Mercy, it was hard to hear this, and she wished she'd been there with him to talk him out of that call. Since he was as stubborn as his father, she likely wouldn't have been able to do that, but at least she could have been there to help him pick up the pieces.

Sophie leaned down to make eye contact with Tate. "You know your mom isn't, well, she just isn't in a mom kind of place in her life right now."

A massive understatement, and Sophie wanted to shake Valerie senseless for rejecting her own son. Of course, judging from the woman's behavior, she already was senseless.

"We know you called her," Sophie continued. "Clay… Chief McKinnon found out. And we also know that it upset you when she told you she didn't want you to come to Santa Fe." Valerie hadn't confirmed that last part, but Sophie had some inkling of what was going on in Tate's head.

Again, Tate took his time before he said anything. "Mom might change her mind."

Again, Sophie wished Valerie were there so she could give her a hard shake. Because the woman had had over a decade to *change her mind*, and she hadn't done it yet.

When they pulled into the driveway, Sophie spotted her car. And the tire was no longer flat. One of the ranch hands had likely fixed it and driven it home.

Roman, Garrett and her mother were waiting on the porch, and the moment Clay stopped, Roman barreled down the steps toward the truck with Garrett and her mom right behind him. Sophie wasn't sure what he was going to say to his son, and it seemed as if Roman wasn't sure, either.

"First things first—you're grounded," Roman finally snarled. "Second, why the hell would you do something like this? And third—you're grounded."

Just seconds earlier Tate had looked seriously defeated, but facing his dad put some of that cockiness in his expression. Sheez. He wasn't just a copy of his dad—Tate could do the I-don't-give-a-crap look as well as Roman could.

"He was upset over his call with Valerie," Sophie reminded Roman, though she'd already told him that over the phone.

"Yeah, I'm upset about it, too." Roman stopped, and even though he didn't curse, Sophie figured there was a whole lot of profanity flying through his head. "Why would you call her?"

Tate just kept up that same expression. "Because she's my mom. I know you don't want her to be, but you can't change that."

Roman opened his mouth, closed it, cursed.

"You shouldn't talk like that in front of the boy," Belle scolded.

"So, I'll ground myself. Stay out of this, Mom."

"No, I won't stay out of it."

Garrett and she groaned. Clay glanced around as if he suddenly wanted to be anywhere but there.

"If you'd just put a ring on Valerie's finger, then this might not be happening," their mother added.

Roman didn't aim the look at Belle, but his expression morphed into a glare that could have frozen Texas in July. "No. She would have just left town with the ring."

Good comeback, but Sophie knew that wouldn't deter

her mother. Whenever Belle was anywhere near Roman, she just had to preach to him.

"I married Meredith, and that didn't turn out so great," Garrett said, interrupting whatever their mother had been about to say.

Sophie interrupted her for the next round. "And I was engaged to be married to Brantley. Didn't work for me, either."

"Thanks," Roman mumbled to them, "but I can fight my own battles."

Clay no doubt heard that, but he was the one who interrupted Belle the third time. He didn't aim his comments at her, but rather Roman. "I'll close out the missing person's report, and if you want me to deal with the follow-up, just let me know. I'll be glad to have a chat with the teenager who gave Tate a ride to Wrangler's Creek."

"Thanks," Roman said, "but I'd like to chat with him myself."

Clay looked at Sophie, maybe silently asking if that was a safe solution. It was. Roman could be a badass, and he might scare this teenager, but he wouldn't physically harm him. Tate, either. But she was betting her brother would follow through on the grounding.

"Hold on there a second, Chief McKinnon," Belle said when Clay started to get back in his truck. "I heard you were kissing my daughter. I'm not sure that's a good idea."

Not this, not now. Sophie would have screamed, but she was too busy groaning. In fact, it was a chorus of groans what with Garrett and Clay joining in. Roman punctuated it with more mumbled profanity.

"It's not a good idea," Clay assured her mother. "But

sometimes people don't always do what's good. Me included."

Belle huffed, obviously seeing that as an attempt to blow her off. "Well, will it happen again?"

"You should ask me that because I'm the one who started the kissing," Sophie spoke up.

Clay gave her an I-can-fight-my-own-battles look that was similar to Roman's. It still didn't stop her mother from prattling on.

"Your sister won't like you seeing Sophie, and my daughter's already had enough drama in her life what with Brantley and the skirt-chasing Shane."

Also as Roman had done, Clay opened his mouth, closed it. Then he nodded. He was no doubt biting his tongue. Maybe literally. He tipped his cowboy hat as a farewell, got in his truck and drove off.

Sophie felt as if he'd driven off with a little piece of her heart.

It was stupid to feel anything for him what with her life and her family falling squarely into the "messy" category. But it hurt to think that she might not get to kiss him again.

"Let's go," Roman said to Tate. He threw open his truck door and motioned for Tate to get inside.

Tate stayed put. "I want to stay here. And I have to pee."

Roman tipped his eyes to the heavens as if seeking divine help. Sophie figured all parents needed a little of that. "I'll stop at the gas station, and you can pee there," Roman answered. "Now get in."

"How about you stay for a while?" Garrett suggested. "You, Tate, Sophie and me could camp out at Z.T.'s old house."

"I'm not rewarding him for pulling crap like this," Roman snapped.

Well, it wouldn't have actually been a reward as far as Sophie was concerned since the place was no doubt crawling with spiders and coated with enough dust to trigger an asthma attack. But she would have done it if Roman had agreed.

He didn't.

"In the truck now," Roman repeated to Tate.

Tate must have realized there was no stall tactic to deter a pissed-off father so he intensified his glare and slid onto the truck seat.

"The boy can stay," Belle piped up. "You're clearly having trouble handling him so you just leave him here."

Too bad her mother hadn't added some maybes and pleases in that demand. Also too bad that it was indeed a demand.

Roman didn't look at her. A couple of muscles flickered in his jaw. "Need I remind you that I own this land and this house…where you live? Think about that, Mother, and stay the heck out of our lives."

It was a hollow threat. At least Sophie thought it was. Roman had a temper, but he also had common sense. He wouldn't sell the place out from under Garrett, Lawson and her. But at the moment he likely wanted to ban Belle from the ranch, maybe from Wrangler's Creek if he could have managed it.

"You see my side of this, don't you?" Belle asked Garrett and her as Roman drove away. She didn't wait for an answer, which would have been no! "I hope Tate gets to pee soon. It's not good for a boy to hold his bladder like that."

Tate's bladder was the least of their problems right

now. Garrett started walking in the direction of the barn. "I'm spending the night at Z.T.'s house, and I'm going by myself," he added, and though he didn't leave any room for argument, Sophie had to give him one anyway.

"I'll go with you. It's not a good idea for you to be out there alone."

"Being alone is exactly what I want," he muttered and kept walking.

Sophie considered going after him but decided instead to call Lawson so he could ride out there and check on him. Garrett wouldn't like that, but it was better than her worrying about him all night. Of course, she'd be worrying about Tate and Roman. About Clay and his family situation, too. Plus, Mila was probably a wreck by now over this whole runaway ordeal, and getting caught in the fantasy.

And then there was her mother.

Belle was sniffling as if fighting back tears, and because this insensitive woman was still her mother, Sophie gave her a hug.

"I think I'll drive over to Mary Lynn's house for some girl time," Belle said. Mary Lynn had been her mother's best friend since childhood and was a yes woman. She would tell Belle exactly what she wanted to hear—which was better than Sophie would be able to do at the moment.

She followed her mother onto the porch, but the moment Belle was inside, she took her purse from the hall closet and grabbed her keys. That's when Sophie saw the pink envelope sitting on the foyer table.

"Oh, Lawson fixed your flat and brought that in for you," her mother said. "He mentioned something about the lube that you left behind worked like a charm."

That improved Sophie's posture a little. Ironic that Lawson had chosen the word *charm* when it had involved something from Vita.

Her mother motioned to the envelope on her way to the door. "I'll be here tomorrow when you open it."

Tomorrow. Her thirtieth birthday.

"Alice has the night off," Belle added, heading out, "but if you're hungry, she left lasagna in the fridge. Don't wait up for me 'cause I'll probably be late."

Sophie shut the door, took the letter and headed to the kitchen. Not for lasagna but for a beer. She might need something stronger, but at least if she had too much to drink and got whiney, there'd be no one around to see or hear her.

No one around, either, to witness her reaction to her father's letter.

Her birthday wouldn't be much of a birthday, but there was no use spoiling what was left to spoil by waiting to read what would almost certainly be sucky news. She sat on the stool at the kitchen island, tore open the envelope and got started.

The letter was typed, not handwritten, and that twisted her gut a little more than it already was. He'd personally written Garrett's and Roman's, but apparently by the time he'd gotten to hers, he'd either been too weak to write it himself or too busy tidying up his empire despite the fact he couldn't take it to the grave with him.

"Sophie," she began reading aloud.

"By now you've followed through on your life plan and are a married woman. Brantley had better be treating you right, though now that I'm dead, it's all right for you to hear that I've always thought he was somewhat of a spineless weasel."

Sophie laughed. She'd only been dating Brantley for about a year before her dad got sick, but even then they'd been talking marriage, kids, growing old together. So much for that. She continued to read.

"Of course, maybe all fathers feel that no man is good enough for their daughters, so if Brantley is treating you right, make sure he doesn't see this letter."

If Brantley hadn't read it already, then he wouldn't get the chance to see it now. Because when she was finished reading it, Sophie was going to light a fire and burn it to ashes.

"Now, here comes the part you're dreading because I'm sure you know there was what your brothers considered bad news in their letters. I had my reasons for doing what I did, reasons they might someday see as a good thing."

Not likely. But Sophie steeled herself up and kept on reading.

"I want you to try to mend the rift between your mother and Roman. I wish I could say it had been mended, but I know your mother, and she'd rather be right than happy. Not a good high road to take, considering Roman's mule-headedness. So, mend it if you can so that Tate will one day be able to call the ranch his home."

If only. After what'd just happened, Roman might never let him set foot on Granger land again.

She pushed that dreary thought aside and got back to the letter. "And finally, Sophie, here's what I'm giving you..."

Sophie stopped reading aloud because she was certain she wasn't seeing the words right. She looked at them again. And again.

But they didn't change.

Although it was hard to tell now that her eyes were filled with tears. Sophie held the letter to her chest and let the tears continue to fall.

CHAPTER TEN

CLAY TOOK A deep breath, which he was certain he would need, and knocked on Brantley's door. No answer so he knocked again. After a repeat of the no-answer, he rang the doorbell.

Every second that crawled by only caused his insides to churn more. If April had talked Brantley into leaving, then there was no telling where they could be. He'd have to go searching for them, and after the day he'd already had, Clay just wanted to go home and crash in bed. However, he couldn't even think about doing that until he made sure his sister and nephews were okay.

He rang the bell a third time and took out his phone to try calling. But that wasn't necessary. The third time worked—the door flew open, and he came face-to-face with a crying pregnant woman.

"I don't want to see you," April snapped through the sniffles.

Clay used his foot to stop her from slamming the door in his face. "Tough. Because you're seeing me and we're talking."

"Nunk!" Hunter squealed and went running toward Clay. Hayden was right on his heels, and Clay scooped them up. The hugs he gave them were for him because the thought of losing moments like this with them had shaken him more than Clay realized.

Brantley came out from the kitchen, and judging from his expression, he'd been through the wringer. Good. Because in a way, this was all Brantley's fault. If he'd just gone through with the wedding to Sophie…

But Clay stopped.

Frowned.

And he silently groaned when he realized he was damn glad that marriage hadn't happened. Of course, he wished that Brantley hadn't wedded April, but that was a different kind of silent groan.

"I was about to put the boys to bed," Brantley volunteered.

Clay looked at his sister to see what she had to say about that. He figured she was about to snarl something about they'd be leaving first thing in the morning, but she only took the boys from Clay and passed them to Brantley. The boys protested and whined until Brantley promised to read them two stories.

April waited until they were out of the room before she said anything. "I'm not happy about you kissing Sophie, but I understand she's probably desperate to find a man. Any man. That's why she used those dating sites."

"She had one date, and it didn't work out." Clay was certain that if there'd been more dates, he would have heard about it. Gossip traveled faster than the speed of light in Wrangler's Creek. "If you remember correctly, you gave me a subscription to a dating site so I guess that means you think I'm desperate, too. I'm not, by the way. In fact, I don't think I'll ever be…desperate."

April looked him in the eyes, and several things passed between them. Unspoken but understood. His sister was one of the few people who knew what had happened two years ago. And because she also knew that it was something he never wanted to discuss, she didn't bring it up.

Since April still had tears in her eyes, something that twisted at him, Clay reached out and pulled her into his arms. "I'm sorry this upset you, but you can't fly off the handle like that. The boys need stability. They don't need to be moved around because their uncle kissed your husband's ex. Plus, you need stability, because you're pregnant."

She pulled back, her mouth still tight. "That's what Brantley said."

Well then, Brantley just went up a notch in Clay's book. A very small notch since the stability thing was common sense. "So, we're okay?" he asked.

"Are you going to kiss Sophie again?" April asked right back.

Was he? Clay wanted to say no way, but he was learning he was pretty weak when it came to Sophie.

"If I kiss her again," he said, "just remember this stability chat we had."

Clay would remember it, too. He'd fought hard for stability in his own life. For his sanity. And while kissing Sophie again would lead to some wonderful things, like sex, it would also lead to other things.

Like talking.

His body was all up for the sex, but talking—*real* talking—was out. He just wasn't ready to let anyone get close to his "shit to forget" box. And Clay had to admit that *ready* might never happen.

"You think it could mean something?" Arlo asked Clay.

Clay shrugged and looked at the lump of bedding in the center of the floor. A dirty floor, Clay observed, and it smelled exactly like Clay thought a fishing cabin would smell when it was owned by a man who seemingly never changed his overalls.

Like fish guts, piss and old motor oil.

"I was right to call you out here, huh?" Arlo went on. "Because if Billy Lee really did take a snooze here, it was without my knowing. Just don't want to get arrested for an old friend taking a snooze."

Yeah, Clay got that when Arlo called him and told him that Billy Lee might be at the cabin. Arlo had repeated it when Clay arrived. And even though this was Arlo's third time mentioning an arrest, Clay wasn't seeing anything to indicate Billy Lee had even been here.

"Though I gotta say, this isn't the usual kind of place Billy Lee would stay," Arlo went on. "Too small. Billy Lee's got that closet phobia thing. Has had it since he was a kid."

"Claustrophobia?" Clay asked. "Fear of tight spaces?" Because if it was a fear of closets, then that was a first for Clay.

"That's right. He got it 'cause all them bigger boys in junior high used to cram him in his locker and fart on him through the vent holes."

Great day. He was learning plenty he didn't want to know and nothing he needed for the investigation. "Speaking of bigger boys, do teenagers ever break in here?" Clay asked him.

"No need to break in. I leave the place unlocked. Sometimes, Ordell Busby's boys come out here to smoke and drink, but they don't leave the covers like that."

Nobody who'd actually used the covers for sleeping would have left them like that. It was like a heap of laundry. Which only made Clay suspicious. Of course, he was suspicious, too, that Arlo had called him out here.

"You're sure Billy Lee hasn't contacted you?" Clay asked. "And by contact, I mean a phone call, visit, email, smoke signals or any other form of communication."

Arlo scratched his head, looked away. "I'm sure."

If there'd been a picture of a liar in the dictionary, it would have been one of Arlo.

"All right," Clay said, "here's what I'm going to assume. You're aiding and abetting a federal fugitive." Arlo howled out a protest, but Clay just kept talking. "I think you brought me out here so I'd think you were cooperating, but since I suspect you're not, then this is the last place Billy Lee would be. So, where is he? And if you lie, I'll know, and I'll arrest you for obstruction of justice."

Arlo shoved his hands in his pocket, kicked a rock and cursed. "I don't know where Billy Lee is, but he called me and said not to believe everything I heard about him. Then, he asked if he could stay here. I hated to turn down an old friend so I told him you'd been out here a lot checking the place. That way, I knew he wouldn't come, and I could stay out of it."

Clay groaned. "You could have told him to come here and then called me."

"Didn't seem a good way to treat a friend even if he's in trouble with the law."

Clay considered charging Arlo with something—anything—but he thought of a better way to work this. "When did Billy Lee call you?"

"Late yesterday."

Apparently, that was the day for all hell breaking loose what with Tate running away, Garrett's wife getting caught with another man and April's meltdown. Still, with all that going on, if Arlo had called him, Clay would have had one of the deputies try to intercept Billy Lee.

"Here's what you're going to do," Clay advised him in the sternest cop voice he could manage. "If Billy Lee calls back, tell him I've already checked out the cabin and that he can come here. Then you get in touch with me immediately." Clay emphasized the *immediately* just to make sure Arlo and he were on the same page.

Arlo kicked more rocks. Cursed some more. Then nodded. "All right. If he calls back, I'll set him up to be arrested."

Clay gave him a stern look to go with his stern tone. "Don't you dare tip him off, or I'll set the feds after you."

Whether or not that would work, Clay didn't know, but he was tired and ready to go home after another long day. He got back in his truck and called his contact, FBI Agent Mike Freeman. Mike didn't answer so Clay left him a voice mail. Maybe, this would be enough for the FBI to get a wiretap on Arlo's phone, perhaps even constant surveillance of the gas station and cabin, and that in turn might lead to Billy Lee's arrest.

Sophie and Garrett might finally get some answers about their former CFO.

But Clay couldn't call or text them to let them know what was going on. If the word leaked, it could spook Billy Lee, and the FBI might never find him. Still, Clay figured he should call Sophie just to wish her happy birthday.

Or he could tell her in person.

That's because Clay spotted her when he pulled into his driveway. She was sitting on his front porch, all bundled up because it was cold. And she was feeding the feral chickens. From her hand. The chickens weren't trying to peck her eyes out or anything. In fact, it appeared one of the hens had brought her chicks to feed on whatever Sophie was offering.

It was already dusk, but thanks to the porch light, he had no trouble seeing her smile. It was a tentative one but still a welcome sight. Well, maybe. With the way this week had been going, she might be here to deliver some more bad news.

He stepped from his truck, slowly, and as always around the beasts, Clay didn't make any sudden moves. Sophie did, though. She got to her feet, and the chickens scattered, waddling their feathery butts toward the back. Clay didn't care where they were going because when it came to these chickens, he went with the "anywhere but here" approach.

"Are you okay?" Clay asked as he got closer. "They didn't try to attack you?"

She shook her head. "I guess I'm a chicken whisperer." She chuckled, dusted her hands, and he smelled something sugary sweet. "I brought you a piece of birthday cake, but I got hungry. The chickens and I shared it."

"It's okay. I still have some of my birthday cake in the freezer." Clay glanced around but didn't see her car. "How'd you get here?"

"On horseback. I put my mare in your barn. Hope that's okay."

"It is." Clay didn't get a chance to add anything else because Sophie continued talking.

"Reena came out to the ranch for a riding lesson with one of the hands, and she mentioned that you'd already left work for the day. I saddled up and rode over because I thought you'd be here."

Since she seemed to be waiting for an explanation

about why he hadn't been there, Clay settled for saying, "I had an errand to run first."

She nodded, obviously accepting that, which was good because he didn't want to get into the details of that errand, aka meeting with Arlo.

"Garrett is still gone on a pseudo campout," she added. "And Mom's recovering from a hangover so I skipped out of any birthday plans they might have had for me and came here. I wanted to find out how things went with April."

"She's not moving. Not happy, either, but she's staying put for now. She knows that's what's best for the boys and her. Brantley, too, since this is his home."

Sophie blew out a breath of relief. "Good. I felt bad that I'd made her life and yours so crazy."

Their lives had already been in a crazy state before that kissing session in the car. Sophie had just added a new depth to the craziness.

He put his hand on her shoulder to get her moving to the door and felt the damp chill on her jacket. He unlocked the door so he could get her inside. "How long have you been out here anyway?"

"Not long."

Like Arlo, Sophie wasn't very good at fudging the truth, but Clay figured she'd said that so he wouldn't feel bad about her sitting out in the cold.

"Hey, the place looks great," she said, sounding as surprised as Clay felt.

"Freddie isn't finished, but he's finally made some headway in the right direction."

Thankfully, this front part of the house looked normal anyway, and with the open floor plan, he could see right into the dining room on one side and the kitchen

on the other. No misplaced toilets. No holes in the floor
with hole signs.

The moment Clay shut the door, Sophie turned to face
him, probably to press him for what had gone on with
April. At least Clay thought that was what she wanted.

It wasn't.

She came up on her tiptoes, put her mouth on his and
kissed him.

Her lips were cold and tasted like frosting, which was
more appealing than Clay thought it would have been.
Of course, this was Sophie so she didn't especially need
the sugar to make this kiss feel like some kind of sexual
appetizer. Just being near her had a way of doing that.

Unlike the kisses in her car, this one didn't go on and
on. Much to his body's disappointment. She eased back,
and he saw something in her expression that he hadn't
seen in the dim light on the porch.

"Bad day?" he asked.

The corner of her mouth lifted, but it wasn't much of
a smile. "You asked me that when I was in your office
on what was supposed to be my wedding day."

"You look considerably better now than you did then,
but there's a glimmer of being shaken up on your face."

"If it's just a glimmer, then I'm doing a good job of
hiding it."

Uh-oh. That couldn't be good. "Is this about the letter from your father?"

She nodded and got that not-much-of-a-smile again.
Even the partial smile was short-lived because she
stepped away, turned her gaze from him. "He made me
CEO of Granger Western. Ironic, huh?"

Clay had expected to hear something, well, bad. This
didn't exactly fall into that category though it was ironic.

Her father had given Sophie exactly what she wanted, but Granger Western was a festering pile of crap right now.

He didn't mention that to her. No need to state the obvious. So, Clay went with the best encouragement he could muster. "You might get the company back, and then you'll have what you've always wanted."

"It's possible."

She didn't sound very convinced of that, and Clay nearly told her that they might have a lead on Billy Lee. But the problem was that finding the CFO might not do any good. It was likely that the damage had already been done.

"I'm sorry," Clay told her, and that covered some territory.

Since she was still shivering, he turned up the thermostat a notch and then started a fire. In the fireplace. There was one already flickering in his body from that kiss, but it was best if he kept a little distance between them until he could get his footing.

"Being the CEO is part of my life plan," she continued. "*Was* part of it, anyway," Sophie corrected. "My plan is pretty much shot. By now, I should have been pregnant."

He looked up from the fireplace and frowned. "That's not why you're here, is it?"

She laughed. "No, your sister is doing an ample job carrying on your genetic line. And as for mine, well, Roman's got that covered."

"You really have a life plan?" he asked.

Sophie took out her phone and showed it to him. There was indeed a list of goals. Marriage was still on there. The CEO part, too. Apparently, she wasn't giving up on that just yet.

"I keep a copy of it on my phone and laptop so I can

look at it. Sort of a way to keep me on track. At least it was until everything derailed," she explained. "So, what about you? Do you have a life plan?"

Yeah, he did. To make it through a day where nobody he knew and/or loved died. So far, so good if he didn't count what'd happen two years ago.

But Clay always counted that.

Killer.

"Other than making sure my sister's present and future offspring are taken care of, I don't have a life plan," he settled for saying.

She stayed quiet a moment, watched him stand after he had the fire going. "You gave up a lot to move here and be with her. Didn't you? And you did that without even knowing if the chief job would be permanent," Sophie tacked on after a few more seconds.

It was a simple comment, but Clay thought she might be fishing for a nonsimple answer. "What are you asking?"

Sophie shrugged, avoided eye contact with him. "Mila said there wasn't much about you on the internet. I mean, about your cases and such. She thought maybe that meant you did undercover work."

It didn't surprise him that Mila had Googled or Yahooed him. Probably everyone in town with computer access had—including Sophie. But Mila was right. There wouldn't have been much to find when it came to his time in Houston PD because most of it was sealed.

"I did some undercover work," he admitted. It was the truth and more than he usually told anyone.

Again, she was clearly waiting for some details. Details that he wasn't going to give her. Clay figured it was time to offer her something to drink. Or maybe say that he had something to do and could give her a ride home.

Or…

He didn't want to let that other option enter his head, but it was already too late. There was one surefire way to put an end to this conversation and not hurt Sophie's feelings. Of course, it would almost certainly end up hurting in other ways, but he would deal with that when the time came.

Clay hooked his arm around her, pulled her to him and kissed her.

CHAPTER ELEVEN

IN HINDSIGHT, THIS was exactly why Sophie had come to Clay.

Of course, she'd wanted to know about April, had wanted to tell him about her father's letter, too. But more than that, she'd just wanted Clay to kiss her and maybe chase away the storm cloud that was hovering over her head. She'd wanted to feel something more than the pity party that had taken hold of her mood.

And she felt something more, all right.

Sophie felt Clay's mouth on hers, followed by the slam of heat when he deepened the kiss and pulled her hard against him. Oh, yes, this was exactly what she wanted. No way would a shred of pity make it into her head now because the only signal that her brain was sending out was that she was going to get what she'd been wanting for weeks.

She was going to get Clay.

Maybe.

Sophie didn't have any doubts what they were doing was wrong. She knew it was. However, that didn't stop her, even though she felt Clay might have some hesitation when he pulled back and looked at her.

Then he cursed. It was pretty bad, but it seemed to be aimed at himself.

"April," she said. She especially didn't want to give him an out, but she had to do that since the stakes for him were sky-high. He could lose spending time with his sister and nephews.

Clay repeated some of that profanity, and this time he included his sister's name in the mix. Brantley's, too. And he stared at her as if debating what to do. What he didn't do was take his arm from around her waist. In fact, he seemed to be tightening his grip just a little and pulling her back to him at a snail's pace.

"This can't go anywhere," he said.

She nodded. He was right. But neither of them backed away. They just stood there, staring at each other. Sophie was waiting for him to grow some willpower, and he was no doubt waiting for her to do the same. And she tried. But willpower was no match for the hot cowboy cop right in front of her.

"What do you think our chances are of keeping something like this a secret?" she asked.

"No chance whatsoever."

She had to nod again. Part of her had wanted him to lie, but that wasn't in Clay's nature. However, it was in his nature to ease her just a little closer to him. So close that the next little adjustment would align their bodies in a special way. A way where she would get to feel a lot more inches of him.

At least if someone drove past his house, they wouldn't see her car so maybe this one time they could get away with it. Unless he got a visitor. Or unless someone guessed because of the satisfied look Sophie would almost certainly be wearing if they followed through on this and did something stupid. But maybe she could conceal that stupid look with makeup.

He leaned in, brushed a kiss on her lips. His muscles

were tight now like a man prepping for battle. Or something.

Sophie was hoping for the *something*.

Clay groaned, and he was so fast that she didn't see the next kiss coming. He made it deep. And perfect. Especially perfect because he finally took the plunge and smooshed their bodies together. The contact was so spectacular that Sophie thought she might get that something even with all their clothes on.

He trailed some kisses on her neck, then slightly lower, all the while moving her again. Not against him this time, though. He kept that delicious contact and backed her against the wall. He didn't stop there. He readjusted their positions, giving her a little nudge with his man parts that nearly caused her to go blind.

Good grief, how could he do that with just some pressure and kisses?

Quite easily, she soon realized, because he didn't just kiss her blind. Sophie thought she might have indeed landed in the middle of next week. It was okay with her if she stayed for a while.

Clay clearly had a different notion about that. He pulled back again. Cursed again, as well.

"I'm weak and stupid when it comes to you," he admitted.

That pretty much summed her up whenever she was around him so she nodded. With that confession out of the way, Sophie took hold of the front of his shirt to pull him back to her. But Clay held his ground. Apparently, he hadn't ventured into the middle of next week along with her.

"And because I'm weak and stupid," he went on, "I purposely didn't buy any condoms."

Because her head was light from all the fire in her body, it took several seconds for that to sink in. It didn't sink in well, and this time it was Sophie who cursed. Clay's forehead was bunched up when he slid his gaze down her body.

To her jeans pocket.

Sophie had to shake her head. "No, I didn't bring one with me. I don't even own a condom. And I'm not on the pill, either."

She didn't add that she was also in midcycle and probably ovulating. Probably as fertile as a rabbit, too. She definitely hadn't come here to get pregnant, and she was positive that was the last thing Clay wanted.

"We could make a run into town," she suggested. But Sophie immediately waved that off. "Someone would see us buying condoms and blab to everyone we know."

That included April, who might have a permanent meltdown this time.

Garrett probably had some in his room, but again, that trip would be risky. Her mother was home and would likely figure out what Sophie was up to after bombarding her with a thousand questions. Besides, by the time she got back to Clay's, this fire would have probably cooled a bit and they would have both come to their senses.

At the moment, though, her senses weren't anywhere to be found. Sensations though, yes, they were plentiful. Her body was still zinging. Begging, actually. But despite the begs, her body wasn't going to get Clay.

He stood there, staring at her, his gaze occasionally drifting to his kitchen. "I could fix you something to eat," he suggested. "And there's leftover birthday cake."

Tempting but not as tempting as the man still standing way too close to her. "It's probably not a good idea to rain check something like this," she mumbled.

He smiled, making that heat fire up even more. Of course, at this point just his breathing was doing that. So, Sophie tried a different angle.

"Tell me it can't work between us," she said.

"It can't work between us." He didn't hesitate, either, and it didn't seem like lip service.

Since the fire was still there, she tried again. "If we're together as lovers, it could mess up your life," Sophie added.

"It could mess up my life." Again, no hesitation.

There it was. She had her answer. It couldn't work and it would create a big festering mess. Since she already had one of those in her life what with the business and her brothers' problems, she didn't need another one.

Sophie fluttered her fingers to the door. "It's probably time for me to go."

Clay moved finally. But it wasn't to free her from his waist-grip. Nope. He snapped her back to him, and the kiss caught her sound of surprise. It wasn't an especially pleasing sound, more like a mix between a gasp and a grunt, but Clay went with it, and Sophie soon found herself in the middle of next week again.

Which wasn't a good thing.

She wanted to remind him about the no-condom, no-pill dilemma, but it was hard to talk while being French-kissed. And she could no longer breathe. Her breath was somewhere in the vicinity of her kneecaps.

"Let's fix this," Clay said.

At least that's what she thought he said, but Sophie had to admit he could have just as easily cited the preamble to the constitution. She was in the fire-hot, me-want mode, and that mode skyrocketed when Clay unzipped her jeans and slid his hand right into her panties.

Sophie gasped again and managed to break the kiss. "I don't think this is going to fix anything."

But she was so very, very wrong.

Clay kissed her again. Not her mouth but her neck. He located the most sensitive spot in that region of her body and went after it. His fingers, however, found the most sensitive spot of all.

He slipped his fingers through the slick heat and touched, and touched and touched. All the while, he kept up those maddening neck kisses while his left hand cupped her butt and held her in place.

It was a sweet assault on multiple erogenous zones. It was also a mind-blowing, leg-melting one. If Clay hadn't kept her pinned between him and the wall, she would have slid straight to the floor.

Instead, she slid straight into a fast, hard climax.

She'd had climaxes before, of course, but nothing like this. Maybe because she'd gone so long without one. Maybe because Clay knew exactly what he was doing. Either way, Sophie made some nonsensical sounds. Moans and whimpers. But most of all, she just let the pleasure blast her into the middle of next year.

The climax rippled through her, making it to her kneecaps and toes, and she held on to Clay while he stroked the last of the climatic ripples. He gave her every bit of orgasmic fun that he could have possibly given her, considering that his erection was still behind his zipper, and then he pressed his forehead against hers.

He was out of breath, too, and practically panting when he finally looked at her.

"Excuse me," he ground out, his voice as strained as his expression. "But I need to take a cold shower now."

ACTUALLY, CLAY NEEDED more than a shower. He needed a hammer so he could hit himself in the head. That might knock some sense into him.

Might soften up his dick, too, though he wasn't holding out much hope in that area.

His dick wanted Sophie, but since it wasn't going to get her, then it would likely just stay hard as punishment. The heart might want what the heart wants, but the dick was, well, a dick, when it didn't get off.

While he dried off from his shower and got dressed, Clay tried to figure out how to handle this. It would be easier if he immediately took Sophie home, but that felt a little like a variation of love 'em and leave 'em. It didn't matter that he hadn't actually "loved her" in that way. Didn't matter that taking her home would be the safer option. Because there was still the factor of her crappy day. She probably needed a little TLC. Too bad, though, that his dick was offering him a dirty version of how to dole out that tender loving care.

Clay mentally prepared himself in case he found Sophie in a puddle of tears. Thankfully there weren't any tears. She was seated at his kitchen island, eating some of his birthday cake. Not an itty-bitty slice, either. This was a sugar-coma-sized portion. And she was drinking a beer with it.

She looked up at him, their gazes connecting for a second before Clay looked away. But he saw enough of her to know there were no tears. She even smiled. And the third thing he noticed: she was fucking beautiful.

His dick wanted to take that last part literally.

"Say, do you know you've got a dirty egg in a plastic bag in your fridge?" she asked. It certainly wasn't the question he was expecting, but it was better than her mentioning what had happened against the wall.

"Vita sent me those. They're chicken repellant. And it's not dirt you're seeing. I'm pretty sure it's shit, and that's why the bag is sealed."

She made a face.

"Don't worry. It didn't touch the cake." He cut himself a slice, grabbed a beer and took the seat opposite her. There was a chair right next to her, but that didn't seem a smart choice especially coming on the heels of the other unsmart choice he'd made—to put his hand in her panties.

"The cake's really good," she went on. "According to the label on the box, it's from the bakery over in Spring Hill. The one that Logan McCord's wife owns. Have you met the McCord brothers yet?"

Clay actually welcomed the conversation. It was normal. Safe. Nonsexual. "I've met Lucky, the bull rider. He was in town on business once, and I ran into him at the café."

For just a second her smile turned a little dreamy or something. "Yes, he was here doing business with Garrett. We buy our livestock from the McCords." She shrugged. "Half the state buys livestock from them. Garrett would like to get to the point where the other half buys them from us."

Clay had known that Garrett was expanding, but he hadn't realized that Sophie's brother had plans to go that big. "Wouldn't you need more land for that?"

She nodded, had a sip of beer before she answered. "As I already mentioned, our cousins—Lawson and his brothers—own the land directly north of us, but they're not likely to sell to anyone, especially us. The town's to the west so we can't expand in that direction, and Vita's and your land are to the south."

"I'm not selling," Clay quickly told her.

"That's what I figured. So, that leaves the land near you. Hermie Winters owns it, and while he might sell to us, that leaves the problem with Z.T.'s old house. It would put it right smack-dab in the middle of what we'd need for pasture, and we can't tear it down or move it."

"Terms of the will?"

"Historic site. Of course, there are worse things than having a really ugly house surrounded by cows so in the end that's our best option."

He couldn't tell if she was pleased about that or not. Of course, now that she was CEO of Granger Western, Garrett could put all his efforts into making the ranch the way he wanted.

"Enough of cow and land talk. Happy birthday to us." She ate another bite of cake, smiled again, then looked away. He didn't want to tell her that the blue icing on the cake was now stuck to her teeth. Also didn't want to admit to himself that it looked kind of cute.

Hell.

First, he'd thought of her as fucking beautiful and now as cute. Yeah, he wasn't in any kind of trouble here.

"That's the first hand job I've ever gotten," Sophie continued. Her voice was practically a whisper, and she didn't look at him. Instead, she had her attention nailed to dragging her fork through the icing. "There's a lot to be said for it."

Yeah, two words came to mind—hard dick.

"You didn't have to do it, you know," she added.

"Wasn't exactly planned." Though he had needed to do something in that moment or he would have exploded.

It relieved a little of the pressure cooker heat to have at least one of them come.

"All the fun for me without the risk of getting pregnant." She paused. "But it couldn't have been much fun for you. I probably should have joined you in the shower."

His dick heard that, got all excited. But Clay shook his head. "Eating cake was the wiser choice." He should just let it drop. He didn't, though, because there was still an air of stupidity around him. "No hand jobs in high school?"

He instantly regretted the question. Because she'd dated Brantley back in those days. Clay really didn't want to hear any sex details about Sophie and his brother-in-law.

She shook her head. "Mila and I had this pact-thing of waiting until we got married. That didn't last for me, obviously. When I was eighteen, Brantley and I broke up, and I lost my virginity to…someone else. Mila, however, has stuck to that pact."

Apparently, she'd reached enough of a sugar high because Sophie pushed the plate with the rest of her cake aside. "How about you? Any hand jobs in your past?"

Even though she didn't say it, Clay thought she might be asking if he wanted a hand job in the near future. Like right now. While his dick liked that idea, Clay knew he had to play the common sense card here.

"One or two." A lie. It was probably closer to six hundred since his high school girlfriend had favored that along with a few blow jobs. No way would he elaborate on his answer, though, so he changed the subject. "Speaking of Mila, how is she?"

"Upset because of what Tate did. Also upset because she thinks Roman's mad at her because maybe she said something to Tate to make him think that she would actually drive him to his mother. Also upset because we walked in on…whatever the heck it was we walked in on. I asked her if she wanted some company tonight, but she said she wanted to watch some movies alone and then crash."

That brought out the cop in him. "You don't think she's meeting another stranger for some fantasy role-play, do you? And you need to tell her to stop leaving a key in her verbena."

"I did fuss at her about the key. And no, she's not seeing anyone tonight. Actually, that whole fantasy thing might be on permanent hold. Though Mila would rather eat glass than admit it, she tends to turn hermit and mope after she's seen Roman. She's always had a thing for him."

Well, that was something the gossips hadn't mentioned yet. Probably because it seemed so far-fetched. Sophie's brother and her best friend were about as mismatched as could be, though Roman probably had had some experience in taking a woman's virginity. But there was a problem when that lover was thirty like Mila. Sex like that almost always came with a commitment, and Roman didn't look like the commitment type.

"This is nice," Sophie said, looking at him.

He knew that look. It was rife with sexual overtones. Clay wasn't sure what to say or do about it, and he didn't have to decide. That's because his landline phone rang, the sound shooting through the house. And it wasn't a pleasant sound, either, since it was a loud, old-fashioned ringtone. Thankfully, it was just two rings. That's the way he had it set before the answering machine kicked in, and he heard his own recorded greeting. A warm and fuzzy welcome, it wasn't.

"Chief McKinnon here. Leave a message after the beep only if you haven't been able to reach me at the station. And only if it's really important that you speak to me."

Clay frowned and wasted a couple of seconds, hoping it wasn't a neighbor calling about some trivial problem, which it usually was, but it didn't take much time beyond those seconds for his gut to tighten. A conditioned response because sometimes it wasn't his neighbors who called on that line.

He practically jumped out of his seat to hurry around the island so he could get to it. But he was too late. He heard the caller. And the message left for him.

"Killer."

There was no mistaking the bitterness in that voice. The pain.

"My God," Sophie said. "Do you get prank calls like that often?"

"It's not a prank call," he said before he could stop himself.

Clay wished he had stopped speaking, wished he could undo the last minute of his life. Hell, undo this whole evening.

Sophie shook her head, and he could tell that she was about to start a string of questions that he didn't want to answer. Besides, the flashbacks were there, and if he had to look into Sophie's eyes right now, he'd see her.

He'd see Delaney.

And everything that he'd done to her.

"Is it something you want to talk about?" Sophie finally asked.

The answer was easy. "No." And the next part was easy, too. He had to get her out of there so he could try to corral this tangled nightmare. "Come on. I need to drive you home and have one of Freddie's boys bring your horse to you later. All of this was a big mistake."

CHAPTER TWELVE

CLAY DUG HIS pen into the report so hard that he tore the paper and broke the pen. He threw the pen in the trash. Missed. And then he kicked the wire mesh can. It flew across the floor, smacking into the wall with a thud. It didn't feel good exactly, but that was asking a lot of a can kick.

Shit.

He'd made a mess of things. First, by what he did to Sophie and then his reaction to the phone call. He had been trained to handle stressful situations, but all that training flew out the window with just a handful of words.

It's not a prank call.

Followed by the even wiser gem of: *All of this was a big mistake.*

Not exactly something a woman wanted to hear after semisex. Definitely not a "call me soon." And Sophie hadn't called.

It'd been a week since that'd happened, and he had heard nothing from her.

Of course, in addition to his words, he had given her the silent treatment when he'd driven her home. That had been necessary, though. Clay had barely been hanging on by a thread, and he hadn't wanted to say or do anything else that would have triggered a full-fledged flashback. No way in hell did he want Sophie to see that.

No way in hell, though, did he want to continue on like this.

He took out the note from his wallet. It was the number of the caller. Clay knew the person. Knew him well, actually. The worst of enemies sometimes started off the best of friends, and that's what had happened in this case. Clay took a deep breath, ready to make the call and ask for a meeting. It wouldn't solve everything, but it would be a start, and maybe a start would be good enough to get the calls or pink envelopes to stop.

Maybe.

He'd pressed in the first two numbers, but before he could finish, there was a knock at the door. "Chief, you got some visitors," Reena called out.

She didn't wait for him to respond; the door opened, and Clay was more than surprised by who he saw standing there. April, Mila, Arlo and Vita.

"Is this some kind of intervention?" he grumbled.

Reena chuckled, but Clay was serious. He couldn't imagine why these four had shown up at the same time.

"I didn't know she was here," April said, sparing Mila a glance.

Apparently, his sister didn't like Mila because she was Sophie's friend. April's cool glance, however, didn't land on Vita. Perhaps like most of the town, April didn't want to risk pissing the woman off. Not because she feared any real retribution but because Vita could be a pest.

"And I didn't know *she* would be here," Mila countered, but she was looking at her mother. "You'd better not have brought any curses or potions with you," Mila added to her in a whisper. Apparently, Mila wasn't as concerned as others about a potential pissing off.

"I had to see the chief," her mother simply said.

"Well so do I." Arlo that time. "And it's important. I need to speak to him in private."

Clay debated how to handle this. Arlo was likely there on business, and while he didn't like putting anything ahead of an investigation, it was best not to leave his sister with Sophie's best friend and a gypsy. He motioned for April to come in.

"We won't be long," he assured the others.

April shut the door in their faces, went to him and kissed him on the cheek. "I just came from my OB appointment and wanted to stop by. Three months along now." She proudly patted her stomach.

"And?" he prompted when she didn't add anything.

"And Brantley and I want you to come to dinner tomorrow night."

Clay didn't have to be a cop to be instantly suspicious. "Are you planning some kind of intervention?"

She huffed. "Why do you keep asking that? Do you need an intervention?"

Yeah. But he didn't want one. Besides, there probably wasn't a cure to get Sophie off his mind.

However, April might think there was.

"Is this some kind of blind date arrangement?" he pressed.

Bingo. He could tell from his sister's huff that he was spot-on. "You didn't use that dating service we got you for your birthday so I want you to meet Brantley's paralegal."

"No."

But April just kept on. "She's beautiful, smart, and it's been ages since you've had a real date. Plus, it would stop those rumors about Sophie and you seeing each other."

"No." And because this could go on and on, he stood,

took her by the arm and led her to the door. "I won't be there and don't set me up again."

April was still arguing with him when he opened the door. "Bye," he told her and kissed her cheek before he motioned for Arlo to come in. "Reena, can you make sure my sister gets out okay?"

It was a nicer way of saying don't let the door hit your ass on the way out. His sister shot him a glare, but she did leave. One down, three to go.

He brought in Arlo next, and once they were alone, the man didn't waste any time taking a note and a cell phone from his pocket. "I found those on my truck seat this morning." He unfolded the note, dropped it and the phone on Clay's desk.

Clay read aloud from the note:

"You have to help me for old time's sake. Call me tonight on this phone."

There was no signature, but Clay figured this had to be from Billy Lee. Well, unless Arlo was having an affair—no, Billy Lee was pretty much the only option here.

"He didn't say what time," Arlo went on, "but I was thinking about doing it around six. Anything special I should say?"

"You won't be making that call alone. You'll wait here for FBI Agent Mike Freeman to arrive, and then he'll tell you exactly what to do." Clay pressed his intercom and asked Reena to come in. The deputy practically came running. "I need you to put Arlo in an interview room."

"Uh, did Arlo break the law or something?" Reena asked.

"No. But someone's maybe stolen some stuff from the gas station. A ring of thieves that the FBI's investigating. An agent will be here soon to talk to him about it." Yes, it was a lie, but it was one of those necessary ones, since Reena and everybody else who worked for him had trouble keeping secrets.

Reena nodded, led a grumbling Arlo away, and Clay made a quick call to Agent Freeman to ask him to get down there ASAP. Once the agent arrived, he'd turn both the phone and the note over to him. For now, Clay put the items in an evidence bag. Arlo had probably already compromised any prints, fibers or trace, and the phone was almost certainly a prepaid burner cell, but the FBI crime lab might find something they could use.

"Next," Clay called out when he was finished bagging. He put the bag in his drawer so that it wouldn't get the attention of his other two visitors.

He was a little surprised when Mila came in and not her mother. "We played rock, paper, scissors, and Mom lost," Mila explained.

Apparently, Vita's fortune-telling skills didn't extend to hand games.

"I don't have much time because I have to get back to the store," Mila said right off, "but I'm worried about Sophie. What did you do to her?"

Clay wasn't sure about the best way to handle this so he went with an old cop's tactic of answering a question with a question. "What did Sophie tell you I did to her?"

"Nothing. That's just it. She usually tells me what's going on in her head, and this time she didn't."

As long as Sophie didn't discuss what had gone on with that phone message, that was all right. And it was best if she hadn't mentioned Clay having his hands in her pants, either.

"I'm worried," Mila repeated. "She's moping around the way she did after the Brantley fiasco, and she won't talk about it."

Hell. Clay hadn't thought he could feel any shittier, but apparently he could. He'd known right from the get-go that it wasn't a good idea to start up anything with Sophie, and this was proof of it.

Mila huffed. "I guess you're not going to talk about it, either," Mila went on. "But Reena says you've been moping, too, and in a really pissy mood."

Clay would have loved to deny that, but it was true. However, he would have a chat with Reena about discussing her boss's state of mind with anyone else.

"I only want what's the best for Sophie," Clay said, just to be saying something. But that was true, too.

Another huff from Mila, who stared and then huffed some more. "All right. So, that's how it is. At least call her and wish her a happy life or something. Maybe then she'll give the dating sites a real shot."

Yes, maybe she would. And that twisted at him in a different sort of way. He wanted Sophie happy. She deserved it after everything she'd been through. Too bad that happiness would have to be with another man who would almost certainly put his hands in her pants.

"I'll call her," Clay finally said. That was possibly a lie, but there was nothing he could tell Mila that was going to make her worry less. And besides, he wanted her out of his office so he could finish with Vita and then have some time to think.

Or maybe he'd just have some whiskey.

Over the past two years, he'd discovered that thinking was highly overrated.

"Let me know how the call goes." Mila headed for the door, but she paused long enough to give him a warning. "Hurt her the way Brantley did, and I'll have a hundred feral chickens delivered to your doorstep."

As threats went, it was effective, and considering the source, it might not be just a mere threat.

Speaking of Vita, she came in next but not before giving her daughter a long, lingering look. "It's a stupid game. I could just smash a piece of paper with a rock. Ain't that right, Chief?"

Clay wisely stayed out of that. "I don't want another egg," Clay told the woman right off. "And no Mighty Lube, either."

"Both worked," she said as if it were gospel. "But no, today I'm here about Sophie."

"Your daughter just lectured me about her." Heck, his sister had, too, but in a different kind of way, by trying to set him up on a date.

"Well, this isn't a lecture. More like a warning."

If Vita put a curse on him, Clay was in an ornery enough mood to arrest her. But no curse. Not a verbal one, anyway. Instead Vita took something from her pocket, put it on his desk.

Clay tried not to choke on his own breath, but he would have given up a kidney for one of those the previous week.

Because Vita's offerings were three foil-wrapped condoms.

SOPHIE THREW OPEN the front door, expecting either Mila or Lawson to be on the other side. But it was Vita. And condoms. Three of them. That's what was in Vita's hand.

A hand she extended to Sophie.

"Uh, is this a curse or something?" Sophie asked.

"Who's at the door?" her mother called out, and she was no longer in the kitchen. Judging from the sound of her footsteps, she was approaching the foyer.

"It's me," Vita answered. "I'm just here to give Sophie something she needs for the chief."

"What is it?" Her mother was moving in even closer.

"Uh thanks, Vita," Sophie whispered, "but it's too late. I don't need them anymore."

"Suit yourself," Vita said on a shrug, and walked away.

Sophie clearly hadn't whispered softly enough and she hadn't closed the door fast enough because her mother had no doubt seen and heard everything. The bleached-out color on her face confirmed that.

"Is there something you want to tell me, Sophie?" her mother asked.

Easy answer. "No." She fluttered her fingers toward the living room. "I was just going to tidy up before lunch."

The house was spotless, thanks to Alice, but it was the only thing Sophie could come up with off the cuff. Too bad it sucked. Her mother was suspicious, and that was never a good thing.

Her mother stared at her awhile longer and then thankfully turned and went back to the kitchen. Maybe there was a sudden scent of burning bread in the air. Thank God for mistimed baked goods.

"Turkey, peas and Sheez Louise," Sophie heard Garrett mumble when he walked past her in the foyer.

Her brother didn't need to explain himself because Sophie knew what it meant. It was a phrase her father used to say for family gatherings. Louise was his late mother, and prime gossip fodder for Belle.

Of course, Belle didn't limit her gossip to her now-late mother-in-law. Nope. And on this Thanksgiving Day, she was already in prime form. In Sophie's short ventures into the kitchen, she'd heard Belle diss Meredith, Roman, April, Reena, two of the ranch hands, the cashier at the grocery store.

And Clay.

Her mother didn't know what had gone on between Clay and Sophie. No one did. Heck, even Sophie wasn't sure what'd happened, but there was no way she could forget the word she'd heard on that phone message.

Killer.

That had been bad enough, but Clay's reaction was what had crushed her. It was a reminder that she shouldn't have allowed herself to be placed in a position of being crushed. And here she'd allowed it only seven months after the last crushing.

That made her an idiot.

Her mother hadn't dissed Clay because she'd connected him to Sophie's bad mood. Nope. It was because she'd seen him in town and thought he needed a haircut. Considering Belle had used the same tone as she'd done with Meredith's sex-capade, it was obvious her mother didn't mind heaping the trivial junk with the life-changing.

Sophie finished setting the table for dinner. In addition to herself, there was one for her mother's friend and gossip buddy, Mary Lynn, Belle, Garrett, Mila, Roman, Tate, Lawson and his current girlfriend, Ava. Sophie would bet her favorite mare, Moonlight, that Roman and Tate wouldn't be there, but it didn't seem right not to include them even if that inclusion was only in the form of dinnerware.

She made her way back to the kitchen to see if there was anything else she could do to help, and she immediately spotted the source of the burned smell. It was actually the cinnamon rolls, her favorite, but now they looked like miniature cow patties.

Sophie also got another serving of turkey, peas and Sheez Louise.

"Vita had no right to come here today," Belle said. "Especially no right to come here with voodoo stuff. It was voodoo, wasn't it, Sophie?"

Even though that particular smell wasn't in the kitchen, this was a fishing expedition, and Sophie wasn't biting. She went with a lie instead. "Foil-wrapped chocolate. It was sweet of her to bring it by, but we already had enough dessert on the menu."

Minus cinnamon rolls, of course.

Her mother clearly wasn't buying that chocolate lie, which meant she'd bring it up again. And again. And again. For now, though, Belle moved on to a different *again.*

"Roman should have at least allowed Tate to come." Belle was taste testing, but she could still talk with a mouthful of stuffing. That whine was directed at Sophie since Mary Lynn had the mixer going to finish up the mashed potatoes.

"Tate didn't want to come," Sophie let her know.

That caused her mother to snap her head toward her. Alice, who had apparently tuned out the world while she basted the turkey, didn't even glance at her. No way could Mary Lynn hear over the mixer.

"How do you know that?" her mother asked. "I tried calling over there this morning, but no one answered."

Sophie could have been mean and said she'd spoken

to both her brother and nephew that morning, that they hadn't ignored her call, but that would only spark another round of Roman bashing so Sophie just shrugged.

"They're going to one of those all-you-can-eat buffet places. Tate sounded excited about it."

A total lie. Her nephew was about as overjoyed as a steer's rump on a red-hot branding iron. Bringing that up, though, would only be gossip fodder, and Roman would get the blame for his son's unhappiness.

"Alice, you need any help?" Sophie asked before her mother could continue.

Alice came out of her hear-nothing trance to answer. "Nope. I'm fine. You can tell Garrett we'll be ready to eat when Mila, Lawson and Ava get here."

"Where are they, anyway?" Belle complained. "They should have been here by now."

Not really. It was twelve thirty, and Belle's invitation had been for one. Since Lawson and Mila were both smart people, they would have wanted to minimize their turkey, peas and Louise time by not showing up too early.

She made her way through the house and found Garrett exactly where she expected him to be. His office.

"No booze?" she asked right off. Because she'd also expected to find a shot glass in his hand. Instead, he was drinking water and reading the latest financial report she'd sent him that morning.

"I considered it, but I thought I might try a Thanksgiving meal with a clear head."

That could be a mistake, but maybe he was worried that he'd been drinking too much. Working too much, as well. He was doing both, but Garrett wasn't someone who needed to be policed about his life. He was already too hard on himself.

"The ranch is doing well," she said, tipping her head to the report. "I'll interview those new hands you want to hire next week. And I talked to Logan McCord about the new cattle shipment."

He mumbled a thanks, made a sound of agreement. "You sent Roman a copy of this?"

She nodded. Even though Roman wouldn't read it, Sophie sent him anything that had to do with the ranch. "Roman's not impressed that you're making him a ton of money."

Garrett made another sound of agreement. "*We're* making him a ton of money," he corrected. "You're handling all this stuff so I can focus on the hands-on part."

Yes, it had worked out nicely that way, but Sophie was always waiting for the other boot to fall. The FBI hadn't found Billy Lee or anything that indicated Garrett and she were involved in Billy Lee's scheme, but it felt as if there was something bad in the air.

Maybe that was just the scent of the Brussels sprouts and burned cinnamon rolls, though.

"Roman made an appointment with another lawyer to see if Dad's will can be broken so he can give us the ranch," Garrett added.

"Yes, he mentioned that when we talked. Roman also asked how you were handling not being the CEO of Granger Western." She paused. "How are you handling it?"

"Better than you are. I'm okay with it. That job should have been yours years ago."

She'd figured that's how Garrett felt, but it was good to hear it aloud.

"And how are you handling everything else?" she asked.

He chugged some of the water as if it were a beer. And frowned. "People are smiling at me and saying nice things."

"The bastards," she joked. But she knew how he felt because she had been through months of it herself. "Folks will get over it soon enough."

Possibly. She was still getting poor-pitiful-Sophie looks from some people in town. Heck, from some people in her own house. Her mother and Alice were guilty of that.

"How about you?" Garrett asked. "How are you doing?"

She doubted he'd missed her mopey moods. Or the gossip that had no doubt gone along with them.

"You're asking me about Clay," she said, filling in the blanks.

He nodded. "It's my brotherly duty to remind you that anything you might be doing with the chief could be a rebound reaction and could therefore get you hurt."

"Rebound reaction, huh?" It was too late to avoid the hurt because that'd already happened.

"Well, I was going to say rebound fuck, but I know you don't like it when I say the f-word."

"Only because when Mom would hear it, she'd start lecturing you about potty mouth, and she'd include me in the lecture. But no, there's no f-word involvement for Clay and me. No rebound, either, because I no longer feel much of anything for Brantley."

He stayed quiet a moment as if deciding whether that was true or not.

"I just want to get on with my life," she added.

"So I gathered. I just got a little concerned when I heard Mila went to chat with Clay. I figured you had to be upset or something for her to do that."

"Mila went to see Clay?" This was the first Sophie was hearing about it.

"Yeah, about a week ago. I heard it from one of the ranch hands who heard it from Reena. She said Clay got a lot of visitors that day. April, Vita, Arlo and an FBI agent."

Heck, where were the gossips when you needed them? She'd get Mila's scoop soon enough, but for now she wanted to hear more about that last visitor. "An FBI agent? Was he there because of Billy Lee?"

"According to Reena, no, the agent was there to investigate some missing items at Arlo's place. But remember I was getting it secondhand so who knows. I figure if it has to do with Billy Lee, then Clay will let one of us know."

Maybe. But Clay wasn't exactly being chatty these days.

"Are you and Clay...on good terms?" Garrett asked a moment later.

Sophie felt her stomach do a little flip-flop. "What have you heard?"

"Nothing that should make that kind of fire in your eyes. I was asking from a business perspective."

Sophie was about to assure him that Clay and business had no perspective, but it came to her. "His land."

Garrett nodded. "I know he doesn't want to sell, but once we buy Hermie Winters's land, Clay's acreage is just on the other side. Then, we could maybe pay Clay to use his back pasture. He's not using it now, and it might take years for him to expand his business. In fact, that won't happen unless he gives up on being the permanent chief and raises horses full-time."

Sophie understood almost all of that. All but the last part. "You think Clay will quit being a cop?"

Garrett shrugged. "The city council still hasn't offered him a permanent position. You know how stand-offish they are about newcomers. And as for whether or not he'll quit, there are times when he doesn't seem to enjoy being a cop."

No, he didn't. And Sophie wondered if it had something to do with that phone call he'd gotten.

She heard the doorbell ring, followed by Mila calling out to her. Sophie hurried to the foyer so she could find out why her friend had visited her semi-ex-lover without telling her. However, the moment Mila stepped inside, Sophie saw something tucked under her friend's arm that had her holding off on the question.

A pink envelope.

"Please don't tell me that's from my father," Sophie said.

Mila shook her head. "I don't think so, but it does have your name on it. It was tucked in the newspaper slot of your mailbox so I stopped and got it. You think it might be from Clay?" she asked, lowering her voice and smiling.

Sophie shook her head, too. "If Clay were to send me a letter, he wouldn't use a pink envelope. He knows I don't have especially good memories associated with that color."

"Then maybe you have a secret admirer." Mila stepped away when she saw Belle, and gave the woman a hug.

"I'll call Lawson and Ava to come on over so we can start dinner early," her mother announced.

Sophie heard her, but her attention was on the envelope. It did indeed have her name on it, but it didn't just say Sophie. Someone had typed Miss Sophie Granger on the front. Much too formal for Clay. Heck, it was too formal for anyone who knew her.

It wasn't sealed so she opened the flap and peeked inside. It was a white piece of paper with something typed on it. She slid it out, sliding out the other papers that were attached to it with a clip.

The message read:

If you want to know all about Clay McKinnon, take a look at these.

Everything inside her went still, and the last thing Sophie wanted to do was see what was behind that note. But she couldn't stop herself, either. She lifted the page and saw it.

Oh, God.

CHAPTER THIRTEEN

Sophie parked up the road a good quarter of a mile from Clay's, pulling her car into an old ranch trail so that it couldn't be easily seen, and she started walking. Her heart was pounding. Her mind racing with what she'd seen in that pink envelope.

It sickened her to think that the photos could be real, and she reminded herself that this could be some kind of prank. Something meant to upset her because of her connection to Clay.

If so, it'd worked. She was upset. And she needed answers.

Sophie hadn't told anyone in her family about what was in the envelope. Not even Mila. She'd let her friend believe it was indeed from Clay though obviously Mila and Garrett realized something was wrong. Still, Sophie had put them off, saying she wasn't feeling well and had then picked and nibbled at the meal.

Her lack of appetite and mood had backfired some, though. Because when she was helping to clear the table, she had heard Mary Lynn ask Belle if Sophie could be pregnant.

Great.

Now that rumor would be floating around town.

Sophie hadn't called Clay because, thanks to Reena's gossip, she knew he was supposed to be at his place with his sister, nephews and Brantley for their Thanksgiving feast. And he was, because the moment Clay's house came into view, she saw Brantley's car.

She ducked behind a tree to see if she could spot Clay through the window. That way she could get his attention, and he could come out for a quick chat.

Hopefully, one with quick answers that would explain all of this away.

Despite the sunny day, the temps were still in the forties, and while Sophie had worn a coat, it didn't take long before she began shivering a little. It also didn't take the chickens long to notice she was there. They came out from the bushes and, pecking the ground, they started in her direction.

There was some movement in the large bay window at the front of his house, but it was only the twins. They appeared to be giggling and were pointing at the chickens.

Oh, no.

She didn't want the twins' attention anywhere near the critters because the chickens were only a few yards away. And they were quickly pecking up the distance between them and her.

Sophie ducked even farther behind the tree and considered texting Clay so he could distract the boys and then come outside to see her. But before she could even get to her phone, April appeared in the window. And Brantley.

Then Clay.

Clay was the only one of the group scowling, no doubt because of the previous chicken attacks. But the boys, April and Brantley seemed absolutely enchanted by the poultry.

Poultry that were now only a few inches away from Sophie.

She couldn't take the chance of peering out from the tree any longer because the humans might see her, so she stood there as still as she could manage. The chickens came, and they must have found some prime pecking material around her shoes because they hovered around her. And hovered. She tried to shoo them away by moving her feet a little, but unruffled, they just adjusted their pecking grounds a little but stayed right by her.

Time stopped—Sophie was sure of it.

The temp must have dropped by thirty degrees, too.

And she had to pee.

Too bad she'd forgotten to go to the bathroom before she'd left the ranch, but she had been in a hurry to sneak out of there after Mila, Ava and Lawson had left. Sophie had feigned a headache and told her mom she needed to go for a drive to see if that would help. It was a lame excuse, but her mother had only quietly agreed.

Quietly and suspiciously.

No doubt because she was now convinced her daughter was pregnant.

Sophie was about to risk a look around the tree to see if Clay and the others were still there, but her phone buzzed before she could do that. Maybe Clay had spotted her after all and had sent a text message to tell her how to get out of this mess. Literally.

Because the chickens were also pooping around her.

She eased the phone from her pocket and silently cursed when it wasn't Clay's name on the screen but rather her mother's.

You know you can tell me anything, her mother had texted.

No, she couldn't. Sophie wouldn't tell a soul about this visit, but her mother was almost certainly referring to her future grandchild that she was now convinced Sophie was carrying.

Sophie texted back a noncommittal thanks, slipped her phone into her pocket and nearly had a heart attack when she heard the voice. Not a faraway voice, either, but one that was very, very close.

"What are you doing out here?" Clay whispered.

She made a few garbled sounds and tried to recover from the surprise of seeing him. She also had to make sure he was alone. Other than the chickens, he was, and Clay was volleying some uneasy glances between them and her.

"I had to come," she said. "I had to see you."

"And it couldn't wait?" He didn't give her a chance to respond and was likely about to tell her to be on her way.

Sophie stopped him. "Someone sent me a pink envelope. And it wasn't from my father."

Clay hesitated, looked away. "You opened it?"

"Yes." Sophie left it at that until his gaze came back to her. "What does it mean? Who sent it? And who was that woman in that horrible picture?"

Now he cursed. "Did the sender threaten you in any way? Did you see him?"

She shook her head. "No. Someone left the envelope on the mailbox, and it wasn't a threat. The letter inside said—'if you want to know all about Clay McKinnon, take a look at these.' It wasn't signed or anything. What does it mean?" she repeated.

This time, he cursed. "I can't talk about it right now, but I'll come to the ranch later."

"No, my mother and her best friend are there. I don't want to start any gossip that'll get back to your sister.

Plus, my mother probably thinks I'm pregnant with your child so if she saw you, she'd bring that up."

Sophie hadn't intended to throw in that last part, but since she was dropping bombshells, she might as well empty her arsenal. That's the reason she added, "And that hand job had nothing to do with a rebound."

Clearly, that was a lot to deal with at once, especially when time was a factor. "I'll text you after April and the others leave. You can come over then, and we can talk." Clay didn't sound as if he were looking forward to that. "I'll go back inside and see if I can hurry dinner along," Clay said. "I'm sorry." And he started cursing again.

At first, Sophie thought the cursing might be aimed at her, but she heard the footsteps. And the voice. Not April, thank God, but that didn't mean she wasn't far behind.

"What's going on out here?" Brantley asked.

No way was Sophie going to tell him the truth, and she didn't want to launch into another fake kiss, either. It was going to be hard enough to convince folks that she wasn't pregnant, and if Brantley saw a kiss, even a fake one, he might buy into what would no doubt soon become a public rumor of Clay knocking her up.

Sophie did the first thing she could think of. She grabbed one of the chickens and thrust it toward Clay. The other chickens scattered, and the one she held squawked and wiggled, but Sophie held on to make her point.

"I was driving by, and this one was on the road," Sophie lied. "I didn't want her to get run over so I decided to bring her home. Here, take her," she added to Clay.

He probably would have preferred taking hold of a rattlesnake, but keeping with the lie, he took the chicken. The squawking got louder, but instead of just wiggling, the hen dug her spurs into Clay's hands. It went after his face with its beak and drew blood.

Sophie quickly snatched it away and put it back on the ground. She stayed stooped down, though, because she heard something she didn't want to hear.

"Is everything okay out there?" April called out.

"Fine," Brantley and Clay lied in unison. Collectively, there was a whole lot of lying going on tonight. Hiding, too, because both Clay and Brantley moved in front of Sophie so that April wouldn't be able to see her.

"Get the first aid kit," Brantley told April. "Your brother needs it."

Finally, someone had spoken the truth. He did need it, and this latest attack wasn't going to help the other thing she intended to find out tonight.

One way or another, Clay was going to give her the answers she needed.

CLAY WAVED GOODBYE to his sister and Brantley, and with the boys sacked out in their car seats, he watched them drive away. The moment they were out of sight, he took out his phone to text Sophie. Since she answered right back that she was on her way, Clay knew he didn't have much time.

He sat on the steps, took out the note with the number and called it. Like his text to Sophie, he got an immediate response. The person accepted the call on the first ring, but he didn't say anything.

"Brody," Clay greeted, and it wasn't a question. He knew Brody Kincaid was there, listening and waiting for something he would never accept from Clay.

An apology.

Clay had tried to give that to him in the past, but that wasn't why he was calling tonight.

"It's all right to send that stuff to me," Clay warned him, "but you keep Sophie Granger out of this."

"I had to do something to get your attention," Brody said. His voice was low, practically a growl, and dripping with emotion. And pain. Especially pain.

"Brody, you've always had my attention. There's no need to drag anyone else into our mess."

"Sophie needs to know. You shouldn't bed a woman until she knows what you did."

Clay couldn't argue with that, and it was one of the reasons he'd resisted Sophie. She really didn't know him. Well, she didn't know what was in his shit-to-forget box anyway, and that was a damn big part of who he was.

What he was.

"I'll tell Sophie the things she needs to know," Clay assured him. "And you're stopping the calls and the letters, not just to Sophie but to me and anyone else you think you might want to reach out to. No negotiation, no second warnings. This. Stops. Now."

"And if I don't?"

"Then, I'll arrest you." Man, it hurt to say that. Brody and he had once been friends. No, it was more than that. Once, they'd been like brothers.

"You'll arrest me after everything you did to me…to my sister?" The bitterness in his tone went up a notch.

Clay adjusted his tone, too, to make sure Brody got this word for word. "Yeah, I will. Delaney was your sister, and I know you loved her, but that doesn't give you the right to do what you're doing now." And he hit the end call button.

If Brody called back on his cell, he'd block the number. But Clay took it one step further. He went inside the living room, grabbed hold of the landline cord and ripped it out of the wall.

One problem solved.

Yeah, he deserved punishment all right, but he was giving himself a reprieve just for tonight. Because if Sophie heard another *Killer* message, it would be punishment for her, too.

While he was at it, he carried both the phone and answering machine to the trash. If his neighbors wanted to get in touch with him, they could call dispatch. Clay was slamming down the lid on the trash can when Sophie walked in.

"Bad day?" she asked.

He wanted to kiss her for the awful joke. And for so many other reasons.

She stepped inside, shutting the door behind her, and he had to give it to her. She didn't avoid making eye contact with him, didn't stay back as if afraid of him. Sophie went to him and did something that Clay had wanted to do to her.

She kissed him.

Until her mouth came to his, Clay hadn't realized just how much he needed it. How much he needed her. It didn't matter that he shouldn't need her. Nothing else mattered right now. She just kissed him until some of the bone-deep cold seeped away.

She pulled back, scrounged up a smile, though, he wasn't sure how she managed it because she'd no doubt had an even worse day than he had.

"First things first." She touched her fingers to the chicken wound on his forehead. "Are you okay?"

"It's just a scratch." A semitraumatizing one because

he'd just started to trust the feathered bastards. "How about you? Are you okay?"

She lifted her shoulder. "You'll probably be getting a visit from my mother. If I can't figure out a way to head her off at the pass, then she'll probably come over here with a shotgun-proposal demand. She has this huge problem with her offspring having babies out of wedlock. Even babies that don't exist."

Yeah, Sophie had indeed had a hellish day. "Why does your mom think you're pregnant?"

"Moodiness. I picked at my food at lunch. I won't use those stupid dating sites. Plus, Vita came by with these condoms, and my mother heard me tell her that I didn't need them, that it was too late. Added to that, she's heard the rumor about us seeing each other."

It was the perfect storm of real information mixed with rumors. He would definitely be getting a visit from Belle Granger.

"And as for my rebound hand job remark," she went on, "Garrett's responsible for that."

"You talked to your brother about that?" Hell. He'd be getting a visit from Garrett, too.

"No. Not that specifically. Garrett was talking about me rebounding with you, and he was serious because he used the f-word." She stopped, looked up at him. "This isn't making any sense."

"It is," he assured her. "Garrett's your big brother, and he's concerned about you. Trust me. I get it since I've had that same conversation with April about rebounding and Brantley."

She nodded, brushed a kiss on his henpecked cheek. And waited. They still had a lot to discuss.

Since there was no easy way around this, Clay just

dived in headfirst. "I called the man who sent you that stuff, and if he sends you anything else or contacts you, I'll arrest him."

That put some concern in her eyes. "He's dangerous?"

"No. Not physically, anyway, but he's hurting, and what he sent you and what he sends me is his way of lashing out. He wants to make sure I hurt as much as he does." Mission accomplished. Of course, Clay hadn't needed the lashing out to hurt. The hurt was always there. "What was in the envelope?"

She reached in her jacket pocket and took it out. She'd folded it in fours so it took him a couple of seconds to open it. There were no surprises. The typewritten note was exactly as Sophie had said.

If you want to know all about Clay McKinnon, take a look at these.

These were two photos that Clay knew well because Brody sent them to him each month. The first was a shot of Clay, Brody and Delaney. Delaney was in the middle, her arms slung around their waists, and she was smiling from ear to ear. Since the shooting, seeing that smile always cut him to the core, and tonight was no different.

Clay needed a deep breath before he went to the second photo. Again, no surprises. This photo had been taken only two hours after the last one.

But in this second picture, she was dead, lying in a pool of her own blood.

Clay refolded both pictures, the note, and slipped them back into the envelope. He dropped it on the end table, but he'd need to bring it to work and add it to the others. He definitely didn't want to leave it in Sophie's hands.

"I'm not sure I can tell you about that last picture," he admitted. "Not tonight, anyway."

She nodded again. "Is the person who sent it to me the same one who left you that phone message when I was here?"

"Yes. And he's the same man in the first photo. The same one who sends me a pink envelope each month."

Sophie stared at him. "All right," she said after a long silence.

Clay was certain he looked stunned. Because he was. *All right?* That was it? He'd expected the third degree, tears, maybe even some observations about her sucky luck with the wrong men. But he sure as heck hadn't been expecting an *all right*.

"One day maybe you can tell me about that." She tipped her head to the envelope. "And I want to hear it when you're ready to tell me."

That sounded like something a woman would say when she trusted a man, something Sophie shouldn't be doing. Not after the heart-stomping Brantley had given her. And she especially shouldn't be trusting him.

"Since we're not going to talk about pink envelopes," she went on. She reached in her pocket, and for one heart-stopping moment, Clay thought she was going to take out something else Brody had sent. But no.

Because it was a condom.

"It's not from Vita," Sophie explained. She dropped it on the end table beside him. "I got it from Garrett's bathroom."

Clay repeated that mental *hell*, but the only part of him not pleased with the sight of that foil wrapper was his brain. Of course, his brain had been present when he'd bought some condoms yesterday. He didn't have to explore why he'd done that.

Because the reason for that purchase was right in front of him.

Sophie looked up at him. "Anyway, if we decided not to have sex, I didn't want it to be because we didn't have protection. I wanted it to be our choice. A choice made by two people who understand just how much sex will totally screw up their lives."

It was a decent argument and a reminder that he should step back. Clay stepped all right, but it was in the wrong direction. Or the right direction if he was aiming for totally screwing up their lives.

He pulled Sophie into his arms and got started on the screwing.

CHAPTER FOURTEEN

SOPHIE HAD PREPARED herself in case Clay sent her home with her condom still unwrapped. But the kiss was a good sign that wasn't going to happen.

Of course, she should be trying to talk herself out of using a condom, something she'd done on the drive to his house, but clearly it was a verbal battle she'd lost. And it felt really, really good to be a loser right now.

Clay kissed like someone in charge. Like a cop. She wouldn't mention that because it might spoil the mood. At the moment she couldn't mention anything, anyway, since he was kissing her blind. She went from the simmering aroused stage to full-blown "take me now" heat.

Sophie wanted more. Still, she wanted a different kind of more. She wanted to touch Clay. To kiss him. To make him as crazy as he was making her. So she slid her hand between them to touch his chest and encountered his hand along the way.

"I'm sorry," he said, lowering those kisses to her neck.

Clay and she had only had two kissing sessions, but he'd already located a couple of the most sensitive parts of her body—her neck and her breasts. He was doing a great job of teasing her neck with his tongue, but his fingers weren't doing a bad job on her nipples, either. In fact, he was doing such a stellar job that it took Sophie a couple of moments to realize what he'd said.

"Why are you sorry?" she asked.

"Because I'm not being the responsible adult I should be."

If she could have shrugged, Sophie would have. In this moment being responsible seemed highly overrated. That likely explained why there were unplanned pregnancies, therapy and regrets. She could avoid the first two, but they might have a serving or two of regret after the orgasms.

And she was bound and determined that this time there'd be two orgasms. Both Clay's and hers.

To get started on that, Sophie lowered her hand to the front of his jeans and did some touching there. Clay cursed, backed her up a few inches, and using just one of his hands, he pinned her wrists to the wall. Since it was the same wall where her other orgasm had happened, it had good memories for her, but without the use of her hands she was going to have trouble with the "making him crazy" part.

Clay, however, had no trouble escalating the insanity. Speed suddenly mattered, no doubt because of the urgency building inside them, and he used his free hand to shove up her top and pull down her bra.

The next round of kisses got very interesting.

He used his tongue again and his warm breath to create a special feeling inside her special place. Too bad that feeling only escalated matters even more.

Since she wouldn't wiggle her hands out of his grip, Sophie wiggled the rest of her body instead. Specifically, she brushed her midsection against his. She found a wonderful surprise.

His erection.

All ready for that condom she'd brought over.

Clay cursed again, but she was pretty sure that's because he was enjoying her wiggling a little too much. In his mind he probably didn't want to put an end to this too soon, but Sophie was up for some quick and dirty sex against the wall. Or on the floor. Maybe even the sofa. And then they could use the second condom in her pocket for a second round of slow and dirty.

Either way, she just wanted dirty.

She wanted this fire to dictate the pace, intensity and even the amount of clothing removal. At this point, she would just settle for getting Clay and her unzipped.

Sophie tried for the unzipping again, and she managed to get one of her hands free. However, her hand got distracted along the way to the front of his jeans because his shirt had come unbuttoned, and her fingers landed on his chest.

Nice.

Very nice.

Pecs, chest hair and all. Everything she wanted in a lover, and it made her rethink the minimal clothing removal. She wanted to see him naked. Wanted to touch him while he was naked. And since she didn't know if there'd be a repeat of this night, she decided to tick off everything on her "take me, Clay" wish list.

Clay had moved his kisses lower, to her stomach, and while he was heading in a good direction, Sophie created a detour. She caught onto his hair, pulling him back up so her mouth could play with his chest. Fun stuff, and it got a lot more fun when she pulled open his shirt.

On a scale of one to ten, he was off the scale so Sophie didn't even bother assigning a number. But seeing all that beautiful manhood only made her want to see and kiss the rest of him. She twisted her body to unpin herself from him, dropped lower and played her own game of kiss the stomach. It was fun but not nearly as much when she kissed the front of his jeans. She made sure there was a lot of breath in that kiss, too.

More cursing. That seemed to be Clay's go-to response when things were moving faster than he wanted. But it was Sophie who was suddenly moving faster. He picked her up, threw her caveman style over his shoulder and headed up the hall. His shoulder hit the wall, so did hers, and her head would have smacked into the door frame if she hadn't ducked at the last second.

Clay dumped her on the bed—and yes, it was a little rough, just like she wanted.

"I've been thinking a lot about how you'd be in bed," she said.

He didn't answer. Not verbally, anyway. Clay shucked off her top, rid her of her bra and gave her some more of those nipple kisses all while getting her out of her jeans. So, this was how he was in bed.

In charge and silent.

And possibly with the sleight of hand of a magician since he had her stark naked in under fifteen seconds.

Except he wasn't actually in bed. Nor was he naked. And now he was looking at her in a head-to-toe kind of way. Since she wasn't used to being under naked scrutiny, she reached for the covers, but Clay stopped her. There he was, being in charge again.

"Perfect," he said.

All in all, it was the perfect thing to say. And it stopped her from making a second attempt to cover herself. Not that there was time to do that. Clay pulled off his shirt, and her girl parts shouted yes! The shouting continued when he unzipped, hooked his thumbs around the waist of his jeans and dropped both the jeans and his boxers to the floor.

He moved toward her, but Sophie caught on to him. Because she was sitting, that meant she caught on to his hips and butt. She wasn't in the best position for her to give him a head-to-toe look as he'd done to her, but she got an up close view of the part that would play a big role in her life.

Well, for the next ten minutes, anyway.

But that part was missing a condom.

Obviously, Clay wasn't in any shape to sprint, but Sophie was about to do just that and get the condom from the living room. However, Clay had something else in mind. He reached into his nightstand drawer and took one out.

"I bought some," he told her. But that was all he said.

With the same speed he'd used to undress her, he got that condom ripped open and on, and he got onto the bed with her. Sophie expected that fast pace to continue, but Clay slowed down considerably. He kissed her. So slow and sweet. Sliding his body against hers. Stoking the fire that needed no such stoking because it was already at full blaze.

Just when Sophie was certain she could take no more of the maddening pace, Clay eased into her. Also slowly. She hated to admit it, but it gave her a few moments to savor this. To savor him.

The savoring didn't stop. It just went up a notch when Clay started to move inside her. And then the savoring climbed and climbed until it was into the "fire, hot" zone.

No way could she tell him how good this felt. No way could she form something as complex as human speech. That's because she was a cavewoman now, all need, no finesse. She just wanted him to keep hitting the right spot to make her come like a nympho after a dry spell.

And Clay didn't fail her.

He hit the right spot until both of them got the intended use from the condom.

It wasn't ten minutes, though.

It was fifteen.

WHEN HE FUCKED UP, he really fucked up. Literally in this case.

Clay figured he wasn't going to have to spell that out to Sophie, though. Now that their animal urges had been satisfied, she was probably hitting her head against the wall.

Or not.

When Clay came out of the bathroom, he found no head hitting going on. Sophie was sitting in his bed, still naked, though she had pulled the sheet over her lap, and she was eating some pumpkin pie.

"Sex makes me hungry," she said. "And I didn't eat any pie at my house."

"Help yourself." Though the invitation wasn't really necessary since she was in already in midbite. However, she stopped eating to give him a long look.

He was naked, too, and she was giving him the once-over. Twice. When he reached to pick up his boxers, she shook her head, smiled and motioned for him to join her on the bed. Clay sighed. It was a mistake, of course, but he did it anyway.

"Let's play a game," she offered.

Since she was naked and looking at him as if he were the whipped cream on that pie, Clay would have agreed to anything. Even if he shouldn't.

"What kind of game?" he asked.

She fed him a bite of pie before she answered. "It's called 'we're not going to feel guilty about this and here's why.' Then, we start naming all the reasons why there'll be no guilt or regret."

Clay drew a blank.

"All right, I'll start," Sophie continued. "I don't regret it because it felt amazing."

"That's the orgasm talking," he concluded, and had another bite of the pie.

She smiled. Shrugged. "Second reason. We both had really bad days and needed to relieve some stress."

Now he shrugged because it was true. To a point. "There are other ways to relieve stress that won't screw up your life."

Sophie gave him a flat look. "Name one. Wait. Name one that won't make me drunk, fat, broke or sweaty."

With those added conditions, he was drawing a blank. That possibly had something to do with Sophie shifting her position on the bed, and he got a glimpse of what the sheet had been covering. Suddenly, he was thinking of another reason not to regret this.

A stupid reason.

It involved curing the regret of the first time by going back for seconds.

She must have seen the attentive look in his eyes because she smiled again. "I have to get back home soon, or my mother might come looking for me. I don't think either of us is up to a chat with her tonight, are we?"

No way. That cured him of the notion of seconds and slapped some sense back into him. It gave him a much-needed reminder of why this was a fuckup. And why he should give Sophie a reminder, too.

"You should be keeping away from me," he said.

She rolled her eyes. "We don't have much willpower when it comes to each other so I'm pretty sure that's not going to happen."

He hated when the truth interfered with what he knew he should be doing. "I might never be able to tell you things that you think you want to know," Clay tried again.

She nodded. "You mean the story behind the pink envelopes. Yes, I think I want to know, but I can wait. But I should tell you that the scenarios I'm creating in my head are probably worse than what really happened."

"No, they aren't. In this case, reality is worse."

Clay thought that might send her running from the bed to get dressed so she could leave, but other than eating another bite of pie, she didn't budge.

"You're a good man, Clay McKinnon," she said. "You moved here to look out for your sister even when that meant taking a job that's almost certainly beneath your skill set."

Clay focused on the two words in the middle of that. His sister. He certainly hadn't forgotten about April, but she was another reminder why being with Sophie like this was a bad idea.

"April will have a cow if she finds out about us," Clay started. "I could just say to heck with it and point out that she's always done what she wanted, even when I didn't approve."

"But she's pregnant," Sophie finished for him. "And in a fairly new relationship with Brantley. This might put too much stress on both April and their marriage."

Sophie had spelled out the big picture. Plus, there was that whole part about his knowing this was a mistake.

"If everyone learns we're together-together," Sophie

added, "and it doesn't work out between us, then I'll have to go through another pity party showered on me by nearly everyone who lives in Wrangler's Creek. Those same people will blame you, and it'll make it harder for you to do your job because you crushed the heart of the town's resident princess." She paused. "Yes, I know they call me that behind my back."

They did. It wasn't flattering since it was beneath Sophie's skill set as a competent businesswoman, but most people said it with affection. And those *most people* would indeed blame him for a breakup.

Hell, he was already thinking breakup, and they weren't even together.

"This doesn't sound pretty, but we could just sneak around and see each other," she went on. "That way, we could keep it between us and at the same time, figure out if whatever *this* is has a chance of working. If not, then no one but us will know about it."

He frowned. Then frowned some more when the sheet fell from her left breast. Instead of doubts, the word *perfect* jumped into his head. His dick did a little jumping, too.

Still, even with his dick's reaction, Clay tried to latch on to some reason. "Certainly, sneaking around and having sex with me can't be part of your life plan."

Sophie smiled that perfect, evil smile and kissed him. "It is now."

CHAPTER FIFTEEN

SNEAKY SEX WAS a huge distraction. Mainly because Clay couldn't stop thinking about it. Maybe after Sophie and he had been together a time or two more, then the desire to have sex with her would fade, taking the distraction right along with it.

Pigs could also learn to fly.

Clay cursed, admitted that it was going to take more than a time or two to get Sophie out of his system and forced his attention back on a budget report he had to review. That worked for a couple of seconds until he saw Sophie outside the window. Not heading his direction but rather to the bank. His office was the last place she would go, since in her mind, being sneaky meant not being seen with him in public. Of course, people would notice they weren't being seen together and draw the same conclusion as if they had been seen together.

And that conclusion was that Sophie and he were lovers.

Clay could no longer deny that to himself. Wouldn't be able to deny it to her brother, either, if Garrett came out and asked. However, everyone else was on his denial list. Who was or wasn't his lover was nobody's business but his and Sophie's, and the only reason he would let Garrett in on it was because they had an unspoken camaraderie as big brothers.

He watched Sophie until she was out of sight and then

went back to the budget report. He got two lines into it when his phone rang, and he saw Agent Mike Freeman's name on the screen. Finally, a real, work-related distraction.

"Please tell me that Billy Lee called Arlo and that you managed to track him down," Clay greeted.

"Not yet. We had Arlo use the phone to call him, but Billy Lee didn't answer. Arlo left him a message, but so far, there's been no response."

Clay tried not to jump to some bad conclusions, but it was too late. He was already jumping. "Billy Lee could have been watching Arlo and could have seen him come here to the police station."

'How hard would that have been for Billy Lee to do?" Mike asked.

"Hard but not impossible. Did you check Arlo's truck for a tracking device?"

"We did. Nothing there."

That didn't surprise Clay. "At least a dozen people could have seen Arlo coming into the station, and it would have taken seconds for that to get around town. If Billy Lee managed to get word that Arlo was here, it could have caused him to back off."

"Any idea who could be feeding Billy Lee gossip?"

"Anybody with the ability to communicate either through speech, writing or sign language. Wrangler's Creek is loose-lips headquarters. And they might not be doing it intentionally. I've had some experience with how fast and wide-reaching info can spread here."

Mike made a sound, one that needed no verbal skills to interpret. The agent knew Clay was right but also knew there was nothing he could do to stop the flow of gossip.

"What about the note Arlo brought in?" Clay asked. "Anything on that?"

"The lab analyzed it, and it's definitely Billy Lee's handwriting. One of the fingerprints on it belonged to him, too."

Hell. Hadn't Billy Lee ever watched an episode of CSI? Apparently not. Maybe he hadn't counted on Arlo turning over the note. But he should have. He should be in the trust-no-one zone right about now. And that's what bothered Clay.

"Why is Billy Lee even reaching out to Arlo?" Clay continued. "If he stole all that money, why hasn't he used it to get out of the country?"

"Don't have a clue about the first question, but maybe Billy Lee lost the cash to the money launderers he was involved with."

Yeah. And if so, that made Billy Lee dangerous. Because he might do anything to get the cash, and that included going to Sophie and Garrett for funds.

"I'm coming to Wrangler's Creek later today," Mike went on. "I want to be there when I have Arlo make another call to Billy Lee. I'll keep you posted if we learn anything new," he said before ending the call.

Clay was about to go back to the budget, but this was apparently going to be his afternoon for interruptions because his intercom buzzed.

"You said you wanted me to tell you if you had a visitor," Reena said, "and not just send them back."

He had told her that—after multiple visits from Vita. He wouldn't turn the woman away, but he didn't like surprise knocks on his door.

Someone knocked on his door.

"Sorry," Reena added, "Belle Granger went back to

your office before I could stop her. But when you're done with her, we could use some help putting up this Christmas tree, and the lightbulb over my desk went out again. You're the only one tall enough to reach it on the ladder. Oh, and Brantley's here. He says he has to talk to you about something personal, that it's real important."

Clay wasn't sure how his predecessor, Sheriff Vern Tripp, had ever gotten any work done. Of course, maybe Vern hadn't gotten involved with the very woman who could create maximum door knockage. And maybe Vern had also bought long-life lightbulbs.

The door opened, and yes, it was Sophie's mom all right. Judging from her tight mouth and slightly narrowed eyes, this was about the other sort of knocking up. Clay decided to nip it in the bud as soon as Belle closed the door.

"Sophie's not pregnant," he said.

Clay could practically see the relief fly out of Belle's body. Too bad the anger didn't fly out with it. He figured there was a lecture coming on.

"Sophie's very vulnerable, and it wasn't right for you to take advantage of her like that," Belle scolded.

He wouldn't mention that it was Sophie who'd started it, especially since he'd been the one to finish it. Well, finish that particular encounter, anyway.

"I can see why she turned to you," Belle went on. "I mean, you look like one of those cowboy models. And you've got that dark, bad-boy edge that appeals to some women. Many women," Belle amended.

If Clay didn't know better, he'd think Belle was coming onto him, but this was probably just her attempt to get on his good side so that she could sway him to her way of thinking. And her way of thinking would be no sneaking-around sex.

Belle apparently wasn't finished with her lecture. "But here's what you have to remember." And she said the two words that could win plenty of arguments. "Your sister."

There was no need for her to elaborate on that, but that didn't stop Belle from doing it. "You don't want April to get wind of…well, whatever it is going on between my daughter and you." She finally paused, probably just so she could gather enough breath to continue. "What exactly is going on between you?"

Protected sex, missionary position with a hand job thrown in probably wasn't the answer Belle wanted to hear. "Sophie and I are attracted to each other," he settled for saying.

Finally, the anger vanished from her face, but Clay saw another emotion that was even more troubling. A mother's concern. "I'm afraid if Sophie's hurt again, that this time she'll break."

Yeah, he was worried about that, too, and there was plenty that could hurt her if she found out about his past. And she would find out. You couldn't bury a secret deep enough to stop it from coming to light. Despite his warning to Brody, that wouldn't necessarily prevent the man from spilling everything to Sophie. Since everything would be the truth, Sophie would be crushed.

That was the reminder Clay needed. There should be no more sneaky-sex with her. No sex, period.

"And if she breaks," Belle went on, "then I'll have to break you. Have I made myself clear?"

Clay nodded and sat there, watching her leave. Watching Sophie, too, because she went past his window again. Still not headed his way. And she didn't even look in his direction. She was doing something on her phone that had her full attention. So much so that she nearly walked right into a decorating crew that was putting up plastic Santas on the street light poles. A moment later, Clay's own phone dinged with a text message.

He doubted it was a coincidence.

Clay took a deep breath, ready to see an invitation for sex from Sophie. It was an invitation all right, but it wasn't from Sophie. It was from his sister.

Dinner at our house tomorrow night at seven. April had texted, I know you'll come because Sophie will be there.

Shit.

Before he could respond with a WTF?, his phone dinged again with a second text message. This one was from Sophie. And she'd taken the initials right out of his mouth.

Your sister just texted to say you and I are supposed to be at her house for dinner. WTF?

Clay had no idea what was going on, but he was about to press April's phone number when the door opened. Brantley. Clay certainly hadn't forgotten about his brother-in-law, but after the two texts, he'd put Brantley on the back burner with the lightbulb change.

"What the fuck is going on?" Clay asked him.

Even though it was forty degrees outside, there was sweat on Brantley's upper lip. "It's April," he said. "She heard Sophie was pregnant, and she wants to talk to both of you about it."

ALL SOPHIE HAD wanted was sex. A couple of stolen hours with Clay, his bed and a condom or two.

Heck, the bed was even optional.

But instead of an orgasm, or two, April was trying to set her up for another turkey, peas and Sheez Louise dining experience in what would no doubt be a hostile environment.

Sophie glanced at her phone. Still no response from Clay, but she needed to watch where she was walking because she bumped into another ladder. One that was holding Freddie's sons who were doing the decorating on Main Street. It was the second time she'd done that in the past three minutes.

"Look out!" one of them yelled, and they nearly dropped the massive six-foot Santa head on her.

Death by Santa was not the way she wanted to go.

It wasn't a good time to be on the sidewalk what with the Santas, the cold and all the people who were starting to stare at her while she stared at her phone and dodged death. Best to minimize the gossip so she hurried to the bookstore, only to remember that Mila had closed early for inventory. The blinds were down, the closed sign up, but Sophie tapped on the door anyway. When Mila didn't answer, Sophie used her key to let herself in so she could wait inside for a response from Clay.

And she groaned when she spotted Mila.

Her friend was peering out the doorway of her office. She was dressed in skintight black leather pants, a black top that was practically falling off her shoulders, and her hair was fluffed into a curly mess. "You're the One That I Want" was playing in the background.

Once Sophie got her eyes unwidened, she rolled them. "Please tell me you're here alone and that you're trying on costumes for a New Year's Eve party."

"I'm alone. But not for long." Mila caught onto the door frame so she could put on a pair of red high heels normally reserved for movie musicals and cheap hookers. "I have a fantasy date coming over, and he'll be here soon. But don't worry. I checked him out, and he's safe. He's a shrink over at the prison, and they vet those guys very well before they hire them."

Sophie so wanted to repeat those key words back to Mila. Prison shrink. One who was apparently into role-playing that involved leather clothing and screw-me heels.

No, there was nothing weird about that.

"You need to come up with a better way to satisfy these fantasies," Sophie scolded. "Maybe wear one of those emergency alert buttons like senior citizens wear. Or keep a window open so that someone can hear you scream."

"I won't be screaming." Mila gave an indignant huff. "I'll be singing and dancing."

"Yes, but you don't know what the prison doctor has in mind."

The next huff was louder and even more indignant. "Outside of my books, I don't have a lot of excitement in my life like you do. I certainly don't have a cowboy cop who probably looks like an underwear model when he's naked. He does, doesn't he?"

That was such a loaded question along with being poorly worded. "Underwear models don't pose naked so I wouldn't know. And what's with you? Why the interest in hearing about Clay and me?"

"Because I'll bet he's the stuff of your fantasies. As you can tell, lately I'm into fantasies."

Sophie wasn't sure how to put this nicely so she just went with blunt. Good thing Mila and she had been friends since third grade. "Maybe it's time for you to find someone special and have sex. I think all of this—"

she fanned her hand over the clothes "—is a manifestation of some deep-seated unfulfilled area."

Specifically, one unfulfilled area. Of her body.

"Are you saying a woman shouldn't still be a virgin when she's thirty?" Mila asked.

"No. But I'm saying it might not be a good idea for *you* to be a virgin much longer. Clearly, being with a man is on your mind. And both the *Dirty Dancing* and *Grease* dances are, well, sexual. I think it's time to start focusing on finding the right man."

Mila squinted her left eye. Or maybe it just got a little stuck because of the glob of mascara clinging to it. "Focus on finding the right man like you're doing?"

Dang it, they were back to her. "Yes, exactly like I'm doing." Sophie didn't bother to take out the sarcasm and frustration, either. And she added a groan.

Mila finally smiled as if they'd just called some kind of truce. "Why are you here anyway? Weren't you supposed to be at the ranch for a cattle shipment?"

"All done, but right now I'm hiding out and waiting for Clay to text me." She lifted her phone to show Mila the text April had sent her.

"Dinner, tomorrow night at Brantley's and my place. Clay will be there, too. See you then," Mila read aloud.

"I'm waiting on a response from Clay," Sophie added.

Mila had the same look that Sophie had given her when she'd walked in on the *Grease* outfit. Except Mila didn't keep the look on hers. She tipped her head to the door that Sophie had left ajar. "Well, you won't have to wait long because there he is."

Sophie spun around so fast that her neck popped. Yes, he was there. Right in the doorway. He glanced at Sophie. Stared and cursed at Mila.

"I've already lectured her," Sophie said, holding to that unspoken truce Mila and she had just reached. "She'll leave a window open in case she needs someone to hear her screaming and come running. And she'll text me every fifteen minutes, sort of like her safe word check."

Mila hadn't actually agreed to do those things, but Sophie would convince her—once she'd gotten this dinner issue cleared up.

"WTF?" Sophie repeated.

He shook his head, lifted his hands, palms up. Not good signs. "I haven't been able to reach April yet. She took the boys to Spike's grandparents, and she's not answering her phone. I did talk to Brantley, though, and he's not sure why April put this dinner together, but he doesn't like the idea of it any more than we do." He paused. "You don't like the idea of it, do you?"

"No way. I don't want to go another round of berate Sophie Granger from a pregnant woman married to my ex." She glanced over her shoulder to make sure Mila wasn't listening. Thankfully, she'd gone back in her office, but Sophie lowered her voice just in case. "Besides, I'd rather spend that time with you."

That didn't improve his expression.

Oh no.

"My mother got to you," Sophie concluded.

This time he shrugged. "She had some good points."

"Yes, for a woman with very narrow views. She no doubt believes you took my virginity so now she's either planning our wedding or telling you to back off or she'll bury your body where it'll never be found.

"It's the latter," Sophie grumbled.

Clay didn't confirm it. Didn't need to, but she knew some kind of threat had occurred. Later, she'd take it up with her mother, but for now, she had more immediate fish to fry.

"So, why do you think April wants us to come to dinner?" Sophie asked.

"Your guess is as good as mine, but I should know something soon. If she doesn't answer her phone, I'll go to their house and find out."

That was the best they could do right now, and it was obvious that Clay couldn't give her any other information on the subject. But he didn't budge. He just stood there, glancing around and occasionally mumbling a curse word. Obviously he was doing battle with whatever her mother had said to him.

Well, Sophie fixed that.

By playing dirty.

She came up on her toes, making sure her body brushed against his, and she put her mouth right against his ear. Warm breath got involved. And maybe a little bit of her tongue, too.

"I could sneak over to your place tonight," she whispered, giving him another body nudge. Right on his nether region. Not very subtle, but it worked. She saw the spark of attraction in his eyes. Felt some hardening in that region she'd nudged. "Then you can tell me in person what your sister had to say."

Oh, he didn't want to agree. At least his brain didn't, but thankfully there were other parts of his body in play here. He didn't say yes. Not verbally, but he said it in a very good way. He snapped her to him, kissed her, and he used more than a little tongue. By the time he let go of her, Sophie had the answer she wanted.

Clay walked out, leaving her flushed but smiling.

"You really are going for it," Mila said.

Yes, she was. She was going for some more sneaky sex with the hottest guy on the planet.

"But you're also falling for him," Mila added.

That got rid of Sophie's smile. "No. I'm just having some fun."

That didn't sound right. Didn't feel right, either. This wasn't especially fun except for the actual time she got to spend with Clay. It was work, but she still wanted to do it anyway. In fact, she was willing to jump through hoops, maybe hurdle over fire and risk a chicken attack to be with him.

Well, heck.

When had that happened? And it wasn't as if they had a clear path to be together. They might never have a clear path.

"Be safe," Sophie reminded Mila. "And text me every fifteen minutes so I know you're okay."

She waited until Mila grunted, and since that sounded like a grunt of agreement, Sophie headed out. She'd left her car parked at the other end of Main Street so that meant a trek back through the decorating land mines and prying eyes, some of whom had no doubt noticed that Clay and she had been behind closed doors and blinds long enough for him to impregnate her a second time.

Sophie lowered her head against the chilly wind and got moving. She didn't make it far, though, because this time she nearly smacked into Arlo. The wind had obviously helped dissipate the stench of motor oil typically coming off his clothes or she would have smelled him before she saw him.

"Just saw the chief come out of the bookstore," Arlo commented. "And now you came out." He grinned. "Your hair's a little mussed, too."

Good grief. "Mussed from the wind. Gotta go. It was nice talking to you—"

"Since the chief and you are close, I guess he's told you all about Billy Lee. Pillow talk," he added with another grin.

That stopped her, and Sophie turned and walked back to Arlo. "Uh, yes. He told me," she lied. Clay hadn't told her squat about Billy Lee, but obviously there was something to tell. "How did your last talk with the chief go?"

"I figured he'd have told you, all things considered." His gaze dropped to her stomach, which was a little puffy because of the sweets she'd been eating.

"He did tell me, but what's your take on it?" Not very subtle, but she just wasn't good at this sort of thing.

"Well, I gotta agree with the chief on this. I think we're real close to catching Billy Lee. I mean, what with the phone call and all. And the note he left on my truck."

Phone call? Note? Until this moment, she'd thought Billy Lee might be in the grave. Or at least in Fiji spending the money he'd stolen. Apparently, he wasn't in either of those places. He was right here in Wrangler's Creek or at least he had been. And Clay hadn't let her know that.

The question was why?

And the answer was something Sophie was going to get right now.

CHAPTER SIXTEEN

RIGHT NOW HAD had to wait.

Not only had Sophie not managed to see Clay, she hadn't even managed to speak to him since he'd been tied up with "business stuff" according to Reena. Sophie had pumped the deputy for information, but Reena either didn't know or she was keeping something secret for the first time in her life. Either way, it could mean Clay was with Arlo, and they were speaking with Billy Lee. So now Sophie had two things to clear up with Clay.

The Billy Lee situation and April's dinner invitation.

And she was only minutes away from getting that done. Having sex, too, though like the *right now*, that would have to wait.

She parked her car on the ranch trail just up from Clay's and started walking to his house. Just as she heard another vehicle. She ducked behind a hackberry and nearly put her eye out when one of the low-hanging branches poked her in the face. She got poked again when she dodged a fire ant bed.

This secret meeting stuff wasn't for sissies.

Her hiding attempts weren't even necessary because one of Ordell Busby's boys went flying past her in the truck, and though he never looked in her direction, something splatted on the other side of the road.

Chicken feed.

He'd tossed what appeared to be a gallon of it.

So, she was right about one or more of the boys salting Clay's property with the feed to keep the chickens around. It was yet something else she needed to tell Clay.

Sophie followed the ditch in case she had to duck behind the nearby trees again to hide. But she made it to Clay's without further incident, only to see a possible incident the moment she arrived. She had to do some tree-ducking after all because when she spotted Clay, he wasn't alone.

His nephews were with him, and they were by the corral fence looking at the horses.

She couldn't hear what Clay was saying to the boys, but they giggled, and he goosed one of them in the belly. She glanced around to see if Brantley or April was there, but there was no sign of them. Of course, that didn't mean they weren't inside so she sent a text to Clay to ask if she should come back later.

He read the text, and then did some glancing around, as well, no doubt looking for her. Sophie gave him a little wave from her hideout behind the tree. Clay gathered up both boys, one under each arm and made his way to her.

"I didn't know the twins were going to be here," she said.

"Neither did I. Spike dropped them off about a half hour ago. It was his evening to be with them, but he said something came up. A hot date, probably. Anyway, April's tired from the visit with Spike's grandparents so Brantley's coming by after work to pick them up."

That sent her gaze back to the road. No sign of Brantley, not yet anyway, but it wouldn't be too stealthy of her if he saw her hiding behind the tree again.

"Come on in," Clay offered. "I'll give the boys a snack so we can talk."

"Snack!" one of them squealed.

She thought it might be Hunter, the more outgoing of the two. Hayden was the one looking at her, though. He'd lifted his head from the football-like hold his uncle had him in, and he was eyeing her with suspicion.

Sophie was about to point out to Clay that the twins might tell April about this visit, but what the heck—his sister would probably find out anyway. ESP seemed to be rampant when it came to Clay and her.

"What if we don't finish talking before Brantley gets here?" Sophie asked.

"Then Brantley will find out that you're here. Something tells me we won't be finished by the time he arrives. And, no, that wasn't about s-e-x. It has to do with me hearing that you saw Arlo today. I believe the word Reena used to describe your expression was shell-shocked."

"Reena…" Her grumbling sounded like profanity. "Does that woman ever get any work done?"

"Not much."

The moment Clay was inside, he put the boys down. "Snacks!" one of them yelled. Or rather "nacks." Clearly, he hadn't forgotten what Clay had said in the yard because he headed straight for the table.

The other one just stood there and stared at her before he lifted his hands in the air.

"Hayden wants you to pick him up," Clay explained.

She'd gotten the gesture, but Sophie couldn't figure out why. Still, she scooped him up in her arms, and the little boy immediately put his head on her shoulder.

All right.

She certainly hadn't expected to feel the warmth. Both

in her heart and on her hand when she touched his fore-head. "Uh, Clay, I think he's got a fever."

"Shit," Clay snapped. He had just served up some milk and a cookie to Hunter, but he came back to her.

"Shit, shit, shit," Hunter repeated.

"Frote hurts," Hayden said in a whisper.

It took her a moment to realize he meant his throat. Poor kid. But with the way her and Clay's luck had been running, they'd all come down with something highly contagious that would make them bedridden.

Clay tried to take him from her, but Hayden shook his head and held on. Apparently, she was the mommy figure right now.

"I don't have any kid's Tylenol or a thermometer." Clay took out his phone. "But I'll text Brantley to bring them. Why don't you sit on the sofa with him?"

Sophie did, and Hayden snuggled into her arms as if he belonged there. It didn't exactly stir her biological clock, but it did nudge it a little.

She heard Clay turn on the faucet in the kitchen, and several moments later, he came back with a wet cloth that he gently pressed to Hayden's head.

"Nunk," Hayden muttered, and he crawled from her lap to Clay's.

"Is there anything I can do?" she asked.

Clay brushed a kiss on the top of Hayden's head. "No. I'm sure he'll be fine. When April was a kid, it seemed like she'd get a fever at least once a week. She hated meds, too, just like this one. Sometimes, it would take me three or four tries to get enough meds in her to do her any good."

"You had to take care of her?"

He shrugged. "It came with the territory of being

eleven years older than she is. Sometimes, it feels like I'm still taking care of her."

She heard the emotion in that, both good and bad, and was about to ask if he wanted her to go, but Clay spoke before she could say anything.

"Arlo or April?" he asked. He glanced into the kitchen where Hunter was sneaking another cookie from the bag that Clay had left on the table. "Which do you want to talk about first?" Multitasking, Clay got up, moved the cookie bag to the top of the fridge, wagged a scolding finger at Hunter and then came back into the living room.

"Arlo," Sophie said. It wasn't really a tough decision. "Are you actually close to finding Billy Lee? And if so, why didn't you tell me?"

A heavy breath left Clay's mouth. "It's a federal investigation, and the agent and I thought it was best to keep it close to the vest. And for the record, we're not close to finding him. But he did leave a phone for Arlo, and Billy Lee told him to use it to call him."

Sophie moved to the edge of the seat. "I want that phone. I want to talk to him."

Another heavy breath. "Sophie, Billy Lee didn't leave you a phone, and if you'd called him, it probably would have spooked him."

"No, it wouldn't."

But that was her emotions talking. Because yes, it probably would have. Billy Lee obviously didn't want to talk to her or he would have gotten in touch with either Garrett or her by now. And he hadn't. Instead, he'd turned to his childhood friend who had no concept whatsoever of laundry detergent.

The next heavy breath in the room came from her.

Clay sank down on the sofa next to her. However, he

didn't look at her. He pointed to his eyes with his index and middle fingers and then turned those forked fingers on Hunter to let the boy know he was watching him. Apparently convinced that the cookie supply had dried up for the night, Hunter came jetting back into the living room, not for a feverish lap cuddle. He went after a basket of LEGO and dumped them on the floor.

Clay turned to her. "All of this with Billy Lee and Arlo might be nothing anyway. And Billy Lee might be doing this just to throw us off his trail. Think about it—Arlo's not Mensa material. Billy Lee maybe knew that his old friend would tattle to me and that I'd tell the FBI. If we take the bait, we tie up manpower looking for him here in Wrangler's Creek, and he's really off somewhere else."

"Fiji," Sophie grumbled.

Since that had been her theory all along, that Billy Lee had fled the country, then it wasn't much of a stretch for her to accept what Clay was saying. Not much of a stretch, either, to see why he hadn't told her. The secrecy was the badge part of Clay McKinnon.

The same part of him that was likely connected to what was in those pink envelopes.

Sophie didn't bring up the envelopes now because she had to move onto important topic number two.

"What's going on with your sister?" She whispered that just in case the kiddos were listening, but Hunter was bashing apart some LEGO he'd just stacked, and Hayden was asleep.

"April says she wants to bury the hatchet with you because she thinks you're pregnant with my baby. She said she saw you earlier, and it looked as if you were showing."

Good grief. Maybe she should start wearing Spanx or

cut back on the sugar cookies that Alice was churning out as part of her preholiday baking.

"Since you're not pregnant," Clay went on, whispering, too, "when she finds out the truth…"

"She might want to dig up the hatchet and throw it at me," Sophie finished for him.

Clay didn't deny it. "I suspect Brantley put her up to it anyway. Half the town turned against him after what he did to you. The other half is riled because he married April and in their minds is rubbing it in your face because April and he started a family so soon."

That did sound like something Brantley would want his new bride to do. Not only for his sake but so that April would fit in better. She was still a newcomer to Wrangler's Creek, and getting people to accept her wouldn't be easy if she kept pitching hissy fits about the town founder's great-granddaughter.

"I've already told April we can't come to this dinner she'd planned, that we both have to work," Clay went on. "She bought that. Or at least pretended to buy it. I also told her that you're not pregnant. I'm not sure she believed it, but she will eventually when you don't start to show."

Yes, she definitely needed the Spanx.

'So, are we good?" Clay asked. "Are you still mad at me for not telling you about Billy Lee?"

After a few more seconds of sulking, she waved it off. "We're good."

"Then, you just need to decide one more thing. Brantley just pulled up in front of the house. If you don't want him to see you here or if you don't want to talk to him, you can wait in my bedroom."

Sophie immediately chose the bedroom and hurried in there.

Not only because she didn't want to face Brantley tonight but also because the bedroom was where she eventually hoped Clay would join her. It was probably wrong of her to think of sex with everything going on, but there always seemed to be something going on in their lives. If she waited for a break, Clay and she might be retirement age before they needed another condom.

Sophie eased the door shut and locked it just in case Hunter decided to come running in there. Or rat her out. His verbal skills weren't at an adult conversational level yet, but it didn't take too many words for him or his brother to tell their stepdad that someone was in Nunk's bed. She put her ear to the door, listened, and it didn't take long for her to hear Brantley's voice.

"You're not feeling good, Hayden?" Brantley asked. "I brought a thermometer, the kind you put on your forehead, and I'm going to take your temp. Is that okay?"

She didn't catch the little boy's response, if there was one, but Clay filled Brantley in on the fever, mentioning that Hayden was okay until the last twenty minutes or so.

"Well, it's not much of a temp," Brantley said a short time later. "But I'll have Sophie look at him when I get home."

"Sophie?" Clay said.

"Uh, I meant April." Mumble, mumble, something else she couldn't decipher so she moved from the wall and to the door so she could open it a bit. She couldn't see Brantley and Clay, but she could see Hunter. He had fallen asleep next to a pile of LEGO.

"Guess I've had Sophie on my mind a lot, and that's why I slipped and said her name," Brantley went on. That was plenty clear enough for her to hear. "Since the boys have both crashed, can we talk for a minute?"

"If you're going to ask me if Sophie's pregnant, she's not," Clay volunteered.

"No, I didn't figure she was. After I thought about it, I realized she's too careful to get caught up in an unplanned pregnancy. And as for the belly, well, she always gains weight this time of year."

She scowled and was so going to get those Spanx. And go on a diet.

"What I wanted to talk to you about was April," Brantley said. "I love her—I really do, but this whole marriage and parenting thing is a lot harder than I thought it would be. I never have any time to myself. It's work, home and work some more to help April out since she's tired a lot these days."

For a second, Sophie got a smidge of satisfaction over Brantley's less than blissful marriage. After all, he deserved some kind of misery for dumping her the way he had. But the smidge was quickly fading. Because he'd done her a favor by calling off the wedding. Still, he hadn't known he was doing her a favor at the time so she held on to the smidge a while longer.

"April's changed since we got married. She was so vibrant and, well, perky before. Full of life. I miss the woman I fell head over heels in love with."

Well, there went that smidge. April likely wasn't perky because she was full of a different kind of life. She was pregnant. And Brantley was the one who'd gotten her that way.

"Are you telling me this for a reason?" Clay asked him. And he didn't sound any happier with Brantley than Sophie was right now.

"Yes." But that's all Brantley said for what seemed like an eternity. "I'm not sure I can make this marriage work."

Sophie got a new smidge, but it had nothing to do with wishing Brantley some misery. It was more about wanting to throttle him, and it billowed into much more than a smidge.

She came storming out of the bedroom, her narrowed gaze going straight to her ex. "You willy-nilly piece of poop!"

Sadly, she didn't intentionally keep her insult G-rated for the boys' sake. Her mind and mouth just turned to silly profanity when she was shocked or angry. Clay's was a lot better than hers.

"You dickhead piece of shit," he snarled. He put his hands over Hayden's ears even though the boy was still asleep. Thankfully, so was Hunter.

Brantley got to his feet. "Sophie. I didn't know you were here," he said before his gaze swung back to Clay. "I didn't say I was leaving April or anything like that." He cursed, scrubbed his hand over his face. "I'm just saying this is harder than I thought it would be."

"Tough titty," Sophie snapped in a whisper. "Lots of things are harder than we think they'll be." Like secret sex with Clay. Getting along with her mom. Life in general. "Suck it up and be the husband and stepfather that April and her sons deserve."

Only then did Sophie realize the tough-titty lecture should have come from Clay. After all, this was his family not hers. And he would have worded the lecture better, too.

"Was there any part of what Sophie just said that you didn't understand?" Clay asked Brantley. So, obviously her wording had been to Clay's satisfaction.

Brantley shook his head so fast that his neck popped,

and he scooped up Hunter from the floor. "I should be going. April will be wondering where I am."

Scowling, Clay stood, and he carried Hayden out to Brantley's car. Sophie didn't follow them and didn't try to listen to what they were saying. Though Clay was certainly saying something. Maybe something that would drill a couple of tons of sense into Brantley's head.

Clay didn't linger. He only talked as long as it took them to get the boys into their car seats, and then he made his way back into the house as Brantley drove away.

"Did you threaten him within an inch of his life?" Sophie asked, closing the door behind him.

Clay shook his head, gave a weary sigh. "I can't make him stay committed to April. And I shouldn't have to. If Brantley's not in this one hundred percent, then he should leave and let April get on with her life."

Oh, mercy. That would send April into a tailspin, maybe shatter her, and Clay would have to be there to pick up the pieces. It was like the medicine thing when she was a kid all over again. Clay was taking care of her, and he would continue to do that even if it meant multiple tries.

Clay gave another weary sigh, pulled her to him and brushed a kiss on the top of her head much as he'd done to Hayden. "I'll walk you to your car. I'm guessing after everything that just went on, you're not in the mood for... anything."

Sophie debated it. A very short debate.

"You are so wrong about that," she said.

She kissed him, and it wasn't on his head. This one was on his mouth. And she led him straight to his bedroom.

CHAPTER SEVENTEEN

A THREE-CONDOM NIGHT. Clay wasn't sure the last time that had happened. Maybe his freshman year of college when he hadn't been thirty-four and feeling sixty. His back hurt.

But the rest of him was humming like a finely tuned Harley.

Or maybe that was just his stomach growling.

He wasn't sure if Sophie was feeling the same because she was facedown on his bed, sprawled out naked. And she'd stolen all the covers. In fact, he'd learned a couple of things about Sophie during the night. She'd definitely been in the mood for sex, was on the adventurous side, and she didn't share bedding.

Clay supposed that was a small price to pay for three orgasms. A small price to pay considering he got to wake up to a very hot naked woman. A woman he should be avoiding.

But that was an argument he'd have with himself another day.

For now, he just enjoyed the view. That's the reason he didn't move or get up even though he was starving and in need of a caffeine fix. If he moved, this moment would be lost. And since he knew a lot about lost moments, he decided to savor this one. Like all moments though, it didn't last.

Sophie opened one eye, peeked at him. And she smiled. It was easy not to notice the color of her eyes when he had that dazzling smile to greet him. A belly kiss, too. She made a sound of lazy pleasure, lifted her head and dropped a kiss on his stomach.

His *lower* stomach.

The woman certainly knew how to start the morning. Maybe he wouldn't need that caffeine after all.

"Ever wonder why people started kissing?" she asked.

Never. And he wasn't wondering it now. That was probably because her kiss went even lower, and to adjust her position, her bare breasts ended up against his outer thigh.

"I mean, think of it," she continued. "Imagine the first time a woman walked up to a man and kissed him. It was probably in a cave. They were likely wearing animal skins. Maybe they were hot, sweaty. Horny."

There was a lot of breath in her voice. Intentional, Clay was sure of it. Because it was hitting him against his dick, which was right there in front of her because she'd stolen those covers.

"Maybe it was the man who walked up to a woman and kissed her," Clay suggested.

She shook her head, letting her hair brush over what was now a full-blown erection. She let her mouth brush over it, too. "No, a woman started it. A man would have just hoisted her against the cave wall and had sex with her."

He made a sound of agreement and would have agreed to anything at the moment.

Sophie looked at him, met his gaze. "I'm not very good at this so bear with me." And she took him into her mouth.

Fuck.

Clay nearly came off the bed. Hell, he nearly came because "not very good" was a big-assed lie. She was extremely good at this. In fact, street hookers could have taken lessons from her. He'd had blow jobs before but never like this. Sophie managed to use her breath, her hair, her breasts and some very clever flicks of her tongue. She tortured and teased him until Clay was certain he could take no more.

And then she stopped.

"Mila and I used to practice this on bananas," she said her breath still bitch-slapping his dick.

Say what? Clay didn't actually get out the words, but he sure hadn't expected bananas or Mila to come up in conversation.

"We read it in a magazine and decided to try it," she went on, taking a condom from the nightstand.

Clay could only watch as she opened it, holding the unrolled condom in her mouth, and she lowered it to his dick. All Clay could think was that she must have practiced it a lot because she nailed it. She got the condom on him and then outstretched her arms as if waiting for applause.

He intended to give her something all right, but it wasn't applause.

Sophie laughed and scampered across the bed away from him. Even with a raging hard-on, Clay had no trouble catching her because she didn't go far. Plus, she was tangled in those stolen covers. He got tangled in them, too, and ended up with his chest against her back.

He took her that way.

Sophie made another of those sounds of pleasure, adjusted herself until she was crouched on her knees, and she caught on to the headboard for support. Normally, Clay didn't prefer this angle of sex since all the interesting parts of a woman were in the front, but he was so far gone that it would take some doing just to get her off before he brought this to a too-quick end.

While he pushed into her, he slid his hand to her lower belly, then between her legs to give her a little help. Apparently, he found the right spot because Sophie threw back her head, moaned, and he felt those slick, tight muscles squeeze him in the right spot, too.

Of course his right spot was a lot easier to find since it was his whole dick.

Even though it'd only been six hours or so since he'd last come, it felt as if he'd been starved for this. Starved for her. So, while he knew this would only add to the regrets that were piling up, Clay let Sophie and her muscles finish him off.

Sophie dropped back onto the bed, taking him with her, and she turned, coiling her body around so they were face-to-face. She kissed him.

"Want to know what else I practiced?" she asked.

Hell, no.

Well, not until he recovered.

"I'm thirty-four," he reminded her. "You've got to give me at least two hours." Or thirty minutes, he amended, when she climbed off the bed, and he got an unobstructed view of her naked body.

She laughed, kissed him again and reached for her clothes. "I practiced how to make an omelet," she clarified. "But once you've recovered, I can try out a lap dance. I've always wanted to do one of those."

With that dick-hardening offer still fresh from her mouth, Sophie took her clothes and headed in the direction of the guest room. Probably so she could freshen up and leave his own bathroom free for him to do the same. Without distractions. Because if they showered together, that would eat up the rest of the morning. Maybe literally. And while it was incredibly appealing, he really did need a couple of minutes.

Clay didn't waste any time. Not because of the lap dance tease—maybe that did speed him up some—but he also knew he didn't have much more time with Sophie. It was seven, and he'd have to be at work in the next hour or so.

He wondered if they could skip the omelet.

Clay showered, fast, and got dressed, but Sophie was even faster. She was already out of the guest bathroom and in the front part of the house when he came out. However, she wasn't in the kitchen. She was at the front door. The *opened* front door.

And she wasn't alone.

Brody was standing there.

Seeing him was the fastest way possible to put an end to Clay's postsex buzz. He hurried to them, stepping in front of Sophie. "What the hell are you doing here?" he asked Brody.

"Dropping this off," Sophie said. That's when Clay noticed that she was holding a cardboard box. It appeared to be filled with files.

And pink envelopes.

"It's not what you think," Brody jumped to say.

That didn't stop Clay from debating if he should just punch Brody's lights out. What the devil had he said to Sophie?

"I didn't tell her anything," Brody added as if reading Clay's mind. "I just got here."

"He's right," Sophie verified. "He knocked on the door, I answered it, and he handed me this just as you were coming out of your bedroom. We hadn't even said good morning yet."

"And you won't say it," Clay snapped. "Because he's not staying."

"No, I'm not." Brody tipped his head to the box. "That's everything I have on Delaney's death. And those pink envelopes are all empty. I'm here to say goodbye and to let you know that you'll never have to see me again. I'm taking a private security job overseas, and I'm leaving the country today."

That was a start, but it wasn't nearly good enough. "You had no right to come here. You could have just mailed the box."

Brody nodded. "I considered it, but I wanted you to see my face one last time. Not so I could apologize," he quickly added. "I doubt I'll ever be able to do that. But I wanted you to see that I was serious. I won't be bothering you again. It's time to let go of this, to let go of Delaney." And he turned to leave.

"Why pink?" Sophie asked him, and that stopped Brody in his tracks.

He didn't turn around. He kept his attention focused on the ground. "It was Delaney's favorite color. Do yourself a favor and have Clay tell you what's in those files. If you hope to have a future with him, you need to know."

Clay stood there, watching Brody drive away. He certainly wasn't in the mood for that lap dance. Not in the mood for much of anything except maybe punching a wall. If he thought it would help, that's exactly what he would have done. But there was only one thing that would help right now.

The truth.

He took the box from Sophie, set it on the entry table and riffled through it until he found what he was looking for. The final reports of Delaney's death. Clay took out the file and handed it to her.

Because Brody was right.

In a way.

If Sophie hoped to have a future with him, then yes, she did need to know. They couldn't have this dark secret hanging between them. But it was a double-edged sword. Because if she learned the truth, then she would know one thing for certain.

That there would be no future with him.

"Take it home and read it," Clay told her. He headed for the door and just kept on walking.

WELL, IT WASN'T in a pink envelope, but Sophie had no doubt the file contained things she didn't want to know. She put it on her bed, unopened, and stared at it.

She'd have to open it, of course. When Mila arrived. Sophie would have to read what she didn't want to know. Because Brody was right. She couldn't have this dark secret festering between Clay and her. She only hoped that the cause of the festering was something that Clay could get past.

Something that she could get past, too.

"Sophie?" her mother called out from the other side of her bedroom door. A door that Sophie had locked. Good thing, too, because her mother tried to open it.

"I'm napping," Sophie lied.

In hindsight, it wasn't a good lie since it was eight in the morning. Her mother almost certainly knew that she hadn't slept in her bed because she'd probably heard her come in just fifteen minutes earlier. And her mother had likely guessed that she'd been with Clay all night.

A wonderful, glorious night.

That had been shot to heck with Brody's arrival.

"Mila's here," her mother told her.

That was the only thing her mom could have said to get Sophie moving. She hid the file under a pillow and threw open the door. Thankfully, Mila was standing in front of Belle, and Sophie latched on to her arm and pulled her into the room.

"Mila and I need some girl time alone," Sophie explained to her mother. Definitely not a lie. Sophie wasn't sure she could get through this without her best friend.

Her mother nodded, eyed them with suspicion. "Alice and I are heading to the grocery store. Do you need anything?" There were several unspoken questions mixed in there. Her mom wanted to talk about the possible pregnancy, about Clay. Maybe even about Christmas cookie recipes.

"No, I just need to talk to Mila," Sophie answered. This lie would probably fuel her mother's notion of the pregnancy, but it couldn't be helped. Sophie needed to read the file. Then, she might need a good cry, and she didn't want her mother around for that.

"Why don't you pick up the stuff to make Grandma's peanut butter brownies and her orange chocolate cookies?" Sophie added.

There were at least sixteen ingredients in each recipe and it might even involve a trip to a larger grocery store in San Antonio. That would ensure Sophie got the time she needed. And it wasn't a total wild-goose chase since both would get eaten.

Probably by Sophie herself.

She really did need a less fattening way to manage her stress.

Her mother finally walked away, but Sophie waited several long moments to make sure she was truly gone. When she heard the car pull out of the garage, she drew in a deep breath and took out the folder.

"What is that?" Mila asked.

It was another level of hell, but Mila was obviously looking for something specific. "A police file. It's the reason someone sent me the pink envelope with the photo and the word *killer*."

Mila's eyes widened, but Sophie watched as her friend reined in all her own shock and nerves. "Here, I'll open it for you."

"No, I can do it. I just wasn't sure I could read it."

Mila nodded and watched as Sophie took out the file's contents. There were pictures, one of which she'd already seen of a woman lying dead. Delaney. The other shots were varying angles of the scene, including some close-up pictures of shell casings. There was also a photo of another body. A man this time, and like Delaney he appeared to be lying in a pool of his own blood.

"Do you know why the woman was killed?" Mila asked.

Sophie shook her head. "But she was someone very important to Clay. Her name was Delaney, and her brother is the one who sent me that pink envelope." Heaven knew how many he'd sent to Clay.

She put the pictures aside, facedown, and went to the paperwork. The reports. There were several of them, including some from eyewitnesses. Since she didn't want to have to read about what'd happened more than once, she thumbed through until she found the final report.

And there it was.

All typed out for her to see. She read through it, skimming over the lines as fast as she could, but her heart was beating so hard that she had to stop a moment. Had to level her breathing, too, because it was out of control.

Mila took it from her. "This might be best in condensed form."

Yes, but condensed would also be watered down. "I want to know what happened. *Everything* that happened," Sophie emphasized.

Mila made a yeah-sure sound and continued to read. Whatever was there had to be riveting because not once did Mila take her attention off the page. It felt as if a week or so had passed by the time she finished reading it.

"Holy shit," Mila mumbled. "You want the good news or the bad news first?"

"Bad," Sophie said without hesitation.

But Mila hesitated, and Sophie was about to remind her about the *everything* when she finally spoke. "Her name was Delaney Kincaid. *Detective* Delaney Kincaid," she amended. "She was killed while on an undercover assignment with Houston PD. Clay was the team leader, and they'd gotten a tip on a drug deal. When Delaney, Clay and another officer, Brody Kincaid, arrived on the scene, they were ambushed."

"A setup?"

"Yes. One of the men involved in the deal grabbed Delaney and tried to use her as a human shield." She hesitated again. "Clay shot and killed her."

Someone sucked all the air out of the room, and it was a good thing Sophie was sitting down or she would have fallen.

"Not on purpose, of course," Mila went on. "Clay was

shooting at another of the dealers, and the one holding Delaney pushed her out into the line of fire. She was killed instantly."

All right. That helped a little with the breathing. It'd been an accident. But Sophie knew that Clay wouldn't see it that way.

He'd blame himself.

"You said there was good news?" Sophie asked.

Mila nodded. "Clay was cleared of all charges, and the drug guys were captured."

That was good. But again, Clay wouldn't see things that way. Even if Houston PD felt he didn't deserve punishment, Clay would still punish himself.

Mila slid her hand over Sophie's. "Are you okay?"

"No." There was no sense lying to Mila. She'd save her lies for her mother.

Sophie couldn't just sit there so she got up. She also couldn't go to Clay, not until she'd reined in her emotions and processed what she'd just learned. Besides, he probably had some reining in and processing to do, too.

"I'm going to take one of the horses out for a ride," Sophie said. She kissed Mila on the cheek. "I'll be okay. Go ahead to work or you'll be late."

"I can stay. I can go for a ride with you."

Sophie shook her head and left, going out through the back of the house and straight to the stables. Thankfully, there were no hands around so she saddled Moonlight and rode out. She held back the first tear until she was certain no one would see it.

Especially Clay.

Not that he was anywhere around, but she wouldn't want him to know this had shaken her to the core. If it was doing this to her, she couldn't imagine what it had done to him. And Delaney wasn't the only victim here. Clay and Brody were alive and breathing, but they'd been victims, too.

Moonlight whinnied and turned her head as if checking on Sophie. "I'm all right, girl," she assured the mare.

And she would be. She just had to steady herself and then go to Clay and talk this out. But she couldn't steady herself at home because there was no telling when Alice and her mom would return. They could spot tear-reddened eyes at fifty paces. So, Sophie kept riding, and she headed to Garrett's favorite thinking place.

Z.T.'s old house.

She climbed from the saddle and looped Moonlight's reins around an old hitching post. Sophie hadn't thought it possible, but the house looked worse every time she saw it. This was despite the maintenance the ranch hands did on it from time to time. The purple paint had blistered and was peeling in spots, and there were squirrels skittering across the leaf-strewn porch.

No one had lived here since the sixties when it'd been occupied by her great-aunt Matilda. According to whispers Sophie had heard, Matilda had agoraphobia and had come here to get help from a doctor at the local hospital who'd dealt with that sort of disorder. Apparently, it'd worked because Matilda left after only a few months.

There'd probably be spiders and other critters inside, but maybe during Garrett's recent visits, he'd cleaned up a bit.

He hadn't.

Sophie got proof of that when she went inside. There was a thick coating of dust on the floor. Cobwebs, confirming her spider theory. Judging from the tiny tracks in the dust next to Garrett's footprints, they had a rodent problem, too.

Clearly, this was not a thinking place after all, and she turned to leave when she took another look at the footprints. Garrett had a big foot, a size twelve, and these were smaller. She considered that maybe one of the hands had been out here.

Or Tate.

She took out her phone to text Roman and make sure her nephew hadn't run away again, but the sound stopped her. Not just any old ordinary sound. But someone's voice.

"Sophie," someone said. And it was a voice that she instantly recognized.

Billy Lee Seaver was no longer missing.

WELL, THE SIGHT of Billy Lee was the cure for her tears, that's for sure. Sophie no longer felt weepy, just really, really pissed off.

"Don't run," Billy Lee told her.

Sophie had no intention of running. But she did consider punching him. Not in his face, either, because she wouldn't be able to hit hard enough to hurt him. But a swift kick to the balls should do it.

"And don't call the cops," Billy Lee tacked onto that. "I hadn't planned on you or anyone else seeing me, but now that you're here, we need to talk before you do anything else."

She wasn't sure how she could see him because her eyes had narrowed to the point of being painful, but she saw him start down the stairs. At least someone with Billy Lee's voice did, anyway.

The person was wearing a billowing white nightgown and nightcap that made him look as if he'd stolen Scrooge's clothes. Except Sophie recognized that gown and droopy hat. It had been in a chest of old clothes stored in one of the bedrooms. She'd seen it there when she was a kid. However, she'd never seen Billy Lee's bare legs. They were spindly and stuck out like hairy pretzel sticks from beneath the gown.

"I had to wash my clothes," Billy Lee said as if this were a normal conversation. "They're not dry yet, and it was cold so I put these on."

Her eyelids weren't the only thing narrowed and tight. Her jaw felt like stone.

"I guess you're wondering how I got here," he added.

"I'm wondering a lot of things," she said through clenched teeth. "Where have you been all this time?"

"A hotel at first. One of those fleabag places that didn't cost too much. After that, I bought a truck and have been sleeping in that." He scratched his head around the nightcap. "I drove the truck here, and it's parked out back. I used the old trails to get here so that nobody from the ranch would see me. I've been staying here for the past couple of nights. There's a decent bed in one of the rooms, and there were plenty of blankets in the attic."

She didn't care a rat's droppings about any of this. "What'd you do with the money you stole from us?"

"I didn't steal anything," he insisted.

Sophie made a show of looking him over from head to toe. "Innocent men don't run, hide out and wear garbs like that."

She hadn't meant to add that last part, but it was distracting. And ugly. If Victorian men went to bed looking like that, it's a wonder how they managed to ever impregnate Victorian women.

"Innocent men do if they don't have any other options." On a heavy sigh, Billy Lee sank down, his knees landing wide apart, and she hoped he'd found some spare underpants in that trunk. This visit was already disturbing enough without adding a gross peepshow. Of course, it would make it easier to kick him in the balls if it came to that.

"The FBI doesn't believe you're innocent," she fired back.

"And what about you?" He lifted his head, met her gaze. "Do you honestly believe I'd steal from Garrett and you? You're my goddaughter, for Christ's sake."

Yes, she was. Sophie gave her own heavy sigh. "I don't want to believe it, but Billy Lee, there's a lot of evidence against you. The FBI found proof of embezzlement and money laundering. Did you know that they could have put Garrett and me in jail for that?"

His eyes widened, and while she wanted to believe it was a genuinely surprised reaction, there were still too many unanswered questions.

"What happened?" Sophie demanded.

"Where do I start?" he mumbled. He did another head scratching, encountered the cap again and yanked it off his head. "Shortly before all of our lives took a ride on the highway to hell, I started noticing some anomalies. There were payments for some custom saddles to a start-up company, and on the surface it seemed legit, but the shipments from that company went missing at least half the time."

That was indeed an anomaly. A suspicious one.

"I called one of the accountants, Martin Crowley," Billy Lee continued, "and I asked him to give me all the records on the company. I wanted orders, invoices,

tracking numbers…everything. That was the Friday before your wedding, and he said he would have it for me
by the end of the day. He didn't. So, the next morning,
that Saturday, I went over to the admin building to see
if Crowley had left the report on his desk."

Not a long trip. The admin building was just around
the corner from the main offices, but it was the first Sophie was hearing about any of this.

"Any reason you didn't alert Garrett or me that there
might be a problem?" she asked.

"Because it wasn't a problem. At least I didn't think
it was. I thought we were dealing with a company that
didn't know how to manage its inventory or shipping
channels. It happens. Plus, you were about to get married, or so I thought, and I didn't want to bother you with
it. At that point, I was just looking for what was going
wrong." He paused. "And I found it."

"Found what?' she pressed when he didn't continue.

Billy Lee groaned softly. "There was no sign of a report, but when I booted up Crowley's computer, that's
when I found all kinds of fake files about sales that I
know none of us authorized. And it was my name on
those invoices. Sophie, it was hundreds of thousands of
dollars."

She tried to process that, but her brain was on overload
after looking through the files she'd gotten from Clay.
Still, she wasn't so overloaded that she couldn't think of
what to say because there was a really obvious thing that
Billy Lee should have done.

"Why didn't you call the cops, Garrett or me right
then and there?"

"I'd planned to do just that," he answered without hesitation, "but I kept looking, to see how far all of this went.

I lost track of time, I guess, and then I got a call from Marcum. He said the cops were looking for me, that they thought I'd committed all these crimes. I didn't."

She looked for holes in that story and soon found one. "Why didn't you show the cops what was on Crowley's computer?"

"Crowley had set up a virus or something because while I was talking to Marcum, they disappeared. He deleted them off the server."

"Those files turned up on your own computer," Sophie pointed out.

"Yes, but I didn't put them there. That's why I ran. I knew I was being set up and would be arrested. I couldn't go to jail, Sophie. You know how I am about closed-in spaces."

She did. Billy Lee was definitely claustrophobic along with being seriously squeamish around anyone who farted. "That doesn't explain why you didn't call Garrett or me."

"Because I was trying to keep you two out of it. I wanted to go into hiding and catch Crowley."

"Trust me—you didn't keep us out of it." She huffed. "The FBI has investigated everyone who had a connection to Granger Western. Including Garrett and me. And I'm sure they've looked at Crowley and every computer ever associated with the business."

"I need them to look again. I was going to tell Arlo all of this so he could pass it along to the FBI, but now that you know, you can tell them."

"Arlo?" That gave her a new surge of anger, and the ball-kicking idea was regaining ground. "You planned to talk to him and not Garrett or me?"

His gaze darted from hers. "I didn't figure either of

you wanted to hear anything I had to say. Plus, I'm... embarrassed."

"Well, you should be. Not just for not telling us this before now but for those god-awful clothes you're wearing."

"Sophie?" someone called out.

Clay.

That caused her to freeze, and she wished Billy Lee had frozen, too, but he didn't. He jumped up from the stairs and wasn't mindful of the way the movement would swish the gown.

And he was commando.

Good gravy. Talk about an image she couldn't unsee.

"Sophie?" Clay, again.

"Put on your clothes," Sophie ordered Billy Lee, and she went outside and onto the porch. She was ready to blurt out that Billy Lee was there, but the words sort of died on her lips when she saw him.

Clay was riding up on one of the horses from the stables. She'd seen him in cowboy mode before, of course, but the sight of him today caused her mouth to go a little dry. Maybe because he wasn't just a cowboy cop, he was her cowboy cop *lover*. And she got a rush of all that attraction that had sent her to his bed.

But it didn't last.

Because that troubled look on his face trumped her lustful thoughts and attraction-rush.

"I was worried about you," he said, getting off the horse. "Mila dropped by the office and said you were upset and crying."

"I didn't cry in front of Mila," she grumbled. But her friend knew her well enough to know the tears would come. She couldn't exactly deny that she'd been crying, either, since her eyes were almost certainly red and puffy.

"I came right over to the ranch," Clay added before she could say anything else. "And one of the hands told me he saw you riding out in this direction. He said you hadn't been gone long so I saddled up and came to find you."

Of course, someone had seen her. Despite the ranch being hundreds and hundreds of acres, it was almost impossible to find a hiding place. Even Billy Lee hadn't found one for long.

Clay came up the steps toward her. "You read the file."

She nodded, and while this conversation was important, it would have to wait. Sophie fluttered her fingers to the inside of the house. "I found Billy Lee."

Clay pulled back his shoulders, cursed and bolted past her. Even over the sound of his footsteps on the creaky floors, she heard something else.

An engine.

Mercy, no. Billy Lee couldn't be running.

Sophie was, though. So was Clay, and they followed the footprints in the dust to the back door. Which was wide-open. About ten yards away, she spotted a black truck. The one that Billy Lee had obviously parked in a cluster of trees.

But it was no longer parked.

Billy Lee was speeding away.

CHAPTER EIGHTEEN

CLAY CURSED AGAIN, something he'd been doing all day. First, over Brody's showing up at his house, then Mila's visit to tell him how upset Sophie was over that file and now Billy Lee's disappearing act.

If Clay had been in his truck instead of on horseback, he could have caught up to the man and hauled him in. Or at least gotten close enough to read the license plate. But the horse hadn't been much competition for Billy Lee's truck, and the former CFO was on the lam again.

Clay cursed now because there'd been no reports of anyone seeing Billy Lee in the four hours he'd been gone, and Rowdy, the deputy, hadn't found anything inside Z.T.'s old house to indicate where Billy Lee might be heading. However, Rowdy had found the man's pants, underwear and shirt drying on a makeshift clothesline in an upstairs bedroom. If Billy Lee was still wearing the garb that Sophie had described, then the moment he stepped out of his truck, he'd draw attention. If there was anyone around with attention to draw, that is. There were plenty of woods and trails where he could hide.

"You still there?" Mike asked, coming back on the line. Clay wasn't sure how long the agent had had him on hold, but he hoped it was worth the wait.

"I'm here. Did you find out anything on Martin Crowley?" Clay had reported to Mike everything that Billy

Lee had told Sophie, including the name of the man that Billy Lee thought was responsible for the financial fiasco.

"I'd already investigated Crowley, of course, but I'm taking another look at him. Specifically looking to see if there's any trace of those computer files that Billy Lee claims he saw."

Mike didn't sound convinced of Billy Lee's innocence. Neither was Clay, but he went back to one of his original questions. "Where's the money? Because Billy Lee certainly isn't living like a man who's sitting on a fortune."

"The money trail might be impossible to trace. Billy Lee, Crowley or whoever's responsible could have it stashed in offshore accounts. Or it could have been laundered in small enough amounts not to be noticed."

Yeah, Clay knew all of that, but it still didn't make sense. "Billy Lee would have held back enough cash for living expenses."

And maybe he had. Maybe he'd already blown through what he had and for some reason couldn't access his other funds. Hell, maybe someone had stolen the money from him. There really wasn't much honor among thieves.

"I'm bringing Crowley in for questioning in a couple of hours," Mike went on. "I can pressure him, make him believe I have some evidence against him, but I've got squat unless something new turns up about those computer files Billy Lee says he saw."

Clay knew that, too, but sometimes people broke during interrogation. Sometimes, they just lawyered up. If Crowley did that, it might put a guilty light on him, but that didn't mean it would clear Billy Lee of anything.

There was a knock on his door, and Clay was about to shout out that he didn't want visitors. But the door opened, and Sophie stuck her head inside.

"Got a minute?" she asked.

No, he didn't, but he nodded anyway. "Call me after you've talked to Crowley," Clay told Mike, and he ended the call.

Sophie stepped into his office and closed the door behind her. Her eyes were no longer red from crying, but Clay figured her troubled look pretty much mirrored his.

"I can't stay long," she said. "I'm on my way to talk to Mila. I want her to start texting me whenever she's on one of her fantasy dates. Just so I'll know she's okay. But I wanted to drop by and see if there was anything new on Billy Lee."

"Nothing. Something might turn up on Crowley, though." He wouldn't get into the slim-to-none chance of that happening.

"I've been going over everything Billy Lee said." She stopped and shook her head. "I want to believe him."

Clay was sure she did, but there was doubt in her voice. "If he's innocent, he probably wouldn't have run," Clay reminded her. "And yes, I know about his claustrophobia. Arlo mentioned it. But he must know what you and your family have been through. That should have outweighed the phobia."

"Yes, you'd think that." Again there was doubt but not as much as Clay had expected there to be. "But Billy Lee's always been an odd duck, which you probably also guessed since his closest friends were a guy who never bathes and my father, a man few people liked."

Yeah, he had guessed that, but he wasn't giving Billy Lee any passes here. "At least we know he's in the area, and if he's as short on cash as he appears to be, he should turn up soon."

Now that Clay had addressed that, he needed to get

something else off his chest. "Mila said you might be suicidal," he explained. "That's why I hurried out to the ranch."

Sophie frowned. "She told you that to get you to do exactly what you did—hurry to me. She wants us to kiss and make up."

He felt the tension in his stomach ease up a bit. Sophie hadn't seemed like the suicide type, but then Clay knew he'd dumped a nightmare in the form of old baggage right in her lap.

"Mila wouldn't want that if she knew what was in that file," Clay pointed out.

"She does know. She was with me when I opened it." Sophie went to him, gripped his arms and kissed his cheek. "Clay, I'm so sorry." Then, she kissed him on the mouth.

Sorry? That wasn't the right response. She should have been disgusted with him. And she darn sure shouldn't have been kissing him. It had to stop, and Clay thought he knew the fastest way to do that.

"You need to know something else about Delaney," he confessed. "I was in love with her."

She nodded. "I suspected as much. That's probably why you took her death so hard."

Again, that wasn't the right response. Clay huffed. "You should be horrified that I shot and killed the woman I loved. The sight of me should send you running to find someone suitable to live out that life plan of yours. Because I'm not life plan material, Sophie."

She waited a second, then two. "Are you finished?" She sounded annoyed or something.

"No. I'm not. You shouldn't have just kissed me, either.

Save your kisses for Mr. Right because I'm as wrong for you as wrong can get. We can never be together. *Never.*"

Sophie waited another couple of seconds. "Never is a really long time."

She moved as if to kiss him again. She didn't. And Clay hated that he felt disappointed by that. After the speech he'd just given her, he should have been glad she was backing away.

And she was doing just that.

"Okay, then," she finally said. "Have a nice life, Clay."

Sophie didn't argue with him. Didn't tell him he could possibly be wrong. She just walked out, leaving him to wonder what the hell he'd just done.

SOPHIE FIGURED SHE deserved some kind of award for holding it together while she made her way out of the police station. Three mental punches in the same day. The case file on Delaney, Billy Lee and now this.

She certainly had the right to cry, but she forced back the tears until she was up the block. Then she ducked into an alley and prayed no one saw her boo-hooing all over the place.

After learning what was in that file, she should have guessed that Clay would push her away. And he had done just that. She'd also figured it would hurt. She just hadn't counted on feeling as if a herd of cattle had just stampeded on her heart. But it did.

God, it did.

She turned her back to the sidewalk just in case anyone came by, and she fished through her purse to find a tissue. She found one all right just as she dropped her purse, and everything went flying. Wallet, makeup, an old candy bar, along with assorted change, cough drops and condoms that she'd snagged from Garrett's room. Condoms that she wouldn't need.

That didn't help slow down the tears.

To reduce her dignity even more, she had to sink down on her knees in the dirty alley while she tried to gather up her stuff. Not an easy feat with tear-filled eyes and a nose that needed blowing.

Part of her wanted to go running back to Clay and try to convince him that he was wrong, that he could be life plan material, that they could put those condoms to good use. But she wasn't certain her heart could stand another round of rejection. And maybe he was right about her needing to move on.

That caused her to sob even harder.

Because she didn't want him to be right. She didn't want to move on.

"Sophie?" someone said.

Bird crap. It was April. The last person in the cosmos that she wanted to see right now.

"Uh, are you okay?" April asked.

April couldn't see her face so her crying must have been pretty darn loud for her to hear it and ask that question. Especially ask that question with a gallon of concern in her voice. April's voice, or any other part of her for that matter, had never had much concern for Sophie.

"I'm fine." The lie just rolled off her tongue, and Sophie tried to make sure there wasn't an audible sob. "I... just have a headache."

She'd started to say she had the stomach flu and was about to vomit. In her experience that usually got people backing away fast, but Sophie didn't want to lie about anything intestinal for fear that it would be taken as a pregnancy symptom. No use continuing to weave that web.

Unfortunately, a headache lie didn't work as well as the vomit threat because Sophie heard April walking toward her. She also heard the pitter-patter of little feet, which meant the twins were almost certainly with her. The only good side to that was maybe April wouldn't have a full-blown hissy fit.

And speaking of blowing, Sophie managed to do that to her nose before April stepped in front of her. Nothing she could do about the red eyes so she kept the tissue in front of her face.

The twins were indeed with April. She had one in her arms. Hayden. And she had her hand clamped around Hunter.

"Soapy," Hayden greeted.

Sophie hadn't been sure the little boy even knew her name, but he obviously did. Or else there was something on her face that made him think of suds.

"He knows you?" April asked. That concern was no longer in her voice.

Sophie didn't feel right lying about this in front of the boys so she nodded. "I was at Clay's when they were there. Briefly there," she added. And she waited for the fallout. No way was April going to like that.

But while April might not have liked it, she didn't launch into verbal fire. She just studied Sophie's face a moment longer though the tissue had to be taking up most of the surface area.

"Is Clay the reason you're crying?" April asked.

Since that sounded, well, almost friendly, Sophie lowered the tissue. Plus, it was making it hard for her to breathe. "It's been a tough day," Sophie settled for saying. "And I really need to be going—"

April sighed. "You can't go out there on the sidewalk

now. Someone will see you crying, then see me, and I'll get blamed for upsetting you again." She looked ready to blink back her own tears. "People in this town hate me."

"No. They don't."

It was only a partial lie. Some disliked her because they felt loyal to the Grangers. Others just liked that the whole April-Brantley-Clay-Sophie quadrangle was giving them some good gossip fodder. But it was true that April would get the blame if anyone walked by and witnessed this.

"You are crying over Clay," April said, and it wasn't a question.

"Nunk!" Hunter hollered, and for another heart-stopping moment, Sophie thought he had joined them in the alley. But he wasn't there, thank God. Right now, only one adult and two toddlers had witnessed her like this.

"We'll see Nunk in a few minutes," April told the boy, maybe with the hopes that it would stop him from trying to tear his hand from hers. It didn't. Hunter was obviously in the all-velocity no-vector mode.

"Clay's had a troubled past," April said to Sophie, and she was no doubt choosing her words carefully.

Sophie chose her response carefully, too, and just nodded.

Apparently that was enough to prompt April to continue. "I haven't helped with that. I guess he told you that he raised me after our folks died? And you probably guessed that I didn't always do what he wanted me to do."

It seemed a good time for another nod. "He loves you."

Now, it was April's turn to nod, and Hunter nearly tore her arm from the socket when he tried to bolt. "I said we'll see Nunk in a few minutes," she repeated to Hunter, but it did nothing to settle the boy.

Though she really didn't want to do anything to prolong this chat, April was obviously struggling. "You want me to hold Hayden so you can hang on to Hunter?" Sophie asked.

Hayden must have taken that as his cue to hold out his arms and go to her. Sophie took him from April but then wanted to kick herself when April got a strange look on her face.

"Most people can't tell them apart," April remarked.

"If they were both asleep, I wouldn't be able to tell, either. And really it was still a guess on my part," Sophie continued. She just kept on continuing, too. "I mean, it's not as if I've spent much time around them or anything. It was only that time outside the café and then that short visit at Clay's."

She wouldn't dare ask if Hayden's fever was okay, but she touched her cheek to his to check. His temp seemed normal.

"I was only with them a few minutes at Clay's," the prattle continued. Sophie wouldn't mention seeing Brantley, either. Or the disturbing, poop-head things Brantley had said. "But even though I haven't been around the boys much, they seem like sweet kids."

April finally interrupted Sophie's babble-thon. "I know you've been seeing my brother. And no, I'm not happy about that." She huffed, glanced around and blinked back more tears. Hunter gave her another hard yank, and she scooped him up in her arms.

"It's over between Clay and me," Sophie assured her.

Just saying it felt as if those cows had returned for another heart-stampede. It was stupid, really, because Clay and she hadn't been together that long. But her feelings for him had been...

Like a lightning bolt.

That's the way Brantley had described how he felt about April, and Sophie got that now. Man, did she get it. And it hurt like the devil.

Sophie gave her eyes another wipe, and Hayden helped, too, by kissing her cheek. "All bebber now," he said as if he'd just kissed a boo-boo.

Sophie brushed a kiss on the top of his head as well and hoped that didn't rile April. It didn't. But April didn't exactly have a pleasant expression. Her forehead was bunched up, and the muscles in her face were tight.

"What's wrong?" Sophie asked, and she glanced around to make sure they didn't have an audience, especially an audience that included Clay and/or anyone with the surname of Granger.

April clutched her left hand to her stomach. "Oh, God. You need to take me to the hospital. I think I might be having a miscarriage."

CHAPTER NINETEEN

THIS WAS YET another level of hell that Sophie hadn't known existed until today. But she was certain it was nothing compared to what April had to be feeling right now.

"Mommy o-tay?" Hayden asked.

Sophie wasn't a pro at toddlerspeak, but she could see how worried the little boy was. He might not be old enough to pronounce okay correctly, but he was certainly old enough to understand that something was wrong. Even Hunter had settled down, and his nervous gaze was darting all around the hospital waiting room.

"Your mommy's okay," Sophie reassured Hayden, and she prayed that it was true.

Immediately after April had started having pains, Sophie had gotten her and the boys loaded into April's car and driven them to the hospital. Sophie had considered calling an ambulance, but since it was deer season, and Burt Monroe, the town's only ambulance driver, was a big-time hunter, she didn't know how long it would take him to respond. Plus, the hospital was only a couple minutes away.

Those minutes had felt like an eternity.

The moments that followed hadn't exactly sped by, either, despite the fact that the nurse had whisked April away to an examining room as soon as they'd stepped into the ER. The nurse's only instructions to Sophie had been to "wait here." So, Sophie was doing just that.

Waiting sucked, though.

Hayden was on her lap, and Sophie had her arm around Hunter so he could be near his brother and maybe get some comfort from that. She also tried calling Brantley and Clay again. Her second attempt for each. But all went straight to voice mail, including the call she'd made to Mila. Sophie left messages for all of them.

"Mommy got boo-boo?" Hayden asked. He looked up at Sophie, and she saw the shiny tears pooling in his eyes.

Poor kid. And even though Hunter wasn't crying, yet, he probably would if his brother started. Sophie glanced around, looking for anything she could use to distract them. There wasn't much. The only magazine within reach had a scantily clad actress on the cover, along with articles entitled: "Hot-Tush Exercises," "Sex Q&A" and "Go For It In Bed!"

She pushed aside the reminder she got of "going for it" with Clay and snatched up the magazine. Certainly, there were some pictures inside that were suitable for kids.

Or not.

It took some thumbing—which wasn't easy with the boys coiled around her—but she finally found a men's cologne ad that featured a shirtless guy in leather pants straddling a motorcycle.

"He looks like my brother Roman," Sophie said. He didn't. This guy looked a little prissy, and there was nothing prissy about Roman, but she had to work with what she had. "And Roman rides a motorcycle like that. It goes really fast and makes a lot of noise."

Until she added that last part, the boys hadn't shown any interest, but they looked now.

She pointed to the handlebars. "That's how you make a motorcycle go fast," she continued. "And Roman's good at making it go fast." He had the speeding tickets to prove it, too.

"Roman coming here?" Hunter asked. Or rather "Roamin' tomin' here?"

"I wish. But no."

Though she did consider calling him. If Garrett and Lawson hadn't been out of town on a cattle buying trip, they would have been on her "get here now" request loop. She didn't have Spike's number so that left her mother, and Sophie would have to reach at least one more level of hell before she phoned her.

"What kind of sound do you think a motorcycle makes?" she asked when Hunter started to squirm.

He attempted it with a *grr grr grr*. Hayden just snuggled closer to her and asked for his mommy. Even though it'd only been a couple of minutes since she'd called Brantley, she tried him again.

Voice mail.

She left another message telling him to get to the hospital faster than ASAP. Where the heck was he, anyway? Of course, since Brantley was a lawyer, it was possible he was with a client or in court. Sophie hadn't spoken to his assistant, Jana Somerfield, since before the jilting fiasco, but she thumbed through her phone, looking for the woman's number. However, before she could find it, the ER doors swung open, and Mila came rushing in.

"Sorry, but I was with a customer and couldn't get to my phone," Mila said right off. "As soon as I listened to your message, I closed up shop and got here as fast as I could." She hurried to Sophie. "Is April all right?"

"Yes." Sophie tried to add a smile to that, but she was

certain she failed. "Mommy will be just fine," she told the boys. "And I'm sure the doctor will tell us that her tummy pains are nothing to be worried about."

But Sophie was worried, and Mila clearly was, too. And her worry apparently wasn't just limited to April.

"You were reading that to them?" Mila asked, tipping her head to the magazine.

"No, not really. I was just showing them a picture of a motorcycle."

"Like Roman," Hunter added.

Mila looked at the picture, frowned and took something from her purse. A kids' book that had bunnies on the cover. Much more appropriate than a bikini model and tush exercises.

"I grabbed this on my way out," Mila said, and the moment she opened the book, Hunter crawled into her lap. Even Hayden perked up a little and moved in closer to her so he could see the pages.

Sophie could have kissed her. Good best friends could make even a level of hell better.

She took out her phone again, ready to make another attempt to call Brantley, but that's when the nurse came out of the examining room. Her name was Wanda Kay Busby, and her brothers were the town's troublemakers. They liked to joke that they picked up the slack now that Roman no longer lived there.

"She's asking to see you," Wanda Kay said.

It took Sophie a moment to realize that Wanda Kay meant her and not the boys. "Me?"

Wanda Kay lifted her shoulder in a yeah-I'm-surprised-too gesture, nodded and motioned for Sophie to follow her. "She first asked for Brantley, then her brother. When I told her they weren't here and that the kids couldn't be with her in the examining room, she wanted you instead. Nothing like being fifth choice to make you feel special, huh?"

Sophie was about to point out that this wasn't a time for snottiness, but she didn't want to get into it with the likes of Wanda Kay Busby.

"I can watch the boys," Mila volunteered.

Sophie thanked her, passed off Hayden to Mila and got to her feet. "Is April okay?" she asked Wanda Kay once they were out of earshot from the boys.

"Can't really discuss it, privacy and such, but knowing the other things she's done, she could be faking it to get attention." Wanda Kay smiled as if Sophie would jump to agree with that.

She didn't. "April was in pain when I drove her here."

"Well, pain can be faked. Anybody who'd steal a woman's fiancé is capable of just about anything."

"Not this," she assured Wanda Kay, but it gave Sophie a glimpse into what April had been dealing with for the past eight months.

Wanda Kay opened the door to the examining room, ushered Sophie inside, but she didn't leave. The nurse hovered in the doorway, probably hoping for a catfight. If there was such a fight, it was going to be between Sophie and Wanda Kay. Sophie didn't like her attitude.

April was lying on the examining table, a thin pillow beneath her head, and she had some kind of monitoring belt across her stomach. She was also crying. Sophie went to her, but since a hug didn't seem appropriate, she took some tissues from a nearby cart and dabbed away April's tears.

"Are the boys all right?" April asked.

"They're doing great. Mila will keep them entertained.

All you need to do is rest and get better. How are you feeling? Is there anything I can get you?"

April sniffed back more tears. "I'm so scared. I don't want to lose this baby."

"And you won't. Women go through this sort of thing all the time and still deliver healthy babies." Sophie had zero knowledge about that, but it seemed the right thing to say.

"Why are you being so nice to me?" April asked.

"Yeah, why are you?" Wanda Kay grumbled.

Sophie shot the nurse a glare. "Why don't you get April some water or something?" she said to the nurse.

Wanda Kay huffed, shot her own glare at Sophie and finally walked away.

"Why are you being nice to me?" April repeated.

"Because I guess I'm a nice person." She lifted her shoulder. "Most of the time, anyway, in situations that don't involve my immediate family." Sophie did some more tear dabbing. "Are you still in pain?"

"Not as much. My OB's on his way to check me out. Deer season," she added in a grumble. "It shouldn't be long now. The other doctor examined me, drew some blood and said he'd be back in here soon to let me know what's going on. God, I wish Brantley was here."

"He will be soon." At least he'd better be. After the things she'd heard him say to Clay, Sophie hoped Brantley had found the pair that she'd told him to grow.

"And Clay," April said. "I want my brother here, too." She stopped, clamped her teeth over her bottom lip for a moment. "I'm sorry. You probably don't want to see him."

Wrong. Sophie would love to see him for no other reason than because April needed him. If she had been going through something like this, she would have wanted Garrett and Roman by her bedside.

April's gaze dropped to Sophie's stomach. "You're not pregnant, are you?"

"No." She was certain April wouldn't believe her since no one else had, but the woman nodded. That gesture was like some kind of green light to Sophie because she just continued with the confession. "But I am sneaking around and having sex with your brother. Well, I was. As you probably already figured out, he broke up with me."

April nodded. "Because of Delaney?"

Sophie's gaze stayed connected with April's for a few seconds before she answered, "You knew her?"

"Oh, yes. I'm pretty sure if Delaney had lived, they would have gotten married. But she was wrong for him. An adrenaline junkie, always taking risks. Clay's not much of a risk taker."

"I noticed."

"Funny, considering he's a cop." April gave her a short-lived smile. "Plus, there's the problem with your eyes. How did Clay get past that?"

Sophie was certain she'd missed something in this conversation. "My eyes?"

"Yes, they're almost identical in color to Delaney's. I'm betting that gave him a jolt when he first saw you."

Sophie didn't have to think hard to remember that meeting with Clay and the ones that had followed shortly thereafter. He'd always looked away from her. And when he'd kissed her in her car, he'd asked her to close her eyes first. Now, she knew why. God, it's a wonder he hadn't just avoided her altogether.

"You think seeing my eyes triggered bad memories of Delaney?" Sophie asked.

"Probably. But he'd never fess up to anything like that on his own. Not Clay. He'd just learn to live with it. Which it seems he must have done." She paused. "He really hurt you, didn't he?"

Best not to admit that whole cattle stampede feeling in her chest. "I cared a lot for him. Still do," Sophie corrected. Obviously, she was still in confession mode, and she hoped that Wanda Kay wasn't outside the door listening to this.

April slid her hand over Sophie's. "I'm sorry. For everything." But April's touch was like her smile. It didn't last long, and she quickly jerked it away and returned it to her stomach. "Oh my God."

And that's how Brantley found them when he came storming into the room. His attention volleyed from Sophie to April and then back to Sophie again.

"What are you doing in here?" Brantley howled, glaring at Sophie. "Did you upset April?"

Sophie was so stunned by the accusation that she could only shake her head. April couldn't clear it up, either, because she was moaning in pain.

"Wanda Kay?" Sophie called out. As expected, the nurse was right there, just behind Brantley.

"I already paged the doctor," Wanda Kay assured her. "He'll be here in a few seconds."

Brantley hurried to April, easing down next to her, but he shifted his glare to Wanda Kay. "How could you let Sophie in here? You know what's gone on between April and her."

All right. Enough of this. Sophie was still stunned but no longer to the point of not being able to defend herself. "April asked to see me."

"I did," April muttered through the groans. "Sophie

had some things to tell me. I know she was with Clay last night when you went to pick up the boys."

The glare Brantley had given Wanda Kay was a drop in the bucket compared to the one he now gave Sophie. He stood and walked toward Sophie. "Did you tell April what I said to Clay? Did you?"

"What did you tell Clay?" April asked. And it was obvious she wanted an answer now because she repeated the "What?"

And that's how Clay found them when he came into the room.

CLAY HADN'T EXPECTED this to be a pleasant visit, what with Sophie's frantic messages to get to the hospital, but he hadn't counted on walking into both a firestorm and a hornets' nest.

First things first, he went to his sister, glancing at the monitor that was next to the table. He had no idea what the device was, but it appeared to be monitoring the baby's heartbeat. The good news was there was a heartbeat. The bad news was obviously something had gone wrong if his sister was here.

Since April looked ready to repeat her question for a third time, Clay stopped her with a question of his own. "How are you?"

That caused some tears to spill down April's cheeks. Not her first tears, either, and since it was obvious that Sophie had been crying, too, he wanted to know what had happened.

"I started having pains, and Sophie drove me to the hospital," April said, and she looked at Brantley. "And she didn't upset me. You have, though. Because you took so long to get here and now you won't tell me what you said to Clay."

"I was in court," Brantley explained. He didn't offer anything else, though, on the second part of April's beef.

"I want to know," April insisted.

She clearly wouldn't let this go. But she was going to have to do just that because while Sophie might not have upset her, hearing what Brantley had said surely would. Brantley and Sophie knew that as well, and they weren't jumping to provide April with an answer. Thankfully, they got a reprieve when Dr. Alan Sanchez came into the room and went to April, checking both her and the monitor.

"I need you two to leave while I examine April again," the doctor said to Sophie and Clay. He glanced at Brantley. "You can stay."

Clay had to hand it to Brantley. He didn't look as if he wanted to be sent out of the room, too, though it would have been a way to stall April. Brantley stayed right by April's side and took her hand.

Sophie and Clay stepped out into the hall just as Wanda Kay entered the examining room, and she shut the door in their faces. It didn't take long for the uncomfortable silence to start.

"I was out at Arlo's cabin, looking for Billy Lee," he explained, though he'd repeat this to April once they had a chance to talk. "No cell service out there so I didn't get your message until I was back in my truck. I got here as fast as I could."

Sophie lifted her shoulder. Didn't look at him. In fact, she looked everywhere but at him. She also didn't ask him if he'd found Billy Lee. Of course, he hadn't expected her to be in a friendly or chatty mood after the conversation they'd had in his office. And after what she'd just been through with April.

"Thank you for driving April here," he continued. "And for arranging for Mila to be with the boys. They really seem to like her."

Another shoulder lift from Sophie, and the uncomfortable silence went up a notch. Clay didn't know how long it would take the doctor to examine April, but it was already starting to feel as if it were taking a week.

"I really didn't say anything to April to upset her," Sophie finally muttered.

"I didn't think you had. You're too nice to do something like that."

A third shoulder lift and zero eye contact. Though it would have been smart just to let this be, Clay wasn't usually in smart mode when he was around Sophie. He took hold of her arm and turned her to face him. Even then she didn't look at him so he lifted her chin.

And she closed her eyes.

"April told me about Delaney," she said. "About her eyes being the same color as mine."

Hell. He hated to curse his sister when she was in the hospital, but he silently did it anyway. "She shouldn't have brought that up."

"No, but you should have. You should have told me that it triggered bad memories for you."

He wasn't sure how to answer that so Clay went with, "I don't like to talk about it."

"Obviously, but if you'd told me, I could have worn colored contacts or put on sunglasses whenever I was around you."

Now Clay silently cursed himself. Yes, Sophie would

have gone to the extreme like that, but it hadn't been necessary.

"At first, your eyes did bother me," he admitted. "But then…they didn't. Delaney's and your eyes aren't identical. They're just similar. And I just started focusing on the parts that were different."

Now they weren't Delaney's eyes. They were Sophie's. That didn't mean it made everything better. This wasn't a boo-boo that could be kissed away.

She finally looked at him, no doubt examining him to see his reaction. Clay tried not to have one. He especially tried not to have one that would give Sophie any hope of this relationship working out.

"Sneaky sex has its consequences," she said, looking away again. This time, though, he didn't think it had anything to do with triggering bad memories.

"Yes, and I'm sorry. I knew it was a mistake to get involved with you, and I did it anyway."

"A mistake," she repeated. It didn't sound as if she agreed with that.

Nope, she didn't.

And when she looked at him again, there was some fire in her eyes. Uh-oh. She was about to blast him for what he'd just said, but whatever she was about to say was put on hold when they heard the voices in the examining room. Specifically, April's voice, and he heard it because it was at a volume slightly louder than the normal conversational level.

"Why would you say something like that to Clay?" April snarled. "Do you really feel that way?"

That was another uh-oh.

Clay couldn't hear Brantley's response, but he hoped

his brother-in-law was doing some serious groveling coupled with some huge apologies.

The door opened, and judging from the doctor's expression, he wasn't pleased about the chat he'd almost certainly overheard between April and Brantley.

"Get out!" April snapped. And she aimed that snap at her husband.

"Yes, get out," the doctor concurred.

Brantley looked as if someone had drained him of any hope, but he walked out into the hall with Clay and Sophie. Both gave him a frosty glare.

"You should have lied," Sophie whispered. "You shouldn't have upset your pregnant wife, especially when she might be on the verge of miscarrying."

Clay and the doctor made sounds of agreement, but Clay wished he could add to that by punching Brantley in the face. The man's timing absolutely sucked.

"I'm fairly sure April's not miscarrying," the doctor said. "The contractions are what we call Braxton Hicks. They're painful, but since she's not spotting, I believe the baby and she will be okay. I am going to admit her to the hospital, though. Just for an overnight stay so I can keep an eye on her and run some more tests."

"Thank God," Sophie mumbled. Clay thanked him, too. Even though the pregnancy wasn't planned, he knew how much April wanted this baby.

The doctor gave each of them a glance. "I think it's for the best if you all leave."

"I'm not going anywhere," Brantley insisted. "I'll wait here in case April wants to talk."

"Suit yourself," the doctor said, "but you won't go within ten feet of her unless she agrees, understand?"

He waited until Brantley agreed before turning back to Clay. "You'll take care of the twins?"

Clay nodded. "I just have to let my deputies know what's going on."

The doctor told April that he'd be right back after he got those tests ordered, and he headed up the hall.

"I have April's car," Sophie said, "and I can drive the boys to your house if you want to say goodbye to your sister."

Everything considered, it was generous of her. He took his house key from his key chain and handed it to her. However, Sophie didn't leave. She caught onto Wanda Kay's arm as the nurse was walking out, and she got right in Wanda Kay's face.

"If you're not nice to April…" Sophie whispered. It was a mean whisper, too. "I'll tell everyone you gave blow jobs to the entire football team…and you did it before they'd even showered."

Wanda Kay's eyes widened to the size of dinner plates. "You wouldn't."

Sophie let go of the woman's arm, and her index finger landed against Wanda Kay's chest. "Yes, I would. And guess what? Everyone will believe me because I'm Sophie Granger."

Clay had no idea what had gone on before he'd gotten there, but he wanted to give Sophie an *atta girl*. He didn't get a chance to say anything, though, because Sophie stormed off.

"I didn't do that to the football team," Wanda Kay said to him. "And I wasn't nice to April because she stole another woman's fella."

Clay gave her the coldest stare he could manage, which wasn't hard to do since right now he was feeling pretty damn cold. "If you're not *nice* to my sister, I'll not only confirm what Sophie said, I'll tell everyone you swallowed."

Wanda Kay gasped, and the color in her face turned an unflattering shade of red before she turned tail and headed up the hall. Clay made a mental note to request another nurse after he talked with his sister.

"Please tell April I'm sorry and that I didn't mean what I said to you," Brantley begged. At least he was following the doctor's rules and didn't go near the door to the examining room.

Clay considered several ways to respond. Most would include some profanity. But one look at his sister's tear-streaked face, and he only nodded. For reasons he didn't understand April seemed to love Brantley, and he needed to help them work this out. Not just for their sakes but for this baby.

"I'll tell her," Clay settled for saying, and he went into the examining room, closing the door behind him.

"I heard him," April mumbled the moment Clay sat down beside her. Fresh tears sprang to her eyes, and since Clay wanted to put a stop to them, he said something that he hoped would help.

"Brantley really is sorry. He wants to make this marriage work." If that wasn't true, then Clay would help April pick up the pieces. Again. Hell, he'd do it a thousand times because she was his sister and even though she drove him crazy, he loved her.

"Are you really okay?" Clay asked her.

"I'm better now. The pain isn't so bad. I just wish I could see the boys, but the doctor said not until tomorrow. Are they all right? Did you see them?"

"I saw them when I came through the waiting room.

They were making bunny sounds while Mila read them a book."

"Bunnies make sounds?"

"According to Hunter they do. They sound like a motorcycle." One that "Roaming" rode.

She nodded, seemed relieved. Clay was a little relieved, too, but it might take a while for his heart rate to settle down.

"You scared me," he admitted. "When I heard Sophie's message that you were in the hospital, I forgot about some of your hardheadedness and ass-wipe mistakes and remembered that I love you."

That got the reaction he wanted. She punched him on the arm. Acceptable violence between siblings. "I learned my hardheadedness from you," she fired back. "And I'm not the only one who makes ass-wipe mistakes."

He suspected they were talking about Sophie now. He wanted to ask exactly what had gone on between the two women to bring on this change of heart, but there were other things on his want-to-know list.

"You told her about Delaney's eyes. Why?" he asked. Clay made sure he didn't sound angry. Easy to do because he wasn't. However, he was frustrated, not just about April's situation with Brantley but also because he'd hurt Sophie. Definitely an ass-wipe mistake.

"I thought Sophie already knew. I just figured you came clean with her before you had sex with her."

Clay figured he shouldn't be surprised that April knew he'd been sleeping with Sophie. Probably everyone within a hundred miles knew. But, no. He hadn't told Sophie about Delaney's eyes. In fact, Sophie and he had had sex several times before he'd given her that file to read. That seemed like a lifetime ago, but it had only been hours in this hellishly long day.

"I broke things off with Sophie," he went on. "Did she mention anything about it to you?"

April nodded, touched her fingers to the tight muscles in his forehead. "She *mentioned* a lot of things. Want me to tell you what she told me?"

Clay didn't like that look in his sister's eyes and was about to decline, but she caught onto the front of his shirt, pulled him closer.

And April told him all right.

CHAPTER TWENTY

THE CHICKENS WERE there when Clay got home. Right by the front porch steps. It was as if fate wanted to punctuate the day from hell with yet one more hellish obstacle.

Sophie was there, as well. At least he thought she was when he spotted April's car parked by the side of the house. She was no doubt inside with the boys. Because it'd been three hours since she'd left the hospital with them, she would probably be ready to run the moment he stepped inside. The boys could be a handful. Of course, Hayden and Hunter might not be the only reason she wanted to run.

She probably wanted to see as little of him as possible.

If what April had told him was right—and the jury was still out on that—then Sophie and his sister had had quite a talk at the hospital. And Sophie had said things that she'd never said to him. Things that he wouldn't have been especially receptive to hearing.

Like, *I love you.*

Why the heck would Sophie have admitted something like that to April? And since he was asking himself questions—why would Sophie have allowed it to happen? She'd known from the start that he was emotionally bad news, and he hadn't exactly been Mr. Sunshine around here.

Yeah, the jury was still out on that *I love you.*

He got out of his truck and didn't even slow down or skulk as he usually did around the chickens. A good fight might help his sour mood, though some would probably think he had lost it if that fight was with poultry. Still, the chickens must have picked up on his "go ahead, make my day" attitude because they squawked and scattered.

Good.

Clay went up the steps, stopped and frowned when he spotted the egg on the welcome mat. Maybe one of the hens had laid it there, but the more likely culprit was Vita. It had her trademark shit streak and tiny feather. He refused to accept that the "offering" might have played some part in the chickens' flight, but he gently rolled it to the side with his foot.

Bracing himself for the chaos that he'd probably see inside, Clay opened the door.

No chaos.

There were no toys strewn on the floor, no signs that Sophie and the boys had been here at all, actually. That revved his heart up some, and he hurried through the house, looking for them. They weren't in his bedroom, but he soon found them in the guest room. Even though it was barely 8:00 p.m., the boys were sacked out on the bed. Sophie was asleep, too, snoozing between them with Hayden cradled in her right arm and Hunter in her left.

Even though Clay didn't make a sound, something must have alerted her because Sophie opened her eyes, yawned and smiled. The smile quickly vanished, though, because she likely remembered that she was pissed off at him. Except it was more than that.

He'd hurt her.

"April said that you told her you're in love with me," he blurted out.

All right, that wasn't how he'd planned this, and judging from Sophie's confused look, the jury had been right to stay out on this. Either April was flat-out wrong or Sophie was still waking up and wasn't sure how to respond.

She put her finger to her mouth in a hush gesture and eased away from the boys, kissing each on the top of his head, as she got up from the bed. She pulled the covers over them, picked up the baby monitors from the nightstand. He'd bought the monitors for when the boys slept over, and Sophie obviously knew how to use them because she flicked them on, leaving one on the nightstand and carrying the other one with her.

Once she was next to Clay, she took hold of his arm much as she'd done to Wanda Kay before giving the nurse a good dressing-down. Then she closed the guestroom door and led him back to the living room.

"Good evening to you, too, Clay," Sophie snarled.

"I'm sorry that sounded so blunt." Was *blunt* the right word? Maybe *like an asshole* would have been better. "But it's just been weighing on my mind. Did you really say that to her? And why doesn't the house look as if the Hunter and Hayden train wreck hit it?"

Clay groaned. He was batting zero tonight in communication skills so he tried a do-over.

"Good evening, Sophie. I'm sorry I'm late, but I got a tip on a possible Billy Lee sighting that I had to check out. No Billy Lee," he added before she could ask. "Brantley wants to stay the night at the hospital and won't be able to pick up the twins, but Spike's folks will come and get them in the morning. I tried to get here as fast as I could since I figured the boys would have set the place on fire by now."

She stared at him, shook her head. "No fires or train

wrecks. They were good for the most part, and I found diapering supplies in the bag in April's car. Plenty of toys for them to play with, too."

Yeah, like the baby monitors, he kept toys for them, and was about to say that, but Sophie just kept on talking.

"After I fed them, I took them to tend your horses, then bathed them—the twins not the horses—and had them help me clean up. I stayed with them while they fell asleep. FYI, Hayden wants a bunny and Hunter wants a motorcycle. You can blame me for the motorcycle and Mila for the bunny."

Then, her stare changed a little. Not quite a glare but close.

"And I didn't say diddly-squat to April about being in love with you." Her tone changed, too. It hadn't exactly been friendly before, but it had a hostile layer to it now even though she was whispering. "I don't know if she assumed it or misheard something I said because she was in pain. Either way, the *l*-word didn't come up. However, I did tell her that I'd cared for you."

Cared. He didn't miss the past tense of the word. Was it a slip of the tongue or did she really no longer care? And why did it feel like a punch to the gut if it was the latter.

Because he was stupid, that's why.

The attraction was still there, swirling around him and making him feel things he didn't want to feel. "Fuck the attraction," he grumbled.

Since he hadn't meant to say that aloud, he was still batting zero and probably shouldn't attempt anything as complex as human speech. That didn't stop him, though.

"It's good that you didn't fall in love with me," he said. "Because that wouldn't have been a smart thing to do."

Sophie's glare got a little bit worse. "Don't you think I know that?" She poked her index finger against his chest as she'd done to Wanda Kay. He hoped she wasn't about to threaten to spread some rumors about him and the football team. "I don't want to be in love with you, Clay McKinnon. I don't want to care for you. Heck, I don't even want to like you."

Well, she told him. Or at least she would have if he hadn't heard something at the end of that mini tirade, and what he heard was something he repeated aloud. "But?"

And he held his breath.

Sophie certainly wasn't holding her breath. It was coming out in short spurts and reminded him a little of a bull that was about to charge. Her gaze darted around. She cursed under her breath. Apparently his communication skills weren't the only thing at zero tonight because he had no idea what was going on in her head right now. She certainly wasn't answering that "but."

"How well do the boys sleep?" she asked.

Of all the questions he'd considered she might ask, that wasn't one of them. "Like rocks. Why?"

Again, no immediate answer, but she still seemed to be stewing.

"Fuck the attraction," she grumbled.

Clay pulled back his shoulders. He'd never heard her curse. Well, other than that G-rated stuff that seemed to come out of her mouth whenever she was upset.

"And fuck you," she added.

They stood there like gunfighters in an Old West shoot-out. Clay figured this would be a good time for him to tell her that she could drive April's car to her house, that he'd arrange to have it picked up later.

But he didn't say that.

However, he did move. So did Sophie. And he wasn't sure who moved first. Either way, he yanked her to him, and they landed against each other. She repeated her last two words of profanity, but Clay didn't think she was cursing him this time. She seemed to be letting him know what she was going to do to him.

Good, because he was going to do it right back.

Even if it was a big-assed mistake. Even if it complicated things worse than they already were. Even if he burned in hell for it.

Clay kissed her, hating that she tasted so good. He hated himself. Hated her. But he just kept on kissing her. Of course, it didn't just stay a kiss with Sophie and him. Their hands soon got involved. He touched her, moving his hand from her waist to her butt. That way, he could align them in the best possible way for a cheap thrill.

Which he knew wouldn't be very cheap. Nope. He'd pay for this for a long while.

Sophie did some touching, too. Her hand on his butt, and she bopped him in the head with the baby monitor when she tried to hook her arm around his neck. It smarted since it landed against the old chicken injury, but pain was the least of his worries right now.

In the back of his mind, he thought of the boys and hoped they really did sleep like rocks. But just in case that didn't happen, he needed to make sure they didn't get out of bed and find Nunk and Sophie naked and doing the nasty. He'd be able to hear them over the monitor, the very one that bopped him in the head again, but best not to drag Sophie to the living room floor for this.

He'd drag her to his bedroom floor instead.

That took some doing, what with the monitor bopping, the kisses, touches and Sophie trying to get him unzipped. Clay scooped her up, and while trying not to bash into the wall, he carried her to his bedroom.

Sophie took full advantage when he was occupied with setting her on her feet and shutting the door. She went after his zipper again while she kissed him. Frantic kisses. He knew they were fueled with the same heat he was feeling, too, but he needed her to understand that she could back out of this mistake if she wanted.

Clay put his hand over hers to stop the zipper lowering, and he looked her straight in the eyes. Definitely Sophie's eyes. Not a trace of flashbacks. Which wasn't necessarily a good thing. A flashback would have stopped him. As it was now, Sophie was his only hope.

They were screwed.

Because she was no hope at all. She pushed his hand away, unzipped him. "If you don't have a condom, this is going to get ugly."

His dick was intrigued by the notion of ugly, but it was just a tad more intrigued by having actual sex with her. Clay fished a condom from the nightstand drawer and pulled her to the floor. The bed was only a few inches away, but it seemed too civilized to take her there. If he was going to do this, he deserved to be punished with rug burns and sore knees.

Sophie started up the kissing again. Man, did she. The woman's mouth and hands were everywhere, but she quickly zoomed in on his zipper again. Clay zoomed in on hers. He pulled off her jeans but didn't bother taking his off. This was a little like a war now, and for some reason speed mattered. Maybe because if they thought about this too long they'd stop.

But neither stopped.

He rid her of her panties and got the condom on in record time. What he hadn't counted on was Sophie flipping him on his back and climbing on top. So, she'd be the one with sore knees, and he'd get the rug burns on his ass. All in all, not a bad price to pay for having his head explode.

That's exactly how it felt when Sophie took him inside her and started to move. Explosions in his head. Thankfully, he didn't in explode other places despite Sophie's attempts to do just that.

She was still in the fuck-you mode, and she put that anger to good use. She rode him hard until Clay could take no more. He reached between her legs to give her some help to hurry along her orgasm, but she batted his hand away. That's when he realized this wasn't just sex for her. She was proving a point. Exactly what point he didn't know because he could no longer think. The only thing he could do was let Sophie's ride give him the mother of all fuck-jobs.

Clay was helpless when he came, but Sophie continued to move, making sure she drained him. Then, she rolled off him, dropping onto her back on the floor.

"I want you to remember that," she said.

Oh, he was certain he would. Once his brain cells started working again. Thankfully, his hand started working before his brain, and he was able to take hold of her when she started to get up. Clay pulled her back to the floor with him. And he kissed her.

Between her legs.

If she wasn't going to let him put his hand there, then he'd see how she reacted to his mouth and tongue.

She reacted all right. She sort of melted, and he could almost feel the anger seeping from her body. Her muscles went slack, and she fisted her hand in his hair. Not pushing him away but pulling him closer. She even lifted her hips off the floor to help him, but Clay needed no such help. He kissed and tasted until she called him a bad name. Until she cursed again.

Until she came.

Clay didn't move. All in all, it was a nice place to rest his head. And he gave her one more special kiss along with it. He didn't say anything, but the words were floating through his head.

I want you to remember that.

SOPHIE WOKE TO the sound of gibberish. Perhaps alien gibberish coming from above. Her eyes flew open, and it took her a couple of moments to figure out what was going on.

She was in Clay's bed.

Naked, from the waist down, anyway.

Clay wasn't there, but in the middle of the alien gibberish she heard his voice. "Shh. Don't wake Sophie."

"Soapy!" the alien squealed, and that's when she realized it was one of the twins, and the conversation she was hearing was coming from the static-y baby monitor.

She jumped from the bed and cursed the rug burns on her knees. She had some on her butt, too, she realized when she pulled on her panties and jeans. Plus, she was a little sore from the rough anger sex. But at least she'd proved her point. That Clay and she were attracted to each other despite how he felt. Despite how she felt, too.

In hindsight, it was a stupid point to prove.

Sophie hurried into his bathroom to freshen up. Thankfully, she didn't look as if she'd had sex on the floor with a cop. She just looked, well, kind of relaxed. A good orgasm could do that, and the orgasm had indeed been good. Now, all that was left was facing the devil who'd given it to her.

"Soapy?" one of the twins called out.

Even though she could have used a shower, Sophie opened the door and peered out. Two sets of little eyes peered right back up at her.

"Soapy!" Hayden yelled and grabbed her legs for a hug. Hunter quickly joined him.

Ignoring the rug burns, Sophie scooped them up for a real hug. That's when she saw there was another pair of eyes on her. Clay's. He was in the living room, watching them from the hall.

He'd obviously showered because his hair was still damp, and when Sophie went closer with a boy on each hip, she caught the scent of his soap. He smelled good. Looked good, too.

Damn him.

After the anger sex, she'd told him *I want you to remember that*. But her slapped-together plan had failed. She doubted it'd left a lasting impression on him, but she sure as heck would remember it.

"It's hard to keep them quiet after they wake up," Clay greeted. "I wanted to let you sleep a little longer."

"I slept plenty long enough." And she'd slept like that proverbial rock. She recalled Clay moving her to his bed shortly after the orgasm to remember, but after that she'd zonked out. Apparently, the zonking had lasted for over nine hours since it was nearly seven in the morning.

Clay took the boys from her and headed to the kitchen. He put them in booster seats at the table where there was already cereal and juice waiting for them. Obviously, there'd been no nine hours of sleep for him. The boys seemed pleased with what was on the menu because they got busy eating.

"Just so you know, Spike's parents couldn't come after all so Brantley will be picking them up any minute now," Clay said.

He didn't have to finish that. If she didn't want to see her ex, and she didn't, then she'd better skedaddle.

"You can take April's car if you need to get home," he added.

Yes, she definitely needed to get home, especially since her mother would want a report. Sophie had called her shortly after she'd arrived at Clay's the night before to let her know what was going on, but that didn't mean her mother wouldn't have questions. Sophie only hoped she didn't have a visible hickey—a sexual scarlet letter—so her mother would know what she'd been up to.

"Have you spoken to April this morning?" she asked.

He nodded. "She's not having any pains. The doctor's going to let her go home later today." Clay paused. "You want to talk?"

She did. But she also *didn't* want to talk. If Sophie thought it would do any good, she'd pour her heart out to him. But now wasn't a good time. Truth was, there might never be a good time for it. Anger sex didn't mend a broken heart.

"I should be going," she decided to say, and she located her purse on the counter, intending to do just that. But Clay's phone rang before she could tell the boys goodbye. Since it could be an update from April, she waited.

Clay didn't put the call on Speaker, and she didn't want to move close enough to hear the conversation so she kissed the boys goodbye.

"See you guys later," she whispered to them.

"Ater," Hunter tried to repeat. Hayden actually stopped wolfing down his cereal and gave her a milky kiss in return. As kisses went, it was one of the best, and stickiest, she'd ever had.

Thankfully Clay's conversation was short but maybe not especially sweet since he looked a little troubled when he hit the end call button on his phone. "Can you stay with the boys a little while longer?" he asked.

Not that she was looking forward to seeing Brantley, but she nodded. "Why?"

"That was FBI Agent Mike Freeman." Clay put his phone in his pocket, already heading for the door. "He's investigating what happened at Granger Western, and he said he found something important. He needs me at the office right away."

"Important," Sophie repeated as she watched Clay practically race to his truck and drive off with barely a backward glance.

Not just any *ordinary* important, either, but something connected to the investigation. She certainly hadn't forgotten about what'd gone on at the company, but with everything else happening in her life, she'd put it on the mental back burner.

While the boys finished their breakfast, she took out her phone to see if she'd missed any calls or texts. She had. There were eight texts from Mila, who was apparently checking in during her *Titanic* fantasy date. Sophie read through them to make sure all was well, and it was. Like the character of Rose, Mila had survived and had gotten safely home around 10:00 p.m.

She was about to put her phone away, but she accidentally hit the note section, and her life plan popped up. It was all there for her to see.

Her failures.

No marriage. No baby on the way. No CEO job. She hadn't even managed to do the traveling, learning a foreign language or zip-lining in Costa Rica.

It was obviously time for a change, and she was about to delete it when there was a knock at the door. Brantley, of course, and he didn't look any happier to see her than she was to see him.

The boys, however, were pleased as punch. They scurried out of their booster seats and ran toward Brantley to give him very enthusiastic hugs. Hunter immediately started to babble about wanting a motorcycle. Hayden got in his bunny wish. Brantley listened to each of them while gathering them into his arms.

"Clay had to go to work," Sophie told Brantley when he looked around. She picked up her purse again, ready to leave.

Brantley nodded. "Thanks for staying with the boys. Thanks for everything." He paused a heartbeat. "Have you got time to talk?"

Sophie huffed and was about to say no. But then she remembered the little ears in the room, and these little ears didn't miss much. She certainly didn't want them to pick up on the tension between Brantley and her.

She went into the living room and put on a movie. One they'd watched the night before, but apparently the twins were eager to watch it again because they bolted from Brantley's arms and plopped down in front of the TV.

"I want to say I'm sorry for how I spoke to you at the hospital," Brantley started. "I was wrong to accuse you of telling April about Clay's and my conversation."

"Yes, you were wrong. And if this is what you want to talk about, then—"

"No, there's more. I'm sorry that I hurt you."

"Old water, old bridge."

He nodded again. "Yes, because now you're in love with Clay."

She was about to dispute that, but Brantley just kept on talking before she could say anything.

"That's good because I really do love April." He scrubbed his hand over his face. "I was just feeling frustrated and inadequate when I said those things to Clay. But I'd walk through fire for April and the boys. For this new baby, too."

Even though she hated to give him the benefit of the doubt, he sounded convincing. "Did you let April know that?"

"I did. And that's why I wanted to talk to you. Is there any way you can let her know that I'm in this with her for the long haul? She's the love of my life, Sophie, and I don't want to lose her."

She gave him a blank stare. "I'm your ex-fiancée, and you want me to convince your wife to stay with you?" Sophie hoped that sounded as absurd to him as it did to her.

But apparently it didn't because Brantley nodded. "She needs a friend, Sophie. And even if you can't convince her to give me a second chance, talk to her because she needs someone. Someone other than her brother," he quickly added. "Because you know from experience that brothers aren't always the most objective when it comes to sisters." He rubbed his jaw. "I remember Roman punching me in the face on the day we were supposed to get married."

Sophie blinked. "Roman punched you? He wasn't even there."

"Beg to differ. He tracked me down within a half hour after I left you at the church."

This was the first she was hearing of it, and it meant she owed Roman an apology and a scolding. An apology because she'd griped about him not showing up on that fateful day and a scolding because she didn't want any violence perpetrated in her name. Even if it made her smile a little to think that Roman had been looking out for her.

"Anyway," Brantley went on, "will you talk to April?"

At that moment the twins giggled over something they saw in the movie, and that sound was a reminder of what this was really all about. It was about them. Maybe it did take a village to raise a child, especially since some of the village was being mean to their mother.

"I'll talk to her," Sophie finally said, "but I can't promise it'll do any good."

Brantley blew out a breath a relief. "Thank you." He went into the living room with the twins and motioned for them to get up. "Come on, boys. It's time to go home."

Hayden and Hunter protested, of course, because it was one of their favorite parts in the movie. But the protest wasn't necessary because Brantley's phone buzzed, and he stepped back out of the living room when he saw the name on the screen.

"I don't recognize this number," Brantley mumbled, and he walked even farther away from the twins to take the call. Maybe because he thought it was Clay calling to chew him out, and he didn't want the boys to hear that.

As with the call Clay had gotten, Sophie couldn't hear any part of the conversation, but whatever the caller was saying to Brantley, it caused his forehead to bunch up.

"Why me?" Brantley asked. "Isn't there someone else you'd rather have do this?"

Uh-oh. That definitely didn't sound good, and Sophie found herself moving closer to him so she could figure out what was going on.

"All right," Brantley said a few moments later. He huffed. "If Sophie can stay with my stepsons, I'll be right there." He ended the call and looked at her. "You're never going to guess who that was? Billy Lee," Brantley answered before she could say anything.

Good thing, too, because she wouldn't have gotten the right answer. She shook her head. "What did he want?"

"To hire me as his lawyer. And from the sound of it, he'll need one. Clay just arrested him."

CHAPTER TWENTY-ONE

THERE WERE TOO many damn people in his office, and Clay couldn't hear himself think. And it was definitely a time when he needed to do some thinking.

Mike, two other FBI agents and Rowdy were at his desk going over what they'd found. And what they'd found was a gold mine. Clay wasn't disputing that. He just wished they'd pan through that gold somewhere else.

Marcum Gentry, the Grangers' legal advisor, was hovering near the agents, questioning every little thing they said. They were saying a lot, too, which meant between the comments and the questions, chatter was filling up the room.

In addition to the three agents and his deputy, Vita was in the doorway doing some kind of chanting to rid him once and for all of the chicken issue. She had feathers that she'd plucked from one of the hens. Mila was behind her, no doubt ready to pluck feathers of a different kind—his—since she'd almost certainly heard about Clay's breakup with Sophie. Hell, maybe she'd even heard about the pissed-off sex Sophie and he had had the night before.

He could add Brantley to the growing number of people who apparently thought his office was the place to be right now. He'd arrived after Billy Lee had made his one phone call, and Brantley was already in lawyer mode.

He was demanding to know the charges against his client, which Clay would give him, but he was still on the phone with the Spring Hill PD who was bringing in yet someone else who'd clutter up his office.

Martin Crowley.

Of course, Clay wouldn't mind having a chat with the former accountant for Granger Western, but that would have to wait until the Spring Hill deputies escorted the man to Wrangler's Creek. Since that shouldn't take long, Clay finished his call, slammed down his phone and motioned to Vita.

"Can you postpone the chanting?" he asked. "Or at least move it to the break room?"

"I can, but the aura back there might throw this all off. It might cause the chickens to get even madder than they are now." And she was dead serious.

"I'll risk it." Though Clay did hope there was nothing to that possibility of escalating fowl behavior.

Vita made a suit-yourself sound, and while still swishing around feathers and mumbling to herself, the woman walked away. Clay pointed to Mila next.

"Is this about Sophie?" he asked. "Because if it is, it'll have to wait."

She shook her head, coming closer, and she stood on her toes so she could whisper in his ear. "It's about Jack from *Titanic*."

And judging from her expression, she was serious, too. "Are you talking about a role-playing thing?"

Mila nodded. "I'm not sure what his real name is because he uses an alias on the fantasy site. Anyway, everything went fine with the ship's bow re-creation and the dance so I left. This morning, though, when I went into the bookstore, I found him there asleep. I'm pretty sure he's drunk. And he's naked. He wasn't like that when I left him last night."

Clay didn't know if she meant the naked part, the drunk part or both. It didn't matter. Mila obviously needed someone to check this out so Clay motioned for Rowdy to come closer.

"If you say a word to anyone about what you're about to see, I'll fire your ass," Clay warned his deputy. "Now, I want you to follow Mila to the bookstore and take care of a problem for her."

Rowdy's gaze swung from Clay to Mila, and even though the deputy likely had plenty of questions, he thankfully didn't ask them. He followed Mila out the door.

Three down, two more to go since the FBI agents could all stay. Clay turned to Brantley next, and the man was more than ready for his turn.

"Why did you lock up my client?" Brantley snapped. "He came here of his own free will, and you know he's not guilty. The FBI found the person who stole the money from Granger Western."

Yes, they had. It was Martin Crowley, just as Billy Lee had suspected. Clay didn't know all the details yet, but apparently the agents had indeed found the money trail that had led them in a very roundabout way to Crowley. Mike was certain he had enough evidence to bring a solid case against the accountant.

"Billy Lee came here of his own free will only after Mike called him on the phone he'd left for Arlo, and Mike told him about what they'd found out about Crowley. Before that, Billy Lee was evading arrest. And, no, it doesn't matter if he's innocent of the original charges, he still should have turned himself in so he could answer questions about the investigation."

That was the law, but of course, Brantley being a lawyer started spouting case references to try to convince Clay to release Billy Lee. That wasn't going to happen, and Clay let Brantley know that with his flat stare. Brantley huffed again and went to the agents to plead his case.

Clay turned to Marcum next and was about to ask him if he'd gotten in touch with Sophie yet, but the question wasn't necessary because Clay looked up and saw her in the doorway. She seemed a little shell-shocked, but the twins might be contributing to that. Hunter was tugging at her left hand as he was trying to reach some candy on Rowdy's desk. Hayden was pulling at her right hand because he wanted to drink from the water fountain.

Clay went to her to take the boys, and Marcum swooped in to scoop up Sophie. Literally. The man picked her up and spun her around. That didn't help the shell-shocked look on her face. In fact, she looked ready to barf when Marcum stood her back on the floor.

"I called Garrett and Roman, of course," Marcum said. "Garrett's on his way back from a cattle auction. Roman's response was, well, you know Roman."

"Yes." Her voice was barely louder than a whisper, and since the twins weren't exactly being quiet little mice, he didn't catch what she added to Marcum.

"Well, are you ready to get out of here?" Marcum asked her. He glanced back at Clay. "You've got somebody to help with those two, right?" He didn't let Clay answer. "Because I've got a mountain of paperwork for Sophie to take care of."

"Do you have someone to help you with them?" Sophie asked.

Clay didn't, not immediately, but there was no way he'd tell her that. Besides, he might be able to convince Brantley to take them somewhere if the boys started pestering their stepdad.

"I'll be fine," Clay assured her. "And congrats. This is great news."

"You bet it is." Marcum was grinning from ear to ear. "Sophie can move back to Austin and pick up right where she left off except this time around she'll be the CEO. There's a lot of sympathy for you, Sophie, and that'll translate to big sales. You'll see."

Sophie glanced back at him as Marcum whisked her away. Soon, it'd sink in that this was exactly what she'd always wanted. To be CEO of Granger Western. She could tick off one very large item of her life plan.

Clay wanted to celebrate for her. And he would. As soon as the sickening feeling of dread eased up in his stomach.

SOPHIE'S BUTT HURT. So did her feet and head. In fact, so many parts of her were hurting that there was no sense identifying them all, but her eyeballs especially were clamoring for a break.

"Only a few more papers," Marcum assured her. The man had no concept of a few since he'd been saying that for the past hour.

She pushed back her desk chair and got to her feet. Not easily. Along with the pain of sitting for hours, some numbness had set in, too. She hobbled her way to the floor-to-ceiling windows of her old office.

Her *office*, she mentally corrected.

In the past, there'd been Director of Marketing beneath her nameplate, but Marcum had called in some favors and had a new one whipped up before they'd arrived from Wrangler's Creek.

Now, it read: Sophie Granger, CEO, Granger Western.

Roman had always called this office the Saddle Palace, and he'd added some snark to it. That's because he'd always seen it as their father's dream. One that he'd tried to shove down their throats. Well, Roman certainly hadn't gone for it. And now neither had Garrett. He'd come back from his cattle-buying trip but had said he'd be by tomorrow in case there was anything he needed to sign. He hadn't said anything about moving back to Austin.

He wouldn't, either.

Sophie was sure of that. He would help her, of course, but he'd be doing that from the ranch.

"Maybe you can groom Tate to step in when he's old enough," Marcum threw out there. "Another Granger to eventually take the reins."

Roman would smother her in her sleep if she attempted it. Or at least he'd threaten her with smothering, but if Tate did show some interest, Roman would eventually loosen his parental grip and let him run with it. But even if that happened, it would be years from now. A decade or more.

"Your dad did the right thing making you the CEO," Marcum went on. He joined her at the window, and while he sipped his scotch, they looked out at the Austin skyline. Incredible view as always.

But something was missing.

Sophie quickly figured out what. She wasn't there. Yes, her hurting/numb butt and feet were in the city, but her heart wasn't. Pieces of it were metaphorically scattered between here and Wrangler's Creek.

"And don't worry about Billy Lee," Marcum continued. "He'll almost certainly get parole for those charges."

Marcum had said a variation of that several times already, maybe hoping for a more enthusiastic response from Sophie. And she was very happy that Billy Lee would soon be a free man. Not just so he could get back to his old life but because he could help her go through all this paperwork.

Her phone rang, and she nearly punched herself trying to get it from her pocket. It wasn't Clay but rather April, and Sophie hated the disappointment that flooded through her.

"I'll pour me another drink while you take the call," Marcum said, stepping away.

"I heard the news about you getting your company back," April greeted the moment Sophie answered. "Are you okay?"

It was ironic that she was the only person who'd asked her that. "Fine. How about you? Did your doctor spring you from the hospital?"

"He did this morning, and I'm right as rain—whatever the heck that means. I wanted to thank you. I don't know what you said to Wanda Kay, but she was nice to me the whole time. Though she did keep mumbling something about her not swallowing. Any idea why she'd say that?"

Sophie frowned. "Nope. No idea." She'd made the blow job threat, but she hadn't mentioned that. Maybe Wanda Kay had just assumed she would add that into the lie-rumor. "By the way, Brantley wanted me to talk to you and tell you how much he loves you. He does, you know? He really loves you."

"Yes, I know, and I love him. We're working it out. So, don't put that monkey on your back. You'll have enough of those now that you've returned to Austin." April paused. "You have returned there, haven't you?"

"Yes." That felt like a lie, as well. "But it might take me a while to get into the swing of things."

April made a sound of agreement. "Are you going to ask about Clay?"

Sophie considered playing dumb, but she'd reached her lie quota for the day. "How is he?"

"Stupid. And I told him that, too. He's stupid to let you just walk away because of your eye color and his old baggage. Heck, you've got baggage as well, because of Brantley, and you were willing to get past it."

She was, but going into the cliché mode again, it took two to tango.

"Anyway," April went on, "I'm sure Clay and you will both be okay, and once he's out of the hospital, he'll head straight back to work."

Sophie thought her heart had skipped a beat. "Why is Clay in the hospital?"

"Oh, I just assumed you'd heard. It was those chickens. He was going up the steps to his house when one of the chickens flew in his face. He fell and got a bit banged up. I tried to stay with him while he was getting stitched up and having tests, but he ordered me home since I'm supposed to be on bed rest."

She could just see all of that playing out. See his trip to the hospital, too. He would not be in a good mood.

"Well, I'd better go and check on the boys," April said. "Brantley put them to bed right before I called you, but they're too quiet. Talk to you soon."

Sophie pressed the end call button and scrolled through her contacts until she got to Clay. It would be so easy to call him. Just one little touch of her finger. Then, she could tell him how sorry she was about the latest attack. She could ask him if he was in pain.

And then what?

There'd be awkward silence because there really hadn't been anything left unsaid between them. Yes, they'd had postbreakup sex, but while it'd been amazing, it still felt post and breakup.

"You need another drink?" Marcum asked her.

Since she hadn't touched the first one he'd poured for her, she shook her head, turned and headed to her desk. Sophie gave her brand-spanking-new nameplate an adjustment that it in no way needed before she sat down and put her numb butt back to work.

CHAPTER TWENTY-TWO

WHEN CLAY GOT home from work, he saw a motorcycle, a dead Christmas tree, six chickens, a chanting gypsy and Roman Granger. The chickens were expected. Ditto for the tree, since his cleaning lady had probably removed it from the house so it could be recycled. But Vita and Roman and his motorcycle were surprises.

Not exactly welcome ones, either.

It was cold, a January damp kind of cold, and Clay was tired, hungry and sleepy. It was only 5:00 p.m., but he had been thinking of eating a sandwich and crashing. Crashing, however, would have to wait.

Vita was prancing around the yard while waving around some kind of smoking clump of stuff that smelled like weed. He hoped like the devil that it wasn't because the last thing he wanted to do was arrest an old woman hell-bent on helping him. After the last chicken attack the month before, Clay had given up dismissing anything Vita did. He wouldn't turn down help even if it was stupid and unconventional, but he would draw the line at narcotics.

"Chief," Roman greeted when Clay shut his truck door and walked toward the porch. Sophie's brother was sitting on the steps, watching both Vita and the chickens as if they were circus acts. "I heard it's permanent now. No more interim label in front of your name."

That was true. On Christmas Eve the city council had offered him a permanent position, and Clay had accepted it. But Clay doubted that Roman had come here to offer his congratulations.

Since this talk with Roman could turn ugly fast, Clay decided to go ahead and just get it started. "If you're here about Sophie and/or Billy Lee, there's no need. Billy Lee's getting probation after a plea deal, and Sophie hasn't contacted me since she moved back to Austin over a month ago. It's over between us, and I won't be seeing her again."

Vita stopped her smudging ritual and stared at him. Roman stared, too. A dark, dangerous kind of stare. Of course, that's how Roman always looked so perhaps he didn't have any other facial expressions.

Maybe because Clay felt the need to defend himself, he just kept on talking. "I know I shouldn't have gotten involved with Sophie in the first place, and I'm sorry for that. Sorry that I hurt her. She deserved better after all the shit she went through with Brantley."

Roman lifted his shoulder. "I'm actually here about your land, but if you want to keep telling me how much you screwed over my sister, I'll listen." He stood, meeting Clay eye to eye.

"My land?"

"Yeah. I'm here on business for Garrett." Along with the dark bad-boy thing, there was some annoyance in his voice, too. "Legally, I own the ranch so Garrett talked me into coming here to see you. Actually, he pestered the hell out of me about it and then used Sophie to browbeat me into doing this."

Clay had been confused enough by the land comment, but Roman wasn't clearing up this conversation any. Worse, Vita had moved closer, no doubt so she could hear, and the weedy smoke was blowing right in his face.

Since he didn't want to get high or go through with an arrest, Clay turned to Vita. "Could you stomp out that smoke-thing and come back to finish this? Roman and I need to talk."

The woman nodded but didn't budge an inch. "Are you really gonna lease your land to the Grangers? And what about Sophie and all those mopey rides she's been taking?"

Clueless. That's the one word that came to mind to describe how Clay felt. "Sophie's mopey rides?" he repeated. The land question was important, too, but he didn't like hearing Sophie and mopey in the same sentence.

Roman opened his mouth to answer, but Vita spoke before he could say anything. "Sophie's been coming home to the ranch nearly every day and taking her mare out for long rides. The hands think she's been crying a lot, too. Of course, that could be allergies."

Clay thought back to Sophie's other "allergy attack" after the Brantley mess. Hell. She'd been crying, and this time it was all his fault.

"You haven't exactly been Mr. Sunshine, either," Vita went on, talking to Clay. "Reena said you've been sulky and moody and that you kicked one of the plastic Santa decorations when it fell on the sidewalk in front of the police station. Then, you kicked the trash can twice."

Shit. He made a mental note to have another talk with Reena about gossiping.

"It's true?" Clay asked Roman. "Is Sophie really moping?"

"Can't say. She does minimal moping around me because she's afraid I'm going to bust in your face the way I did to Brantley."

Clay hadn't known about the Brantley face busting, but he approved. Which made him a hypocrite since he'd hurt Sophie just as Brantley had done. After he got rid of Roman and Vita, he'd drive over to the Granger ranch and check on Sophie. Of course, he could make things worse by doing that since he was probably the source of the moping, but he needed to see for himself that she was all right.

"Are you going to bust me in the face?" Clay wanted to know. He took off his jacket and tossed it on the table in the entry.

Roman kept his leather jacket on. "I'll keep my options open on that. Especially since you've been sulky and moody. Are you that way because of my sister?"

"No," Clay snarled. "Maybe," he admitted. "You don't know the whole story."

"I do," Vita piped up. "Reena said you don't get those pink envelopes anymore, but that you're in the same kind of bad mood that you were when you did get them. This bad mood lasts all the time, too, and everybody's a little tired of it."

He was surprised Reena didn't report how many times a day he took a piss. Clay huffed, and since it was obvious Vita was staying put, he motioned for Roman to follow him inside where they could have a private talk. One that might end in a face bashing, but at least Vita wouldn't be witnessing it. He unlocked the door, ushered Roman inside and got yet another huge surprise.

Sophie.

She was peering out from the hall and cursing under her breath. "I rode my mare over here and put her in the barn, but I didn't know Roman was coming," she said as if that explained everything.

"I didn't know you were coming," Roman answered as if he knew exactly what was going on.

Clueless went through Clay's head again.

"Why are you here?" Roman asked Sophie at the very moment she asked him the same thing.

"The land," Roman answered. "You?"

"Sex. And to return Clay's key."

Clay decided it was a good time to stay quiet, listen and try to figure out what the heck was going on. However, his body zoomed right in on the word, *sex*. Maybe because Sophie looked good. No allergy eyes. She looked good enough to…

He purposely didn't finish that thought.

Especially since it was sex that had gotten him into this position.

"You go first," Sophie prompted her brother.

Clay would have preferred to hear what Sophie had to say, but it probably wasn't a good idea to address that sex comment in front of Roman.

Roman dragged in a long breath, turned to Clay. "Garrett wants me to ask you about leasing the back part of your land to us. He needs to expand now and could use the acreage. In exchange for what I'm sure will be a generous payment, he'll also take down the fence between your place and the pond so your horses can water there."

Clay was about to ask why Garrett hadn't made this request himself, but this went back to Roman owning the ranch. Plus, it would involve paperwork, and Clay was already well aware how much Garrett disliked that particular part of his job.

"I'll need some time to think about that," Clay said.

Best to think when Sophie wasn't completely distracting him.

Roman nodded, turned to his sister. "Now, it's your turn. Why are you here?"

"I told you already. Sex and keys. I forgot to return that." She plucked said key from her front jeans pocket and handed it to Clay. It was the house key he'd given her the day April had been hospitalized. "I thought I'd just sneak in and leave it since I know you wouldn't have wanted me to hide it in the verbena." She paused, smiled, then quit smiling when Roman scowled. "But before I could leave, I saw Vita and Roman drive up."

"And you didn't want me to know you'd come here," Roman finished for her. He made a circling motion with his fingers. "Now, explain the sex part. And FYI, *sex* isn't a word brothers like to hear coming from their kid sister's mouth."

Clay made a sound of agreement but wished he hadn't. It got him a scowl from both Sophie and Roman.

"I wanted to talk to Clay about sex," Sophie explained.

Talk? Well, his man parts had gotten all excited for nothing. They didn't get un-excited, though, because Sophie was still there, and as long as his eyes could see her, the rest of him wanted more of her.

"Clay and I didn't have a smooth parting of the ways," she said. "I needed some…closure. Yes, closure." She punctuated it with a nod that wasn't any more convincing than the remark had been. It sounded as if she'd just filled in the blank with the first word that'd popped into her head.

Roman looked at both of them. "Closure, huh? Never heard it called that before." He huffed, put his hands on his hips and looked at Sophie. "Just assure me that whatever you're about to do will not add to that snit you've been in for nearly a month."

"A snit?" she howled.

"Snit," Roman confirmed and brushed a kiss on her forehead. "Let me know if I need to kick Clay's ass for you."

Damn. They'd moved on from face-bashing to ass-kicking. Of course, if it came to that, Clay would have to face-bash and ass-kick right back, which definitely wouldn't improve things.

"I'll call you in a day or two about the land," Clay told Roman when he headed for the door.

"Call Garrett instead. In the future you can keep me out of the land loop. Out of the sex talk loop, too." Roman paused, looked at them from over his shoulder. "Was the verbena some kind of sex reference?"

"Yes," Sophie lied with a straight face. "And if you don't want me to describe it in complete detail, you won't ask any more questions."

The corner of Roman's mouth kicked up into a smile, and he strolled out. Clay only got a glimpse of the yard before Roman closed the door, but Vita was nowhere in sight. Maybe she'd taken her smoky chantings elsewhere.

With Roman gone and no sounds from Vita, the house got very quiet. Clay waited for Sophie to say something, but when she just stood there, he decided to start.

"It's good to see you," he said. "And you were right—we didn't have a smooth parting of the ways. Rug burns," he added in a grumble.

She nodded. "And I got a bruise on my left butt cheek."

Clay couldn't help it, he smiled. "I'm sorry about the bruise. Sorry about a lot of things." He was about to launch into a remixed version of why he should have never started up an affair with her, of why he was no good for her. For anyone. And why she was better off without him. But Clay decided to start with a simpler question. "How do you like being CEO?"

She lifted her shoulder, not exactly an enthusiastic response. "It's a lot of work, but Billy Lee is helping. Plus, it'll be easier when I move my office to the ranch. That way, I can rope Garrett into helping more. He's one hundred percent cowboy these days and not much into the business."

So he'd heard. But he hadn't heard about Sophie moving her office. "Can you do that, work from the ranch?"

Another shoulder lift. "I'm actually taking over the guest cottage at the back of the house. My mother will still be around, but it'll give me a designated work space."

"What happened to make you want to move back to the ranch?" Clay wanted to kick himself for the question though, because it sounded as if he were fishing for an answer that involved him.

He wasn't surprised that he wanted it to involve him. No matter how much he told himself that this wasn't a good thing, it was. Sophie was very much a good thing. Now the real question was, what was he going to do about it?

Sophie came closer, but she slipped her hands into her back pockets as if to anchor them there. "I want a date."

Clay was surprised. "Haven't we had this conversation before?"

"Yes, but that was for a ruse so that my family wouldn't kill Brantley. This time, I'm asking because I want a date. A real one. With you. No strings attached."

No such thing.

"Look, I can't make this perfect," she continued before he could speak. "You have a past. I have a past. I'll always be your brother-in-law's ex-girlfriend, and you'll always have pink envelopes. Maybe not physical ones, but they'll always be there."

Yes, they would.

She came even closer. So close that if Clay wanted, he could reach out and pull her to him. He would have done that, too, if she hadn't continued talking.

"I know there's no such thing as no strings attached. Dates often lead to commitments…and other things."

She finally stopped talking and Clay was about to pull her to him, but she did some pulling of her own. Not with him but rather her phone. She took it from her pocket, opened the note that was titled LIFE PLAN and showed him the screen.

It was blank.

"The way I figure it," she went on, "I've got two choices. I can fill that in with stuff that might end up being what I really want, or—"

Clay was about to kiss her, but instead he took the phone from her and typed in something. A life plan goal that he really hoped she would consider. He turned the screen and showed it to her. It got the reaction he wanted.

She smiled.

Then Sophie launched herself into his arms and kissed him. All in all, not a bad kiss but Clay figured they could do a whole lot better. Especially with the life goal he'd just suggested.

I'm in love with you. What do you say to that?

Sophie took back the phone and typed in her answer: *I say I love you right back.*

Clay hadn't been sure how he would feel if and when

Sophie ever said that to him, but it felt pretty damn good. That's why he said it out loud.

"I love you, Sophie."

She took hold of his shirtsleeve, pulled him back to her. "And I love you, *Chief* Clay McKinnon." She smiled again. "Say, I've never had sex with an actual police chief before. You think he's better at it than the interim was?"

"Much, much better." And Clay took her to the bedroom to prove it.

* * * * *

Now, turn the page for the special bonus story
LONE STAR COWBOY, also from USA TODAY
bestselling author Delores Fossen!

LONE STAR COWBOY

CHAPTER ONE

It wasn't every day that Lily Rose Granger walked into a barn and found a naked cowboy, but apparently this was her day for ticking off that particular box. All in all, it was a nice box-ticking experience, too.

Or at least it would have been if the cowboy hadn't been glaring.

Jake Monroe, aka naked cowboy, was clearly not a happy camper right now.

She barely glanced at his glare, though. That was because there were so many other things to grab her attention. Like Jake's damp cocoa-brown hair, his narrowed blue eyes. That tough, gorgeous face. The very tight muscles in his neck, chest and stomach. And then there was the most eye-catching thing of all.

That towel he had wrapped around his cowboy package.

It was a little towel, barely fitting around his hips, and the way Jake was clamping on to it, it created a gap where she could possibly get a glimpse of something really interesting if he shifted just a little.

She found herself hoping he would shift or maybe there'd be a sudden breeze. The breeze might help with the flash of heat she was having, too, and Lily Rose didn't think that flash had much to do with the steamy July temps.

Even though it'd been a while since she'd seen that particular part of Jake's anatomy, she knew it was worthy of a gawk or two. What Lily Rose couldn't understand, though, was why he was here to give her even the possibility of such a gawking.

The straight-laced Jake wasn't the sort to stand around in a barn wearing just a towel. Especially these days. He was the boss and owned the place. This looked more like a stunt he would have pulled when he was a teenager and worked on her cousins' ranch just up the road.

"Did you see anyone when you drove up?" he asked.

Surprised that would be the first thing he'd say to her, she shook her head. It was barely 6 a.m., a little early for the ranch hands to start arriving, but they'd be there soon. "Is this your version of a casual workday outfit?"

That didn't cause his scowl to ease up any. Of course, she hadn't expected it would. Jake had obviously had either a bad night or an equally bad start to the morning and wouldn't appreciate the humor. Or the wink she added to it.

"I need to get in the tack room," he snarled. Since he was standing right next to the door, that wasn't much of a shocker destination. "There are some clothes in there, but it's locked."

And she had the key. A brand-spanking-new one since this was her first week of working for Jake. A position she hadn't exactly counted on having—and wouldn't have for long. She was supervising the training of some champion cutting horses and was midway through that process. Since Jake had bought those particular horses from her former boss, Ian Keller, Lily Rose had followed the equine trail to Jake's equally brand-spanking-new ranch, Sugar Hollow, named for the trail on the back-side of his property.

Lily Rose pulled the key from her pocket, and Jake

nearly knocked her down getting inside. She didn't mean to watch, but it was hard to focus on anything else when Jake dropped that towel, and she got a look at his butt. He could win prize buckles with a butt like that if they gave out such awards.

"When I got out of the shower, I discovered I wasn't alone in the house," he grumbled as he yanked on a pair of jeans. They were dirty, muck on the bottom and probably weren't even his, but they fit him the way jeans should fit a championship butt. "There was a naked woman in my bed."

The little pang of jealousy bitch-slapped her before Lily Rose could stop it. It was no grand revelation that Jake had sex, and for that to happen, it required at least some level of nudity. Still, it wasn't something that Lily Rose liked to think about.

In her mind, Jake was, well, still *hers*.

The proof that he wasn't hers, though, was right in front of her. He had been mostly naked when she walked into the barn and he'd left a naked woman in his house, which was only about twenty yards away.

"Please tell me this isn't some kind of sexual scavenger hunt," Lily Rose said, trying to sound nonchalant.

"No." He stretched that out a few angry syllables. "The woman is Marcie Jean Garza, and I didn't invite her into my house or my bed. She was there when I got out of the shower."

All right, that helped a little with the jealousy, which apparently had decided to set up residence in several of her body parts. "So, why didn't you just ask her to leave?"

He huffed as if the answer were obvious. "Gee, why didn't I think of that? Oh, yeah. Because it doesn't work with Marcie. Or half the women in town who've decided that I'm the catch they've been waiting for their whole lives."

"Well, in a way you are. The catch, I mean. To them," she added just so he wouldn't think she was in on that particular fishing expedition. "It isn't every day a single guy inherits a lot of money and it brings out the barracudas."

But that was exactly what'd happened. In the week since Lily Rose had returned to Wrangler's Creek, she'd heard plenty of gossip about Jake and the women after him. If the gossip was right, he'd let a couple of those women "catch" him, too. So, Marcie probably wasn't the first naked woman he'd recently had in his bed.

"Funny, though, that I wasn't such a catch when I didn't have the money my grandparents left me," he grumbled on.

Oh. That. "Yeah, as a Granger I know a little about gold diggers. And, no, you didn't try to gold-dig with me so don't get offended. That was just sex between us."

He didn't disagree with that, though her family certainly had at the time. A Granger dating a ranch hand. One who'd been six years older than her at that and with a reputation for having a quick zipper on his jeans.

Now that she was twenty-seven, the age difference wasn't such a big deal, but it had been mighty big to her brothers and male cousins when she was eighteen and Jake had been twenty-four.

"Marcie hid my clothes," he went on. "And when I tried to get to the dresser and closet to grab something else, she would pop me with this stupid BDSM riding crop. I would have called to have her arrested, but I didn't want it all over Wrangler's Creek that I was running from a naked woman."

She made a sound of agreement. In a cowboy town, that wouldn't have been good PR for a rancher, and it would have cost him some major ribbing the next time he walked into the Longhorn Bar.

"Thank God none of the hands saw me." Jake pulled on a white T-shirt as if the fabric were at fault for his predicament. He did the same to a mucky pair of boots. "Not a good impression for a boss to make."

"True." And because Lily Rose thought he could use some levity, she added, "but it gave me a nice start to the day." She chuckled.

Jake didn't.

He looked at her, meeting her eyes with those scorching baby blues, and it caused other parts of her to scorch as well. Jake could do that to her with just a simple look. Or touch. Actually, he could manage it just by breathing.

"*This* can't happen," he said.

Too bad she knew what he meant. Probably because he'd already spelled it out for her the day she'd arrived with the horses. He had a rule about getting involved with people who worked for him. Since his other employees were four male ranch hands and Jake was straight, the rule was meant solely for her.

Sometimes, rules sucked.

Hormones didn't give a rat's toot about rules. At least *her* hormones didn't. They only wanted hot naked cowboys, especially if that particular cowboy was Jake. It didn't help that she had made some pretty incredible memories with him. Nope. Because she had rules about that sort of thing, too. In her case, it was a rule she'd learned the hard way. No sleeping around with the boss.

She gave a dismissive wave of her hand to respond to his *this can't happen* and tried to appear focused on work. She needed to get in the tack room so she could drop off her supply bag. Normally, that would have been a start to getting her mind on work and leaving to check on the horses, but she went through the doorway at the exact moment Jake was coming out.

His chest brushed against hers.

The zing of heat was so fast and intense that it could have qualified as foreplay. Jake must have noticed it as well because when their eyes met again, she saw all the things he didn't want her to see.

Mainly lust.

But there was some profanity mixed in with it.

This would have been a good time to mention that she'd had a bad experience sleeping with the boss. A good time to mention, too, that she was coming off a relationship and didn't do rebounds well. Not with men anyway. Chocolate and binge-watching TV were the cure for that.

At least that was what she kept telling herself.

It was getting harder and harder to make herself believe it when Jake lingered there, almost touching her. His mouth almost close enough to kiss. Those *almosts* felt like foreplay, too.

There were plenty of reasons for her to move away from him. For one thing, she really did need to get to work, and for another, there was also the sound of some vehicles in front of Jake's house. Probably the ranch hands. No way did Lily Rose want the hands seeing her and their boss in a semi-intimate position.

"Woohoo!" someone called out. "Jake?"

Crud, it was Marcie. Jake's profanity, however, was much worse than hers, and he cursed out loud.

Lily Rose went to move away from him so she could give him time to tell Marcie to get lost, but he took hold of her arm, anchoring Lily Rose in place. Again, more foreplay because the front of his zipper brushed in the general region of hers. It didn't help that he hadn't fully zipped up when he'd put on the spare jeans.

"Jake?" Marcie was much closer now, and it only took a few seconds for her to come into the barn. "There you are…" But her words sort of died on her lips when her attention landed on the two of them standing so close together.

It took Lily Rose a moment to figure out the exact reason for the word-dying, but then she noticed what was going on. Jake still had hold of her wrist, but his hand was now in the vicinity of her lower stomach. He was also leaning in, his mouth hovering just a couple of inches from hers. It looked as if they were about to kiss.

"Play along," Jake whispered.

Ah, this was so Marcie wouldn't come after him for more riding crop games. Since Marcie was indeed aggressive along with being generous with her womanly parts, Lily Rose could indeed play along.

She kissed Jake.

In hindsight, that probably wasn't what he'd been expecting her to do. He had probably just planned on faking the kiss. He went stiff, all of him, even his hand, and since it was still in her panty region, she almost got an accidental orgasm.

"Oh," Marcie said, sounding not at all happy about what she was seeing.

But Marcie's disapproval was an itty bitty drop in a big ol' bucket compared to the voice Lily Rose heard next.

Lawson, Lily Rose's brother.

The mean, mule-headed one.

And he wasn't alone. Her cousin, Garrett, was on one side of Lawson. Her ex-boss, Ian, on the other side.

Lawson cursed, and his profanity was even worse than Jake's had been. It cast doubts on Jake's IQ and his paternity, and Lawson, Garrett and Ian followed that with similar questions they all asked at the same exact time.

"What the hell are you doing with my sister?" Lawson asked.

"What the hell are you doing with my cousin?" That from Garrett.

But Ian's was the loudest voice of them all. "What the hell are you doing with my girlfriend?"

CHAPTER TWO

BY TRYING TO avoid one pitfall—Marcie—Jake had ended up stepping in something he shouldn't have had his boots anywhere near.

Lily Rose.

Great day in the morning. Lily Rose and he always created a swath of trouble whenever they were together, and that swath had apparently led these four right to the barn.

Jake checked his watch—yeah, it was only six-thirty—and because of the hour, he decided to go on the defensive. "It's a little early for a visit," he said.

But he kept his tone as friendly as he could manage since he had to do business with Garrett and Lawson. Plus, on most days he liked them.

Not this day, though.

Garrett's brother, Roman, owned the ranch, but Garrett, their sister, Sophie, and Lawson were the ones who ran it. They were also Jake's former bosses and people he needed so he could keep a steady supply of livestock. No way did he want to piss them off.

Ian was a different story.

Jake would like very much to start some pissing off with him.

"Why are you here?" Jake snapped. "And since when are you Lily Rose's boyfriend?"

That was the real question, and even though Jake had heard rumblings that Ian and Lily Rose had been involved months ago, that was a far cry from slapping the girlfriend label on her.

None of his visitors got a chance to answer. That's because Lily Rose stepped forward, folded her arms over her chest and managed to look even more riled than all of them put together.

"None of your business," Lily Rose said to Lawson, obviously answering his question of what the hell Jake was doing with his sister.

"None of your business," she repeated to Garrett.

"And it's *really* none of your business," she snarled to Ian.

Marcie scurried away, probably so she could text every human in the tri-state area and let them know that Jake was carrying on with Lily Rose and that her brother, cousin and yet-to-be-determined boyfriend wanted to pulverize him for it.

"If you don't mind, and even if you do," Lily Rose added to the men, "I'm going to check on the horses." Huffing and grumbling something under her breath that Jake didn't catch, she headed out the back side of the barn.

All of them watched her leave. Garrett and Lawson, probably because they were considering going after her. Ian looked at her—specifically her butt—with lust. Jake had some thoughts like that about her, too, and he hoped her brother and cousin didn't notice.

They did.

Jake drew in a long stream of air that he figured he'd need to start this explanation. "Yes, I remember the talk we had about your sister being hands off," he said to Lawson. "And nothing happened. She's hands off. What you saw wasn't what you saw."

He probably should have rehearsed what he was going to say. Probably should have made sure his jeans were zipped, too, but Jake didn't realize they weren't until he glanced down in that area.

"What I saw was two people who've always had a thing for each other," Garrett added. "A thing that shouldn't have happened because of this dirthead." He hiked his thumb in Ian's direction.

"Hey!" Ian protested. "You don't know what happened between Lily Rose and me."

"I know she arrived at the Granger ranch all upset," Garrett answered just as quickly.

"Because I sold the horses she'd been training, but that was just business. Lily Rose knows that."

It might be business to Ian, but Jake had seen her with the horses. That wasn't her job. It was her life. He knew that because he felt the same way about the ranch he now owned.

"I'll deal with you later." Lawson aimed that snarled threat at Ian, but he directed his glare at Jake. "Lily Rose was grumpy at breakfast this morning, said it had nothing to do with the dirthead so Garrett and I drove over to have a little chat with you to see what was going on. We didn't know the dirthead would be here."

"Hey!" Ian repeated. "Hold off on the name-calling. Lily Rose and I had a falling out, but now I'm here to patch things up with her."

They all turned to scowl at Ian. He was an easy target since no one liked him much. Well, no one but women. Ian's rock-star looks often made women forget the fact that he was an asshole. Of course, they didn't forget it for long.

Lily Rose was proof of that.

"I'm going to find Lily Rose and talk to her," Ian said to no one in particular, and headed out the way she'd left.

Jake considered stopping him. Considered punching him, too. Because if what he'd heard about Ian giving Lily Rose a heart-stomping was true, then her ex-boss deserved a wallop or two. That still might happen, but first he needed to smooth things over with the Granger men.

"I've had some trouble with women lately," Jake explained. "Not that kind of trouble," he added when Lawson and Garrett glanced at his crotch. "It's just women keep pestering me, and that's not pestering in a good way. I can't get any work done. They sneak into my house and my truck. I can't go into town without one of them throwing herself at me."

"Marcie?" Garrett asked.

Jake nodded. "And that's why Lily Rose was kissing me, to get Marcie off my scent."

Well, that was part of why Lily Rose had kissed him. The other part, the one that had caused some stirrings behind his zipper, was because of the attraction. Garrett and Lawson weren't fools so they'd no doubt sensed it. Seen it, too, because that kiss had involved a little tongue.

Lawson and Garrett exchanged glances. "So, you're faking a relationship with a woman who works for you?" Garrett said.

"A woman too young for you," Lawson added, "who's just coming out of a bad relationship with a dirthead jerk?"

"Yeah, pretty much." But when they put it like that,

Jake could see flaws the size of Texas in his off-the-cuff plan.

Lawson had a follow-up question. "Are you the reason Lily Rose was crying this morning?"

Hell. Crying? This was the first Jake was hearing about it, and he honestly didn't know if he was the reason or not. "I told her yesterday that there couldn't be anything between us, but she didn't seem upset. In fact, she agreed."

Both Garrett and Lawson huffed. "Lily Rose would agree to a root canal without painkillers if *you* asked her. She's a smart woman, but her brain turns to mush whenever she's around you. That's why it's up to you to make sure nothing starts up between you two again."

Jake hadn't known for sure about the brain-mush part. Probably because he had a similar problem when it came to Lily Rose. But there appeared to be something else happening here. Yes, Garrett and Lawson were on the protective side, but this seemed above and beyond the call of genetic responsibility.

"Is there something going on with Lily Rose?" Jake came out and asked.

Garrett and Lawson gave each other an uneasy look. Not a good thing. Because it made Jake anxious, too. "Ian didn't knock her up, did he?" Because if he had, Jake was indeed going to beat the crap out of him.

"No," Lawson answered, and he paused. "Ian broke off things with Lily Rose months ago. The only reason she continued working for him was because of the horses."

"Then, why the hell does Ian still think she's his girlfriend?"

"You'd have to ask dundernuts that question." Lawson glared at him again. "I just don't want you piling anything else on Lily Rose right now. And sleeping with her and getting her hopes up about you two would be piling it on. Just keep your distance from her, okay?"

Jake should have just made a sound of agreement, said goodbye and got to work. He had fences to check and paperwork to do. But he stayed put.

"Is Lily Rose upset because of something going on in your family?" Jake asked Lawson.

It was a legit question. There always seemed to be some feuding going on with the Grangers. It had started two generations ago as a dispute over some ranch land and continued today between Lawson's family and Garrett's clan. Despite that feud, which often turned bitter, Lily Rose and Lawson had managed to stay friendly with their cousins.

"Lily Rose is already going to be madder than a hornet because we came here," Lawson said. "Anything else you hear should come from her."

Hell. So, there was something to hear. Something that apparently Lawson and Garrett weren't going to tell him because they walked away. Jake did some walking, too, straight out the back of the barn so he could find Lily Rose. He didn't have to go far. She was in the corral with the horses and the horse's ass—Ian.

Lily Rose had her arms resting on top of the fence, her left foot on one of the lower slats, and she was having a whispered conversation with Ian. An angry one, judging from her tense shoulders.

Since pretty much anything Jake could say to them would make him sound A) jealous B) nosy or C) a horse's ass equal to Ian's status, he just went with sounding like a boss.

"I want you to work with Zeke and the chestnut today,"

he said to Lily Rose. Zeke was one of his hands and due at the ranch any minute now, and like all the hands, Lily Rose was training him on the cutting horses. Of course, once she was done with that training, her job would be finished here, but Jake was beginning to think that wasn't a bad thing. Lily Rose and he played a little too well together for her to stick around.

"Lily Rose and I were talking," Ian protested. He said it as if Jake cared even a little about that.

"Tough. She works for me now, and she can't do that if you're around here yapping in her ear. Chat her up on her off time."

"Just go," she said to Ian. "I'll be fine. I'll work it out."

Okay, that didn't sound like a conversation about a broken heart or her considering getting back together with this clown. Good. Because Ian didn't deserve a second chance to give her any more misery. Too bad he'd already caused plenty of that, though.

Or maybe something else had put that troubled look on Lily Rose's face.

"I would have never sold you these horses if I'd known you were going to act like a jerk," Ian said to him.

"You wouldn't have sold them if you hadn't been trying to get back at Lily Rose," Jake countered. It was a guess on his part, but it must have been a good one because the corner of Lily Rose's mouth lifted in a smile. Ian, however, didn't smile.

"I'll call you," Ian told her, and stormed off.

Lily Rose moved as if to leave, too, to go into the corral with the horses, but Jake stepped in front of her. "You want to tell me what's going on?" he asked.

"No," she answered right off. Then, she groaned. "Obviously, Ian is trying to get back together with me."

He waited for her to add that there was no way in hell that was going to happen. But she didn't. What she did do was groan again before she continued.

"It's tricky," she said, "because more than anything I just want to train cutting horses from champion bloodlines. Well, guess who controls a lot of the buyers and stock for that?"

Ian.

Even Jake had had to do business with the moron.

"You're not saying you'd get back with Ian just so you'd have a job?" he asked.

"No," she snapped just as quickly as she had before. "But I have to walk a fine line with him. Until I can start my own business, that is, and then I'll give him some competition to take him down a notch."

Jake shrugged. "Seems like you could start that business now. Well, after you finish with these horses. You could put that Granger trust fund to good use."

She made a sound that could have meant anything. Or nothing. And she looked at him. "You and I have similar problems. We both have someone trying to put strings and rings on us. Of course, what with all the women after you, you have a lot more people trying to do that to you than I do, but Ian's not the sort to just give up."

No, he wasn't, and Jake thought he knew where she was going with this. "You want everyone to think we're together. That way, you can keep Ian at bay without outright telling him to get lost."

She nodded. "And it would work for you, too. It would put a stop to all those women chasing you. It would certainly stop Marcie from surprising you in your bedroom. That in turn would prevent you from having to buy bigger towels."

Lily Rose winked at him.

That wink shouldn't have caused a frenzy in his jeans, but it did. He'd definitely given her an eyeful when she'd walked into the barn to find him naked, but that wasn't a good thing. They already had enough heat between them without adding eyefuls and nakedness to the mix.

"Just think," she added. "No more having to duck and cover when you go to the Longhorn Bar."

Yeah. Not having to do that was an upside he wanted to latch onto. But there were also a couple of really big downsides. "Your brother and cousin won't like this," he reminded her.

"I can tell them what's going on and swear them to secrecy." She answered fast enough to let him know she'd given this a little thought. "Of course, we can't let too many people in on it or it'll get out. In other words, your hands are going to think you're breaking a cardinal rule by playing around with me."

Interesting word choice—playing around—and Jake's body was already coming up with ideas as to how to do that. Those ideas weren't for a fake relationship, either. They involved sex.

Which couldn't happen.

At least not until Lily Rose had finished working for him, that is. Even then it would be plenty hard to convince Lawson and Garrett that he wasn't out to stomp on Lily Rose's heart the way Ian had.

"So, do we have a deal?" she asked.

He was still debating it, thinking about all the angles, especially those that could come back to bite them in their butts. But then he made the mistake of turning toward her. The sun was barely up, but it was hitting her face just right. Or just wrong if he hadn't wanted to be reminded that Lily Rose was a mouth-watering woman.

And she noticed the way he was looking at her.

Worse, she started looking at him the same way—as if she'd like to have him for breakfast.

"For this to work, people would have to see us together," he said more to himself than to her. "Playing with fire usually turns out bad."

She smiled. "But it can be fun, too." Lily Rose laughed, dropped a kiss on his cheek and headed back into the barn. "Think of all the cold showers in our future."

He was, and Jake was also thinking about something else.

Just how fast and how hard they were going to fail.

CHAPTER THREE

"You are so going to fail at this," Sophie said to Lily Rose.

It was exactly the response Lily Rose had expected from her cousin after she'd told Sophie that Jake and she were going to pretend to be lovers.

"Don't you remember what happened between you and him when you were eighteen?" Sophie added. She had a sip of her margarita and looked at Lily Rose from over the top of her salty rim.

"Of course, I remember." In wonderful perfect details. Jake hadn't been her first lover, that'd happened a year earlier with her then high school boyfriend. But Jake had a way of branding himself into her memories.

Triple orgasms could do that.

"And don't you remember how you cried when Jake broke things off because he said you were too young?" Sophie kept on.

Her cousin was obviously trying to drill home that this fake relationship was a bad idea, but Lily Rose needed no such convincing. It was bad, and yes, she would fail. Heck, she'd probably get another broken heart out of it, too.

"I remember all of it," Lily Rose assured her. "And there are a lot of reasons why I should back away from this." Solid reasons, too. That didn't mean she was going to play it safe. Not when she had such a hot fire to make sure she got good and burned.

Lily Rose sighed, drank her wine. "Maybe I feel as if I need to be punished."

Sophie's eyebrow came up. "You're not going to borrow Marcie's riding crop, are you?"

Lily Rose dismissed that with another huff, but it might be fun to smack Jake's butt with it. Actually, it might be fun just to see his butt. Along with the rest of him.

"I can set you up on a date with one of Brantley's lawyer friends," Sophie suggested. "That way you can maybe have a real relationship rather than a fake one."

Brantley was Sophie's longtime boyfriend and fiancé. Lily Rose had always thought he had the personality of a generic potato chip bag. Which wasn't much personality at all. But since Sophie seemed to be in love with him, Lily Rose held her tongue. However, tongue-holding wasn't a good idea when it came to matchmaking. She might end up with someone like Brantley.

Lily Rose shook her head. "Thanks but no thanks. Actually, I think it's a good idea for me to take a break from men. It hasn't been that long since Ian broke up with me—"

"Over four months ago," Sophie provided. "That's plenty of time for you to move on especially since you don't want to get back together with him." She paused. "Do you?"

"God, no. Lesson learned." She should have learned it sooner, though.

After the breakup, Ian had made her work environment as hellish as possible, but she had been under contract. Walking away from that would have hurt her future prospects in the business along with making her look like a wimp for not being able to handle the pressure. Plus, it wasn't as if she had a lot of options.

"I'd prefer a guy not cheat on me after demanding that we be in a monogamist relationship." Lily Rose stopped. "But just because I don't want Ian, it doesn't mean I should jump in bed with someone else."

Sophie gave her a flat look. "If you stay around Jake, bed jumping will happen. That's why you should just give up this ruse and start dating for real."

It made too much sense, and it was taking Lily Rose a while to come up with an argument to counter such logic. Thankfully, she got a distraction to interrupt the conversation. And the distraction was yet another hot cowboy.

Sophie's brother, Roman.

It seemed as if time stopped when he walked in. Women certainly stopped anyway, and those seated at the bar and in booths all turned in his direction as if their eyes were metal, and he was the magnet.

Simply put, Roman got people's attention.

Lily Rose's, too. Even though he was her cousin, she'd always loved him like a brother. Since she rarely got to see him, it was a little like a visit from Santa Claus.

Roman spotted them and headed their way, the eyes in the room following him. When he made it to their booth, Sophie moved over to make a spot for him, but he kept standing.

"I can't stay," he said. "I'm heading to the ranch to do some paperwork, but Lawson asked me to check on you." He directed his concern at Lily Rose. "He mentioned that you'd cried. And that you had hooked up with Jake again."

In addition to eyes being on them, ears were, too.

"The crying was allergies," Lily Rose lied, "but uh, yes, I'm back with Jake. We're very happy."

Roman's hands went on his hips, creating some sighs in the room. Probably because it caused his jeans to tighten over all the right parts of him. "Bull crap," he snarled. "You don't have the look of a satisfied woman, and I just saw Jake because he's out front trying to fend off one of the Busby sisters. No satisfied look on him, either. So, what's going on?"

"Jake's out front?" Lily Rose repeated. Of course, what concerned her more was the Busby sister. Marcie was tame compared to that Busby gene pool.

Roman blocked her from leaving when she got up. "Look, I don't like putting my nose in your business. Especially when I've got better places for my nose to be. But I need to know if I should be worried about you."

He gave a bad-boy glower to Candy Mercer who was inching closer, batting her eyelashes and looking ready to jump him where he stood. Roman's glower, however, was the equivalent of a wink for most women because Candy kept coming

"You don't have to worry about me. But thanks for checking." Lily Rose kissed his cheek to reassure him that all was well. It wasn't, of course. Maybe Roman knew that, too, but he didn't stop her when she hurried out.

It didn't take long for Lily Rose to find Jake. He was parked just up the street about a half block away from the bar and was standing next to his truck, his back against the driver's side door. He wasn't alone, of course. Nelly Busby was there right in front of him. However, it wasn't exactly the scene Lily Rose had expected to see.

For one thing, Jake was laughing, and while Nelly

was indeed leaning in a little too close to him, her body language wasn't of a woman who was on an aggressive prowl. This was more like flirting.

Jake stopped laughing when he saw Lily Rose, and he started toward her. Nelly's flirting expression vanished, and she gave Lily Rose the stink eye that many single women in town had been giving her.

"I was just looking for you," Jake said, giving Lily Rose a quick kiss. It was very similar to the one she'd given Roman. Similar in quickness and pressure anyway, but it still packed a wallop. "I saw Roman, and he said you were inside with Sophie."

Lily Rose nodded. "Are you here for a drink?"

He tipped his head to the lawyer's office just up the street. "I had some papers to sign."

Papers that probably had to do with his inheritance. Depending on who you talked to, that inheritance was worth a million or more. Other folks thought it was much less than that and that Jake had used every penny to buy the ranch and get it going.

"I probably shouldn't say anything," Nelly grumbled, "but it's hard to believe you two are back together. I mean, neither of you look very happy about it or anything."

Since Roman had just told Lily Rose something similar, she immediately tried to change her expression. She also hooked her arm through Jake's and kissed him. Not one of those for-show pecks, either. Lily Rose made it count.

They ignored Nelly, and even though Lily Rose broke the kiss and eased her mouth from Jake's, they continued to stare into each other's eyes. Hopefully, it looked intimate as if they were starved for each other and couldn't wait for Nelly to leave.

"Fine, be that way," Nelly finally snapped. On a loud huff, she turned and walked off.

"Thanks," he whispered with his mouth still so close to Lily Rose's that she could easily go back for seconds. Well, she could have if Jake hadn't stepped away and let go of her arm.

Lily Rose had to level her breathing some just so she could speak. "You didn't look as if you needed to be rescued from Nelly."

His eyebrow came up. "She said she was thinking about making a homemade porn movie, and she wanted me to star in it."

Oh. So, perhaps that's why Jake had been laughing. Sheez. Maybe this hadn't been a wasted trip to save him, after all.

"The kiss did the job," he pointed out, sounding unaffected by the lip-lock. Unlike her. Lily Rose was certain she sounded asthmatic, and her whole body felt flushed. "But I need to come up with something else. Something that works. Because it didn't work when I told Nelly I wasn't interested in not only the sex tape but also her."

Lily Rose shrugged. "You might have to be rude. I know that's hard for you, though."

He looked away from her, dodging her gaze. "I don't like being mean to women."

"Because of your mom." His dad had been mean, both verbally and physically abusive, and Jake had been the one to try to soothe things over, and most of the time it'd worked. Though Lily Rose did remember his mom, Pam, once sporting a black eye. Jake had had a couple of those, too, before he'd gotten old enough to fight back.

"By the way, how's your mom doing?" she asked.

"Good. She finally got it right when she divorced my dad and found a guy who'd treat her right. They've been married about five years now and live in Tennessee where he works."

Yes, Lily Rose had heard that. Good for Pam. The woman deserved some happiness. Too bad, though, that Jake's father had done so much damage, not just to Pam but to Jake as well. Even now, she could see the pain in his eyes when he turned back to her.

Jake forced a smile, and she could see him pushing all that old baggage down deep inside him. "Did Roman come to tell you to stay away from me?"

"Pretty much. My brother and cousins don't think I can survive a broken heart, and they're fairly sure that's what'll happen if we 'date.'"

Jake lifted his shoulder. "If I can't be mean to Marcie, why would I break your heart?"

"Because you did it before." Oops. She hadn't meant to just blurt that out. "You didn't break it intentionally," she quickly added. "I was just too young, got too close. You weren't looking for Ms. Right."

"You were eighteen," he pointed out. "You weren't looking for Mr. Right, either."

"True." Well, maybe it was true. The fact was that all men since Jake had paled in comparison so even if she hadn't been on the hunt for the right guy, it was highly likely she'd found him.

And lost him.

She would lose him again, too. If she ever got him back, that is. Because she wasn't in a good place to be in a relationship, and it was highly likely being with Jake would blow up in her face. Unless she limited it to just sex, that is.

Of course, sex with Jake didn't seem like much of a limit.

"You had dreams," he went on. "You wouldn't have fulfilled those dreams if you'd committed to a ranch hand when you were just weeks out of high school."

"Dreams," she repeated. Yes, she'd had them all right. "Dream number one was not to work for my brother, Lucian." She loved Lucian, but no way did she want to get sucked into running his cattle empire. "Even back then I knew I wasn't an office person."

"Then you probably shouldn't have been born with a trust fund." He added a smile to that, and Lily Rose quickly tried to smile right back. "Or you shouldn't have been born a Granger. Family expectations and all that. I'd imagine it's easy to choke on a silver spoon."

It was. And that was what Lily Rose had done. Soon, she'd need to tell Jake all about that. But not until she'd finished working for him.

"So, what's your dream these days?" he asked.

Lily Rose finally managed that smile, but she avoided looking him straight in the eyes. Too easy for him to see that something was wrong. Instead, she looked at his chest, the way his denim shirt stretched against all those muscles. Then, her attention drifted slightly lower.

"That's your dream?" he asked, chuckling.

"At the moment, yes, but I think the kiss is responsible for that."

He smiled, that incredible smile that somehow made her go even hotter than when he'd kissed her. "Other than *that*, what's your dream these days?"

"To own my own cutting horse operation. Nothing big,

but I'd like it to be where I not only supervise the cutters but also do it all from start to finish. That includes hand-picking the horses..." She stopped when she noticed he was smiling again. "What?"

"Your eyes just lit up. The only other time I've seen that happen was when you..." Now, he stopped.

Good thing, too, because she was pretty sure he was about to say "have an orgasm." Lily Rose didn't need that reminder, especially coming so soon after she'd gawked at him. And kissed him. And thought about having sex with him.

"Are we going to fail at this fake stuff and end up in bed?" she asked.

But at the same moment Jake asked his own question. "Why don't you just buy a cutting horse operation like that—"

He stopped, no doubt because he'd finally heard what she'd asked. Jake cursed, scrubbed his hand over his face. "Probably. But only after you no longer work for me."

So, two weeks, tops. Part of her wasn't sure she could wait that long, but the sane logical part knew that after the job was finished, she should just walk away.

She wouldn't just walk, of course.

When it came to Jake, she was never sane and logical.

"Marcie," Jake said, adding more profanity.

It took Lily Rose a moment to realize he'd said the woman's name because she had come out of the Long-horn, her attention immediately zooming in their direction. She was probably cursing Lily Rose under her breath for being with Jake, but she still came toward them.

"Your *boyfriend* just came in through the side door of the bar," Marcie told her. There was some smugness mixed with glee in her voice. "He's looking for you."

Crud. She was so not in the mood to deal with Ian today. But apparently, Ian was in the mood to deal with her. Because he came out the front door, and as Marcie had done, he immediately started toward Jake and her.

Lily Rose was about to tell Jake that it was show time, but he was already one step ahead of her.

"Let's stop Ian in his tracks," Jake said.

That was the only warning Lily Rose got before Jake yanked her to him and kissed her. There was no leading into this kiss. And it was definitely no peck. It started off hot and quickly jumped to whatever temperature was beyond scalding.

The memories came. Of other kisses. Of other things they'd done together after the kisses. Lily Rose's pulse revved up. So did her body, and despite the fact they were standing on Main Street, a certain part of her body thought she was about to get lucky with Jake.

Lily Rose had no idea if it truly did stop Ian in his tracks, but she was reasonably sure of one thing.

The kiss had melted her toenail polish.

CHAPTER FOUR

JAKE REINED IN his horse and climbed from the saddle to take a look at the creek. If anyone had asked him why he was there, he would have said it was to check the water level, but the truth was, he just liked this spot. If he looked behind him, he saw his pastures.

His.

Something he never thought he would have owned when he was growing up just a couple of miles away. As it always did, he felt the little catch in his heart. Good thing he didn't have to mention that to anyone. Cowboys didn't have heart-catches.

It was hot, the air heavy with humidity, and it wouldn't be long before rain moved in. The pastures needed it, but if he didn't hurry back, he was going to get caught in what could turn out to be a downpour. Still, even with that threat looming, he didn't budge.

He couldn't wait for his mom to see the place, to know that he'd gotten exactly what he'd dreamed about as a kid. So many times he'd looked at the Granger Ranch and thought something like this was out of his reach. Now with the passing of his widowed grandfather and the inheritance the man had left him, Jake had reached it.

So, why did it feel as if he still had an empty spot inside him? Why did he still feel like that kid who was getting the hell beaten out of him while trying to protect his mother?

And why did he feel as if he needed sex?

The answer to the last question was easy. That was because he spotted Lily Rose riding out toward him. Seeing her always brought sex to mind. Probably because of the kiss that'd happened a week ago on Main Street. He should have never done that. Instead, he should have settled for a pretend kiss. If he had, he might be feeling pretend sex urges right about now.

"You're gonna get wet," she said. She was smiling, and she pointed up to the thick iron-gray clouds.

"I don't see you carrying an umbrella," he joked.

She shrugged, got off the bay mare and made her way to him. "I like getting caught in the rain." Lily Rose glanced around. "So, are you out here surveying your kingdom?"

"Something like that."

She turned, looked at the same view of the pastures that he'd just been admiring. Now though, he was admiring something else. Lily Rose, in those jeans. Mercy, that didn't cool down his thoughts about sex.

"You've been avoiding me," she said. Not a question. And it was true.

He could have lied and said he'd been busy. He had been, but he still could have managed to run into her. Jake had just made sure, though, that he was in his office around the time she'd be arriving and leaving.

"I thought we both could use some space," he settled for saying.

She didn't argue with that, but she certainly could have. After all, they were pretending to be a couple. Hard to do that when they weren't with each other. But then, it'd worked for him. At least there hadn't been any naked women turning up in his bedroom.

"Any contact from Ian?" he asked.

She sighed and re-gathered her hair into a fresh ponytail. "Daily emails and texts. In one of them he gave me permission to have sex with you so I could get you out of my system."

There it was again. That word—*sex*. It made his groin tighten. Of course, Lily Rose's butt in those jeans was likely responsible for that. He was thankful when she finally turned around to face him.

"Permission?" Jake repeated. "This guy does know that he doesn't own you, right?"

"Ian has a problem with boundaries. And being faithful. Oh, and sharing. FYI, never take a French fry, even a limp greasy one, off his plate. You'll end up getting a lecture about boundaries."

This guy was sounding like an even bigger tool with everything Jake was learning about him. And Jake was feeling like a randy teenager with every passing second as well. The front of Lily Rose was just as groin-tightening as the backside of her.

"What about you?" she asked. "Any contact from Marcie or the other women?"

"Peace and quiet. I can thank you for that."

"Well, actually you can thank the kiss outside the Longhorn. We might have broken a few laws doing that."

Yeah, and they'd broken something else. Barriers that should have stayed in place. At least another week or so, anyway, when he was no longer Lily Rose's boss.

He felt the first few drops of rain and started for his horse. He didn't make it far, though, because Lily Rose caught on to his hand when he went to walk by her.

"Look, a rainbow." She pointed to the spot on the horizon where there was just a sliver of colors. That wasn't a sliver of a smile, though. It was dazzling, and when she turned that smile on him, Jake thought maybe he'd forgotten how to breathe.

Hell.

He reminded himself of why they needed barriers. Lily Rose had already done the deed of sleeping with her boss, and that hadn't worked out so well. Even though it was something he'd never done, he had seen it create some very sticky situations.

Like now.

They were standing there in the drizzle, staring at each other, and the fire was already snapping at him. The best thing he could do was get on his horse and ride back to the house.

But he didn't.

The rain was already falling on her face, but despite that she wasn't moving, either, and she was still smiling. A smile that now seemed to say "take me."

So, that's what Jake did. He kissed her, knowing that it was a dangerous thing to do. Unlike when they were on Main Street, there was no one around to make him put on the brakes. But the only saving grace was that he didn't have a condom with him. That and that alone might stop this from turning to full-blown sex.

Lily Rose kissed him right back, and she didn't pull any punches. She went deep from the start, and she grabbed on to handfuls of his shirt to drag him closer. Not that she had to work hard to do that. Jake was already moving in her direction, and that direction ended up with her back against a sprawling oak.

The tree was full enough to give them some cover

from the drizzle, but even if it hadn't been, that wouldn't have stopped them. The kiss seemed to have a momentum of its own, and it fired up a heat that was already too hot.

Jake figured that heat was why this turned into some kind of race. A race where speed mattered, because the kiss became frantic pretty fast, and with frantic kisses came frantic touches, and he slid his hand between them to cup her left breast. She was wearing a bra, but her nipple was easy to locate since it was puckered, and he swiped his thumb over it. That caused a nice reaction.

She cursed him and made a silky sound of pleasure. So, he did it again. When he got a similar reaction, he gave her other breast the same attention.

And more.

He pushed up her top, shoved down her bra and replaced his thumb swiping with his tongue. Now, that got a very special reaction from Lily Rose. She cursed him again and ran her hand down into his jeans. He got a reaction of his own.

Jake cursed, too. And he went rock-hard.

Since rock-hard made it impossible to think straight, he took hold of her, gripping both of her wrists in one hand, and he pinned her to the tree. She protested, of course, whimpered, and tried to grind her zipper against his. Not a bad place to do some grinding, and again, it wasn't helping with that whole thinking straight thing he needed right now.

Jake quieted her by kissing her neck and pushing his leg between hers. It was a high school move because it basically meant she was riding his thigh, but it gave him a moment to regroup.

The moment didn't last.

She got one of her hands free and went after his zipper.

"We can't," he assured her. "Even if that's what we want really, really bad." He could have added a few more "really's" in there, too. "I don't have a condom."

Lily Rose stared at him, blinked. And her hand went between them. Not to go after his zipper this time. But to take a foil-wrapped packet from her pocket.

"I wanted to be prepared," she said. She said it tentatively as if she weren't sure if it'd been the right thing.

It wasn't.

Because that condom was a massive temptation right now.

"One of us would get splinters on our butt," he reminded her. Or bruises from the rocks on the creek bank. Plus, there was the rain. It was coming down harder now, and it wouldn't be long before they would be soaking wet.

"The splinters might be worth it," she said.

In other words, she was giving him the green light. A light he couldn't take. But that didn't mean he couldn't do something about this fire. Well, about the fire inside her, anyway. Jake did a repeat of what Lily Rose had done earlier and slid his hand into her jeans.

"The condom," she said, but it only took him a second to find the spot that hushed her protest.

It wasn't a pretty way to finish this, but it was a way that would get him into the least amount of trouble. It also didn't mean he couldn't enjoy it. He kissed her, letting the taste of her slide right through him. Of course, the heat was doing some sliding, too, and urging him to make use of that condom.

He didn't.

Jake kept touching her. Kept up the kissing, too, and when he felt her getting close, he eased back so he could watch her face when she came.

It was a mistake.

Because her face was even more amazing now with that dreamy look of pleasure. It made him harder than he already was. Made him curse himself for having a stupid-assed rule about not having sex with someone who worked for him. Because this was a hundred notches above that long kiss they'd shared on Main Street.

And that was when he knew that he'd just screwed up big-time.

"I'm sorry," he said, resting his forehead against the tree.

"Regrets already?"

Yeah, but not for the reason she thought. "I'm sorry because next time I'm going to put that condom to good use."

LILY ROSE KNEW there was a surefire way to kill an orgasm buzz. It wasn't the rainy ride back to the ranch or even that Jake was seeping with sullenness over what had just happened. No. It was the fact that she saw Ian in the barn when Jake and she rode up.

Jake's sullenness was a drop in the bucket compared to the riled look that Ian was giving them.

"Nice ride?" Ian asked in a tone laced with sarcasm.

"Very," she answered, knowing it was like poking at a wasps' nest with a stick. She reminded herself that Ian could hurt her six ways to Sunday when it came to business, but since she had a backbone and a mouth that often got her into trouble, she wasn't in a butt-kissing mood.

Lily Rose turned to Jake as they led their horses into the barn. "Can you give me a minute with Ian? I need to get some things straight."

Jake didn't budge, but he did glare at Ian. She really

didn't want this to turn into a testosterone match so she stepped between them. "I'm not going to punch him," Ian snarled. His eyes narrowed. She doubted Ian could get off a punch before Jake could knock him cold, but what annoyed her was that Ian obviously thought he had some reason to be upset about her going off riding with another man. Or that the man had given her a nice, rainy climax against a tree. Lily Rose really needed to set him straight, but since Ian could play dirty, it was best to do the straightening when Jake wasn't there. Plus, she really didn't want this to come to blows, and with Ian's penchant for irritating people, it could easily happen.

"Could you please give Ian and me a minute?" Lily Rose asked Jake again.

Before she even looked at him, she knew his eyes would be narrowed, knew that her request wasn't going to make him happy. Of course, he was already unhappy about what had happened so her request only added to his scowl. She partly expected him to bark out some kind of order about which horse and which hand he wanted her to work with today, but he didn't. Jake just walked away, leaving his gelding with her and heading out the front of the barn and toward his house.

Ian turned to watch him leave, and didn't say anything until Jake was out of earshot. "Does he know?" he asked.

Lily Rose understood the question, knew exactly what he meant, but she didn't want to hear it all spelled out. "No."

Ian made a sound, the kind a person would make when they knew someone had screwed up in a big way. "He'll think you're like all those other women he's trying to avoid."

Yes. He would. But again, this wasn't something she

wanted to rehash. "Are you here for a reason or is it just to state the obvious?"

"Both," he readily answered. He smiled. "I want you to come back to work for me."

Now, Lily Rose made a sound, the kind a person would make when they'd just heard something ridiculous. "You fired me, remember?"

He lifted his shoulder. "You and I both know I did that out of anger."

"Anger?" she repeated. "You did it because I found out you were having sex with another woman."

He didn't dispute that. In fact, Ian nodded. "It was a stupid business decision on my part. You're an excellent trainer, and I can give you the opportunity to rise to the top."

These were words she had desperately wanted to hear. Four months ago, anyway. "You want me to go back to the way things were before? I can't—"

"No," he interrupted. "I don't want to hire you just as a trainer. I want you to supervise a huge cutting horse program. After a couple of years, I'll make sure you have your own operation. I can supply the horses and you can focus on the training. I've already lined up buyers for them, too. Logan McCord over in Spring Hill."

She knew Logan. He had the cream of the crop when it came to cutting horse stock. And having her own business was exactly what she wanted. But none of this felt right—probably because it wasn't.

"Ian, why are you doing this?" she asked. "And please don't tell me it's because you're in love with me."

"No," he repeated. "This isn't about love or sex. It's business. You can make me a lot of money and vice versa. We can both get what we want out of this venture, and if we decide to start seeing each other again, then it'll have no bearing on the cutting horse operation."

Maybe, but she still wasn't convinced, and Lily Rose reminded herself that Ian loved to wheel and deal. He wanted things he couldn't have, and maybe now that he thought she was interested in Jake, this was his attempt to win her back. But there was a huge problem.

She was interested in Jake.

Not just for a fake relationship, either. She was thinking she wanted the real deal. Too bad she might have blown any chance of that happening. Even after her job was finished with him, he almost certainly wouldn't want her if he thought she was like all the other women in Wrangler's Creek.

"I can see you're thinking it over," Ian said. Yes, she was, but probably not in the way he believed she was. "Good. Because this is your dream job. Just remember that."

She stared at him. "What's the catch? And yes, I know you said this was strictly business, but I know you, and there has to be something else."

Bingo. His hesitation let her know that she'd been right. Ian was up to something.

"People are talking about me," he finally said. "About us. About how you ditched me for another man."

"I didn't," she interrupted. "You ditched me, and what does this have to do with the offer you just made?"

"It has everything to do with it." Another long pause. "This situation with you has made me look like a wronged man. And yes, I know I'm the one who ended the relationship, but some people don't seem to believe that."

"Some people?" she questioned.

He lifted his shoulder. "Some folks I do business with.

They think less of me because they're under the impression that my woman ran off with another man. It's hurting my company."

Lily Rose was certain she looked at him as if he were crazy. "That doesn't make a lick of sense."

"Not to you," he readily agreed. "Not to me, either. But it's just the way things are."

Maybe, though she did think that was shortsighted of these business associates. But even if what Ian was saying was true, she still had no idea where he was going with this.

Uh-oh.

Lily Rose suddenly got an idea, though.

"You want me to walk away from training Jake's horses?" she asked, hoping that wasn't it.

However, Ian nodded. And he didn't hesitate with that nod. "To get the dream job you've always wanted, you have to leave here *today*."

"Today?" Lily Rose questioned, but that was all she got to say because Ian kept on talking.

"I'm sure you'll want Jake to have a steady supply of the livestock he needs. Like what happened a few hours ago. He lost out of a deal because someone paid above market value for a herd he wanted."

Oh, mercy. She had no trouble filling in the blanks on this one. "You bought that herd." And it wasn't a question. "Let me get this straight. Are you threatening to hurt Jake's ranch if I don't go back to work for you?"

"You're a smart girl. Figure it out." And with that, Ian strolled away.

CHAPTER FIVE

JAKE WAS REASONABLY sure his mood couldn't get any worse. He'd lost a cattle sale that he needed to increase his herd. The nonstop rain had slowed down some fence repairs and some other ranching chores. And the training on the cutting horses had ground to a halt. That was because Lily Rose had told one of his hands that she'd needed to take some personal time.

Personal time was code for her regretting that hand job he'd given her against the tree.

Jake had known it was a mistake right from the start, and now Lily Rose might be thinking of leaving. That wasn't a guess, either. Delbert, one of this hands, had seen her after she finished her conversation with Ian in the barn, and Delbert had said she looked upset. Ian, on the other hand, had looked pleased with himself. Of course, Delbert wasn't an expert in body language so who the hell knew what was going on.

He ducked his head under the shower, hoping it would help clear the dull ache there. It didn't, and he finally gave up after a couple of minutes. He dried off, pulled on his boxers and went toward the kitchen for a beer and whatever he could scrounge up in the fridge to eat. However, he only made it a few steps before he heard a sound he didn't want to hear.

Someone was moving around in his bedroom.

Hell. He didn't want to go another round with Marcie so Jake put on the toughest scowl he could manage and went to face her down. But it wasn't Marcie.

It was Lily Rose.

Not naked, though she was sitting on his bed.

Jake hadn't thought there was a cure for his bad mood, but the sight of her sure helped. For a couple of moments, anyway. During those moments, he remembered just how good those kisses had been. How much he wanted her. But after those moments passed, he remembered something else. That she was probably here to tell him that it was over between them. Not that it'd actually been *on*, but she probably wanted to ditch even the fake relationship.

She fluttered her fingers in the general direction of his living room. "Your front door was unlocked. You really shouldn't keep doing that, or you might find Marcie in here again."

True, but that didn't explain why Lily Rose was here. Jake was about to ask her that, but he got distracted when he realized she was looking him over from head to toe. Probably because there was a lot of bare skin in between those body parts. Jake could have reached for some clothes, but he figured he'd have plenty of time to do that after she left.

"Are you here to tell me that you're quitting?" he asked. She blinked as if surprised by that conclusion. "One of the hands mentioned you looked upset or something after Ian left," he added.

She stared at him. "You find a woman on your bed, and the first thing you think to ask is if she's quitting." Lily Rose shook her head, smiled, but the smile didn't quite make it to her eyes. "I must be losing my touch."

No, she wasn't. He'd felt her touch, and everything was just fine in that department.

She stood, walked to him. It was probably a bad idea since they always did stupid things when they got close to each other. Lily Rose knew that, too, but it didn't stop her. She just kept coming until she was only a few inches away.

"I wish things were different," she said. No smile, and he saw something in her eyes that he didn't want to see. Sadness. Maybe even regret.

Hell.

She was quitting.

Delbert had apparently been right after all about her being upset. Jake reminded himself that her leaving was a good thing. Lily Rose wasn't someone who should be working for him. Still, he figured there was more to this than just her ending her employment.

"Are you going back to Ian?" he asked.

She gave another blink of surprise. "No. Not like that. But he wants me to work for him again."

Clearly, she was considering doing that, but he couldn't understand why. And he didn't get a chance to understand it, either. That was because she kissed him. Oh, man, she tasted good. Like all those things he'd been dreaming about for a long, long time.

Jake had had plenty of kisses, and he'd always seen them coming but not this one. Probably because he'd been expecting an answer to his question.

Are you going back to Ian?

Obviously, Lily Rose thought that could wait because in addition to the kiss, she leaned in, brushing her body against his, and she deepened the kiss.

"I don't want to talk about Ian," she whispered against his mouth.

Suddenly, Jake didn't want to talk about the man, either. The effect of the kiss kicked in, knocking out of him what little sense he had left, and he multiplied Lily Rose's mistake by hooking his arm around her. He snapped her to him, not that much snapping was required.

Jake continued things from there.

And Lily Rose let him do that.

In the back of his mind, he knew this was another mistake, but it was obvious this was why she'd come here. Perhaps this was her way of saying goodbye. If so, it was a darn good way—with one exception. When he had her in his arms like this, he wasn't wanting goodbye to play into it. Of course, that was the lust talking. It was doing some talking for Lily Rose as well, but when the heat cooled, she might be more than ready to tell him what was eating away at her.

For now, though, he just slid right into the flow of that heat.

Lily Rose did her part. She kissed him right back, all the while tugging and pulling him closer. It was hard to manage that since they were already plastered against each other, but all that tugging and pulling upped the urgency. So did the French kisses. And it didn't take long for them to start moving in the direction of the bed. All in all, it was a good direction if this were going to lead to full-blown sex. Judging from Lily Rose's kisses, that was her plan, but Jake had to be sure this was what she truly wanted.

He pulled back, his eyes meeting hers. "Are you sure?"

Or at least that was what he intended to say. Jake got out the "are" and a little of "you" before Lily Rose latched onto the back of his neck and went after his mouth again. Jake pretty much gave up asking questions after that. Heck, he gave up any notion of common sense, too, and he figured if he was going to make a mistake, then it might as well be a good one.

He backed her to the bed, pushing her onto the mattress, and since they were coiled around each other, when she fell, he fell with her.

Maybe it was the pressure of his body against her, the wild kisses or the fact they'd already worked each other up from what had happened against that tree. It didn't seem to matter why, only that Jake decided he had to have her now. Lily Rose seemed perfectly fine with that decision. In fact, she started in on his clothes. Of course, she didn't have much to remove since he was only wearing his boxers, but she stripped those off while he was going after her top.

He'd kissed her breasts earlier. Years ago, too. But it was even better this time around. Maybe because she made that needy sound when he took her nipple into his mouth. Maybe because she latched on to his ears and pulled him to her. He lingered there a moment and then gave her other breast the same kissing attention. It caused her moans to get louder. Her grip got harder, and when she lifted her hips to his, Jake knew he had to do something fast.

Fast involved getting her out of those jeans. No easy feat when it was clear he had a woman who wanted him bad. Lily Rose kept kissing, kept touching and kept driving him crazy while he rid her of her jeans and grabbed a condom from the nightstand drawer.

Jake intended to enter her slowly so he could make this last longer than a certain part of him had in mind.

But Lily Rose had other plans. She did that hip lift again just as he pushed into her, and it damn near caused them both to come right then and there.

He had to grind his teeth and think "pure" thoughts just to get him past the "blowing off the top of his head" stage to where he could pace this out better. He was doing fine with that, the pleasure slamming him in all the right spots, but then Lily Rose said something.

His name.

Normally, that wouldn't have done anything to spiral him toward a climax, but it sure as hell worked now. It also didn't help when Lily Rose shattered, the muscles of her body latching on to him and giving him only one place to go.

Jake shattered right along with her.

LILY ROSE HAD never regretted a mistake so little as she regretted having sex with Jake. Not only had it been wonderful, it had given her some memories to take with her.

Too bad those memories were bittersweet.

It was also too bad that she was an idiot.

She cursed her screw-ups, cursed her situation, which was of her own making, and she cursed again because this wasn't going to end well for anyone. Well, perhaps Jake would get a happy ending out of this, maybe because for him this had just been sex. But if it had been more, then he was just another casualty of this road of hers that she'd paved with mistakes.

Lily Rose eased from the bed, brushing a kiss on his mouth. Jake stirred a little, but he didn't wake up. Ditto for when she gathered up her clothes and tiptoed into the living room. She got dressed there, hurrying and trying to figure out how she should tell Jake the truth. Of course, she should have told him before the sex, but that was water under the bridge now.

She glanced around, looking for paper, and found some on the kitchen counter. Lily Rose considered leaving a full-out confession, but that should probably keep for a face-to-face conversation. Though it could be a short conversation indeed once Jake learned the truth. Instead, she settled for telling him that she had to get back to the Granger Ranch and that she would call him in a day or two.

Keeping as quiet as she could, Lily Rose slipped out of the house and went to the stables so she could say goodbye to the horses. Thankfully, no one was around so it gave her a moment to clear her head.

Unfortunately, the head-clearing only reminded her that there were no easy fixes for this. She would either have to go back to work for Ian or suck it up and go to her brothers. Either was about as palatable as tangoing with a rattlesnake, but she was fresh out of good choices.

One of the horses, Sapphire, whinnied when Lily Rose approached and turned, eyeing her as if questioning why the heck she was there. Lily Rose couldn't quite get out the word goodbye because it cut her to the core to know that she wouldn't be able to finish the training. She wasn't a quitter, especially when it meant leaving a job she loved.

Lily Rose touched the horse, rubbed gently. "You've probably never been between a rock and a hard place, have you, girl?" she whispered.

"If she answers you, I'm leaving," someone said.

The voice shot through the barn, causing Lily Rose to gasp, and she spooked the horse. She whirled around to see Lawson leaning against a stall. She wasn't sure how long he'd been standing there, but it seemed as if he had been waiting for her. Knowing her brother, he probably had.

"We can go two ways with this," Lawson said. "You can tell me what's bugging you, and I can try to fix it. Or you make me pester you until you tell me what's bugging you, and I can try to fix it. Your choice."

She gave him a flat look, to let him know that she didn't appreciate the brotherly bullying. But actually she did. Lily Rose went to Lawson and hugged him. She hadn't realized she was crying until she felt the tears burn her eyes.

Lawson must have heard her sniff because he cursed. "Am I going to have to kill Jake?"

"No." She couldn't say that fast enough. "He's not the reason I'm crying."

Her brother eased back from her, lifted his eyebrow. "You came sneaking out of Jake's house, and I doubt you're upset over losing a game of dominoes."

At least he wasn't browbeating her for having sex with a man he'd warned her about. However, that might be part two of this visit.

"Why are you here anyway?" she asked. Not exactly a diversion tactic but maybe it would work.

"Sophie sent me. She's worried about you. Said she tried to call you a couple of times but you didn't answer."

No way could she have answered considering what was going on between Jake and her, but it was best not to mention that to Lawson.

"Anyway, Sophie was going to drive over here and check on you," Lawson added, "but I told her I'd do it. That way, if Jake's ass did need kicking, I could take care of it. That's my version of multitasking."

"No kicking required. I was just leaving." And she

would have headed toward her car if Lawson hadn't stepped in front of her.

He sighed in frustration. "Don't make me hound you into talking. Just tell me what's wrong, and then we can both go home and do whatever else it is we want to be doing other than standing here in a barn."

Lily Rose figured there was no way she would be able to ditch Lawson or this conversation so she just went with what would get her out of there the fastest. "Ian is being... Ian." Aka turd-head. "He's jealous of me spending time with Jake, and now he's trying to woo me back."

Lawson cursed. "Hell, the butt I need to be kicking is Ian's."

Lily Rose nearly said she wouldn't stop him, but Lawson might take that to heart and go pulverize her former boss. Who might end up being her current boss. Or she might just kick his butt herself. Growing up with four brothers had her a few things about standing up for herself, but in this case, that would only end up hurting Jake.

"I hope you told Ian to go to hell," Lawson growled.

"Not yet." But if she thought she could get away with it, she would. "Anyway, I think it's best if I cut my losses and leave. That'll be better for anyone."

Lawson gave her a look that only a big brother could manage. "Better for Ian, you mean."

She shrugged, nodded. Paused. "There are some things you don't know."

He gave her a second of those looks, this one more intense than the other. "Are you pregnant?"

"No!"

"Dying?" he tacked on before she finished even that short response.

"No. It's just I've had some, well, setbacks. I'd rather

not get into it with you right now, but suffice it to say that I might be moving home."

Since neither Lawson nor she had lived "home" in years, he was probably surprised. Maybe even shocked. Because home meant being back under Lucian's thumb. Lawson's big-brother looks were tame compared to Lucian's. However, Lawson didn't get a chance to express any of that shock because the sound of footsteps got their attention.

Lily Rose groaned softly. It was Jake, and she shouldn't have hung around for him to find her. Especially find her when he seemed riled about something. His mouth was tight, his eyes narrowed.

"What the hell is going on?" Jake asked, and it didn't take Lily Rose long to figure out that the question was meant for her. She didn't think he was talking about Lawson being there, either.

"I have to leave," she said, hoping Jake didn't ask for details.

He didn't.

Instead, Jake held up his phone. "I just finished a chat with Ian. According to him, you're flat broke and that's the reason you just had sex with me."

CHAPTER SIX

JAKE HAD HOPED like the devil that everything Ian had just told him was a lie. But he could tell from the shell-shocked look on Lily Rose's face that it wasn't.

Crap.

"Start talking," he demanded at the same moment Lawson said, "What?"

Clearly, her brother was in the dark on this, too, but Jake intended for there to be some light-shedding very, very soon. Lily Rose seemed to have less urgency, though, to speak because she stood there, staring at him all the while Lawson was glaring at her. Jake figured his own expression wasn't exactly pleasant because hell in a handbasket, it hurt to think that Lily Rose was like half the other women in town and only after his money.

"I am broke," she finally said. She had to add the rest over Lawson's and his groans. "I made some bad investments. Well, one really bad one anyway, and I lost almost everything. But I didn't sleep with you to get your money. That was purely about sex and your hotness."

Lawson added another groan to go with his glare. "I don't want to hear about my kid sister having sex. What I do want to hear about is how you lost your trust fund."

It was obvious Lily Rose didn't want to get into this, but it was equally obvious that Lawson wasn't going to give up. Well, Jake wasn't going to give up on being convinced that it had "purely" been sex between Lily Rose and him. After he'd been burned time and time again by some of the Wrangler's Creek women, he wanted to be sure.

"You know I've always wanted my own cutting horse operation," Lily Rose said to her brother. "Well, I found one I could buy, but it turned out to be a scam. The cops and FBI are investigating it, but they aren't hopeful I can get back the money."

Lawson cursed. "When the heck did all of this happen?"

"A year ago."

Lawson cursed some more. "And you didn't come to me?"

There were tears in Lily Rose's eyes now. Tears that cut away at Jake, but he resisted the urge to go and comfort her. For one thing, he was still pissed off that she hadn't volunteered any of this information, that he'd had to hear it from Ian. Plus, he doubted Lawson was going to want to see Lily Rose wrapped in his arms so soon after learning about them having sex. After all, Lawson had warned Jake to stay away from Lily Rose.

"I was embarrassed. Ashamed," she corrected. She slashed her fingers over her cheeks to wipe away the tears. "And I didn't want to hear 'I told you so' from Lucian or from you."

Jake knew all her brothers and figured a couple of them would have indeed said it, too. That was the problem with being a little sister to four alpha brothers. In their eyes, she would never grow up, and she certainly shouldn't be sleeping around with him.

"This is why you said you'd be moving back home," Lawson grumbled. He didn't wait for her to confirm that.

"Don't. I'll talk to Sophie, Garrett and Roman about you staying indefinitely at the Granger Ranch."

She was shaking her head before he finished. "I don't want you to fix this." Lily Rose tapped her thumb against her chest. "I got myself into this mess, and I'll get myself out of it." She snapped toward Jake again. "And no, that doesn't involve getting money from you because we had sex."

The tears returned, and she couldn't wipe them away fast enough. "I can't believe you'd think that about me."

At the moment, neither could he. But Ian's call had hit him like a Mack truck. Not just the revelation of Lily Rose being broke, either, but the other thing Ian had told him.

"Are you really going back to work for Ian?" Jake snapped.

Judging from the way she dodged his gaze, the answer to that was yes. "He offered me a once-in-a-lifetime business opportunity."

"Oh, man." Lawson groaned. "He's offering you the opportunity to be at his beck and call."

She certainly didn't argue with that. "I have my reasons for considering his job offer."

Lawson started cursing again. "There is no reason for you to work for that turd."

Lily Rose stayed quiet several long moments. "You're wrong. I have several good reasons. And I don't intend to discuss them with you," she quickly added. "Or you," she said, turning to Jake.

She stopped again, shook her head and mumbled her own profanity.

She pointed to her brother. "I don't want you to bail me out. I want to work for a living just the way you do."

"Obviously, that didn't work so well for you," Lawson grumbled. "You let yourself be scammed, and then you didn't bother telling us the truth. No wonder Jake thinks you've turned gold digger."

It was the wrong thing to say, and it put some fire in her eyes because it had that whole "told you so" ring to it. It also didn't help that Lawson was giving her that "Me, big brother; you, little sister" look.

Jake wasn't sure how Lily Rose could see with her eyes narrowed like that, but she pointed her finger at him next. "As for you, I can't believe you thought so little of me."

Another swipe of the tears, and she hiked up her chin. Jake could see that she was trying to steel herself up. Or at least that was what he thought. But he was wrong. She dismissed them both with a wave of her hand.

"I'm in love with you," Lily Rose snarled to Jake. "And now, you can just go to hell."

Jake just stood there, unsure of what he should do. Lawson didn't budge, either.

"Did she say she was in love with you?" Lawson asked, sounding none too happy about that.

Jake wasn't happy about it, either. What the heck? "When did that happen?"

"Maybe about the time you took her to your bed. You know, like an hour or so ago." Lawson cursed and shook his head. "I suspect this has been a long time coming. Lily Rose has always had feelings for you. I just didn't know they ran this deep."

Neither had he.

Well, hell.

This was a night for revelations. First, the fact that Lily Rose was broke and about to return to work for a jackass. Then, him accusing her of gold digging. Now, this.

Except there was more to it than her saying she was in love with him. Apparently, Jake had done exactly what Lawson and Garrett had thought he would do.

He'd broken Lily Rose's heart.

ON A SCALE of one to ten, Lily Rose figured her anger was a hundred and six. Maybe more. Worse, in addition to being pissed off, she felt as if someone were sitting on her chest, crushing her.

How the devil could she have let herself fall in love with Jake?

True, she'd always been crazy about him, but she'd contained that craziness with a hefty reminder that he would always think she was too young or not right for him. It had been that way years ago, and it was the same tonight. It didn't matter that Jake and she had had sex. Didn't matter that said sex had been mind-blowing and incredible. It only mattered that now things were a big mess.

"After his money," she grumbled, punctuating it with plenty of cursing. "Right." The only way she would have been interested in his money was if it'd been in his boxers and her interest would have only been to move it aside so she could put a condom on him.

But he didn't believe that.

Even if he did, it didn't matter. The damage had been done, and she could thank Ian for setting that particular ball rolling.

However, it wasn't a thank-you she had in mind when she called his number as she went into the guesthouse at the Granger Ranch. While she waited for Ian to answer, she went straight to the fridge and poured herself a glass of wine. She didn't put away the bottle because she might need every drop to get her through this conversation.

"Lily Rose," Ian said when he finally came on the line. "I'm guessing Jake told you I'd phoned him?"

"Go to hell," she snarled. She probably should have rehearsed that a bit so she could convey her anger while not ruining things for Jake. After all, Ian had said he would blackball the livestock purchases that Jake needed to make a go of his ranch.

Ian gave what sounded to be a heavy sigh. "You're upset. I get that, but Jake needed to know about your financial problems."

"Yes, but he didn't need to hear it from you. Why would you tell him, Ian? Why would you even call him?"

"I thought you might need some encouragement to accept my job offer. I mean, it was obvious you were having doubts because you didn't jump at the chance—"

"I didn't jump because you threatened Jake."

"It wasn't a threat. It was just business."

She was already riled to the boiling point and rather than do something that would cause this to blow up for Jake, Lily Rose took a gulp of wine. Then, another. She refilled her glass, grabbed the bottle and headed for the bathroom so she could soak in the tub. She might do some head-soaking as well while she was in there.

"Jake's a big boy," Ian went on. "He understands this isn't personal."

"But it is, isn't it? Honestly, would you have offered me that dream job if I hadn't been with Jake?"

Ian paused. "Maybe. I admit I realized the mistake I'd made by letting you go. Not just from my life but from my business, too. But that's all water under the bridge now. You'll come to work for me and all will be fine with Jake."

Yes, the only thing she had to do was give up on the man she loved. Easy peasy. Well, except for that heart-crushing pain. And the tears. Once more they were threatening.

"I have to go," she said to Ian. Best to end this conversation now than say something she might regret. "Please don't call Jake again." And with that, she hit the end-call button.

The tears came while she ran the bathwater and continued while she had that soak. It didn't help, but then hot water wasn't exactly a good cure for a heartbreak. But wine might be. Without drying off, Lily Rose pulled on a robe and headed back to the kitchen.

But the sound stopped her cold.

Someone was in her bedroom. She peeked around the edge of the bathroom door and spotted Jake.

Naked.

Well, almost. Like the time she'd been waiting for him in his house, he was wearing only a pair of boxers.

Just like that, the jolt came—the attraction mixed with the hurt. As bad as the hurt was, the attraction still won out, causing the ache in her heart to intensify.

"I wish I could find a cure for you," she mumbled.

The corner of his mouth lifted, though in her mind there was absolutely nothing to smile about. He tipped his head to the wine bottle that she had clamped in her hand. "It appears you've been looking for cures, though."

"I have," Lily Rose readily admitted. "So far, no luck." She dragged in a deep breath so she could continue. "Did you lose your clothes?"

Another smile. "I stripped down in the living room.

Thought it might break the ice if we talked while I was just wearing this."

Jake didn't break ice. He melted it. Melted her, too, but Lily Rose figured it was best not to admit that especially so soon after her "cure" remark. Jake already knew he had her hormonal number so she should minimize the sexual references. Maybe if she didn't talk about it, she could rein in her lust and have a meaningful conversation.

Of course, her body was urging her more in the "meaningful sex" direction.

"FYI, if I don't go to work for Ian," she confessed, "he's going to try to screw you over six ways to Sunday."

Jake nodded, shrugged as if that were old news and walked toward her. Well, it wasn't old news to Lily Rose. It still felt fresh and raw…and judging from the look in Jake's eyes, it was also the last thing on his mind.

"Are you wearing anything under that robe?" he asked, but he didn't wait for an answer. He slid his hand inside over her right breast and flicked his thumb over her nipple.

Great day in the morning. It was hard to stay focused when multiple parts of her were quivering. One part in particular was a little past the quiver stage and might start whining at any moment. That was perhaps because she could see the outline of Jake's erection contained in his boxers.

"Didn't you hear me?" she managed to ask. "Ian will ruin you."

"He'll try." Jake leaned in and brushed a kiss just below her ear.

And her lower body whined began.

It would be so easy to slip right into this. Or rather have him slip right into her. That became even more plausible when he moved closer, putting his body against hers and kissing her. Since she was still holding both the wine bottle and glass, Lily Rose couldn't latch on to him. Which was probably a good thing.

"Ian will do more than try," she assured Jake when he broke for air.

He scowled. "Obviously, I'm not kissing you the right way if you're still talking about Ian. So, let's clear the air. I know you're not after my money, though it is possible you're after my body."

"Not possible. That's a given. I am after it." Now, here was the hard part. And no, she wasn't talking about his erection. This was about what she'd blurted out to him in the barn. "But I'm also in love with you. I have been for years."

He nodded, again as if that were old news. "Not years for me, but I'm catching up with you. I've always been a little in love with you, too, but that little leapt up a bit when I realized you were willing to work for a horse's ass to save me."

"Not just willing," she said around the sudden lump in her throat. "I will work for him. I don't want my ex ruining your life."

"Yet you'd let him ruin yours." He opened her robe and dropped a kiss on her neck. Then, her breasts. "You do know that he's not going to give you that dream job because it could never be a dream if it's tied to Ian."

Yes, she did know that though Lily Rose had wanted to believe it could come true. Still, the dream job had been way secondary to the big picture here.

She had to latch on to his hair and pull him back up so they could have direct eye contact. "Ian. Will. Ruin.

You." There. She couldn't spell things out any clearer than that.

"No. He. Won't. Because before I came over here, I had a chat with Logan McCord over in Spring Hill, and he's going to supply me with as much cattle and cutting horses as I need. Turns out that Logan isn't very happy with Ian and would like to bring him down a notch. Actually, Logan's exact words were that he wanted to bury the jackass."

Oh.

Lily Rose let that sink in, and it sank in well. Logan was capable of crushing Ian so maybe this could indeed work out. At least work out as far as Jake's ranch was concerned.

"So, here's my offer," Jake continued. He went back to kissing her breasts, and when he talked his warm breath created more quivering on her skin. "It's not exactly your dream job, but it's a job all right. You keep working for me, keep training the horses, and we have frequent sex."

It sounded more and more dreamy, especially when he pulled her closer, wedging his knee in between her thighs. Wedging was especially good because it added some pressure to one of her whining parts.

"But you have a rule about not sleeping with your hired hands," she reminded him. However, she gave him that reminder while she slid her hand over his erection. Lily Rose figured two could play at this game.

It seemed as if his eyes crossed. "Then, we won't do much sleeping." And Jake finished that promise with a clothes-melting kiss.

* * * * *

REQUEST YOUR FREE BOOKS!

2 FREE NOVELS FROM THE ROMANCE COLLECTION, PLUS 2 FREE GIFTS!

YES! Please send me 2 FREE novels from the Romance Collection and my 2 FREE gifts (gifts are worth about $10). After receiving them, if I don't wish to receive any more books, I can return the shipping statement marked "cancel." If I don't cancel, I will receive 4 brand-new novels every month and be billed just $6.49 per book in the U.S. or $6.99 per book in Canada. That's a savings of at least 18% off the cover price. It's quite a bargain! Shipping and handling is just 50¢ per book in the U.S. and 75¢ per book in Canada.* I understand that accepting the 2 free books and gifts places me under no obligation to buy anything. I can always return a shipment and cancel at any time. Even if I never buy another book, the two free books and gifts are mine to keep forever.

194/394 MDN GH4D

Name	(PLEASE PRINT)	

Address		Apt. #

City	State/Prov.	Zip/Postal Code

Signature (if under 18, a parent or guardian must sign)

Mail to the **Reader Service:**
IN U.S.A.: P.O. Box 1867, Buffalo, NY 14240-1867
IN CANADA: P.O. Box 609, Fort Erie, Ontario L2A 5X3

Want to try 2 free books from another line?
Call 1-800-873-8635 or visit www.ReaderService.com.

*Terms and prices subject to change without notice. Prices do not include applicable taxes. Sales tax applicable in N.Y. Canadian residents will be charged applicable taxes. Offer not valid in Quebec. This offer is limited to one order per household. Not valid for current subscribers to the Romance Collection or the Romance/Suspense Collection. All orders subject to credit approval. Credit or debit balances in a customer's account(s) may be offset by any other outstanding balance owed by or to the customer. Please allow 4 to 6 weeks for delivery. Offer available while quantities last.

Your Privacy—The Reader Service is committed to protecting your privacy. Our Privacy Policy is available online at www.ReaderService.com or upon request from the Reader Service.

We make a portion of our mailing list available to reputable third parties that offer products we believe may interest you. If you prefer that we not exchange your name with third parties, or if you wish to clarify or modify your communication preferences, please visit us at www.ReaderService.com/consumerschoice or write to us at Reader Service Preference Service, P.O. Box 9062, Buffalo, NY 14240-9062. Include your complete name and address.

ROM15R